DO YOU BELIEVE IN LOVE?

"Men and women have their needs, Meagan." The sound of her name as it tumbled from his lips left her aquiver. "It is not uncommon for a man to satisfy his needs when there are willing maids underfoot. But my heart is chained to no woman. They offer physical pleasure, and in the past I have accepted it."

"Then you do not believe in love," she speculated as her eyes lingered on the rugged features of his face that were carved from years of experience and trials.

"Do you, Meagan?" Trevor asked.

"I pray that love exists," she told him softly, a whimsical glow in her eyes and a tender smile on her lips. "I seek a man who earns my respect without demanding it, one who is strong yet gentle. I wish to marry for love, not wealth. . . ."

"And so you shall, little one," Trevor replied as he bent over to kiss her firmly on the lips. . . .

ANGEL'S FIRE

Connie Drake

ZEBRA BOOKS
KENSINGTON PUBLISHING CORP.

ZEBRA BOOKS

are published by

Kensington Publishing Corp.
475 Park Avenue South
New York, NY 10016

First printing: August 1987

Printed in the United States of America

To:
Bill and Cheryl Dawson
Jerry and Barbara Johnson
Rick Roberts
Larry Warren
Thanks for giving me the space to create.

Prologue

Strong and invincible, William, duke of Normandy, sat upon his steed, his astute gaze surveying the countryside that sprawled before him. He and his army had crossed the English Channel to make his claim on the English crown, one promised to him by his cousin, King Edward the Confessor. Saxon England had offered the challenge by ignoring King Edward's command to deliver the crown to William of Normandy. William was furious that the arrogant English witan, members of an assembly of notable aristocrats, had offered the throne to their own Saxon knight, Harold, earl of Wessex. It further infuriated the duke that Harold, while shipwrecked on the coast of Normandy in 1064, had sworn allegiance to William and had acknowledged his claim to the Saxon throne.

The insolent bastard, William mused irritably. Harold had accepted the English crown, knowing full well that it was not his, could never be his. William shifted restlessly in the saddle, impatiently waiting for the appearance of Harold and his Saxon army. He knew Harold would come to offer resistance, but William was determined in his purpose. He had come ashore at Hastings, prepared to claim the throne that was his by two promises—the late King Edward's and that of the traitor himself, Harold Godwinson.

Approaching from the north, preparing to defend the

English shore, rode Harold, accompanied by his family and his brothers-in-law, Edwin and Morcar, earls of Mercia and Northumbria. Harold was battle weary. Only too recently he had been engaged in combat with the Scandinavian invading army. His victory over that foe seemed insignificant when he received word that William, duke of Normandy, had ferried his army across the English Channel. Harold and his fatigued army had come south to tackle William as soon as possible. He had come not to relinquish the throne, but rather to proclaim it as his own. It had been awarded to him by English noblemen who detested the thought of a Norman, especially the notorious descendant of a Viking chieftain, ruling Saxon England.

During the journey to the southern shores, Harold had asked for reinforcements from Saxon barons and their stable of knights. He had warned his fellow countrymen that if they did not take arms against the duke of Normandy, they would lose their land and titles to the mercenary warriors who rode beside their sovereign. Aided by fresh troops and surrounded by his own exhausted army, Harold mustered his failing strength. He knew the Saxons would not have a prayer for victory if they did not thwart William of Normandy before he took a foothold on English soil.

When Harold climbed the hill overlooking Pevensey, a grim frown clouded his brow. The couriers' reports were true, he dismally realized. The duke had not only surrounded himself with his vassals and knights from Normandy, but had also enlisted the services of mercenaries and adventurers from northern France and even farther away. Harold had seen his share of seaborne invaders, but never had he viewed an enemy force as ominous as the army William had brought with him. The Scandinavian invasion was nothing compared to Duke William's amphibious group of men and equipment!

Resolutely, Harold organized his troops. He was forced to gamble his claim to the throne of England on the outcome of a single battle. The destiny of Saxon England rested upon his shoulders and on those who dared to defy the powerful duke of Normandy.

"M'lord, Harold comes." Trevor Burke, the duke's most valued knight, indicated the Saxon army that had dismounted from their horses to make their stronghold on the hill.

William glared at the resisting soldiers, who had begun to form their customary shield-ring and had armed themselves with Danish battle-axes. How he hungered to settle this feud with Harold. William had extended his hospitality to Harold, had even knighted him! The conniving traitor had even seen the way William led his men into battle. Harold should have been riding *beside* William when he came to claim the throne of Saxon England. Instead, Harold had encouraged other Saxon earls and barons to join in battle to deny William's rightful claim to the English crown.

"I will show the traitor no mercy," William growled spitefully. "Remain by my side, Burke. Together we will bring down Harold for his treachery. England is mine. If the Saxons will not accept my claim, they *cannot* deny the right of force."

Trevor Burke drew his sword, prepared to defend his duke. He would fight to the death to protect his sovereign, he vowed solemnly to himself. William had been a generous, devoted friend, and Trevor had sworn his allegiance to the duke. He did not take lightly the prestigious position of riding by William's side.

When the command was given to charge, the Norman warriors stormed the hill six miles northwest of Hastings. William and his mounted knights were supported by volleys of arrows loosed by the ranks of archers that followed the infantry. The arrow fire whittled down the number of resisting Saxons, leaving them vulnerable to the powerful Norman assault.

Although Harold and his troops of Saxons fought valiantly to keep the crown upon an Englishman's head, they were no match for the skillful Norman army. Norman horsemen, pretending to flee from battle, drew the Saxon warriors down from their advantageous hilltop position. The superior arms and fighting tactics of the Normans proved to be too much for the English defenders.

By deepening dusk, when the long, intense battle had ended, Harold and the men of his bodyguard lay dead at the foot of the English royal standard. They were surrounded by hundreds of slain comrades who had fought to protect their way of life. The Saxon survivors scattered in all directions before they, too, were cut down by the merciless Norman cavalry.

Duke William had led the front ranks into battle and had three horses killed beneath him. But his loyal knight, Burke, had been there to protect his sire, offering his own mount, defending William while he swung upon another steed's back. When the dust cleared and the fierce battle ended, William glanced about his courageous troops and then broke into a proud smile. Those who had aided him in the acquisition of the English crown would be generously rewarded for their heroism and allegiance.

"England belongs to us!" William shouted to his conquering army. "And to the victor belong the spoils of war. The land that once belonged to the fallen English barons will be awarded to my loyal knights. We shall reap the wealth of the defiant Saxons and prove to them that Normans now rule their precious England!"

And so it was proclaimed by the Norman monarch. The conqueror apportioned the land among his followers, and the aristocrats of England fell beneath their Norman lords. William, duke of Normandy, became king. The throne was his by heredity and by conquest. Those who defied his rights fell beneath the swarm of marauding Norman invaders.

While William took Edwin and Morcar captive, hordes of mercenaries and adventurers ravished the once-peaceful countryside. When the new king marched toward London to erect a palace worthy of its Norman lord, the Saxons' worst fears became reality. English land was no longer the property of its Saxon barons, and the Saxon barons were merely servants to the foreign king.

The bitterness the English Saxons felt toward their Norman rulers could not be buried with the fallen soldiers. It festered and grew, feeding on the memories of the defiant defenders and the bloody, ruthless invasion. The threat of rebellion increased with each heavy tax levied by William the Conqueror. The new mound-and-palisade castles with their invincible foreign garrisons were loathsome symbols of alien rule.

The Saxons could not forget the humiliation when the English countryside bore the marks of a civilization that lived by the land, erected fortresses of stone and timber, and thought in the barbaric language of military force. The country had been blemished with monstrous Norman castles and infiltrated by ruthless mercenaries who had little respect for the Saxon way of life.

Even time could not erase the resentment. There were those among the conquered Saxons who would not bow to their powerful Norman lords, even in fear of their lives. The hostility continued to fester like an unhealed wound. The inevitable storm would break, and the thunder of rebellion would echo about King William and his newly appointed Norman lords, who had fed on the defeated Saxons of England. Although they had been conquered by a superior force, there were those among them who would not accept William as their king. They would band together in an attempt to overthrow the reigning sovereign and return the crown to a true Engishman's head. . . .

Chapter 1

August 1069
Wessex County, England

It was with tempered patience that Edric Lowell bowed when Trevor Burke, the overlord of Wessex, strode across the stone floor of the Great Hall, his boots clicking as he swiftly closed the distance between them. Edric's gaze flooded over the emerald green tunic Trevor wore and then focused on the tight black leggings that revealed the muscular shape of Trevor's legs. For three years Edric had sized up the raven-haired Norman, but even the most particular connoisseur of human bodies could find no flaw in Trevor's physique. There was nothing about the tall, handsome overlord to criticize, except that he now ruled as baron of Wessex. It was the position Edric would have held if the British had warded off William the Conqueror's invasion in the fall of 1066.

Edric had not taken arms against William's army. Because of his apathy he had been allowed to remain on his own land. He could not help resenting the intimidating overlord, nor could he overcome the feelings of guilt that plagued him. Many Saxons had fought and died in defense of their country, but Edric had not been one of them. His father had not permitted his knights to band with Harold, because he did not approve of Harold's politics. Because Edric had not carried the Lowell shield into battle he had lost part of his dignity. Now Edric was caught in the middle of the Norman-Saxon conflict. He felt pressured by Saxons who had lost their land and titles, and he was embittered by the Normans who had forced him into submission. Although Edric was forced to accept his lot, he could not be forced to *like* it. And he did not! He merely tolerated his demoted position and his domineering overlord, hoping that one day the situation would be remedied.

Masking his resentment, Edric tacked on the most civil smile he could muster and offered his hand to the muscular overlord, who towered several inches above him.

"I trust your trip was pleasant, m'lord." Edric practically choked on the title, which stuck in his craw. His eyes faltered on the rows of sparkling jewels that were embedded in Trevor's leather belt. Gifts from the reigning king, no doubt, he mused bitterly.

"Yea, Vassal Lowell. 'Twas pleasant enough." Trevor sent the fair-haired Saxon a faint smile, but he continued to measure him with his keen gaze, wondering why Edric appeared so ill at ease. "I inspected the tithing barn to find that your tenants have already brought the share of their crops owed to our king. You are very efficient and punctual, Edric."

Edric nodded appreciatively and then gestured toward the two massive chairs that sat perched on stone at the far end of the hall. "Would you care for some wine to wash away the dust, m'lord?"

A muddled frown captured Trevor's dark features as he ambled toward his chair and listened to Edric summon the pantler, ordering him to retrieve the refreshments. The vassal had something up his sleeve. Trevor could sense it. He was cautious by nature and suspicious by habit. The Saxon vassals of his county were polite to him because they feared for their lives and their lands. Trevor was no man's fool. He knew that beneath those pretentious smiles murderous thoughts were formulating. A Norman baron was an annoying pain in a Saxon's side, tolerated because necessity dictated it. Edric was being more polite than usual, Trevor mused as he planted himself in the oversized chair. During

14

previous visits to Lowell Castle, Trevor had been forced to request food and drink. Never had it been willingly offered.

"What is on your mind, Edric?" Trevor blurted out, cutting to the heart of the matter to appease his impatient curiosity.

"M'lord?" Edric's expression was masked behind a carefully blank stare, as if he hadn't the foggiest notion what Trevor meant by his blunt question.

"Why this royal treatment? What is it you want of me?" Trevor demanded to know.

Edric detested Trevor's forthright manner. The man possessed power that required little diplomacy. The baron was in a position to freely speak his mind, while Edric was forced to resort to tact—something he awkwardly utilized, but still despised.

Squirming beneath Trevor's assessing golden eyes, Edric tugged at his mantle and pasted on another smile. "I have sent for my sister, Meagan, who has been living at the convent north of Pevensey these past three years, and . . ." His voice trailed off as he reorganized his thoughts and struggled to find just the right words to present the proposal to Trevor.

"Go on," Trevor prompted, his tone registering impatience. He had not ridden the better part of two days to listen to Edric stammer and wrestle with his tongue.

"Meagan is a rare young woman of seventeen," Edric continued, fighting to keep the irritation from seeping into his voice. "She has been given a proper education in all facets of life and has grown into a very lovely young lass." At least he was hoping she had. Edric had not seen Meagan since he stashed her away from the invading Norman marauders. At fourteen she had been breathtaking, and by now he expected her to be a ravishing beauty. By damned, she had better be, Edric thought to himself. If not, this scheme would meet with disaster.

Trevor's dark brows went up as he lifted the mug of wine to his lips and peered at Edric over the rim. "I am pleased to hear that you have a lovely sister, but I fail to see the point of this idle prattle."

Edric could have cheerfully choked the baron for antagonizing him, and he clamped a stranglehold on his own mug, wishing he could curl his fingers around the Norman's thick neck.

"I have a request, m'lord." Edric was striving for a humbly pleasant tone, certain his voice would crack if Trevor persisted in needling him. "Meagan will be arriving home this very day. After a brief reunion, I wish to send her to your castle on approval."

Trevor's brows shot up even higher and he strangled on his wine. He knew what Edric was hinting at. "You want me to marry her," he predicted between coughs and then rammed his fist into his chest to save himself from choking to death, since Edric had not lifted a hand to come to his aid. Trevor would not have been the least bit surprised if Edric was delighting in watching his lord gasp for breath.

And Edric was. It did his heart good to see the mighty Norman lord struggling to regain his composure. "Only if Meagan meets your expectations," he insisted before biting into a hunk of cheese and silently chuckling at the red-faced baron. "'Tis my way of affirming my devotion to you and the Crown, a gesture of friendship between two nations that must learn to live in peace."

"But I—" Trevor was still having difficulty breathing, and Edric pounced on the opportunity to elaborate.

"England will only become a strong, unified nation when Normans and Saxons wed and produce heirs who bear the heritage of both backgrounds," he pointed out. "The king wishes peace and tranquility among his subjects and in generations to come. I cannot think of a more efficient way to ensure cooperation than through contracts of Saxon and Norman marriages."

"I have no need of a wife," Trevor insisted. "I—"

Edric was pressing his luck by interrupting the baron, but he was determined to convince Trevor of the importance of such a marriage. "Do you prefer a bastard heir to reign over your lands? Even if you cannot love Meagan she can give you strong, healthy children, ones with royal ancestry, ones who will command the respect of Normans and Saxons alike."

16

Although Edric may have had a logical point, Trevor was skeptical of the vassal's motives. He was willing to bet his right arm that Edric had some devious plan in mind. He would never offer such a proposal if he did not stand to gain from it. Was he counting on Trevor's allegiance, even though they would only be bound together by a loveless marriage?

Trevor wished he could have consulted with his seneschal, Conan. He was a wise sage and soothsayer whom Trevor had befriended among the Norman troops. Conan had an answer for every question and sound logic in all matters. But the aging Conan had remained at Burke Castle, and Trevor was not allowed his years of experience.

"I have heard of several overlords who have married the widows of fallen Saxon warriors. They have gained the respect of the servants and have taken command of the existing manors," Edric tactfully reminded him. "'Tis not an outrageous suggestion. What could it possibly hurt to send Meagan to you? If she does not meet with your approval you can return her to me and I will strike up another match. She is past the usual marrying age and I must ensure my sister's future."

A thoughtful frown plowed Trevor's brow. This discussion closely resembled the lecture he had endured the last time he was in William's palace. He had been in court to discuss the rebel uprisings that sprouted in various parts of the kingdom. But it was not the outbreaks that had been on William's mind, and their conversation still rang in Trevor's ears, one so similar to this one with Edric that he felt irritation swelling up within him. William had complimented him on his successful management of his demesne, and then out of the blue he had inquired why Trevor had yet to take a wife to rule at his side. Trevor had been caught off stride by the king's remark and annoyed that William had used the same line of logic that Edric had just voiced—the necessity of mixed marriages to ensure both Saxon and Norman loyalty to the Throne. It was a cruel twist of fate for William to suggest that Trevor saddle himself with a wife, and he found himself rebelling against the possibility of taking Meagan Lowell home on approval.

What Trevor wanted from the fairer sex had nothing to do with weddings or commitments of love. Most women were shallow creatures like Daralis, the young serving maid of Burke Castle, who clung like a leech, expecting favors for joining him in bed. Trevor swore he could sail to the edge of the earth and eventually drop off without ever finding a woman who wanted more from life than the security of her husband's domain and the wealth he could acquire for her.

No woman had truly set fire to his blood since he was a young lad on the threshold of manhood, seeking to conquer the unknown with those of the feminine persuasion. Trevor had enjoyed his thirty-three years of freedom, and the king's and his vassal's pressuring hit upon an exposed nerve. Nay, he would not tie himself down until *he* was ready, and he wasn't ready yet. But what was he to do about William's blatant suggestion to select a bride and produce an heir?

Trevor's pensive frown settled deeper in his chiseled features while his probing gaze riddled Edric, making him squirm uncomfortably beneath his scrutinizing regard. What harm could come of having Meagan Lowell underfoot temporarily, Trevor asked himself, giving the matter second consideration. At least Edric would think he had out-maneuvered his overlord. Let the man gloat, Trevor mused as he gave the fair-haired young man the once-over, twice.

Edric was having difficulty accepting his demoted position in the Norman feudal system, and Trevor did not wish to risk rebellion in his domain. Rumor had it that many disgruntled Saxons were anxious to take arms against their Norman lords after the initial uprisings in the far corners of the kingdom, and Trevor preferred to avoid trouble whenever possible. He had seen enough killing and fighting to last him a lifetime. Perhaps an ounce of prevention could ease Edric's disorder. Yea, he would consent to the lady's presence in his castle until he spoke with Conan and interpreted Edric's true motive. Then Trevor would find a way to counteract the offer and present gifts to the young vassal, hoping to soothe his ruffled feathers.

"Very well, Edric, I shall have a look at your sister,"

Trevor agreed as he gathered his feet beneath him and started down the steps, but Edric's dismayed voice halted him in his tracks.

"M'lord, you cannot leave yet!" Edric frantically called after him. "Meagan should arrive from the convent before nightfall. Do you not wish to stay for a formal introduction and join us for our evening meal? I have had your room prepared for you."

Stay the evening and chance being stabbed in his sleep, Trevor snorted cynically to himself, but he decided against voicing that particular thought. More than once he had spent the night at a new fortress during inspections and had found some bitter Saxon poised to carve his heart from his chest. Trevor had endured many fretful nights, sleeping with one eye open and a shield protecting his vital parts. He had not enjoyed a peaceful night's sleep since he waded ashore beside William the Conqueror.

"I appreciate the invitation, Vassal Lowell, but I have several rounds to make before I journey to London to counsel with the king. He has summoned me and I cannot keep him waiting." Trevor continued on his way, tossing his parting remark over his shoulder. "Send your sister to me at the end of the week. I should be home by then."

Edric slumped back in his chair and heaved an exasperated sigh. He had hoped that Trevor would take one look at Meagan and fall helplessly in love with her. It would not be until after the wedding that Trevor learned of her stubborn nature and strong resentment of Norman lords. Damn, he had carefully calculated this meeting, and now he would be forced to send Meagan to Trevor on approval, just as he had suggested. But one way or another he would have revenge on that arrogant Norman baron. If Trevor took Meagan to his bed and spawned a child, Edric would have just cause to insist upon wedlock. Meagan was a lady of noble birth, and if Trevor treated her as a harlot, Edric would have firm grounds for making demands. Yea, Trevor Burke would pay one way or another, Edric vowed to himself as the muscular form of a man disappeared into the shadows of the corridor.

Meagan Lowell's blue eyes registered shock and dismay when she glimpsed the mammoth castle that was perched on the man-made hill in Wessex. It had been three long years since Meagan had viewed her home, and now she was painfully aware that it wasn't there at all. The changes were so staggering that for a moment she wondered if she had taken a wrong turn.

The craggy towers of stone and timber cut a jagged slash across the mid-August sky. The manor she had once referred to as home was now a massive, barbaric structure encircled by a deep ditch. A huge mound of earth had been raised inside the circular moat, and upon it sat a guard tower. Beyond the rock fortress was yet another stone structure to house what was left of the Lowell family and servants. A drawbridge had been lowered in anticipation of Meagan's arrival, but she was having serious misgivings about setting foot upon it.

Her wide, disbelieving eyes flew to Barden Keyes, the aging knight whom her brother had sent to fetch her home. "Has Edric agreed to this preposterous transformation?" she questioned aghast.

Barden's chain-mail shirt rattled as he shrugged his sagging shoulders. "Your brother had no choice but to comply with the changes. Edric is only a vassal. The new baron, Trevor Burke, ordered Edric to build a fortress to fit the king's specifications or forfeit his fief to a Norman mercenary," he explained.

"William the Bastard, you mean," Meagan spat resentfully, her lovely face puckering at the mere mention of the powerful duke of Normandy. "He is not *my* king and I will not bow to him."

Barden ducked away from the hissing sound of her voice and threw a cautious glance about him, hoping the trees had not sprouted ears, waiting to uproot and carry her blasphemy to the new king.

"He is every Saxon's king, m'lady, by right of force."

Meagan silently smoldered. The *king* was nothing more

20

than a brutish Norman. William the Bastard—as she would continue to call him—had appeared in Pevensey on September 28, 1066 to claim the throne that Harold Godwinson had taken after Edward's death. A thousand longboats had converged on the English coast, and Meagan shuddered, imagining what a fearful sight it must have been. As the boats had run aground, seven thousand armed soldiers had waded ashore. They were mercenaries and adventurers whom William had collected and paid a handsome price to aid in his acquisition of the English throne. Three thousand horses had been ferried across the channel from France. Besides their prize mounts, the Norman army had floated their own fortress across the channel. Cut timbers had been framed and pinned together in France, dismantled, packed in huge barrels, and then transported by ship to be raised on British soil.

The Saxons had considered the timber fortress an omen of impending doom, and loyal subjects had cringed when messengers brought word that the Normans had reassembled their stronghold the very same day they set foot on British shores. Although Harold Godwinson, the newly crowned king, had gathered his forces to defend England, his brave knights were no match for the skilled mercenaries who swarmed the southern banks.

Meagan squeezed her eyes shut and trembled uncontrollably as she recalled that fateful night when the flaming comet had blazed across the heavens and the bleak news had reached them. Harold Godwinson and both of his brothers had perished on the battlefield, tricked by a Norman ploy. There was no other force to confront the invading conqueror and his heathen band of marauders and pilferers who marched toward London to claim the throne.

Edric had feared for his sister's safety and had quickly whisked her off to the convent. And then the Normans flooded the countryside like a devastating tidal wave of terror, plundering and looting the manors of the English lords who had taken arms against the bastard duke.

When the news of the invasion spread like wildfire, Meagan's father had been seriously ill. Burgred Lowell had refused to send his knights to join Harold, a man he looked upon with contempt. Harold had managed to form the largest landholding party in England, using his power to induce King Edward to exile men who ruled land Harold conveted. Burgred Lowell had not lived to hear that Harold had been slaughtered or that the Normans reigned in England. Meagan had wondered if his passing was a disguised blessing. Her father could not have tolerated either outcome, and he died seeing his manor intact.

Although Edric had been forced to kneel before William and his newly instated overlord, Meagan could well imagine how it galled her proud brother to pledge his devotion to the Norman king and his mongrel overlord, a man rumored to have dozens of skeletons rattling in his closet, a man who lusted for power and who eagerly followed the conquering king for personal gain. The man was of questionable breeding, the scum of the earth. The Dark Prince, as the villagers had nicknamed him, probably had the tough hide of an elephant and the irascible disposition of a wild boar, Meagan mused sourly. Trevor Burke was said to have shiny raven hair and golden brown eyes, setting him apart from his fellow Normans. Meagan had only second- and thirdhand information about the Dark Prince who now ruled her family's fief, but already she despised him. He had been described as a strong, handsome warrior, but she could not fathom how anyone in his right mind could label the savage Norman, or whatever he was, as attractive by any stretch of the imagination.

A faraway look swam over Meagan's delicate features as she gazed back through the window of time to recall the days of happiness, ones she had enjoyed before the vicious marauders swarmed her native land to turn her world upside down. Her father had promised her to Reid Granthum when she was but thirteen years old, and she would have been wed on her fourteenth birthday the following spring. But Reid had united with King Harold, and the Dark Prince had confiscated the Granthum manor, banished Reid from his own lands, and assumed control of the farm ground west of Pevensey. Meagan's fiancé had fled for his life, her father had died, and she had been unable to pay her last respects to

22

him before Edric carted her off to the convent. Now her brother had been forced to pledge himself to the bastard and his Dark Prince, who had the power to tell Edric when to jump and exactly how far. Meagan cringed at the thought of her brother swallowing his pride and stooping to the arrogant Normans who flounced around the English court, proclaiming themselves the mortal gods of Saxon England.

A frustrated sigh tumbled from Meagan's lips, but then she mellowed into a smile when Garda, her devoted falcon, fluttered down to perch upon her shoulder. It seemed the only friends she had left in the world were her pet falcon and the great shepherd that trotted alongside her mount. Meagan had no inkling what to expect when she confronted her brother, and she felt very apprehensive about returning to a world that seemed as foreign as France. Would Edric be as bitter as she was? Had his noble arrogance crumbled after his demotion from baron to vassal? Or had he accepted his fate?

"How did you fare at the convent, m'lady?" Barden inquired, drawing her from her troubled musings.

A smile traced her lips, carving dainty dimples in her creamy cheeks. "Just as you might expect," she teased the aging knight.

"Even the gentle nuns could not tame your contrary nature," he speculated, flashing the comely blond a wide grin. "I cautioned Edric that, although a great many things have changed, some things forever remain the same. 'Tis true of you, m'lady. You have always been a handful. Your father sought to domesticate you, but even *he* failed. I seriously doubt that Edric can accomplish the feat. You were born feisty and as free as the wind." His pale gray eyes anchored on the falcon that sat regally on her shoulder beside the shiny mass of platinum blond hair that tumbled down Meagan's back. "I suppose you saw fit to continue to hunt with Garda and Lear, despite Edric's strict orders to cling to the safety of the convent walls."

Barden knew it was not uncommon for ladies to follow the hunt, but it was rare for a woman to be as skilled as Meagan had been, even at thirteen. She had robbed a nest and

23

painstakingly trained her falcon to swoop down on its prey and then deliver the game to her. She had befriended the vicious stray shepherd that Barden had sworn was part wolf, and she had reduced him to mellowed mush with her throaty, coaxing voice. Now the falcon would fly to the ends of the earth to retrieve any game Meagan requested, and the shepherd would kill or be killed protecting his mistress. Meagan had insisted, as a young lass of twelve, that she be allowed to participate in the hunt, just as her brother did. And her father had granted her most every whim when she batted her sapphire eyes at him and graced him with one of her angelic smiles that could reduce any man to duck soup.

Yea, Meagan had grown sinfully bewitching the past three years, Barden thought as his astute gaze sketched her flawless features and shapely figure. Now Edric would struggle with the difficulty of holding a tight rein on his spirited sister.

Meagan nodded slightly in response to Barden's question, and the old knight was not too slow to catch the flare-up of mischief in her eyes. "I even hunted in the royal forest, just for spite," she announced saucily.

Barden swallowed his breath, the color seeping from his weather-beaten features. "M'lady," he gasped. "Are you not aware of the consequences of trespassing on the Crown's woodlands? Men have been maimed and castrated for wandering through the king's forest without permission."

"I knew of the punishment, but I was discreet," she assured him.

Barden rolled his eyes heavenward, certain that Meagan's guardian angel had been working overtime to keep the feisty lass out of trouble. "But you deliberately defied the law," he crowed.

His stern expression mellowed when Meagan reached over to smooth away his frown. "Do not chastise me, Barden. I thought I would go mad if I did not venture into the woods as I did as a child. 'Twas the only place on God's green earth that did not bear the stamp of the Norman mongrels."

The old knight wilted in his boots when she touched him.

24

He had always been overly fond of the pert young beauty. She was like a breath of spring air, her eyes twinkling like stars, her hair sparkling like the sun. She was a pleasure to watch when she bounded through the manor or ran like a doe across the meadow. Nay, he would not inform Edric that Meagan had flirted with disaster. Edric would be furious to learn that she had disobeyed him. She was just returning home after a three-year absence. 'Twas not the time to tattle, he decided. Edric would see for himself that Meagan Stanley Lowell had not become submissive during her stay at the convent. Indeed, it seemed she had become even more independent—if that was possible.

Chapter 2

When Edric heard his name echoing through the rock chambers, he glanced up, a bewildered gasp escaping his lips. There before him stood Meagan, her silver-blond hair streaming about her alluring figure, her face alive with pleasure, her eyes dancing with that lively sparkle Edric always associated with his younger sister. Her falcon was perched on the leather strap on her forearm, and Lear, the huge black shepherd, was poised beside her, inspecting his new domain. Meagan needed no flowing robes or adorning jewels to enhance her beauty. She had blossomed into a dazzling, delicate rose, and the transformation was spellbinding.

Edric gathered his wobbly legs beneath him, but before he could approach her, Meagan darted across the hall and flew into his arms, sending him sprawling in his chair to shower him with kisses until he chuckled at her overzealous greeting.

He pried her arms from his neck and held her away from him for a final inspection. "Let me look at you, my little bird. My, how you have grown up." Edric gave Meagan the once-over, twice, and then silently chided himself for allowing the Dark Prince to give him the slip without witnessing this scene. Trevor would have become sentimental mush if he had laid eyes on this rare gem, Edric mused.

"Oh, Edric, 'tis good to see you again," she sighed happily and then placed one last peck on her brother's cheek. "So much has changed since I left, but the picture of you that I have carried in my mind is just the same." Her gaze left him to scan the cold, impersonal hall. "This looks nothing like home. Is this frightful castle equipped with dungeons and dragons?"

"Nay, little sister," he assured her as he brushed his knuckles over her flawless cheek and then peered solemnly at her. "But there is . . ."

"M'lady?" Devona Orvin moved silently toward her mistress, lifting pale green eyes to Meagan. "Welcome home."

Meagan squealed in delight and then bounded from her brother's lap, leaving him in midsentence to give the strawberry blond a loving squeeze.

"Devona, I have missed you so!" she exclaimed as she held her at arm's length to study the servant who was only two years her senior. "I thought you would have been wed by now, as lovely as you are." Her dancing blue eyes circled back to Edric to flash him a mocking glance. "You could not give her up, could you? You really are a beast for keeping Devona underfoot when some fortunate man could have taken her for his wife. How many men have you turned away who asked for her hand, Edric?"

Edric flushed up to his blond eyebrows and Devona turned every shade of red at Meagan's outrageous remark. But Meagan knew the two of them only had eyes for each other and always would. Edric was moldy with tradition, afraid of being ridiculed for taking a servant for his wife, and Meagan had insisted on teasing him on that sensitive point. Now that she was home she intended to take up where she had left off. It seemed to Meagan that all Saxons had become servants to the Norman louts, and Edric had little reason for clinging to antiquated customs of noble breeding and courtly marriages. If he didn't marry Devona he was every kind of fool, she thought to herself. There was too little happiness in the present world, and he should grasp pleasure where he found it. Marrying Devona would ease his frustrations.

"Really, Edric, you should make a respectable woman of her before . . ."

"Meagan! That is quite enough!" Edric barked as he bolted to his feet to stalk toward her, itching to shake the stuffing out of her for her brash remarks. But he caught his tunic on the pointed edge of the table, ripping a wide gash in the cotton fabric. His frustration mounted as Meagan giggled at his clumsiness. "Now see here, young lady." Edric wrestled to free himself and then stormed down the steps to wag a lean finger in her beaming face. "I expect you to behave like a lady and mind that reckless tongue of yours. I had hoped the peaceful, unhurried ways of the nuns would wear off on you. I prayed that your stay at the convent would smooth your rough edges, but apparently it did not gentle you. My only alternative is the lash."

Meagan sized up her red-faced brother and his shredded tunic and then shot him a devil-may-care smile. "You have always had a nasty bark, Edric, but Devona and I know that you are as tender as a lamb. You will not lay a hand on me. I am your loving sister who has your best interests at heart."

His brow raised acutely and then returned to its normal arch while his gaze flooded over the saucy lass. "You think not?" His tone held a hint of challenge.

"I know not," she assured him confidently. "You breathe the fire of dragons, but you have never struck me, even when I yielded to the temptation of a mischievous prank." She moved gracefully toward the table to summon the falcon that had roosted there to peck at the crumbs of bread that remained from Edric's brief, unsuccessful encounter with the Dark Prince. "And if you dared to thrash me for speaking the truth, I would sic Garda and Lear on you."

Edric drew himself up to a proud stature and regarded his persnickety sister and the blushing Devona. Then he made his regal exit, flinging his last remark back at Meagan as he pranced toward the door. "Do not overtest my patience, Meagan. The Normans have preyed heavily on my good disposition until there is very little left of it."

As Edric marched away, Meagan turned a quizzical gaze to Devona. "Has he changed so much?" she queried softly.

Devona gestured toward the rock steps that wound upward to the living quarters on the second level. "I have

prepared your room for you, m'lady. We can talk privately."
She glanced discreetly about her and then broke into a wry
smile. "This castle has ears. 'Tis best not to discuss Edric or
his Norman lord unless we are behind locked doors."

Meagan would have been on the edge of her seat if she had
been sitting down. She was itching to know how her brother
had fared in his confrontations with the Normans. She and
Devona had been confidants and Devona would tell her all
she wanted to know, but it could not come quickly enough to
suit Meagan.

As they walked into the upstairs chamber, Meagan's eyes
flew about the room, registering her surprise that the
sleeping quarters could appear so homey when the Great
Hall reminded her of an aboveground dungeon. Long,
colorful tapestries lined the walls to combat the drafts. A
small fireplace was built into the far wall to ward off the
winter chill. Near the hearth was a fur-covered bed that was
surrounded by blue velvet drapes.

"Edric gave me permission to decorate it as I would prefer
it," Devona informed her as she closed the door behind
them.

"You have been using this room," Meagan guessed,
smiling at Devona's bowed head and guilty grin.

"Yea, m'lady," she confessed. "I hope you do not object."

"My only objection is that Edric has not married you
when everyone knows how much he loves you," Meagan
sniffed as she wandered over to lift the lid of the trunk.

"I made you some gowns," Devona murmured, tactfully
avoiding the previous subject. "They will need to be altered,
but Edric wished you to have a proper lady's wardrobe when
you returned from the convent."

Meagan lifted the long tunics and chemises from the trunk
and brushed her hand over the expensive fabric. "I hope
Edric has taken note of your fine stitchery." Her sooty lashes
swept up to stare solemnly at Devona. "My brother is a fool.
Your talents are endless. Your loyalty to him is faultless and
yet he refuses to see that neither of you will truly be happy
until you are man and wife. I marvel at your patience with
him. If I were you, I would have turned my attentions to

30

a man who was willing to offer me more than an occasional rendezvous in the shadows."

"Why should he marry me? I am already his possession," Devona pointed out. "Your brother has faced many humiliations these past years. He is at the king's mercy. If Edric wishes to retain your family's land, he must remain in good standing with the overlord. If Edric stoops to marry someone of my station, he might suffer greatly because of it. Trevor Burke might suggest a replacement and Edric could become a seneschal who handles domestic matters for some Norman vassal. Edric is walking on eggs, and I will not add to his misery by demanding that he marry me."

Meagan listened carefully to Devona's explanation and, although she was aware that Edric was treading on pins and needles, it disturbed her to see Devona used as his amoret.

"And just what does my brother propose to do if you bear his child?" she questioned point blank. "I am not so naïve as to think that you spend *every* night in this chamber."

A hot blush worked its way up Devona's neck to stain her cheeks, and she was far too embarrassed to meet Meagan's probing stare. "We have been careful," she murmured.

Meagan cast the comely servant a withering glance. "How long do you suppose it will be before *cautious* will not suffice?"

Meagan's blunt remark had Devona's composure coming unwound like a ball of yarn on a downhill roll. When she had collected her scattered senses, she countered with a wry smile. "Since when have you become an authority on lovemaking? I would not think that subject would be openly discussed at the convent."

"Well, I . . ." Meagan stammered as she stared at the tapestry that hung on the far wall, seemingly attracted by some intricate design that had suddenly caught her attention.

Silently, Devona moved up behind her. "Do not condemn your brother for his actions, Meagan. He is a man who has been forced to swallow his pride. I do not know what he is planning, but I think he is devising some scheme to avenge his fate. He summoned the Dark Prince this very day and he would allow no one in the Great Hall while they spoke."

A curious frown knitted Meagan's brow as she glanced back over her shoulder at Devona. "What is he like, this new lord?"

"I have only seen him from a distance," Devona admitted. "Edric will not allow me near him."

"He is jealous, I suppose," Meagan mumbled under her breath. Edric was as possessive as a mother cow with her newborn calf, but he also behaved like an ass, seemingly ashamed of the love he harbored for the shapely strawberry blond.

"The Norman is very handsome," Devona went on to say as she took the tunics from Meagan's arms and carefully replaced them in the trunk. "I have heard it said that the castle wenches who live in the walls of what was once the Granthum manor eagerly accepted him as lord and lover. Indeed, they fight over the opportunity to share his bed. If his prowess equals his striking looks I would be prone to believe the rumors."

"The Norman pig," Meagan sniffed distastefully. "I can think of nothing more repulsive than surrendering to that shameless mongrel."

Devona chortled at Meagan's explosive tone as she helped her mistress shed her traveling clothes and don fresh garments. "You may be singing a new tune when you lay eyes on the virile Lord Burke," she teased playfully.

"Nay, I will be gritting out the same melody, second verse," Meagan scoffed as she settled the black chemise over the curve of her hips. "All Normans are one notch above the devil since they are descendants of the eternal furnace." She tossed her silver-blond hair over her shoulder after donning her blue velvet tunic. "Enough talk of the Dark Prince. I am anxious to tour the castle and reacquaint myself with the other servants. It has been so long since I have been home that I do not wish to spoil my return by babbling about that brutish knave, Burke."

"May I join you?" Devona questioned hopefully. "I have completed my chores for the day."

Meagan raised a perfectly arched brow, her blue eyes

dancing with mischief. "I would love to share your company if you think you can tear yourself away from Edric," she mocked lightly.

"You haven't changed a mite," Devona observed. "You thrive on teasing. I can remember many a time when you had Edric gnashing his teeth to keep from strangling you for your taunts."

Meagan's shoulder lifted in a careless shrug and then she turned to summon Lear, who had planted himself in a corner and patiently waited his mistress's command. "Edric always invited teasing," Meagan defended. "Father raised him to be calm and reserved. I thought 'twas necessary to ruffle his feathers occasionally and keep his blood circulating."

Devona reluctantly broke into a smile as Meagan swept out of the room like a whirlwind. And that was what she was, Devona mused as she followed in Meagan's wake. Lady Lowell was lively, uninhibited, and vibrant, a tempestuous young woman whose daring attitude would inevitably get her into trouble. But at least Meagan was quick-witted enough to wade out of it when she found herself stewing in her own juices. Now that Meagan was home to brew up her mischief, the quiet castle would never be the same.

After Devona showed Meagan around the other chambers on the second level, she led her to the basement storage rooms and then to the bailey, a sprawling courtyard that sat between the Great Hall and the servants' quarters.

Meagan came to a halt when she spied the small, gleaming face of the young lad who limped toward her. Almund Culver had changed very little in three years, she mused. He had always been small for his age, and despite his clubfoot handicap Almund had never spoken a bitter word to anyone. Meagan had been particularly fond of the stable boy who had been in charge of Poseidon, the sleek black stallion her father had presented to her on her thirteenth birthday.

Unfortunately, most of the prize stock had been confiscated by Norman marauders and then sold for profit, sometimes to the original owners, bringing further humiliation to the defeated Saxons. Meagan's coal black steed had been one of the many horses stolen, never to be returned, and Meagan had been heartbroken when Barden informed her that Poseidon was not among the mounts left in the Lowell stables.

Almund knelt before his mistress to pay his respect and then struggled back to his feet, lifting his radiant face to survey the breathtaking change in the young lass who had been whisked off to safety at the first sign of impending doom.

"The years have been generous to you, m'lady," he breathed, his gaze wandering over her as if he were viewing a cherished portrait that had been stashed out of sight for endless years.

"And you are looking well, Almund," Meagan complimented him, dispensing with propriety to place a greeting kiss on his cheek.

Almund was dumbstruck, a warm tingle darting down to his toes. When Meagan withdrew after sufficiently squeezing him in two, he backed away to ease the surge of excitement that bubbled through his veins. His bewildered reaction had Meagan giggling, and she yielded to the impulse of hugging him again.

"Have you trained another steed for me, Almund?" she questioned as the lad pried himself loose and took another retreating step, even though he could have remained in the clinch with the lovely lady for the rest of the day. "Have you found a replacement that is as magnificent as Poseidon?"

"I fear there are no others as priceless as your mount, m'lady." A secretive smile settled on his boyish features. "Except perhaps for one . . ."

A muddled frown puckered Meagan's brow as Almund grasped her hand and limped toward the stables. "I hid the stud colt that I believed to be Poseidon's in my own quarters when the Normans swarmed the manor," he explained excitedly. "The steed is the image of his father, but he is only three and is still lean and lanky. I have trained him for you."

Meagan slowed her step when she spied the steed, which truly resembled Poseidon, except for the jagged white streak

34

that trailed down his face and the white stocking on his hind leg. "He is beautiful," she murmured, her appreciative gaze sketching the glistening black colt.

"And he loves to run," Almund assured her as he reached up to rub the horse's soft muzzle. "I have been dreaming of watching you thunder across the meadow with him, as you often did with Poseidon."

Impulsively, Meagan reached for a halter and slipped it over the colt's head. "Then I shall not disappoint you."

Almund hurried along behind her as she led the steed through the courtyard and then vaulted onto his back. Lowering her hand, she waited for Almund, who hesitated, glancing cautiously about him, hoping Edric was not watching and that he and Meagan could escape unnoticed.

"Come on, Almund," Meagan encouraged.

"But if your brother . . ."

"Nonsense," Meagan scoffed impatiently. "Climb on."

Satisfied that he would not be reprimanded for galloping off across the drawbridge with Lady Lowell, Almund pulled himself up behind her and hung on for dear life when she gouged the steed and sent him lunging into his swiftest pace, leaving a cloud of dust at his heels.

Edric muttered under his breath as he watched his sister race across the bridge and fly across the meadow at breakneck speed. But then, giving the matter further consideration, he chuckled to himself. What had he expected, after all? Meagan was as flighty as her mount and every bit as high-spirited as she ever was. Watching her left him with the warm feeling that she would succeed when Edric had failed. Soon Trevor Burke would meet his match, and Edric would bide his time, waiting for the right moment. A self-satisfied grin spread across his lips as he pivoted and strode toward the arched corridor that led to the Great Hall.

Devona walked silently beside Edric, miffed by the expressions that had passed across his handsome face. She did not dare question him, but she would have given most anything to know what was buzzing through his mind.

Devona was suddenly stung by a premonition that whatever Edric was planning involved Meagan, but she could not fit the pieces of the puzzle together. Edric had that same calculating look about him, just as he had the past two months, and Devona feared it spelled trouble. It worried her to watch him fall silent, acting as if she was no more than a stick of furniture.

Breathing an exasperated sigh, Devona followed him through the corridor, wishing he would open up to her and explain why he had spent so many nights sitting by the window, staring off into the distance, preoccupied as if he were meticulously plotting a scheme. Occasionally, he would dismiss her and then ride off into the darkness without telling her of his destination. It distressed her to think that the Edric she knew and loved had shut her out when they had always been as close as two people could get.

Chapter 3

Meagan had gloried in her freedom for four days, behaving like a child who had just escaped the dungeon and was anxious to pour a fortnight of living into a few days. She bounded from bed at the crack of dawn and burned her oil lamp until the early hours of the morning, leaving Edric to wonder if she ever took time to sleep. Several times he had reminded her of the hazards of burning one's candle at both ends, but Meagan paid him no heed. She seemed determined to compensate for her three-year absence in the span of a month.

Edric's gaze settled on Meagan, who looked as radiant as the sun as she fed the falcon that perched on the back of her chair. Meagan was rarely seen without falcon or shepherd, and even while she dined her guardians were looking over her shoulder or sitting at her feet. When she slept the creatures retired to her room. Edric was slightly envious that his sister possessed such a skilled fowl and devoted dog, since he had been forced to take an apprentice hawk when Meagan had hunted with him the previous day.

He would have sworn that damned falcon of hers was grinning at him after swooping down to pluck up the prey the weaker hawk had pursued. When the novice hawk had finally captured a smaller bird, he had been stingy with his catch, and Edric found it necessary to chase down his contrary fowl and pry the game from his beak. And of course, Meagan had cackled, making Edric furious.

With a cold glare, Edric focused his attention on the molting hawk, which was eyeing his tray of food with considerable interest. Edric was toying with the notion of hurling his useless bird through an unopened window to retaliate. Before he could put actions to his thoughts, the music of the psaltery, harp, and oliphant filled the room, easing his irritation.

Three sparsely dressed dancing girls weaved toward them, and Meagan leaned close to draw her brother's attention from the seductive movements of the dancers.

"You are gawking, m'lord," she teased wickedly. "What will Devona think when she sees you undressing these women with your eyes?"

"Must you forever pester me?" Edric grunted before taking a healthy sip of ale and allowing his eyes to wander at will.

"You are an easy target, Edric," she insisted, flashing him an impish grin that made her eyes glow like sapphires.

Edric unglued his eyes from the provocative dancers and anchored them on his sister. "And if you were to wed, would you refuse your husband the pleasure of minstrel dancers?"

"But of course. I would give him little reason to look elsewhere," she assured him breezily.

A devilish smile caught the corner of his mouth, curving it upward. "Do you intend to make your future husband your slave, insisting that he bow down to the stronger force?"

Meagan tossed her long hair over her shoulder and leaned back to offer Garda a treat. "He shall be henpecked. The poor man will molt as often as my falcon does," she chortled, delighted that Edric relaxed enough to engage in teasing banter.

"And what if this powerful lord were as headstrong and persistent as you are?" he questioned hypothetically, knowing full well that Lord Burke perfectly fit the description of being as solid and immovable as a mountain.

"Then I suppose we shall battle for his crown of authority. It would most likely become a morning ritual." Meagan sank back in her chair on the dais to observe the hypnotic movements of the dancers.

"I do admire your spunk, little bird. I only hope you do not misplace it when you encounter the Dark Prince," he muttered under his breath, his voice drowning in the music. But then, he knew Meagan wouldn't buckle, not when she laid eyes on the bronzed warrior while he sat upon his prize steed. She would be further reminded of her low opinion of the Norman lords who had conquered and claimed England and all that stood within her boundaries.

Edric had postponed announcing his intentions to cart Meagan off to Burke Castle until the eve of her journey, and he was hoping she would be dumbstruck. He was delighted that the traveling troubadours had arrived earlier than he had anticipated. Surely, Meagan would not make a scene if he sprang the news on her when the hall was bulging with guests.

When the dance ended, Edric summoned the harpist to him and directed his attention to Meagan. "Accompany my sister, my good man. Her voice is sweet music to my ears."

"But Edric, I . . ." Meagan tried to object, but Edric waved her off with a flick of his wrist.

"I demand a tune, songbird, something from years past to remind me of better days that seem lost to me forever."

Meagan nodded agreeably and then watched Edric down another mug of ale, his fifth that evening. His lackadaisical manner was evidence that the drinks had gone to his head, and she would not have been the least bit surprised if he dozed off halfway through her song.

As her husky voice hovered about him, Edric slumped back in his chair and closed his drooping eyelids, drifting with the hypnotic melody. Meagan had been blessed with a voice that could soothe the wildest beast, while Edric could only chirp like an ill sparrow.

When the song had ended, Edric pried one eye open, graced her with a quiet smile, and then dragged his mug to his lips, mustering his courage, wondering if Meagan would come apart at the seams when he informed her that she was leaving for Burke Castle early the following morning.

For over two hours Edric drank and listened to the troubadours serenade him, and then he called their leader to

39

his table to present him with food and drink. Marston Pearce bowed before Lord Lowell and then scooped up the bread, meat, and cheese that had been offered to him and his troop of entertainers.

"You are very generous, sir," he murmured, his eyes fixed on Edric with a look Meagan failed to notice. Then he glanced at the comely beauty. "And you, m'lady, could bring pleasure to the ears of England if you would join our vagabond band of troubadours."

"My aspirations for the lady do not include traveling with musicians," Edric slurred out before Meagan could respond to the compliment.

"But 'tis a pity nonetheless," Marston countered.

"You are very kind, sir," Meagan wedged in before Edric could interrupt her again. "I shall keep your offer in mind."

When the musicians filed out of the hall, Edric propped himself up in his chair and peered at Meagan. "You will need no other offer, for I have selected your husband and soon you will have an obligation to fulfill."

Meagan would have fallen through her chair if it had not been made of solid oak. It was as if Edric had catapulted a boulder into her lap. She turned wide blue eyes to her drunken brother, her jaw sagging.

"What?"

"Tomorrow you will ride to the former Granthum manor to meet Baron Trevor Burke. Since your former fiancé has vanished, I have decided to offer you to another man."

Meagan's ears were ringing as if she had been trapped inside a church bell the size of the one that hung in Canterbury. The vibrations jarred every nerve in her body. "Surely you jest," she croaked, leaving Edric to wonder how such spellbinding melodies could tumble from her lips.

"I have never been more serious in my life," Edric insisted.

Meagan caught sight of Devona out of the corner of her eye and watched the servant wilt as if Edric had knocked the props out from under her. It was obvious from the expression on Devona's face that she knew nothing of Edric's matchmaking, since she was staring at him as if he had just sprouted another head, one equipped with

40

devil's horns.

"I fear my brother is afloat with ale and does not know what he is saying," Meagan choked out, her eyes darting frantically between Edric and Devona. If Trevor Burke had been the last man on earth, Meagan would have bypassed the opportunity of propogating the human race. Although she had yet to lay eyes on the overlord, she knew she could never accept him as her husband. He was a loathsome Norman, the enemy, the epitome of all she despised, the cause of her bitterness, and the source of Edric's aggravation. "You must be mad!" How could he promise her to the Dark Prince when there were available vassals for her to wed!

"I know exactly what I have done and I know what I am saying," Edric assured her, although his slurred tone belied his words. "And do not look at me as if I had lost my sanity. I know exactly what I am about. Believe that!"

But Meagan and Devona were at a loss to understand his outrageous demand. He might as well have instructed Meagan to fly to the moon and slice him off a piece.

"You will leave on the morrow and will remain at Burke Castle until he has decided if you will suit him, and you *will* suit him," Edric ordered firmly.

"Until *he* decides!" Meagan was livid with rage. Her fist hit the table, rattling the plates and sending Garda fluttering above her perch.

"'Tis the custom," Edric reminded her, concentrating on conjuring up a stern frown when his facial muscles refused to respond to his silent command. "If you do not please him it will be a reflection on the name of Lowell. You are the liaison between Norman and Saxon."

"I'd rather be dead." Meagan's flaming blue eyes narrowed on her brother. "You have become selfish, Edric. Do you anticipate personal gain from his preposterous match?"

"Yea," he answered honestly. "I expect to keep our family lands intact and to remain in the baron's good graces until . . ."

"Swine!" she hissed as she bolted from her chair, startling

41

the falcon, who had just nestled down on her perch. "Do you see me as some subservient wench who will bend to that lout's will? I assure you, Edric, I will make his life a living hell."

"M'lady, lower your voice," Devona's gaze darted about the room, certain that the less loyal servants would be buzzing off to report Meagan's remarks to the Dark Prince.

Meagan was seeing red, and she didn't give a fig who heard her. "You will pay for this, my brother. If I must go then I will take Devona with me."

"Nay, she remains with me," Edric argued, their confrontation having a sobering effect on him.

"If she does not accompany me I will not go," Meagan assured him harshly. "Hear me and hear me well, Edric. If you intend to sacrifice me then you will also relinquish something precious and dear to you. How badly do you wish to secure your position with the Norman Throne?"

Edric gritted his teeth. His argument with his fiery sister set his stomach to churning. "You are in no position to make demands. Since Father is dead, I am the one who must see that you are properly wed, and there is no need for stipulations."

"Wed a Norman mongrel?" Meagan wailed. *"That* dictates stipulations, plenty of them!"

Edric's fingers clamped around her wrist and with a forceful yank he sent Meagan sprawling into her chair. "You will do as I command, woman. Do not forget that 'tis *I* who have authority here."

"I will not go without Devona," Meagan persisted, her eyes drilling into her brother, who looked so distant and remote that she wondered if she really knew him at all. "Not without Devona." Her voice was quieter now, but Edric had no difficulty detecting the obstinancy in her tone.

His gaze circled to the strawberry blond, whose face was as white as a sheet. "Only until the wedding," he compromised begrudgingly. "And then she will return to me."

But there would be no wedding, Meagan vowed to herself. Edric would have both of them back in a fortnight. She would not play Edric's pigeon. He would have to find another way to ensure his position during William the Bastard's reign, and Meagan prayed that it would be a short one.

"Agreed." She pried Edric's hand from her wrist and massaged her arm to revive the circulation.

A victorious smile surfaced on Edric's lips. He had won the first skirmish, and whether Meagan realized it or not she would soon be doing battle for him in her own subtle way. Trevor Burke would not be able to resist the likes of Meagan, not with her overabundance of beauty, talent, and liveliness. Normans thrived on challenges. Taming Meagan would be the incentive Trevor needed. Meagan would lead him on a merry chase, and the arrogant warrior would pursue her, only to fall headlong into a carefully planned trap. Soon, very soon, Edric reminded himself. There was more than one way to conquer the Norman pigs. When force failed, a resourceful man considered his alternatives.

As Meagan flounced toward the steps that led to her chamber, Edric eased back in his seat on the dais to sip the last of his ale, but his smug grin evaporated when Devona gave him the cold shoulder and marched away. He would sleep alone this night, he realized. Devona would adjourn to her own quarters with the other servants, and it would take a crowbar to pry her out. Even a lord's demand would bring no results tonight, he mused disconcertedly.

And he was right. Meagan and Devona had just unanimously voted him the most despicable beast in the world, and Trevor Burke ran a close second. If looks could kill, Edric would have dropped dead twice after both women paused to fling him murderous glowers.

The pensive expression on Meagan's face and the dark circles under her eyes alerted Devona that Lady Lowell had not bothered with sleep the previous night. The cogs of Meagan's mind had been working overtime, and she was not about to accept Edric's decision without putting up a fight. Meagan was the mistress of her own fate, and her brother would not summon her from the nunnery and deposit her in a Norman's bed before the first week was out.

As Meagan's blue eyes settled on her, Devona gulped hard. She had seen that mischievous look once too often; she knew it signified trouble. Meagan was plotting, and Devona had the uneasy feeling that she would be no more pleased with Meagan's plan than she had been with Edric's.

"What are you thinking, m'lady?" she questioned warily.

Meagan beamed in satisfaction as the worried frown carved deep lines in Devona's soft features. "That you have long been denied your true station in life."

Devona's frown grew more puzzled by the remark. "What are you ranting about?"

"I intend to avoid this ridiculous marriage and have my revenge on Edric," she explained as she settled herself more comfortably on the seat of the cart that carried her personal belongings and those of her two servants. Meagan twisted around to glance at Almund, who was edging up beside her on the black colt he had stashed away and then trained for her. "And both you and Almund are going to help me."

Almund tossed her a conspiratory smile even before he learned of his part in her plan. "Your wish is my command."

Devona couldn't share his complete devotion. Almund had always trailed after Meagan like a blind pup, unconcerned about the consequences of being caught up in one of her pranks. Meagan had embroiled herself in a peck of trouble when she was young, and Almund had usually been one step behind her, never profiting from his follies. Meagan had snapped her fingers and Almund had danced like a puppet on a string.

"'Tis not mine," Devona blurted out, her jaw set stubbornly. "I have seen you in trouble up to your neck, and I demand to know what mischief you are brewing before I lay my life on the line."

Meagan released a reckless chuckle. "Do not be so pessimistic. You are the one who will profit most from this plan," she assured her as she darted her an ornery smile. "You are going to become Lady Lowell, as you should have been years ago."

"Me?" Devona squeaked, her eyes bulging from their

sockets. "But I am a servant, not a lady."

"Nay, my friend," Meagan countered. "Your manners have always been more polished than mine. And if my father were here he would attest to the fact. He was constantly comparing your gentle ways to my less desirable qualities. As a matter of fact, he often suggested that I follow your example in behavior."

Despite the compliment, Devona had serious reservations. "I do not wish to deceive the Dark Prince, and you know that I am in love with another man," she reminded Meagan. "What could I possibly have to gain from this charade?"

"If Trevor Burke considers you to be a suitable mate for a baron, how can Edric argue the point?" Her delicate brow arched, and she paused a moment to allow Devona to digest her meaning. "When Edric learns that Trevor intends to wed me and that you are *me*, he will be forced to withdraw the contract. His heart will not allow him to give you up to another man."

"Or perhaps he is so determined to secure his place in the Norman ranks that he will sacrifice whichever one of us that necessity dictates," Devona parried.

"I think not." Meagan drew the food basket onto her lap and rummaged through its contents to offer a snack to her companions. "You told me yourself that Edric stashed you beneath his own bed when the Normans swarmed the manor. If he would sacrifice you to a Norman for his own gain, he would have done so three years ago. He sees you as indispensable. I, on the other hand, am not. He is using me for bargaining power with the Dark Prince."

"And what do you propose to do? Exchange places with me and become *my* servant?" Devona gave her head a negative shake. "I could never do that. 'Twould seem unnatural and awkward."

"You simply must adjust to the idea. You have always adapted well to most all situations. I have no doubt that you can stand in my stead and be a more convincing replacement than the original Lady Lowell."

Devona muttered under her breath. Meagan was calculating, considering every angle, preparing an answer for all of her arguments, making her plot sound as simple as a Sunday afternoon stroll in the meadow.

Meagan cast Almund a hasty glance, and then her gaze circled back to the disgruntled Devona. "Almund will be in charge of Garda and Lear. He will keep them on the leash. If they are hovering around me instead of you, the baron might become suspicious."

"'Tis insane!" Devona blurted out. "You cannot fool the overlord and I cannot portray a lady. Lord Burke will see through this scheme and suspect Edric of attempting to trick him. And I could never . . ."

"I have made my decision," Meagan interrupted, thrusting out a determined chin. "If you do not agree to help me, I will steal off into the night and neither of you will know where to search for me. That is my alternative plan of action."

Devona was between a rock and a hard spot. She was damned if she aided Meagan and she was damned if she didn't. Edric would be breathing fire when he learned of the switch.

Even Almund was having serious misgivings about agreeing to the scheme. If something *did* go amiss, Meagan would have difficulty cooling the fires of Edric's temper. Her eloquent explanations would not keep the vassal from blazing hotter than the summer sun.

"M'lady, it does sound a bit risky," Almund said gently as he reached down to stroke the black colt's neck. "What if one of the Granthums' former servants recognizes you and informs the baron? A fortnight is a long time to play this charade without drawing suspicion."

Meagan shrugged off his concern and focused her gaze to the south where Burke Castle waited like a looming reminder to the conquered Saxons. "And a lifetime is a long time to spend with a man I could never love. When Father betrothed me to Reid Granthum, I was too young to realize that I might not ever learn to care for him. But now that I am old enough to know what I desire in a man, I could never wed a knave who stands for all that I detest," she sniffed distastefully.

"But you have yet to meet the man," Devona reminded her. "He is a virile specimen, and he may be more to your liking than you might have imagined."

"He is Norman," Meagan bit off. "Nothing can disguise that major flaw, even if he is otherwise perfect. William the Bastard surrounded himself with hardened men who were willing to forfeit their lives for the wealth they might acquire if they survived. The Dark Prince has killed many of our fellow countrymen for his materialistic gain. Nay, Devona." Her blue eyes anchored on her servant, cold and unrelenting. "I could never fall in love with a man whose heart is made of stone and whose eyes glow with the greed of gold coins."

The threesome fell silent as Barden Keyes held up his hand to halt the entourage that accompanied Lady Lowell to her destination. When the knight clambered from his steed to massage his aching backside, Almund tugged on Meagan's sleeve.

"How do you propose to fool Barden?" he questioned quietly. "He will be making the introductions."

Meagan's eyes twinkled devilishly. "You will detain Barden outside the castle while Devona and I make our entrance without him. We will immediately request being shown to our quarters to rest from the journey. Edric gave Barden orders to return to him when I have arrived safely. He will never know the switch has been made."

Devona's gaze soared toward the heavens. It would take a miracle for her to play the charade Meagan had dreamed up, she mused disconcertedly. If the plot was uncovered, Devona might find herself dangling from the tallest tree in England. Lord have mercy on her wretched soul. Why had she ever been born, she asked herself miserably. It had been nothing but an uphill battle and the next few weeks had every indication of being disastrous.

Despite her fear of oncoming calamity, Devona held her

tongue while Meagan laid out suitable clothing for her to wear the following morning and offered last-minute instructions. She watched warily as Meagan settled herself on her pallet, smiling like a weasel who had just feasted on a plump chicken.

Meagan drew the fur quilt over her shoulder and prayed that the time would pass quickly since she was itching to see the look on Edric's face when Trevor Burke returned to Lowell Castle with Devona in tow. Let him steam and stew, she thought vengefully. He deserved to find himself in such a predicament after he had deviously plotted to make Meagan his pawn by throwing her at the Dark Prince like a sailor flinging raw meat to a starved shark. Marriage indeed! Meagan had no intention of wedding *any* man unless he bore *her* stamp of approval, not Edric's.

Laughter bubbled from her lips as she imagined Edric attempting to talk his way out of a scheme that had backfired in his face. It would teach him an important lesson, she thought smugly. Edric could not tamper with her life without suffering repercussions, and she knew her brother well enough to know that cutting off his right arm would be less painful than giving his permission for Devona to wed another man.

Her gaze drifted to Devona, who flounced on her straw tick, grumbling to herself. Now if she could only convince Devona that things would not go awry . . . If wishing could make it so, Meagan would have waved her fairy godmother's wand to give Devona the confidence she needed. Sighing heavily, Meagan closed her eyes, hoping the next two weeks would not become a nightmare from which she could never wake.

Chapter 4

Meagan felt the tension mounting as she peered at the castle that made her brother's fortress appear a miniature model of the foreboding stronghold that rose against the horizon. Double guard towers spiraled on either side of the drawbridge. Just beyond the entrance stood a monstrosity of timber and stone that sprawled in all directions. The fortress appeared indestructible with its broad moat and towering walls.

It would take a skilled army an eternity to discover a vulnerable point to attack, but even then Meagan doubted that a siege would meet with victory. Baron Burke had surrounded himself with enough rock and timber to discourage the most patriotic Saxons from revolting against their Norman overlord.

Her gaze slid to Devona, who wore one of the extravagant long tunics she had made for Meagan. Devona looked the part of a lady, while Meagan's simple attire left her position questionable. Now, if only Devona could keep a tight rein on her composure, Megan mused as the horses rumbled across the bridge.

When Devona jabbed her in the ribs, directing her attention to the awesome knight who led his steed from the stables, Meagan growled furiously. Edric knew and he had not informed her! Meagan was silently fuming, wondering if Edric's ulterior motive was to have her slit the Norman's throat when she saw the truth. Not only was Trevor Burke on hand and waiting outside his castle to greet them, but he had taken possession of *her* stallion! God help her. If she had had something lethal in her hand, she would have aimed it at the thieving rooster who strutted about his domain.

When Barden swung from his steed to approach the overlord, Meagan felt her heart come to a screeching halt. Her plan had already fallen flat on its face, and her nose was severely out of joint. She had the impulsive urge to leap from the cart and dash across the bridge into the woods, forgetting that she was about to be delivered into the arms of disaster. Never in her worst nightmare had she imagined that she would be forced to confront the Dark Prince as the true Lady Lowell. This couldn't be happening! Dammit, it wasn't fair!

"M'lord." Barden knelt before Trevor and then gestured back to the cart. "May I present Lady Meagan Lowell."

Trevor's eyes locked with a pair of blue eyes that were burning a scalding blue flame. Her gaze was potent enough to melt metal, and Trevor was acutely aware that the shapely blond detested him on sight. A mutual dislike, he mused sourly. He had been dreading this moment since Edric sprang the idea on him.

Despite her stunning beauty, Trevor felt resentment welling up inside him. Pasting on a reasonably pleasant smile, Trevor handed Barden the reins and strode over to the wagon. On closer inspection, he found the lady's features flawless. He had expected to meet a hook-nosed, cross-eyed termagant after Edric had raved of his sister's beauty. Most men would be quick to compliment a woman's comeliness where he was anxious to get the misfit off his hands, but Meagan was a prize fit for a king.

Before Meagan could protest, Trevor's lean fingers clamped around her ribs. The muscles of his arms bulged as he effortlessly swept her from her perch and set her on her feet. Meagan flinched, stung by the potential strength and size of the bronzed warrior who now towered over her like a looming mountain that blocked out the sunlight and all hope of switching places with her servant. Her gaze flew over her shoulder to see Devona sagging in relief and Almund dropping his head to comb his fingers through the black colt's mane.

Despair closed in on her, and she felt so frustrated that she wanted to scream at the top of her lungs. Now what was she to do? Play the genteel lady while the mighty overlord stood there raking her up and down as if he were closely examining merchandise that he might be willing to purchase, deciding if the quality of goods was worth the price?

Meagan instinctively snatched her arm from his lingering grasp and flashed him a look that would have sent a lesser man on a one-way trip to hell. Though Trevor was every bit as handsome as Devona had described, Meagan saw him as a beastly dragon rather than her champion.

"I demand that you show me to my quarters," Meagan gritted out to keep from shouting the castle down around them. "I wish to freshen up after our long journey."

"Demand?" Trevor's dark brow quirked at her harsh tone, vaguely amused by her daring. Lady Lowell had not crept in like a lamb, but rather like a lioness who was hungry to chew on something—preferably Trevor.

"Your wish is my command," Trevor replied, the faintest hint of sarcasm in his tone as he bowed before her.

I wish the earth would open and swallow you up, Meagan thought to herself.

As Trevor curled his hand around her elbow to usher her toward the forebuilding that led to the entrance of the Great Hall, a low growl erupted from the back of the cart. Trevor's head swiveled around to meet the black eyes of the wolflike shepherd that seemed to be considering Trevor for his midday meal.

"Not yet, Lear," Meagan called to her four-legged guardian, who was poised to pounce on the man who was about to lead his mistress away. Although she had no objections to Lear tearing off one of Trevor's legs for an appetizer, she considered his timing poor. "Come, Lear."

As the shepherd leaped to the ground to come to heel, Meagan heard another growl as vicious as Lear's. Hesitantly, she darted a quick glance to the greyhound that loped from the stables, the hair on his back bristling when he spied the beast that had invaded his territory.

"As the lady said . . . not yet." Trevor gestured to the dog and then firmly ordered him to stand his ground. A devilish smile hovered on his lips as he bent his gaze to Meagan and then propelled her forward. "They will be at each other's throats until they have become better acquainted. Odd, is it not, that the animal instinct runs deep in both man and his beast?"

Meagan was itching to smear that haughty smirk all over his face until he tired of wearing it. And she found nothing strange about a gnawing hunger to exterminate her enemy. Meagan had thought she only hated the overlord sight unseen, but she vehemently loathed the swarthy brute who swept her along with his swift, impatient strides, making her trot to keep up with him or risk being dragged.

"Bring the lady's belongings and follow us inside." Trevor barked the order over his shoulder to Meagan's servants.

"You stole my horse," she hissed, unable to keep the silence as she wormed from his grasp, repulsed by his touch.

Trevor's brow shot up, his gaze swinging to the stallion he had hoped to ride before the entourage arrived to spoil his late morning excursion. "You are mistaken, m'lady. The steed was a gift from one of my loyal knights."

"Nay, Poseidon was *my* gift from my father, stolen by marauders three years ago," she argued.

Clamping his mouth shut, Trevor chose to bide his time until he had this little firebrand alone. Then he would air his griefs and bring the persnickety Lady Lowell under thumb. It was little wonder Edric was anxious to find this minx a husband, he mused, casting Meagan a cynical glare. She had probably caused her brother a great deal of mental anguish. Although Meagan was distractingly lovely, she was as unpleasant as a poisonous snake and just as deadly, giving every indication that she hungered to sink her fangs in Trevor's flesh.

Trevor shoved the door shut with his boot heel and then abruptly slammed Meagan up against the wall with his hard body. "You have shown your bravado to my knights and squires." His breath was hot against her cheek, making her

52

heart thump so furiously against her chest that she feared it would leap out. "And you have insulted me by allowing your maid to dress better than yourself, as if our first formal meeting held no significance." His body pressed closer, his chain-mail shirt leaving imprints on her skin. "We shall dispense with the formality of trying to be gracious and civil to each other in private. Shall we get this over with?"

A puzzled frown knitted her brow as she stared into his amber eyes, trying to decode his meaning.

"You expected to endure my bungling embrace and then rush back to your brother, claiming I have made outrageous advances toward you which must be followed by a proposal of marriage," he said bitterly. "That is what Vassal Lowell anticipated from his heathen overlord, is it not?" An intimidating smile thinned his lips as he bent closer, his mouth only a few breathless inches from hers. "I am to be so enamored with the sight of you that I fall upon my knees and beg for your hand and your undying love."

His biting words infuriated her, but the arousing feel of his muscular body molded to hers brought a reaction that baffled Meagan. She wanted to strike out at him, afraid of the odd sensation that rippled through her naïve body, but he backed her against the wall like an invading army, leaving her no way to fight or retreat.

"You could never be enamored with anyone because you are overflowing with love for yourself," Meagan spat, struggling to free herself from his viselike grip, and then ceased her struggles when she realized she was wasting valuable energy. When he finally did release her, she would be prepared to pounce like a wildcat.

He laughed humorlessly. "If that be true, I would guess that you also suffer the affliction. Shall we see which one of us is more affected by the kiss?"

Before Meagan could reject the suggestion, and she most certainly would have, his mouth swooped down on hers, forcing her lips apart to savagely plunder the softness of her mouth. His teeth gnashed against hers until she gasped in pain. But the initial forcefulness ebbed and his embrace became compellingly persuasive as his lips skimmed over hers, teaching Meagan things she never knew about kissing. Indeed, more than she wanted to know, especially when the Norman lord was her instructor. His fingers no longer bit into her wrists. His hands wandered up her forearms and then tenderly folded around her waist, bringing her thighs in intimate contact with his.

Meagan was shocked by the warmth that rose from somewhere deep inside her, like a blossom opening to the heat of the summer sun. He was kissing her senseless, taking command of her body with skillful hands that glided over her supple curves, discovering unclaimed territory that no other man had dared to touch.

His lips clung to hers in languid exploration until Trevor realized that his forceful embrace had become a web of pleasure. Trevor dragged his lips away from hers and retreated a step, feeling as if he had been scorched. His entire body burned with a need he did not expect to feel when he clutched this spitfire to him. He had intended to teach her a lesson—that she was no match for his overpowering strength and that the strong would forever rule the weak. But suddenly his goal had become one of self-conquest. His body had violently reacted to the softness of hers. The stunning blue-eyed blond with the razor-sharp tongue had stoked a fire that the castle wenches had yet to ignite without complete seduction.

Trevor breathed a ragged breath as he met her bewildered gaze, and he remembered Conan's vision that this woman's appearance was a forewarning of danger. But Trevor had misinterpreted the sage's words, unaware that the enemy came from within—his weakness for a woman's soft, tantalizing body.

Wheeling away from the stirring sight of her heaving breasts and kiss-swollen lips, Trevor stared at the shaft of light that stretched across the planked floor, fighting to maintain his composure when his knees were threatening to buckle beneath him. He had been overly aroused by the feel of her shapely flesh, he told himself. 'Twas just that he had abstained from lovemaking for more than a week. If his passions had been appeased, he would not hunger like a starved beast.

"That will be our first and last embrace, m'lady," he promised, his voice trembling with the aftereffects of his bout with desire. "You can give brother Edric your story and it will not be a lie. But when he comes to voice his indignation, there will be no marriage. Edric craves what he cannot have. He must learn to be content with his station. I will furnish him with gifts to appease his singed pride, and he will find you a more suitable mate. You know as well as I do that all the two of us have in common is our dislike for each other."

If Trevor had not spoken the truth about her brother's scheme, Meagan would have been more outraged than she already was. She, too, had sought to twist fate, hoping to give Edric a dose of his own medicine.

"Edric baited you for his own material gain," Meagan assured him. "But do not think for one minute that I came willingly to your castle. Indeed, I would have preferred to be whipped," she added acrimoniously.

A wry smile cut deep lines in Trevor's craggy features as he slowly turned to face Meagan. "You found my embrace distasteful, then?" he questioned, his golden eyes flooding over her with such intensity that Meagan felt herself quivering all over again.

"Distasteful? Nay," she replied, a honey-coated smile glazing her lips, disguising the undertaste of sarcasm. "It could more aptly be described as repulsive or offensive."

Trevor chuckled at her attempt to insult him. It still miffed him that the woman was so free with her tongue when he could have ordered it bobbed for voicing such disrespectful remarks to her overlord. "Have you ever been kissed by a man before this moment?" he interrogated, closing the distance between them.

Her chin tilted upward as she stared him straight in the eye. "Yea, by men, but never a beast . . . until now."

Meagan was souring his good disposition with her stinging remarks. Instinctively, his hand snaked out to apply bruising pressure to the tender flesh of her arm, causing her to grimace in pain.

55

"Although there is no love lost between us, we will make an effort to be civil to one another until I deposit you on your brother's doorstep. Antagonize me and you shall reap the wrath your insults have sewn. Do I make myself clear, m'lady?" he gritted out between clenched teeth.

A timid rap on the door broke the clash of their smoldering eyes. Meagan was thankful for the interruption, knowing that they would come to blows if they were forced to endure much more time together.

"Give me back my arm, m'lord," Meagan demanded. "I have heard of tenants being maimed for breaking your laws, but I did not realize that we Saxons face amputation for merely offering honest answers to direct questions."

Trevor had confronted his share of contrary Saxons, but Meagan was plagued with enough belligerence to equip an entire infantry. Why hadn't he reached for his whip to leave her with a painful reminder of their conflict, he asked himself. Indeed, she deserved it. But something had stopped him. He would have to study their argument in retrospect before he determined what had deterred his violence.

"Entrez-vous," Trevor ordered as he released his punishing grasp on Meagan's arm and tarried beside her as Devona, Almund, and two of his squires toted her belongings into the lavishly furnished chamber that was to be Meagan's home for only God knew how long. And that was a question that Meagan wanted answered the moment the servants made their exit.

"How many days must I remain here before I return to Edric with the news that you and I are incompatible?" she blurted out.

Trevor lifted a lock of shining, silver-blond hair from her shoulder, seemingly preoccupied with the feel of the lustrous strands that splayed across the back of his hand. "I should think a week will be ample time to satisfy Vassal Lowell. If I cart you home tonight he will claim that I have not given our relationship a sporting chance. We cannot humiliate Edric, now can we, m'lady?"

While Meagan was stewing about how she was to endure seven tormenting days with the mighty overlord breathing

56

down her neck, Trevor strode toward the door and then pivoted to bow curtly to her.

"When you have had reasonable time to cool down and freshen up, you may join me on the dais for food and drink."

"You are most gracious," Meagan lied through her pretentious smile as she stiffly curtsied to him. Actually, she considered him to be a rude, brutish heathen who made a woman appreciate the chivalrous ways of Saxons. "But, pray, tell me if you have equipped my chair with sharpened spikes. I may wish to select heavier garments for padding whilst I partake of my meal." One delicate brow arched, and Trevor was quick to catch the twinkle of deviltry in her beguiling eyes. "And speaking of the meal, will my portions be sprinkled with poison, m'lord?"

The faintest hint of a smile found one corner of his sensuous mouth and tarried there for a moment. "Nay, m'lady. But I cannot honestly say that I have not entertained both thoughts."

With that he turned and walked away. Meagan made a face at his departing back. Her spiteful expression dwindled to a carefully blank stare when he shot her a condemning glance.

"I saw that," he said brusquely.

"But I hope you did not misinterpret it as a gesture of disrespect," she purred all too sweetly. "I was but exercising the facial muscles." Meagan contorted her face into several comical positions, her eyes crossing as she stared at the puffed-up lord. "One must take precautions if one does not intend to be plagued with sagging flesh and double chins in her declining years."

Trevor's measuring gaze assured her that he had not been duped. "M'lady, if you continue to press your luck at the same reckless speed you have pursued it since you set foot in my demesne, you may never live to see your declining years."

For the life of him, Trevor did not know what to make of this blue-eyed tigress. Her tongue was sharp and her temperament feisty. The chit was much too daring for her own good. While he stood there glaring at the insolent wench, he was mulling over their conversation, trying to

57

determine why he had not punished Meagan for her stinging insults and deliberate ridicule. Perhaps it was because she seemed to know just how far to push him before he completely lost his temper. A wry smile pursed Trevor's lips as he recalled the ridiculously amusing faces she had made at him under the pretense of preventing the formation of double chins. The lass could infuriate him one moment and have him biting back a grin the next.

Never had he met a woman who had touched off so many conflicting emotions in the short span of a few minutes. Trevor felt as if he had been strung out on a torture rack. His patience had been stretched until it had come dangerously close to snapping. His very thoughts had been distorted, and his primitive male urges had been sorely put to the test. The fact that he was even giving this Saxon wench a second thought disturbed him.

Trevor had carefully calculated his first meeting with Meagan, intending to put her in her place. But the moment he touched her, tasted her sweet lips, his brain had ceased functioning. Egod! That blond-haired she-cat had turned him wrong-side out, leaving Trevor to wonder if he had just met a woman he could not handle. Meagan was different from the other women he had known. She was an exasperating combination of alluring beauty and torment-ing frustration. *Her* opinion of where she belonged in the Norman feudal system was in direct contrast to Trevor's.

He would have to keep a watchful eye on this misfit, Trevor cautioned himself. He had the uneasy feeling that this distractingly attractive silver blond would derive wicked pleasure from stealing his heart—for no other purpose than to feed it to a pack of starving wolves.

When Trevor slammed the door shut behind him, the sound ricocheted off the walls to echo about Meagan. She glowered at the dragon's lingering image. "And may God strike you down with a bolt of lightning, leaving you a pile of charred ashes," she muttered acrimoniously.

The man disturbed her in more ways than one. He had kissed her senseless, applied brute force, and issued several threats. But if Trevor Burke thought he could subdue her, he had made a serious error in judgment. No doubt one of his many, she thought huffily. Meagan intended to needle Trevor until water ran through him like a sieve. He was not battling some simple-minded twit who could not debate her way out of a feed sack. She was a reasonably intelligent being, she complimented herself. And that was more than she could say for Lord Burke. He did not have an ounce of sense or a shred of decency in that virile body of his.

While Meagan was glaring daggers at his image, wishing she had planted her fist in his face, wondering how the arrogant knight would look with his nose mashed on the left side of his face instead of glued squarely in the middle where the good Lord saw fit to put it, Devona poked her head inside to cast Meagan an apprehensive glance.

"I trust you and his lordship are on friendly terms," she murmured, dragging Meagan from her spiteful contemplations.

Meagan motioned for her servant to join her and then she nodded cynically. "We shall get along fine as long as we are not within ten feet of each other. At closer range I will require a crossbow and sword," she insisted, her tone laced with hostility.

"I hope you did not offend him." Devona tossed her a worried look and walked over to fetch fresh garments for her lady.

"We have been discussing the rules of civilized warfare." Meagan unpinned her brooch, shed her tunic, and then, with Devona's assistance, she slipped into a trim-fitting bliaud.

Meagan glanced down to see that the garment outlined her figure like a clinging glove. She tugged to free herself of her apparel and then had a change of heart. Let the heathen gawk. He had promised not to lay another hand on her, so she could be recklessly seductive with her appearance if she dared. And she did.

"Lace me up," Meagan requested as she held her breath and waited for Devona to cinch up her waist. "We must not keep his lordship waiting. I suspect that he is not a patient man."

"But a very attractive one," Devona added. "Is he not?"

"I suppose he might be attractive to one of his kind," Meagan sniffed. "If that were not so, we would see a scarcity of lizards and snakes."

"Guard your tongue," Devona beseeched. "Do not overtest Lord Burke. 'Tis not your brother you confront. Remember that."

Meagan nodded mutely as she walked toward the door. "Yea, I will try, but that blasted Norman is like a tempest breathing on a crown fire. Once the flames of my temper have been ignited, it will be difficult to keep the blaze under control, and I fear that all the water in the English Channel will not suffice if Lord Burke and I truly clash."

"M'lady?" Devona ducked her head and then slowly raised it to meet Meagan's inquisitive stare. "I cannot say that I am sorry that we were unable to exchange places. I know you will be able to handle the baron much better than I. But please, do not annoy him. I fear for your safety." Devona crossed her fingers and said a silent prayer as Meagan walked to the door and then disappeared from sight.

When her wandering gaze fastened on the shriveled, white-haired man who was swallowed up by the oversized chair that sat on the dais, Meagan broke stride. His dark eyes drilled into her like a probing scalpel, picking her apart from inside out, making her flesh tingle. Mustering her composure, Meagan raised a proud chin and approached the dais, taking time to make the semblance of a curtsy before she seated herself on the left side of Lord Burke.

As she sank down in her chair, Trevor swallowed air, his astute gaze swimming over her delicious figure and then circling back to ensure that he had not missed something. It was a long, fanciful moment before he came to his senses and thought to introduce his guest to his trusted friend.

"Lady Meagan Lowell, I would like you to meet Conan Merrick." His attention settled on the elderly sage whose narrowed eyes were still fixed on Meagan. "My friend is wise in the ways of the world and has rarely misjudged my competitors or enemies."

The comment hung like the air around a stagnant pond and Meagan could see for herself that the heavily bearded counselor had as much use for her as he had for the rats that scampered about the buttery. Resigning herself to the fact that she could not battle both Trevor and his unfriendly right-hand man, Meagan took her meal in silence, finding that all of her food tasted like sour grapes. She quickly excused herself to wander around the fortress to seek out a pleasant face. She wound up in the stables to brush down her long-lost stallion and converse with Almund, who was anxious to hear how she had fared with the powerful overlord.

The remainder of the day she spent meandering about the fortress, avoiding Trevor like the plague. She had the misfortune of passing him in the corridor on her way to bed that evening, and when he blocked her path she felt her irritation and resentment festering like a boil.

"I trust you will sleep well tonight, m'lady," Trevor murmured as his golden eyes traveled over her, his gaze lingering overly long on her bosom before ascending to her exquisite face.

"I have no doubt that I will," she assured him all too sweetly. "I can think of things far worse than sleeping under the same roof with a Norman." Meagan was pressing, giving him the opportunity to snap back at her so she could retaliate with a cutting remark.

"Such as sleeping in the same bed with me?" he speculated, flashing her a wry smile that revealed even white teeth.

"An excellent example," she replied with a bittersweet grin.

Trevor edged closer, forcing her to look up at him, knowing that would agitate her. "You are a very lovely young woman, Meagan," he rasped, unable to contain the hint of desire that trickled into his words. "But you will never be of any use to a man until you climb down from your pedestal."

Meagan gasped at his quiet insult. *She* was not the one who was dizzy from the lofty heights of the throne, *he* was!

"I do not consider myself better than you. I see myself as your equal."

"Oh? In what respect?" he challenged.

"In all respects." Her chin tilted a notch higher.

"Even as a lover?" he baited, flinging her a provocative grin.

Meagan detoured around him and marched toward her room. "Goodnight, m'lord."

His taunting chuckle nipped at her heels until she shoved the door shut behind her. Fie on him! She could have met him on any other battlefield and considered herself worthy competition, but the lout had fished out one facet of her education that was sorely lacking. It galled her that he had had the last word, but Meagan vowed never to let it happen again.

Chapter 5

Summoning her composure, Meagan strode down the corridor to Lord Burke's chamber to rap on the door. Three days had elapsed since she had come to the castle, and she had developed a critical case of cabin fever, certain she would go mad if she were not allowed fresh air and privacy. There had been a chilling tolerance between her and the overlord, and Meagan had come to request a day's freedom.

Meagan swallowed her breath when the door swung open and Trevor stood before her with nothing but a towel draped over his hips, evidence that he had just stepped from his bath. Although she was doing her damnedest to prevent it, her eyes feasted on the broad expanse of his chest, the crisp matting of dark hair that ran down his lean belly, and the muscular shape of his bare legs. When she realized that she had been caressing him with her gaze and silently admiring his brawny male body, embarrassed red flooded into her cheeks.

A roguish smile dangled on the corner of Trevor's mouth as he watched Meagan study him in an altogether different light. "M'lady, I do believe this is the first time you have looked upon me without contempt," he taunted unmercifully. "Am I to assume that in my state of undress you like what you see?"

Meagan blushed profusely at that, mortified that she could find nothing about him to criticize even though she tried. His ribs were carved with scars, but his virile physique would put the mightiest of warriors to shame.

Once she had located her tongue, she raised a proud chin and swept into the room to stare off at some distant point in his sprawling chamber. "I did not come to discuss you, but merely to make a request, one which should be a delight to you as well as to me." She inhaled a quick breath and then blurted out, "I wish to spend the day hunting. I ask your permission to leave the fortress."

Trevor nodded agreeably as he strode up behind her. "I shall inform two of my knights and squires that they will be escorting you, and you may . . ."

"I want to go alone," she insisted as she turned to face him, careful not to allow her gaze to drop below his neck for fear she would be sidetracked by her straying thoughts.

"Nay," Trevor said firmly. "I will not invite Edric's wrath by allowing something disastrous to happen to you while you are in my care."

"I am quite capable of taking care of myself. While I stayed at the convent I always hunted alone, and as you can plainly see I have survived the woodlands without a scratch."

"The answer is nay," Trevor ground out, emphasizing each word.

Meagan's shoulders slumped as she heaved an exasperated sigh. She *was* going hunting without an escort, even if she had to get on her knees and beg. "M'lord," she began, her tone softer now. "I have grown accustomed to reverie after living with nuns and priests. There are times when one must be alone with one's thoughts. I feel caged inside these massive walls and I hunger for the freedom to wander at will."

His finger curled beneath her chin, lifting her face to meet his level gaze, drawn by the soft, tender woman who lay just beneath Meagan's defiant exterior. "Then I will grant you your wish, Meagan. There will be no large escort to protect you from the wilds."

A pleased smile blossomed on her bewitching features, and Trevor felt himself melt a little inside. Perhaps she had used the wrong approach with Trevor, Meagan thought to herself.

64

"But . . ." His thumb brushed leisurely over her cheek, enjoying the feel of her creamy skin beneath his hand. "You must endure my presence." When Meagan flinched, her eyes turning a darker shade of blue, Trevor continued before she lost control of her quicksilver temper. "I will not hamper you. 'Tis just that I will be in the vicinity should you require my assistance. We shall hunt separately and then meet again at dusk."

His stipulation eased her irritation, but his straying caress was sending her heart hammering against her ribs until she feared it would beat her to death. Standing too close to Trevor did strange things to her, making her acutely aware of his manliness, filling her senses with the musky fragrance that clung to him. His face was dangerously close, his golden eyes probing deeply into hers. His fingertip traced the gentle curve of her lips in such a provocative manner that Meagan felt herself tremble, so suffocated by his nearness that she could barely draw a breath without choking on it. Why did he affect her in such a physical sense when she despised him and all he stood for?

The quick rap at the door and the maid's barging entrance left Meagan feeling very self-conscious.

Daralis froze in her tracks when her jealous eyes came to rest on the handsome overlord and Lady Lowell. It did not take much imagination to conclude what the lady was doing in Trevor's room at this early hour of the morning and why Trevor was still scantily attired before sending his amoret on her way. Damn that witch! Daralis had her sights set on the virile Lord Burke, and until the last two weeks she had been his favorite lover. It angered her to see Trevor hovering about another woman, especially one as shapely and attractive as Lady Lowell.

"Forgive me, m'lord," Daralis apologized, striving to keep the annoyance from filtering into her voice. She was in no position to appear outraged that he had turned his attention to another woman, and she was not yet sure enough of herself to make demands on the powerful lord.

Meagan retreated, her face flushing six shades of red when Trevor raised a dark brow and flashed her a devilish grin, knowing what the servant was thinking and refusing to inform her that looks could sometimes be deceiving.

"The lady and I do not wish to be disturbed. You may advise the pantler that we shall be down for breakfast as soon as I have dressed, Daralis."

When the servant exited Meagan wheeled back to Trevor, her eyes snapping with indignation. "She thinks we have spent the night together," she spouted furiously. "Why didn't you set the matter straight?"

His shoulder lifted in a careless shrug as he swaggered over to don his clothes, forcing Meagan to present her back or gawk at Trevor, who dropped his towel to stand naked in the middle of the room. Meagan chose to stare at the window, mortified that Trevor had not one ounce of modesty, adding to his extensive list of flaws.

"I do not have to answer to my servants. What I do is none of Daralis's business," he informed her flatly as he shrugged on his chemise and then reached for his tunic.

"But she is your harlot," Meagan blurted out, and then chided herself for giving tongue to the thought. She had seen the comely, dark-haired wench hovering over Trevor on several occasions and had witnessed her slipping into Trevor's chamber the second evening. Meagan was not foolish enough to think the two of them were engaged in a casual game of chess at that late hour.

A low rumble erupted from Trevor's chest as he clasped his belt around his midsection and ambled toward her. "How do you know that?" he inquired, muffling a chuckle.

"I have heard it said that the chambermaids hover about your door in swarms and that you have to beat them off with a stick. I have no doubts that Daralis is among your doxies."

Trevor stood directly behind her, his warm breath tickling her neck, sending a rash of goose pimples skitting across her flesh. "Men and women have their needs, Meagan." The sound of her name as it tumbled from his lips left her aquiver. "It is not uncommon for a man to satisfy his needs when there are willing maids underfoot. But my heart is chained to no woman. They offer physical pleasure, and in the past I have but accepted it."

"Then you do not believe in love," she speculated as her eyes lingered on the rugged features of his face that were carved from years of experience and trials.

"Do you, Meagan?" He put the question back to her as he continued to sketch her flawless face with his warm gaze.

For a moment the anger and hostility between them evaporated, and Meagan studied him as a woman assessed a man, speaking frankly without antagonizing him as she was prone to do. Usually Trevor brought out the worst in her—her fierce instinct to cling to her pride and rebel against her Norman lord.

"I pray that love exists," she told him softly, a whimsical glow in her eyes and a tender smile on her lips. "I seek a man who earns my respect without demanding it, one who is strong and yet gentle. I would wed for love, not wealth, as Edric would prefer. There must be more to a man and woman's relationship than a tolerant existence, and I am determined to find it or become a spinster." With that she graced him with an impish grin that left her face radiating like the sun.

Trevor chuckled as he stared down at the feisty minx, seeing in her something that he had never taken time to notice in a woman. It was her zest for life and uninhibited vibrance that left him basking in a strange warmth that blossomed somewhere in a shadowed corner of his heart. But, reminding himself that he was a confirmed bachelor, Trevor stepped away before he found himself delving deeper into this enchanting maiden than necessary and then gestured toward the door.

"Perhaps we should partake of our meal and seek out our game before I am cornered by my tenants and their domestic disputes. If they detain me, I do not know if I will be able to slip away."

The spell was broken by his businesslike tone, and Meagan stiffly drew herself up in front of him, attempting to smother the wave of tenderness that had flooded over her. She had her heart set on disliking the Dark Prince, and she could not allow herself to be swayed by the occasional gentleness he displayed. He was still her enemy, and only a fool would permit herself to forget that.

Silently, she followed the powerfully built warrior through the corridor to meet Conan's unpleasant stare and Daralis's envious glare.

Trevor eased back in his massive chair on the dais and cast his sage a sidelong glance. "Lady Meagan and I intend to spend the next few days hunting," he casually announced and then tensed when Conan's disapproving frown drilled into him. "I have also decided to mix business with the pleasure of the hunt. It has been weeks since I have paid a visit to Ragnar Neville's fortress for inspection. With the unsettled relations in the kingdom it is best that I keep a watchful eye on the far corners of my demesne." Trevor sighed and then shrugged his broad shoulders. "At any rate, there will be no reason for you to grow concerned if we are away from the castle for as long as a week."

"Do you think it wise to take this—" Conan turned his silvery white head to rake Meagan with piercing scrutiny— "this young woman with you? Must I remind you, m'lord, that Saxons are alike, one and all? The general consensus of Saxons is that a good Norman lord is a dead one. She is a bad omen, one whom I cannot trust, and I am still battling the premonition that she would like to make you a corpse and present you to the rebels."

Meagan tensed like a she-cat waiting to pounce on her prey, and she would have bolted from her chair to voice a loud objection to Conan's derogatory remark if Trevor hadn't clamped his hand on her arm and forced her back into her chair. Although the outspoken oracle had dug up some of her spiteful thoughts, she felt obliged to protest. Her only purpose for the hunt was to enjoy the freedom of wandering at will, not to stab Lord Burke in the back as Conan had suggested. The nerve of that old buzzard, she thought huffily. How dare he make such slanderous remarks to her face!

"If your lord is not man enough to protect himself against a mere wisp of a woman then he certainly is unfit to reign as overlord of Wessex," Meagan flung at the aging sage, along with a taunting smile that served to stoke the fires of the old

68

man's temper. "Are you suggesting that Lord Burke is incapable of defending himself against a woman? Do *you*, his appointed seneschal and confidant, dare question your lord's abilities? It seems to me that you are the one surrounded with suspicion, great sage and seer."

Trevor bit back an amused grin. Meagan had the uncanny knack of going for a man's throat with a feather, rather than a dagger. She could fuel the fires of a man's temper, and yet she appeared so angelic and innocent while she was doing it that it seemed unreasonable to punish her. Trevor found it far more enjoyable to *watch* his seething sage match wits with this clever nymph than to argue with her himself. Anticipating Conan's counter, Trevor settled himself more comfortably in his seat.

Two graying brows formed a harsh line on Conan's wrinkled forehead as he glared holes in the insolent young woman's tunic. How dare she question his loyalty. Indeed, it was *her* devotion to her overlord that they were disputing. Conan would have bet his right arm that this cunning vixen was biding her time until she could dispose of Trevor Burke. He didn't trust the bright-eyed minx, not even a smidgeon, especially since she was a dyed-in-the-wool Saxon.

"I have never doubted my lord *or* his great abilities," Conan assured her in a grating tone that would have made a lesser woman cower as if she had confronted a timber wolf. "But I have grown suspicious of Saxon rebels who do not bat an eye at resorting to devious means to destroy their Norman rulers." Cold, penetrating eyes peered into Meagan as if he sought to read her mind, pluck out each traitorous thought, and then bring it to Trevor's attention. "You, Lady Meagan, could well be part of a subtle scheme that aims to destroy my lord. It would not be the first time a comely young woman employed her feminine charms to gain favor and trust before she betrayed her lord."

Meagan blushed up to the roots of her blond hair, infuriated by the insinuation that she would spread herself beneath this Norman lord and *then* stab him in the back. If Conan had taken the time to know her before he proposed such ridiculous speculations, he would have known she would rather be stretched on a torture rack than sleep with Trevor Burke!

"You have sorely misjudged me," Meagan spewed, her blue eyes snapping. "Your almighty lord's bed is the *last* place I intend to sleep! And if it were my purpose to run him through with my dagger, I assure you, he would see it coming. I am no coward, Conan. I would fight my battles fairly."

"Even if you could not match your enemy's superior strength?" he sniped, his lips thinning into a sly smile. "Who can honestly say what one would do to ensure victory, m'lady? Perhaps you have yet to be tempted by the possibility."

Meagan opened her mouth to voice a sarcastic rejoinder, thought better of it, and then slammed her jaw shut to glare at Conan. She would not allow him to bait her, she told herself as she counted to ten to gain control of her volatile temper. She was fencing words with a man who held an influential position in Trevor's demesne. And if she didn't carefully guard her tongue she might spoil any chance of a pleasurable outing in the forest, one in which Trevor had promised to leave her to her own devices as much as possible.

"No icy retort or indignant protest, m'lady?" Trevor mocked lightly as he raised a heavy brow. "Do you consent to awarding this round to my illustrious sage?"

Long, thick lashes swept up as Meagan regarded the aging oracle. "I will admit to nothing except to further add that I *am* a Saxon who has long lived with the bitterness of watching my way of life destroyed by marauding Normans. It takes time to heal the wounds of war and to offer respect to my Norman lord." Her eyes swung to Trevor, who was watching her as closely as the oracle was. "My request to hunt does in no way imply that I intend to make *you* my intended prey," she quietly assured him. "I still prefer to go alone."

"She has openly admitted that you have yet to win her loyalty and admiration," Conan hastily pointed out and then leaned close to Trevor to convey a confidential comment. "I still do not trust this woman. If you take her with you, at

70

least consider your blind side and protect it from attack."

A wry smile pursed Trevor's lips as he nodded agreeably. "Your suggestion is well taken, Conan. I shall keep it in mind."

Meagan was itching to know what had transpired in their secretive conversation, but she didn't have a snowball's chance in hell of finding out. Heaving a frustrated sigh, Meagan glanced away, only to find Daralis reentering the Great Hall with a spiteful frown stamped on her comely face. It was obvious the castle wench was battling jealousy, furious that Meagan would be spending several days in seclusion with the powerful overlord Daralis had her sights set on. Meagan was sorry Daralis hadn't been in the room when she had assured Conan that she had been sleeping in her own chamber and had every intention of continuing to do so. There would be nothing intimate between her and Trevor, Meagan told herself. Her only purpose was a breath of freedom and the challenge of the hunt. The very last thing she wanted was a rendezvous with the lord of Wessex. Indeed, he was the last man on earth she intended to bed!

Loud, argumentative voices from the forebuilding drew Meagan's attention and she frowned in disappointment when several outraged tenants stalked into the hall behind one of Trevor's squires.

"M'lord, I tried to settle their differences, but these farmers insist that you can be the only one to successfully resolve their dilemma," Yale Randolph explained. "Forgive the intrusion, but I fear this matter requires your immediate attention."

An apologetic smile trickled across Trevor's lips as his gaze momentarily shifted to Meagan, who was trying very hard to hide her blighted hope. "It seems we are forced to postpone the hunt until the morrow." His calloused finger brushed over her satiny cheek and then curled beneath her chin, forcing her to meet his spellbinding golden eyes. "Meet me at dawn, little dove, and we shall make our escape before we are set upon by more squabbling tenants."

Nodding mutely, Meagan rose from her chair to return to her room, frustrated that she would be forced to spend

71

another day pacing the confines of her chamber.

"Do you think it wise to abandon your castle with so many domestic disputes waiting on your doorstep?" Conan lifted an eyebrow, watching Trevor devour Meagan with his eyes as she gracefully strolled through the hall. "It would be unseemly to shrug your responsibilities and frolic in the woods with that blue-eyed troll."

"But you forget that I am leaving my fortress in competent hands," Trevor countered as he dragged his eyes off Meagan and bent them to the meddling sage. "Were you not so capable, I would not allow this comely maid her request to hunt."

"*Her* request?" Conan's wary glance circled back to Trevor. "Beware the lady. She is far from the usual maid, and it would grieve me to learn that the hunter had become the hunted."

"I will keep a watchful eye on Meagan," Trevor assured him and then turned his full attention on the three tenants who were still glaring murderously at each other. He listened to each one speak and then set out to determine who was at fault and who deserved the overlord's pardon. But just when Trevor had judged where the guilt lay, another surge of tenants flooded the hall, and it was late afternoon before he could flee the Great Hall to take a breath of fresh air.

As he ambled through the bailey, a slight movement from the covered passage that led from the castle to the chapel tower high above him caught his attention. A wry smile pursed Trevor's lips when one bare leg glided over the railing and then slid to the supporting beam beneath the elevated ramp. And then a woman's entire body appeared from the passage to crouch on the lofty beam, as if a dove had flown to its perch and sat stately watching the activities that were going on below her.

So it was true that this lovely misfit was so bored that she was literally climbing the walls, Trevor mused as he strode over to park himself beside the rock wall to watch this restless bird's acrobatic maneuvers. Shapely legs and thighs protruded from the hem of her tunic, and the shaft of sunlight behind her silhouetted the curvaceous figure beneath the thin fabric. Trevor felt the hunger of desire gnawing at him as his sharp eyes sketched Meagan's alluring form. He had never met a woman like this quick-witted, sprite young beauty, who preferred daredevil maneuvers on lofty beams to sitting in her room, chatting with her maid while she labored over her stitchery.

Impulsively, Trevor strode over to grasp the supporting beam above him and then agilely swing upon the rough post, making his way along the ladderlike beams that steadied the passageway to the chapel.

A contented sigh escaped Meagan's lips as she peered across the countryside. Oh, how she longed to straddle her steed and race the wind. The strain of having Conan and Trevor breathing down her neck was almost too much to bear. Despair had closed in on her when Trevor had informed her that they would have to postpone their hunting trip until the following day. But there was no guarantee that even the morrow would offer her freedom. The overlord's duties were numerous, and she doubted that he would be able to escape for even a day. Why couldn't he have allowed her to hunt alone? What did he think she was, some mindless twit who could not defend herself in the wilds? Meagan sniffed distastefully at the thought. She had faced her fair share of danger with the beasts that prowled the forests, and she had returned unscathed from her solitary hunting trips at the convent. Although the nuns had presumed she was in her room, fasting and praying, Meagan had been munching on the wild game she had snared and praying that swarms of hornets would swoop down on the Normans and drive them back to the channel from whence they had come.

"Do you also make a habit of perching in treetops?" came the low, amused voice from so close behind her that Meagan nearly jumped out of her skin.

Her startled shriek caught in the wind as she lost her footing and teetered precariously on the beam. When her hand slid off the plank above her, she was overwhelmed with the feeling that she was about to plunge to her death. But then a sinewy arm snaked out to curl around her waist, catching her the split second before she lost her grip and fell into the bailey in a crumpled heap. Meagan found herself dangling in midair before Trevor clutched her to the solid wall of his chest, and suddenly she found herself preferring to risk the fall than to be held captive in his powerful arms.

"Let me go!" Meagan insisted, alarmed by the wild sensations that shot up and down her spine.

"If I let you go you will surely fall," Trevor laughed softly, his warm breath sending an infantry of goose bumps marching across her skin as he whispered against her neck, "Can you not endure my touch when your only alternative is plummeting to your death?"

Meagan gasped for air as Trevor dragged her onto his lap, molding his hard, male contours to the softness of hers. Her heart was slamming against her ribs so furiously that she was certain they would crack beneath the fierce pressure. She was assaulted by the same inexplicable sensations that had consumed her the day she arrived at Burke Castle and Trevor had kissed her senseless. Those feelings frightened Meagan. She was quite comfortable with her dislike for the powerful overlord, and his touch only served to crumble the barriers of her defense.

"Well?" Trevor prodded when she did not immediately respond.

"I am but considering which is the lesser of two evils," Meagan tossed over her shoulder, not daring to twist around to face the handsome knight who had caught her behaving in a most unladylike manner.

A low rumble rattled beneath his chain-mail shirt, and Meagan felt the vibrations ricocheting through her tense body. "I have yet to hear a complaint from any woman when she finds herself nestled in my arms, daring dove."

"Except one," Meagan amended as she squirmed to brace one hand on the beam above her and, she hoped, pull herself away from Trevor's strong arms. But when she tried to put a safe distance between them, his viselike grip crushed her back against the hard wall of his chest and muscled thighs. "I think I prefer to trip along the borderline of disaster rather than cling to you for assistance." Her half-strangled voice betrayed the crosscurrents of emotion that were churning inside her. "I can climb back to safety if you will kindly unhand me, m'lord."

Trevor was experiencing the same sensations that plagued Meagan. The feel of her shapely body mashed into his stirred longings that Trevor was usually able to control . . . but not with Meagan. She could send his blood pressure soaring with the birds that sailed above them, and she could make his heart prance like a stallion anxious to break into a run. This sapphire-eyed beauty could take his strong convictions about sending her back to her brother untouched and turn them into mush.

As his arm moved higher to ensure that she didn't escape his grasp it collided with the undercurve of her breasts and Meagan flushed crimson. If she didn't escape him, and quickly, he would be doing far more than *protecting* her from the fall!

"Let me . . ."

"M'Lord?" Conan's raspy voice wafted its way up to them, cutting Meagan off in midsentence. "What are you doing?"

Trevor peered down to see the darkly clad sage looking up at him with shock and disbelief written on his wrinkled features. It was apparent that the old oracle believed he had taken leave of his senses, judging by the expression that was plastered on his face. He and Meagan must surely look a sight, perched on the beams below the pentice that led to the chapel.

"I am surveying the perimeters of my demesne," Trevor said with a sheepish smile.

"With the lady poised on your lap?" Conan snorted sarcastically and then shook his graying head in disgust. "I should think you could obtain a better view from yonder guard tower. I tried to warn you that this woman could become a dangerous distraction. She has you behaving like a reckless young squire who climbs around in trees like an ignorant ape." Conan tossed the undignified overlord another condescending frown. "If you can tear yourself away from your limb and that chit, I would like to speak with you."

Meagan inwardly groaned. The old buzzard already

thought she was a menace to his lord, and no doubt he was having misgivings about *her* intelligence. Why hadn't she remained in her room? Because the walls were closing in on her and Meagan feared she would go stark raving mad if she didn't escape the suffocating confines of her chamber, she reminded herself. But the price she had paid for a breath of freedom was far more than she had bargained for. Here she was, draped in Trevor's arms, perched like a pigeon while Conan glared up at her, suspicious of her every move.

"I will join you in the hall in a few minutes," Trevor assured the disgruntled seer and then flicked his wrist to send the old man on his way. "Well, m'lady, it seems we have made a spectacle of ourselves." Laughing golden eyes held her hostage when she dared to glance back at him.

"It wouldn't have happened if you had left me alone," Meagan muttered resentfully as she pushed away from his muscular frame to loop both arms around the beam above her. "I was perfectly content . . ."

"Argh!" Trevor groaned as her foot slipped from his thigh and struck him in the groin. "Egod, Meagan, I will be of no use to any woman if you do not watch where you step!"

His blunt remark had her blushing profusely, and she hurriedly found another place to set her foot besides in the middle of his lap. But then a spiteful thought hatched in her mind and she smiled wickedly as she pirouetted on the narrow beam to follow the path Trevor had taken to climb beneath the pentice.

"Forgive me, m'lord. I would never intentionally cripple a rutting stag. It would be a shame to prevent him from pursuing that which he considers his main purpose in life."

Trevor gnashed his teeth at her taunting rejoinder and then pulled himself to his feet to follow in the persnickety wench's wake. "At least I have the ability to please women," he hurled at her. "But you, naïve imp, can do no more than antagonize a man."

Meagan stiffened defensively against his implication and whirled around on the beam to face his mocking smirk. "I am a woman of discriminating taste," she assured him tartly. "I do not offer myself for a man's lusty pleasures, and I do not intend to until I have found a man who moves me to passion." Snapping blue eyes raked him with contempt, wishing she could find even one flaw in his virile body to ridicule. "You could not find contentment if you slept in every wench's bed in every fortress in Wessex."

"You dare to say too much, minx," Trevor growled as he made a grab for the rebellious young woman who had him walking the fine line between anger and desire so often that Trevor was never certain which way he would fall until the moment was upon him. A few minutes earlier he was having second thoughts about keeping his hands off this lively lass, and now he wondered if it wouldn't bring him greater pleasure to put a stranglehold on her swanlike neck. "If you cannot keep a civil tongue in your head, I will refuse to take you with me on the hunt and you can sit in your room and rot until I return to unlock your chamber door!"

His lean fingers bit into her forearm, cutting off the circulation, and Meagan grimaced in pain. *He* had invited the insult and she had but given it, she thought huffily. But with the power of his position he had bribed her into submission, and it galled her to yield to her Norman lord. But relent she did, when faced with the choice of galloping through the woods or counting the cracks in her chamber walls.

When Trevor finally released her from his bone-crushing grip, Meagan hopped to the ground and then curtsied before him. "I must apologize for my disrespective outburst, sire." Her tone was soft, but void of emotion. It was neither mocking or sincere, but rather bland and expressionless. "Neither of us can help what we are, and it appears that we simply bring out the worst in each other. If you will still allow me the pleasure of the hunt on the morrow, I promise that neither my arrows nor the lance of my reckless tongue will fly in your direction. I trust that Ashdown Forest will be big enough for the both of us and that we will not cross paths until dusk. At that time we will make mention of the game we have snared and then bed down upon our *own* pallets and our own separate territory."

Trevor's irritation dwindled to mild amusement as he

surveyed the exquisite features of Meagan's face, the delicate structure of her jaw, the proud tilt of her chin. She had tactfully apologized for her barb and then set the ground rules for the hunt, as if *she* were the ruling sovereign and *he* were her lackey. Could any man tame this vixen's wild spirit and earn her utmost respect? Trevor was beginning to doubt it. Meagan never backed down. She only backed away . . . temporarily. And each time she considered it in her best interest to retreat from battle, he had the uneasy feeling that she was not surrendering ground, but rather regrouping forces for another attack. Ah, but he enjoyed the challenge this lively wench presented. She was like a wild bird caught in captivity, a dove who would not accept treats from a man's hand and refused to have her free spirit broken, no matter how long she remained caged.

Like a jungle cat hopping to its feet, Trevor bounded down in front of Meagan, bowed before her, and then brushed his lips over her wrist as he took her hand in his. "Although I know your only motive for apology was to ensure the freedom of the hunt, I will accept it—and your terms—except for one." Amber eyes twinkled like sunbeams radiating from the morning star. "We will make camp *together* for our protection against the creatures that stalk the night. You are in my care until I deposit you on Edric's doorstep."

Meagan bristled, mistrusting his intentions of sleeping under the same blanket of stars. "In separate bedrolls, I assume?" One delicate brow lifted as she raked him with uncertainty. He had promised that their first kiss would be their last, but she wondered if this heathen would be opposed to a tumble in the grass if the situation presented itself.

"Naturally, ladylove," Trevor replied, his endearment laced with the slightest hint of mockery. "Although you are not prone to believe it, I am a man of discriminating tastes. Why bother with a naïve maiden when there are a score of women who delight in pleasing a man?"

He was inviting another insult and Meagan was hard pressed not to give it to him. That lout! She should let loose her arrow and let it quiver in his hard heart, she thought spitefully. It would save the Saxon rebels a great deal of trouble and free her from her brother's ridiculous attempt to tie her to an unworthy husband.

"Why indeed," Meagan managed to say without shouting in his arrogant face. "I will rest easier knowing there will be no amorous attack on my person during the nights we must endure together, and I know you will sleep like a trusting child, content in the knowledge that I would make no attempt to seduce you until long after hell froze over," she added in such a sticky-sweet tone that Trevor did not feel the bite of her words until the glazed coating had dripped over her remark and she had pivoted away to dart into the forebuilding.

When hell froze over? Trevor snorted disdainfully, sorely tempted to follow that exasperating chit to her chamber and force himself upon her, just to prove his domination over her. He entertained the spiteful thought for only a moment and then discarded it. What would rape accomplish with a woman like Meagan, he asked himself. He had decided to tote that gorgeous misfit back to her brother just as he had found her, he reminded himself. If her tantalizing figure aroused him, he would turn his attention on another woman to ease his needs. But he would *not* bed that troublesome wench.

And then the vision of long, shapely legs and soft thighs darted across his mind as the memory of Meagan sitting upon her lofty perch returned to haunt him. The feel of her supple body pressed intimately to his flooded over him, and he found himself wondering what it would be like to kiss and caress her bare flesh and knowing it was suicide just considering it. Growling at the arousing direction his thoughts had taken, Trevor shoved away the vision that had leaped into his head and discarded any intention he might have had of dallying with that blond-haired hellion. He would take her hunting the following morning, but that was all he would do with that curvaceous wench with eyes the color of the morning sky and hair of spun silver and gold.

Conan was right, he harshly reminded himself. Meagan Lowell brewed trouble and suspicion, and the less he had to do with that witch the better. He would find her a husband who suited her, and once she was out of sight, she would be out of mind as well. The last thing he needed was a wife who would spite him at every turn. If William finally forced him to wed he would seek out a woman who would not be a thorn in his side, Trevor promised himself. And as for Meagan Lowell, it would serve her right to find herself saddled with some barbarian who would punish her for allowing her tongue to run away with itself by closeting her in a castle tower until she was wrinkled and gray!

Tossing every thought of Meagan from his mind, Trevor stalked toward the Great Hall, certain that his conversation with Conan would distract him and allow him to forget his irritation with Meagan. But even while Conan lectured him about using common sense, he found his mind wandering to the shapely little bird who had taken roost beneath the pentice.

As Meagan rounded the corner in the corridor and moved swiftly toward her chamber, Daralis appeared with a tray to offer her a glass of wine. A wary frown knitted Meagan's brow when she met Daralis's carefully blank stare.

"I have brought you food and drink to sustain you until the evening meal, your ladyship," she murmured.

All that Meagan wanted at the moment was Trevor's head on a platter. He had made her so angry that vindictive thoughts were darting around her mind. "Thank you, but nay," Meagan muttered as she aimed herself toward her room.

"But, m'lady . . ." Daralis called after her. "It will be another hour before our meal."

"I am not the least bit hungry or thirsty," Meagan assured her, wondering why the servant was being persistent, but too irritated after her encounter with Trevor to give the matter further consideration.

When the door closed in her face, Daralis wheeled away, muttering several epithets to the lovely lady who seemed to have caught the overlord's attention.

"You look distraught, m'lady," Devona observed as Meagan buzzed into the room, madder than a hornet, and then flounced over to retrieve another tunic from her trunk.

"'Tis because I am," Meagan grumbled as she yanked off the garment that was heavily perfumed with the scent of Trevor Burke. "The mighty lord of Wessex distresses me."

Meagan looked as if she had bit into something sour when she mentioned Trevor, and Devona choked back a smile as she watched her lady storm about her chamber like a whirlwind looking for a suitable place to unleash its fury.

"Have the two of you been needling each other again?" Devona inquired as she wandered over to assist Meagan with her garment.

"It seems we are constantly at each other's throats," Meagan assured her huffily and then cast her gentle servant an apologetic smile, silently informing Devona that her fit of temper was not aimed in her direction.

"Can you not find some subject of discussion that does not bring the two of you to arms?" Devona questioned as she handed Meagan her mantle. "I strongly suggest that you and Lord Burke bury the hatchet before all your squabbling breeds disaster. Edric will be furious if he learns that you have been argumentative and unpleasant to the man who rules over your fief."

"Then *he* should have married the arrogant lout," Meagan grumbled caustically. "Trevor and I seem incapable of burying the hatchet anywhere but in each other's backs, and the only topic of conversation between us is who will be the first to accomplish that feat."

"Meagan, you must control your temper," Devona insisted as her lady stomped around the room in a huff, attempting to walk off her pent-up frustration. "You are pitting yourself against impossible odds."

Devona's soft words had a soothing effect on Meagan, and finally she breathed a heavy sigh and made the attempt to get herself in hand. "Lord Burke has promised to take me hunting for a few days," Meagan informed her. "Perhaps the tension between us will ease during our trip and we will learn to tolerate each other."

"Hunting? In the woods? For a few days?" Devona eyed Meagan curiously. "And where will the two of you be spending your nights?"

The servant looked as if she was chewing on a thought that had every indication of containing sinful speculations, and Meagan shot forth an annoyed frown. "He will be in his bedroll and *I* shall be in mine," she hastily assured Devona. "I cannot think I would enjoy sleeping with that pompous knave any more than I appreciate arguing with him."

The smug smile on Devona's soft features remained intact as she gracefully knelt to retrieve the tunic Meagan had hurriedly tossed on the floor before her senses were attacked by the manly fragrance that clung to the garment. "Perhaps his invitation was his subtle way of insisting that the two of you become better acquainted without a swarm of servants and knights hovering about you."

Meagan grasped a brush and rearranged the unruly strands of golden hair that had come unwound during her encounter with Trevor. "I have no desire to become better acquainted with Lord Burke. We intend to hunt, nothing more. He is as anxious to return me to Edric as I am to be home, but he will not insult my brother by carting me home before a week is out. This hunting trip will only serve to while away the hours until we can travel to Lowell Castle. So you can toss those lurid thoughts from your mind and fetch my combs," Meagan commanded. "And I will hear no more talk of a tête-à-tête with that annoying lord of Wessex."

Devona nodded agreeably, but she continued smiling to herself over the possibility of Meagan becoming fascinated with the handsome baron while they were in seclusion. After all, he was a most dashing specimen of virility. Devona had been appalled by Edric's suggestion when he had first sprung it on her and Meagan, but perhaps Edric was right. Trevor Burke was just the type of man who could handle a free spirit like Meagan once he had earned her respect. But it would be slow in coming, Devona reminded herself as she cast Meagan a sidelong glance. The lady had a stubborn streak as wide as the English Channel, and she was determined to drag her feet, simply because this was Edric's idea and not her own.

As darkness settled over the countryside, Edric made his way through the dense underbrush for his secretive appointment. "The plan has been set in motion," Edric announced when he spied his conspirator among the swaying shadows.

The man nodded mutely at the news that Meagan had been sent to Burke Castle, and then fell into step beside Edric as he strode along the creek. "Reinforcements are coming from Ireland within the next few months. Harold Godwinson's illegitimate sons were forced from England two years ago, but they have every intention of returning. Now that King William has met with hostility from the Northumbrians, we can attack his flank. The men in Devon are preparing to strike at Exeter, Somerset, and Dorset. Our only hope is to begin our crusade simultaneously and surround the bastard."

"If only Meagan can catch Lord Burke's eye," Edric mused aloud. "Once Burke is disposed of, the castle will fall into my sister's hands and our warriors can move northward without having a lay siege to Wessex."

The man smiled in satisfaction. "Our plan is simple, so much so that Burke will not know he is staring death in the face until *after* he has made Meagan his wife."

After further discussing their arrangements, Edric swung back into the saddle and threaded his way out of the thick trees to return to Lowell Castle, feeling his anticipation mounting. Soon he would be in control of his own demesne, and Norman rule would come to an end, he told himself confidently. He must not become impatient. Meagan held the key to Wessex, and he must wait for fate to run its course. She had to entice Trevor into marrying her. Without the match, Wessex could again fall into Norman hands, and it would take a full-scale attack to gain Burke's stronghold.

While Edric was weaving his way back to his fortress, Meagan was tossing and turning in her sleep, haunted by a pair of dancing amber eyes and a mocking smile. It was as if the man had taken up permanent residence in her mind and refused to allow her peace, even while she dreamed. Twice Meagan awakened in a cold sweat, wondering if her hunting expedition the following morning would prove disastrous. She didn't want to know one more thing about Trevor Burke, she told herself firmly. He was Norman and she was Saxon and that made them incompatible. No hunting trip could end this feud, nor did she intend it to. Indeed, nothing would make her happier than for her and Trevor to part company on the outlining perimeters of Ashdown Forest and to see nothing of each other for several days. The only possible way they could be compatible was if they never saw each other, Meagan thought as she squirmed in bed and willed her eyes to close without Trevor's rugged features materializing before her. But he was there, holding her steadfast against his masculine torso, forcing her to endure sensations that rocked her like waves tossing her on a turbulent sea.

"Get out of my mind, arrogant knave," Meagan muttered as she punched her pillow, wishing she could deliver the blow to the source of her frustration—Trevor Burke.

"Did you call, m'lady?" Devona queried drowsily.

"Nay, I was only talking to myself," Meagan sighed as she flounced beneath the quilt and stared up into the darkness.

Devona's soft chuckle drifted across the room to curl around Meagan. "Have a care that you do not answer yourself," she warned. "'Tis the first symptom of madness."

"Do I not have enough difficulty falling asleep beneath my enemy's roof without your heckling me?" Meagan muttered grouchily.

"When the enemy is as handsome and appealing as yours, I suppose you could do without my harassment," Devona agreed with a taunting smile that would have offered enough light to lead a lost traveler through a blizzard.

Meagan flung her all-too-cheerful servant a withering glance and then presented her back. "For a woman who claims to be in love with my brother you certainly seem aware of Lord Burke's physical attractions. Perhaps we should have exchanged places and you could have spent more time drooling over him."

"I have found the light and love of my life," Devona assured her quietly. "I think 'tis time you found yours."

"He will not be among these heathen warriors and he will most certainly not be leading them," Meagan sniffed disgustedly. "All your hinting will not make the Dark Prince a champion in my eyes. Now I bid you to dream your own dreams and cease this attempt to drag Trevor Burke into mine."

"As you wish, m'lady," Devona murmured as she drew the fur quilt about her neck to ward off the evening chill.

"As you wish"? Meagan laughed bitterly at Devona's last remark. Nothing had been as Meagan wished since Edric deposited her on the cart and sent her to Burke Castle. And with that depressing thought, Meagan fell asleep, wishing she had refused Edric's summons to return home. If she had any sense she would have remained at the nunnery, where her only problem was sneaking off into the Royal Forest without being discovered.

After riding for more than an hour in silence, Trevor halted his steed and glanced over at Meagan, who had already begun to enjoy solitude by pretending that her companion did not exist. "I will grant your whim to hunt alone throughout the day, but you must promise to circle back to this point before nightfall."

Meagan offered him a fleeting glance that barely acknowledged his presence. "I will return before the sun descends on the horizon," she assured him as she lifted her arm, entreating the falcon that sat upon her wrist to soar as Meagan wished she could do.

Before Meagan galloped off to follow the falcon's flight, Trevor caught the sparkle of anticipation in her eyes. It was as if he had flung open wide this wild bird's cage and granted her the freedom upon which she thrived. For a moment he sat upon his magnificent stallion, watching Meagan disappear into the forest with her faithful shepherd trotting along beside her.

A thoughtful frown plowed his brow as he reined his steed to the north and ducked beneath the low-hanging limbs that sought to reach out and snag him. Before he realized it, his wandering mind had strayed off to consider the stunning blond nymph who had been forced upon him, one who goaded him, taunted him unmercifully, and yet stirred his blood when he would have been perfectly content to let it flow through his veins at a reasonable speed.

Trevor's absent gaze swept the clearing that opened before him, and he veered his horse toward the shafts of sunlight that sprinkled through the canopy of trees. As he swung to the ground to lead his stallion along behind him, Trevor kicked at the grass, uprooting a clump. Damnation, why did that blue-eyed chit distract him so, he asked himself. She had made it clear that she wanted nothing to do with him, and he certainly wanted nothing to do with her. That little witch was a thorn in his side, and the fact that he found his eyes and thoughts straying to that fiery vixen who had stormed his castle disturbed him. He had sworn not to lay another hand on her, but he often found himself undressing her with his gaze, wondering how her supple body would feel if it was pressed intimately to his.

And how was he to say "thank you, but nay" to Edric without mortifying a man who could easily be swayed to rebellion? Trevor was no fool. He knew Edric only tolerated his overlord because he lacked the manpower to overthrow his enemy. Vassal Lowell was an excellent manager of his fief, and he had a rapport with his tenants. Losing Lowell would be a distressing headache. A suitable replacement, one who was accepted by the local farmers, would take time, and Trevor was not anxious to begin such a search. He had no complaint with Edric, except that he had shoved his sister into his lap.

Trevor had been walking an emotional tightrope since Meagan had been deposited in his care. He had avoided the castle wenches who continued to buzz about him, ordering them from his room when they found some flimsy excuse to disturb him at a late hour, and he despised himself for wishing it had been Meagan who rapped upon his door, seeking more than just a request to hunt in the royal forest near the castle.

When the stallion pricked up his ears and whinnied uneasily, Trevor dragged himself from his contemplations. His blood ran cold when he heard a familiar grunt from the underbrush. The stallion reared in fright and then thundered off with Trevor's bow still tied to the saddle, leaving Trevor to confront the shaggy, four-hundred-pound boar that charged toward him, its sharp tusks lowered like a knight aiming his lance.

Trevor wheeled and drew his sword, since it was too late to run. The wild boar approached him at incredible speed, and it thirsted for blood. Their eyes met for that split second and Trevor gritted his teeth, his body braced and tensed, his heart pounding in his ears so loudly that he could hear nothing else, see nothing but the dark eyes of forthcoming doom.

"Lear!" Meagan bolted from the cover of the underbrush when the boar she had been tracking rumbled toward the foolish lord, who had stumbled into the clearing to stand like an open target for the vicious swine. Although she was very nearly tempted to let the dolt struggle with his own devices or die trying, she could not help remembering seeing two of her father's friends ripped to shreds by boars. A wild boar could slay its victim with one stroke of its tusk, and a young swine was capable of rapid maneuvers before slitting its quarry with deadly lashes.

At the sound of her sharp command, the powerful shepherd leaped from the thicket to distract the charging boar, and the falcon swooped down to pester it while Meagan clutched her bow and took careful aim. Although she found her target, the bloodthirsty boar stabbed Trevor with a tusk, causing him to cry out in pain. Meagan grabbed a second arrow and prayed that she could drop the boar in his tracks before his deadly tusks struck Trevor in the abdomen. As the boar fell to the ground, Meagan dashed to Trevor, seeing his tunic stained with blood.

Meagan snatched up Trevor's sword to slay the wounded

boar and then turned back to him, reading the agony in his eyes as he clutched at his thigh. Meagan grimaced as she cut away his legging to inspect the wound, finding that the gash laid flesh open to the bone.

Trevor's thick lashes swept up as perspiration beaded his brow. His eyes were glued to the lovely face that hovered over him as darkness circled like a looming vulture.

"I owe you my life," he whispered in forced breaths and then surrendered to the silence that settled over him.

"You are still dangerously close to losing it," Meagan muttered under her breath as she cut the hem of her tunic to serve as a tourniquet.

When she had completed her ministrations, she sank back on her haunches and then groaned when she glanced over to see that Lear had also suffered from his confrontation with the boar. The dog lay on his side, whining miserably. Meagan crouched down beside Lear to inspect the gash on his ribs, and then said a thankful prayer that the shepherd had not sustained a fatal wound.

"The fool," she muttered, flashing Trevor a scornful glare. "What kind of man leaves himself prey to such beasts? He came to protect me?" She scoffed at the irony. Her brows narrowed thoughtfully when Poseidon emerged from the underbrush to return to Trevor, nudging him gently.

Trevor's agonizing groan drew her sharp glance, and indecision etched her brow. Should she take her stallion and return to the castle for help, knowing that Trevor might perish if she left him alone in the woods? It was what he deserved, she mused bitterly. If she abandoned him, Edric would no longer be scheming to find a way to unite the two of them in marriage, because Trevor would die without attention. If she attempted to transport him back to the castle, the journey would kill him. To do nothing at all would dissolve her connection with the Dark Prince.

Again Meagan frowned as the black stallion tarried beside the bleeding Norman. "Pray, tell me what you see in him?" she demanded of Poseidon and then knelt beside Trevor to see fresh blood staining the makeshift bandage. "He is my enemy, a Norman pig, wounded by one of his own kind.

88

Why should I come to his aid? Indeed, why did I come to the oaf's defense in the first place? If I had stood aside he would have perished, and Edric could have placed none of the blame on me for returning home without a marriage proposal."

Another pitiful groan escaped Trevor's lips when Meagan's utterances seeped into his clouded thoughts. Try as he may, he could not find the strength to drag himself up to a sitting position. "Give me your hand," he rasped.

Meagan hesitated until those golden eyes anchored on her. They were glazed with pain, but they still held her spellbound for what seemed an eternity. Her hand folded around his and she found herself wrapping a supporting arm around him as he staggered to gather his feet beneath him. Meagan was certain her clothes would be ripped away as he floundered and then fell, leaving her sprawled beneath him. His weight was awesome and she was helpless, stung by odd sensation that sizzled through her as if she had been struck by the bolt of lightning she had wished on Trevor the first day they clashed. The feel of his male body crushing into hers was frightening, and the side effects were playing havoc with her emotions. She hated Trevor, she reminded herself as she writhed and squirmed to ease the fierce pressure upon her. Trevor was her enemy and he was wounded! Why was she stirred by his touch when he was out of his mind with misery and had no idea what he was doing?

Finally, she wormed her way free and assisted him to his knees, a task that drained both of their strength. Trevor gazed up at her and then clasped his hands on her shoulders to pull himself to his feet. With that accomplished, he flung an arm over his steed's back and waited a breathless moment for the world to stop spinning so he could tuck his boot into the stirrup. Meagan offered her hands as a stirrup, but as he pushed upward, she was sent sprawling backward, tripping over the boar's carcass to land in a heap.

A faint chuckle trailed from Trevor's lips as he looked down to see Meagan lying spread-eagled on the ground. "Forgive me. I seem to have made clumsy oafs of both of us."

Meagan was set to throw a snide remark at him, but the

words died on her lips when her gaze locked with his. There was a boyish quality in that lopsided smile.

"Apology accepted," she murmured as she struggled to her feet. "I . . ." Her voice trailed off as Trevor slumped in the saddle, his strength depleted.

Cluching the reins, Meagan swiftly tied the boar behind Poseidon and then wound her way deeper into the woods to the abandoned shack that she had seen earlier that morning while she had been tracking game. Trevor could not endure a return trip to the castle in his condition, but he might survive if she could get him to the shack and properly tend his wound.

Meagan heaved a weary sigh after she had managed to help Trevor from the saddle and lay him on the pile of straw and leaves that had once served as a bed in the crude, thatched shack. A troubled frown clouded her brow as she eased down beside Trevor to remove the bandage. If she didn't apply cleansing poultice to the jagged gash that was covered with dirt, infection would set in and he would risk losing his leg. Painstakingly, she cut away the remainder of his legging and then went to fetch water and wild herbs to prepare the medicinal paste that would lessen the risk of infection.

Trevor watched her from beneath drooping eyelids and then called to Meagan when she left him alone for a second time. "Stay with me," he breathed raggedly. "I feel so cold and alone. . . ."

As his voice trailed off and his eyes fluttered shut, Meagan peered down at the pathetic expression that settled on his handsome face. His rugged features were soft in repose, and he did not appear the invincible mercenary she had met when he strode out of the stables the day she arrived at his fortress. His soul cried out to her and Meagan knew that if she left him to die she could never face herself. It would have been in her best interest to walk away without looking back, but she couldn't do that. Resolutely, she strode outside to build a fire and stir up the concoction to coat his wound, knowing she would stay at his side, even if he was her enemy.

Chapter 6

For two endless days Meagan remained by Trevor's side, listening to his feverish ravings, sponging his body, feeding him sips of water when he roused. She had nothing to ease his pain, and it tormented her to watch him suffer night and day while she became more attached to the Norman she had sworn to despise. It disturbed her that her antagonistic feelings toward him had dwindled to pity, but that was exactly what had happened.

Each time she removed his tunic to bathe him, she found her hands gliding over his muscled flesh in an absent caress. There was not an ounce of flab on his swarthy body, and Meagan was vividly aware of why his castle wenches found him attractive. His chest was broad, covered with thick hair that trickled down his abdomen, and he was narrow at the hips. His thighs and calves were finely tuned. Masculinity radiated from him, and women were aroused by him simply because it was impossible not to be. His bronzed features were surrounded by thick raven hair that curled at the nape of his neck, unlike the cropped, unattractive hairstyles worn by most Norman barons. There was something different about Trevor, something that set him apart from his compatriots besides his dark skin and coal black hair, and Meagan suspected that it was that bit of mongrel in him that had spawned from his heritage.

Meagan glanced down to see her index finger trailing over the full curve of his pallid lips, and she stumbled on the thought of how he had kissed her until her knees went weak and her heart catapulted to her throat to strangle her before tumbling back to its normal resting place. Never had a man swept her into his arms to plant a kiss that burned hotter than a thousand suns. A faint smile skimmed over her mouth as the scene flashed before her eyes. Even Trevor had been affected by their embrace, although he had attempted to disguise it. Meagan may have been naïve, but she knew when a man was aroused.

The dawn of the third day found Trevor fully awake, his fever gone, and the faintest hint of color in his face. Meagan smiled in relief as he propped himself upon an elbow and glanced about the thatched shack.

"How long have I been unconscious?" he questioned huskily.

"More than two days." Meagan knelt beside him to offer him a drink from the crude cup she had whittled from a hollowed branch.

Trevor glanced down at the bandage around his thigh and cautiously touched the tender flesh. "You have nursed me back to life even when I doubted that I would ever see another sunrise."

Meagan was unable to stare into those amber eyes for any length of time without becoming mesmerized, and she rose to busy herself with the task of dipping up his breakfast to occupy her rambling thoughts. "Do you feel up to eating, m'lord?"

"Yea," he sighed tiredly as his watchful gaze lingered on the shapely blond who had hovered over him like a guardian angel. That thought caused him to frown curiously. "Why did you save me, Meagan? If your looks could kill I would have died numerous times this past week. Opportunity was staring you in the face and you . . ."

Meagan rammed the spoon in his mouth to shut him up. Damn, why had he asked that question? She had no answer, except that she was too kindhearted to stand and watch another human being perish when she was there to intervene. That was the only explanation she could give without delving into her soul, and she dared not do that for fear of what she might find.

"'Tis only that I chose not to let the beast dispose of you when I had been considering seeing to the task myself. It would have brought me no pleasure to see you fall unless you were cut down beneath my sword," she replied, striving for a tone of indifference and surprising herself with her success.

"Your hatred for me runs deep," he mused aloud, mustering a meager smile, although he was weak and vulnerable to her insults. "Three years is a long time to bear a grudge. One day you must accept my authority and treat me with respect."

One dainty brow arched as she stuffed another spoon of broth in his mouth. "Why should I respect the Normans who have stampeded into England, stripping families of their lands and raising fortresses for the almighty William the Bastard?" Meagan sniffed disgustedly. "Do you think we Saxons will respect Normans because we fear your power? Dying is more honorable than living beneath the sword and paying taxes that burden even the wealthiest of men."

Trevor felt as if he had been stabbed and gouged from all directions. He had met with obstinacy from the Saxons since the day he had marched into England, but never had he been ridiculed with such fierce intensity, especially by a woman. And despite his annoyance with her razor-sharp tongue, he could not help but admire a woman who could fend for herself and save him from certain catastrophe. Trevor leaned back to study the stunning maid, raking her with deliberate thoroughness.

"Despite your obvious hatred for me and my people, I have become fond of you," he announced.

Meagan's mouth dropped open and she stared bug-eyed at him until she managed to find her tongue. She had brazenly attacked Trevor and all he stood for and he still offered a compliment? The fever had charred his brain, she decided. Only a week ago he would have cheerfully tossed her off the cliffs of Dover and voiced the silent plea that she would sink like a rock.

"You do not begrudge my bitterness?" she questioned, her tone hinting at incredulity.

His golden eyes took on a faraway look as he stared at the opposite wall. "I have been guilty of harboring a bitterness," he admitted quietly. "But bitterness breeds a hatred that can only feed and destroy the soul. 'Tis best not to dwell on inner angers. Nothing good can come of it."

Meagan frowned at his philosophical remark, wondering what tragedy could have befallen him. It seemed to Meagan that he had met with a great deal of success while she and her countrymen had very little for which to be thankful. And being the inquisitive imp she was, she demanded to know what he meant by his remark.

"I cannot imagine why you would be bitter. You are one of the king's favorites, as I have heard it told. You claim the vast land of Wessex as your demesne and you want for nothing, not food, wine, or women."

"You seem to know a great deal about me, considering we only met one short week ago." Trevor eyed her speculatively, wondering if perhaps Conan's vision and his reservations about Meagan were accurate after all.

A wry smile skipped across her lips, setting her blue eyes to sparkling with deviltry. "You are preceded by your reputation, Dark Prince, especially one that hails your prowess with women. Even at the convent I heard rumors of the Dark Prince who had earned his king's respect and who left a long trail of conquered hearts behind him."

Trevor countered with his own roguish smile as he reached out to trace the delicate curve of her face. "If all those rumors were true, you and I would know each other far better than we do now," he pointed out.

Meagan slapped his hand away and abruptly changed the subject. "You still have not told me why you were bitter," she reminded him as she came to her feet to feed Trevor's leavings to Lear, who had been hobbling at such a slow pace that he had been unable to seek out his own meals.

Easing back on his pallet, Trevor breathed a heavy sigh and then clasped his hands behind his head. "My father died when I was fourteen and our land fell to my uncle, Ulrick Burke. Since I, the eldest son, had not come of age to

94

manage the chateau on the Lys River, Ulrick took it upon himself to rule, and within two years he had drained my father's funds and we were penniless. My uncle despised my mother, who had been no more than a servant in a friend's manor, a shy, retiring captive from Spain who caught my father's eye and soon became his bride, despite her previous station in Normandy. To humiliate my mother, Ulrick gave her in marriage to a dreadful heathen, and she was abused, mistreated, and dead within a year. My brother . . ." Trevor paused a moment to ask himself why he was spilling his life story to Meagan. Because he had kept it pent up inside him for two decades, and he ached to speak of it and then put it from his mind forever. "My brother and I were cast out to fend for ourselves. We met another young lad who struggled for survival, and he was bound for the palace in Normandy to train for battle and sell himself to the Duke as a mercenary soldier of fortune. My brother and I traveled to the palace with Gunthar Seaton in hopes of gathering enough funds to buy back the land that was stolen from us and to even the score with Ulrick. We survived on thoughts of revenge for so many years that it became our existence, our purpose for obtaining wealth." Trevor sighed, his eyes clouding momentarily before he masked the sentimental emotion. "But Ulrick's servant brought word to us that his master was dead and that the lands would be handed over to a deserving man of Ulrick's chosing. 'Twas just before we embarked for England," he added as he gazed back through the window of time. "When my brother perished at Hastings, and Gunthar was severely wounded, there was but one to continue onward and all I had struggled to gain was lost to me forever. My brother was gone and I have not heard from Gunthar since I watched him fall beneath the blade. Each of us had our dreams, and suddenly they no longer mattered." He glanced up at the shaft of light that splintered through the thatched roof. "There was a time when I would have forsaken all else to avenge my family's tragedy, and I carried my hatred within my heart, never daring to voice it to anyone except my brother. Even Gunthar was unaware of the bitterness that plagued me. We spoke of dreams, but never of motives. The pain of my loss was impossible to share and I did not dare try. Now the tender memories of childhood are gone, as well as the chateau that I called home. There is nothing left to fight and I wasted years working toward a goal that I can never hope to make reality." Trevor's gaze circled back to Meagan. "Mark my words, m'lady. You will also waste your best years if you allow your hatred to fester and destroy you like a deadly poison. Harold Godwinson was sent to France by King Edward. It was *he* who brought the formal promise that England would be passed to William when Edward died, and Harold pledged his allegiance to William. When the throne was vacant Harold hungered for supreme power and proclaimed himself king when he knew that it rightfully belonged to William. That is the truth of the matter, Meagan, and all your bitterness cannot change royal decree."

"But that did not give William the right to place his money-hungry mercenaries in the manors of his fallen foes," she argued, her voice rising testily.

"War breeds a certain amount of injustice and to the victor go the spoils. 'Tis a fact of life; one that you must learn, just as I have."

Trevor could talk until he was blue in the face, but he would never convince Meagan that the warlike Norman ways could be justified, not by a long shot. Trevor had been offered another man's land, and he had accepted it. He was no better than his cruel uncle, she mused cynically.

"Swallowing your philosophy still leaves a sour taste in my mouth," she muttered and then turned her attention to her ailing shepherd. "Perhaps you can forget your uncle's treachery, but I cannot forget the cruelty and injustice that have befallen the Saxons since the Norman hordes invaded England. You are still . . ." Her narrowed eyes settled on Trevor, but he had drifted off to sleep and her words had fallen on deaf ears.

Meagan heaved a frustrated sigh and then wandered outside to let Trevor rest in peace. Why? She wasn't certain. She should have shaken him awake to give him a good piece of her mind. Later, she promised herself. Later they would finish their debate.

As the cool morning air settled about Trevor, he came to his senses and then flinched when he found the beady eyes of Meagan's falcon glaring down at him. Trevor dragged himself to his feet and glanced about him, wondering what had become of Meagan. He knew that she had begrudgingly come to his aid, and after their argument Trevor wondered if she had left him to his own devices now that he was regaining his strength.

Trevor shuffled to the door and leaned heavily against the wall to keep himself in an upright position. His breath caught in his throat when his sharp gaze focused on a vision that left him wondering if he was still dreaming. There beside the stream, a stone's throw from the shack, was Meagan. Her shimmering hair was a mystical intermingling of the color of the sun and moon as she glided across the water like a swan. Her bare flesh glowed like honey, and Trevor felt the quick rise of desire, even in his weakened condition. He squinted, afraid he might miss some minute detail of her alluring figure, and then sighed appreciatively, hypnotized by the bewitching sight of her. She was like a goddess who had descended from the heavens to bathe in the creek, and Trevor sizzled with the reckless urge to hobble down to the stream, tear off his clothes, and spend an eternity with the lovely angel.

He was reminded of the story he had heard about William the Conqueror's mother, a fetching young woman whom Robert, duke of Normandy, had seen dancing by the side of the road. Robert had been so enamored of Arletta that he made her his chattel, and their love child had come to rule England.

Trevor tarried by the door for several minutes and then smiled to himself when Meagan disappeared into the shadows to dress. In that moment Trevor found himself wishing he could sprout wings and flutter around Meagan in another form, one that did not disgust her. To the creatures

97

of nature Meagan was tender and loving. But to her overlord she was spiteful and aloof. Then, giving the matter further consideration, Trevor realized he had not helped the situation, because he retaliated each time she needīed him with one of her pride-pricking jibes.

And because of the constant friction between them, Trevor was at a loss to explain why the belligerent sprite had come to his rescue. If she had patiently stood aside, he would have been a dead man. His fatal accident would have solved her dilemma. Meagan could have returned to Lowell Castle without being forced to endure this necessary waiting period required to pacify Edric.

Why *had* Meagan granted him life, Trevor asked himself again. It was obvious that Meagan felt no fond attachment for him. A muddled frown plowed his brow. Yet she had shown him compassion. Could it be that beneath that rebellious, defensive exterior lurked a woman with a tender heart? Meagan had claimed that when he fell, it would be by her own hand, not from a boar's tusk. Did she voice that spiteful remark to annoy him or had she actually meant it?

Trevor heaved an exasperated sigh. He wasn't certain what to believe when he confronted that lovely enigma—Meagan. Egod! How could he find that she-cat so enticing and desirable when he wasn't certain what she thought of him? He must be mad! And yet, how could any man overlook this fair Saxon beauty, especially after he had seen what lay beneath her concealing garments? England had many spellbinding sights and Trevor had seen his share of them. But the one that baffled and impressed him most was the vision of Meagan. In his mind's eye he could see her glaring at him with disdain. Then the image changed and she was hovering over him, tending his wounds like a gentle guardian angel. The vision faded and the sight of Meagan's alabaster skin sparkling with water droplets clouded his mind. The mere thought of her exquisite beauty warmed his blood, leaving him aroused and hungering to satisfy the craving she had instilled in him.

Perhaps he could mellow her contempt for him, Trevor mused pensively. There were ways to woo a woman, and he

98

had yet to employ those tactics on that feisty minx. The thought caused a troubled frown to settle in Trevor's craggy features. He had vowed to keep his distance from Meagan and here he was, devising a scheme to entrap her in his arms. Promises be damned, Trevor decided when he saw Meagan emerge from the shadows. The wench intrigued him. If he wanted her she was his for the taking. Trevor did not have to answer to anyone except King William, he reminded himself.

When Meagan approached the shack to see Trevor propped against the door, a wary frown knitted her brow. Why was he grinning at her as if he harbored some secret and he was about to burst with it?

"There are many enticing sights in the forest this morning," he remarked, a wide smile stretching across his handsome face, affecting each rugged feature.

"Enticing sights?" Meagan repeated. Pausing, she glanced back over her shoulder. There was nothing unusual in their surroundings, she thought to herself. Perhaps Trevor's soaring fever had addled his brain and he was still hallucinating, she diagnosed as she pivoted to face him.

"I roused this morning to be greeted by a vision that left my heart rattling around in my chest." His amber eyes flowed over her like a wandering caress. "The sight was so spellbinding that it took my breath away."

"Not entirely," Meagan sniffed caustically when she realized that he was referring to her and that he had been peeping on her while she bathed. Turning up her dainty nose, she brushed past him. "I do not appreciate the fact that you were spying on me."

Meagan practically jumped out of her freshly cleaned skin when Trevor's husky voice came from so close behind her.

"But *I* did," he whispered, his hands curling about her waist, his touch branding her with fire. "You have a delicious body, Meagan. 'Tis a pity that you have been so stingy with it."

Meagan was suffocating, strangling for breath. Trevor was standing too close for her comfort, and she did not like the way her heart was doing back somersaults around her rib cage. Trevor moved her in ways that she never realized existed, and she was afraid to let him melt the bitterness she felt toward him. If she did not guard her emotions with the fierceness of a knight, the desires that lurked just beneath the surface could sprout and take root. Meagan had no intention of becoming another notch on his bedpost. He had his share of castle wenches at his beck and call, and Meagan was too proud to be labeled as his amoret.

Squealing indignantly, Meagan sidestepped and then put a safer distance between them. "You promised that you would never touch me again and you have broken your word," she snapped harshly. "What I expect for saving your worthless neck is not a toss in the straw with the baron of Wessex County."

Trevor's thick brows formed a hard line over his eyes as he studied her suspiciously. "Are you hinting for some payment of your noble deed?"

Come to think of it, she was in a perfect position to demand compensation. Trevor owed her his life and she would never let him forget it. "Yea, in return for my services for slaying the boar, feeding him to you for nourishment, and nursing you back to health, I ask that you inform Edric that you wish to wed my servant, Devona."

"What!" Trevor crowed like an indignant rooster that had been attacked by a chicken hawk. "I barely know the woman, and she cowers in the cracks of the walls each time I go near her."

"Then you refuse?" Meagan arched a taunting brow, raking the handsome lord with scornful mockery. "I wonder if your knights and squires will continue to see you as their invincible leader when I inform them that you were ambling about the woods like a starry-eyed lad. Will they not be disappointed to learn that their mighty leader had to be rescued by a mere woman and that she dropped the charging beast before it could slay the foolish overlord?"

Her remark set Trevor's teeth on edge. He could well imagine Meagan's rendition of the incident. She was intent on making him appear a clumsier knave than he had been in the first place. His gravest mistake was allowing Meagan to see his foolish side. She would never let him live down his stupidity. But then a thought struck him, and he found that he could swallow his pride if he could live the fantasy that had gripped him while he stood gawking at Meagan as she glided across the water.

"I will ask Edric for Devona's hand if you will consent to share my bed before you return to Lowell Castle," he stipulated.

Meagan could not locate her tongue after practically swallowing it. The man was as crazed as a loon! He had informed her in no uncertain terms that he wanted nothing to do with her, and now he had done an about-face. "I should rather burn in hell!" she declared emphatically. "*You* are the one who owes a debt, not *I.*"

His shoulder lifted in a nonchalant shrug as he sank down on his pallet to give his throbbing thigh a rest. "And I would have complied with your request if you had met my simple terms," he countered in a bland tone.

A hot blush worked its way up her cheeks to stain her hairline as Trevor flashed her a rakish grin and undressed her with his eyes.

"Do you fear that you are not woman enough to satisfy me?" he intimidated.

Meagan was dangerously close to splitting apart at the seams, and she found herself regretting that she had spared this haughty warrior's life. Oh, how she itched to clamp her fingers around his neck and shake the stuffing out of him.

"I doubt that any woman can appease the lusting beast within you," she snapped, her tone threaded with contempt. "You are a dragon, Trevor Burke!"

Trevor sniffed the air, remembering the smoldering coals he had seen on the campfire Meagan had built in front of the shack. "Do I smell our meal burning, m'lady? If I am not allowed to satiate this ravenous craving you suggest I have for women, may I at least satisfy my hunger for the pork you are roasting before 'tis charred beyond recognition?"

Before wheeling and stalking outside, Meagan cast him an icy glare and then muttered under her breath. Damn that man! Where did he find the gall to make such an outrageous request, as if they were discussing something as harmless as the weather? Never in her wildest dreams did she imagine that her first encounter with the temptation of lovemaking would come in broad daylight, from her worst enemy, as part of a bargain. Trevor Burke had successfully shattered her childish whims and romantic fantasies. She had hoped to hear soft music playing somewhere in the distance, feel the heady sensations evolving from soft kisses, and inhale the subtle male fragrance that entangled her senses when the man of her dreams attempted to lure her into his bed. But nay, she was not to be granted even the simplest of pleasures. The music that reached her ears was the sound of a panther calling to its mate. The sensations that stirred her were anger and frustration, and the fragrance that infiltrated her nostrils was that of the burning boar that had been too long on the fire.

Trevor had spoiled her entire world, Meagan mused sourly. The Norman pig should have been roasting at the stake, and she would have derived excessive pleasure from jabbing him until he squealed. Sleep in his bed, indeed! Meagan muttered several unrepeatable epithets to his name as she retrieved the smoldering pork, tossed it on a platter, and offered it to the ruttish boar who sat upon his throne of straw.

When they had finished their meal, Meagan vaulted to her feet and summoned her falcon and shepherd. "I intend to hunt the rest of the day. I suggest you spend the afternoon recuperating so that you can endure the journey back to the castle. It would grieve me to have you suffer a setback from your bout with the boar," she sniffed, her voice dripping heavily with sarcasm.

As Trevor watched her storm out the door, he muffled a chuckle. Meagan was fire and ice. When he stood too close to her, his body caught fire and burned. And when she lashed out at him, her words as harsh as the arctic winds, he could feel icicles forming on his flesh. But for some unknown reason Trevor found himself drawn to her, visualizing the sight of her in his arms. The very thought had his pulse racing, and Trevor decided to take Meagan's advice to catch a nap before he worked himself into a passionate frenzy. Yet had he known of the spiteful thoughts that were buzzing through her mind, he would not have dared to close his eyes without the protection of a coat of armor. At that moment, Meagan was feeling positively murderous, torn between the vivid awareness that Trevor Burke was all man and the deep-rooted hatred that she had carried for Normans for three years.

When Meagan returned to the shack with a skinned rabbit, Trevor propped himself up and offered her a welcoming smile. "I see you have been successful. Your falcon and shepherd seem to be well-trained assets."

Meagan was quick to take offense and sniffed indignantly. "Although Garda and Lear aid in the hunt, I stalk my own prey," she informed him curtly. "But I would imagine that even your poor hunting skills would be camouflaged with their assistance."

Trevor felt as if the minx had drawn her sword and run him through, slicing a nasty gash in what was left of his decaying male pride. "You need not take my remark as an insult," he muttered sourly. "I only sought to make idle conversation."

Meagan heaved a frustrated sigh. Why was she wearing her feelings on the sleeve of her tunic? Because she was trying so hard to despise the handsome warrior whose charisma clung to him like fragrant cologne. She had no desire to become involved with this Dark Prince, who was the symbol of all the wrong her countrymen and family had suffered.

"Humor me, Meagan. I am not a well man," he coaxed and then directed her attention to the bandage. "Could you spare me a moment to assist me with my injury? 'Tis beginning to itch."

Leaving her bitterness on the threshold, Meagan ambled over to kneel beside Trevor and inspect the wound. "'Tis a good sign," she mused aloud. "The wound is beginning to heal."

A strange tremor rippled down her spine as he leaned

close, his muscular shoulder brushing against hers. His male scent wrapped itself around her warping senses. What had come over her? Why was she so vividly aware of his masculine aroma, his virile body, and the arousing way he smiled at her? Meagan had the odd wish to be temporarily struck deaf, dumb, and blind until she completed her ministrations so she could remain immune to his magnetic presence.

Several minutes of agony passed as she touched his thigh with trembling hands and awkwardly unwound the rest of the bandage.

Trevor peered at the neatly stitched flesh and then his wondering gaze swung to Meagan. "'Tis evident that you are also efficient with a needle and thread. You surprise me, m'lady. Your talents are inexhaustible," he commented, a hint of awe in his voice.

"One must be proficient at many things if one is to survive these troubled times," Meagan shrugged, regaining a few shreds of her raveled composure.

"And Normans must be equipped with an extra set of eyes in the back of their heads to observe their enemies," Trevor grunted and then winced when Meagan's fingertip found tender flesh.

"So you are not popular among your Saxon tenants," she surmised as she peeled the last bit of clinging cloth from his thigh.

"Most Saxons carry your resentment." Trevor eased back against the wall while Meagan climbed to her feet to retrieve her medicinal salve and returned to pack it on his wound.

"We will never accept Norman rule as law," she assured him flatly. "England is ours and shall remain so, even while a foreign king treads the halls of London's court."

"Meagan, you have not told me why you would see me wed to your maid." Trevor refused to be dragged into another debate. The lady was sharp-witted and his mind was dulled by injury. At the moment he didn't give a damn who ruled England's roost. He wanted a direct answer. "You knew that I had no wish to wed you or anyone else, but after this . . ."

"You do not have to wed her," Meagan interrupted as she reached for more salve to pack into the wound and concentrated on the conversation rather than the feel of his bare flesh beneath her hands. "I only ask that you propose the contract to Edric so that I may see him squirm in his skin." A devilish smile skitted across her lips, making her eyes glow like polished sapphires, ones that left Trevor mesmerized by the depths he saw in them. "My only intention is to watch my brother fumble his way out of the proposal. He is in love with Devona and I should like to see the tables turned on him."

"Edric and Devona?" Trevor leaned back against the rough wall to conjure up a picture of the shy maid with her lord.

"Yea, 'twas love at first sight. They only have eyes for each other, but Edric refused to wed her," Meagan explained as she wiped away the excess salve and then wound a fresh bandage around his thigh. "When my brother begins to make excuses to convince you that Devona would not suit you, then you can withdraw your proposal. He will see that 'twas not I who made an impression on you, but rather his gentle Devona."

"You believe your maid to possess the qualities that become a lady?" Trevor broke into a wry smile as his wandering gaze caressed Meagan's tantalizing figure, which her tunic and mantle could no longer disguise since he had witnessed every delicious inch of her flesh while she bathed in the stream.

Why was he staring at her like that? Meagan gulped nervously. It was as if he could see through her. The man was hard on her blood pressure, leaving her heart pumping so furiously that she could feel an inner heat, as if another log had been tossed on top of an already blazing fire.

"Devona is more suited for a gentleman than I am," Meagan assured him, intent on their discussion rather than the subtle seduction in those fathomless pools of burnt amber. "She is docile, even-tempered, and very devoted."

"While you could be described as flighty, short-fused, and belligerent," Trevor teased as he impulsively reached over to

105

trail a dark finger over her ivory cheek.

Meagan winced as if she had been snakebit, fearing his touch now more than ever. She was vulnerable to this man who set her confused emotions afire. If Trevor had any lingering doubt that Edric's initial proposal might somehow be practical, Meagan intended to set the matter straight, dashing any thoughts of reconsideration. She could not marry a man like Trevor because her heart had begun to soften toward him. If she made the tragic mistake of falling in love with the handsome lord, she would become a hypocrite. That would never do! She still had her pride, and she clung fiercely to it.

"Yea, guilty as charged," she confessed, her lashes sweeping down to shield her from his measuring gaze. "I have always chased my own rainbows. I am much too independent and set in my ways. The times I have allowed my tongue to outrace my brain are too innumerable to count. I envy men like you, who have the freedom to come and go as they please, and my brother would readily agree that I am as spoiled as a three-day-old dead fish. No man in his right mind would ever wed a woman like me." Meagan was laying it on thick, but on second thought, there needed to be several coats as a buffer between her and Trevor.

"At least you are honest, and you are not blind to your faults. There are so few who will admit a weakness in character," Trevor murmured, envisioning his lips fitted to hers. Egod! He was fantasizing again. If he didn't get a grip on himself, Meagan's underlying charms would have him wallowing at her feet!

"I am not always honest," she corrected, deciding to explain her original plan and assure Trevor that she would never be suitable for any Norman lord, just in case he decided to groom her for one of his countrymen. "I had intended to switch places with Devona before you and I met. I wanted you to think she was Lady Lowell so Edric would find himself hopping from the frying pan into the fire to retract his agreement and have his beloved Devona back by his side."

Trevor crossed his arms over his broad chest and

scrutinized the comely blond for a contemplative moment. Now he understood why Meagan had been dressed so casually for their first meeting. "I realize now that you were as much against the marriage as I was," he chortled. "You would have stooped to portraying a servant to save yourself from me."

"And even lower," she hastily assured him. Her eyes met his penetrating gaze, leaving Meagan wishing she hadn't looked at him at all. He could hold her spellbound, willing her to do things to which she objected. Staring at him caused a riptide of emotion, making her want what she knew she must never have. "I would have escaped into the forest to take my chances in the wilds if Devona had not agreed to switch places. Unfortunately, you were on hand to greet us outside the castle."

"Nothing could save you from me if I intended to have you, my lovely vixen," he told her, his voice soft but rustling with confidence. "But what I want now is for you to kiss me."

Meagan blanched. She could not! Her attitude toward him had changed drastically since the first day they met when he had pinned her to the wall to teach her the difference between a kiss and a *kiss*. If she was swayed by his kiss then she hated to venture a guess what she might experience now. Why, she would probably melt all over him when he set her on fire. Nay, the risk of surrender was too great. She could not submit.

When her frantic gaze darted to the wolflike shepherd who lay near the entrance with his large head resting on his front paws, Trevor grinned wryly. "You once called off your dog, but I wonder if you are toying with the idea of letting him make a meal of me."

He had read her mind like an open book, and Meagan smiled sheepishly. "The thought did cross my mind," she admitted.

"I will not hurt you," Trevor assured her huskily, holding his ground even when he was aching to clutch her to him and ravish her. "Is it so much to ask? I am an ailing man who sees you as an enchanting nurse and guardian angel. Is the price too high when this noble lord intends to ask Edric for

107

Devona's hand so that you may have your revenge on your brother?"

"You will?" Meagan beamed in delight, and before she realized what she had done, her arms flew about his neck to rain grateful kisses on his unshaven cheek.

But Trevor was uninterested in *grateful*. He sought to quench the thirst of desire that tarrying with this beautiful maiden evoked. His hands tunneled through her hair, holding her face to his. He drew her against his chest, branding her with a fire that scorched her flesh at every sensitive point where their bodies touched.

Meagan felt her heart melt in her chest and then drip over her ribs. Her common sense was buckling beneath the barrage of emotions that ached for release. His tongue traced her quivering lips and then probed deeper to savor her response. He took her breath away, like air currenting toward a fire to feed the blaze.

Her eyes were wide as she watched him like a wary hawk until his thick lashes fluttered up to see her staring at him in unmasked bewilderment. His mouth twitched in amusement as he bent to nibble at the pulsating vein in her throat, loving the creamy softness of her skin against his cheek, making him vividly aware of the difference between his body and hers.

"'Twas not so bad, was it, Meagan?" he rasped, his husky voice triggering a fleet of goose pimples that opened full sail and cruised across her skin. "Have I given you just cause to order Lear to sink his sharp teeth into my neck, m'lady?"

The feel of his lips was like a moist flame skimming across her flushed cheek. The gentle pressure of his sinewy arms encircling her waist was like a blanket of pleasure. But the wild thundering of her heart, matching the accelerated beat of his, left Meagan feeling as though she were perched on a towering cliff. One careless step could send her plummeting, and she feared the fall. Once she had been pushed past the point of resistance, there would be no turning back with Trevor. Dragon's blood spurted through his veins, and she sensed that his appetite for passion compared to that of a beast. Though he had shown himself to be a gentle lover thus far, Meagan did not quite trust him in the advanced stages of an embrace. There was always a hint of devilishness, even in his smiles. Charismatic and contagious though they were, Meagan could never decode the thoughts that remained hidden in those glistening golden eyes. She knew that what he wanted from a woman had more to do with lust than love, and she would not become his pawn for a reckless moment of passion.

Pushing away from the broad expanse of his chest, Meagan held him at bay when he would have preferred to lose himself in the tantalizing sight and feel of her. "Nay, m'lord," she rasped in belated response to his question. "But do not press for more than your bargain." Her voice crackled from the aftereffects of his persuasive kiss, one that left her feeling as helpless as a drowning swimmer going down for the third and final time.

"My original bargain was far more than a kiss." Trevor brushed the back of his hand over her stubborn chin, bringing it down a notch. "This will never be enough to satisfy me now. Your lips melted like summer rain on mine. They held a quiet promise of something more fulfilling than an embrace."

Meagan glanced away, but her eyes landed on the bulge at the base of his abdomen and she blushed profusely when she realized how close she had come to bracing her hand on his thigh to keep from teetering backward. Trevor's low chuckle brought her gaze around to his grinning face for further mortification.

"Does it surprise you that you have the power to stir me, little dove?" he queried softly.

"Nay, any woman would move you to desires of the flesh," Meagan insisted, fighting like the devil to keep a tight grip on her shattered composure.

"And you still see me as a lustful dragon," he guessed, chortling as he wound his hand in the platinum tresses that tumbled over her left shoulder like a river of silver gold. "But you are angel's fire to me, Meagan." His voice weaved a satiny web that caught and held Meagan like a fly entangled by a black widow spider. "You seem as soft and lovely as a seraph, and yet you kindle a fire in me that I am left to wonder if I can extinguish until the flame has run its course."

It was not like Meagan to turn tail and run at the first sign of danger, but she feared herself as much as she feared Trevor. He could make her forget her vow to keep a safe distance from him. Meagan tore herself from his arms, rose to her feet, and snatched up the skinned rabbit. "I must prepare our meal, m'lord. It will be our last before we journey to your fortress."

Trevor folded his hands behind his head and sighed heavily as Meagan disappeared outside. She had become a compelling challenge that Trevor was having difficulty ignoring. He had meant to have nothing to do with her, and she with him, but they had both overlooked the possibility that a physical attraction could sprout and grow beneath a veil of contempt. Meagan had felt the spark leap between them, but she was skeptical of the pleasure she might find in his arms. She was like a cautious doe, her body poised to flee when she felt cause for alarm. And there *were* hazards awaiting them, Trevor reminded himself. He had seen the fire in her eyes and he had felt the flames scalding his flesh when he held her reluctant body against his. They had fought the inevitable, but fate had thrown them together for more days and nights than two people who were unwillingly attracted to each other could resist.

Somewhere deep inside him a blossom opened, and a thought crept in from the shadows of his mind. He could never be satisfied until he had possessed this wild, free bird, not as chattel that was his for the taking because of his rank, but as a woman whose softness and beauty could take his breath away. Yea, Lady Meagan Lowell posed a threat as Conan had claimed, but not the kind the wise sage had suspected. Meagan was a subtle danger to the intangible emotions Trevor had buried when he lost his home and family. She could give rise to a bond that Trevor wondered if he could sever, even with the sharpest sword. Would his need for her wither once he had satisfied his overwhelming craving for her passion? Could he be healed once he found himself consumed by this angel's fire?

"The time is coming, Meagan," he mused aloud. "And when it does, neither of us will be able to halt it. Not even your proud determination will withstand the storm that billows between us. There is thunder and lightning in the air. Can either of us walk away unmoved once we have weathered this storm of desire that threatens to engulf us?"

Chapter 7

Inhaling a deep breath, Meagan focused on her chore of preparing supper. Life had been simpler when she and Trevor were antagonists and competitors. But now they stood on another threshold, one Meagan refused to cross. She would *not* give in to passion for passion's sake. Trevor had conquered his fair share of Saxons, male and female alike. She was not some common castle wench who would throw herself at a man, yielding to the stronger force just because there was an attraction between them. Love must accompany desire, she reminded herself. Although she was curious about the passion that passed between a man and a woman, she feared that experimenting with Trevor Burke would prove disastrous. What did she have to gain? Not nearly as much as she stood to lose, she told herself.

"Yea, I can resist him," she said aloud as she placed the rabbit over the campfire to roast. "He lures me, but he sees me as just another woman, not as Meagan Lowell. And even if he did it would not matter."

Meagan tended the horses and wandered about the woods until the meal had cooked, not daring to spend a moment longer than necessary with the Dark Prince, who seemed to possess the magical power of passion. When she ambled back inside, Trevor was asleep and Meagan could not strangle the smile that melted her stern expression. Trevor seemed an altogether different man when in repose, she mused. His rugged face lost its harshness, giving him a boyish quality that was never allowed to develop when he was a child. His tousled raven hair lay across his forehead and curled about his ears, and Meagan stilled the urge to comb her fingers through the thick mass.

But the whimsical moment evaporated when Trevor tensed and then came awake with a start. His cold amber eyes anchored on her and then mellowed as his gaze traveled over her shapely curves and swells.

Meagan squatted in front of him to tear away the meat and then shoved it at him. "Feast on this, m'lord. I have grown tired of your devouring glances," she snapped more harshly than she intended. But dammit, how was she to maintain her sense of dignity when he stripped her naked with eyes that raked her like golden talons?

Obediently, Trevor munched his meal and kept silent until he had eaten his fill. Then he rose to his feet and tested his leg, finding it stiff and still a mite tender. As he walked toward the door, forcing himself not to limp, Meagan stared at him in astonishment.

"Where are you going? You have not completely regained your strength," she reminded him.

"I intend to bathe," he called over his shoulder. "Perhaps that is why you find my presence so offensive."

"But, m'lord. What if . . ."

Trevor dragged himself onto the stallion's back and pressed his good leg to the steed's flank to urge him toward the stream. "You need not fuss over me, Meagan. I have sustained worse wounds than this and I have managed to survive. In the past I had no lady in attendance. I will grow soft if you dote over me, even when I know 'tis not your wont to do so. Indeed, you would have been pleased if I had buckled and died on the spot," he snorted derisively.

Meagan heaved an exasperated sigh as Poseidon trotted toward his destination with that fool Norman careening on his back. It would serve Trevor right to become light-headed and fall face down in the stream. Egod! The man had cobwebs in his attic, she muttered under her breath. Did he wish to risk his life for a mere bath when he was hailed as a valiant warrior? Meagan could imagine his epitaph: The

114

mighty Norman soldier was not taken by his foe's lance or battle-ax to die a proud death. He drowned in his bath to be nibbled on by curious turtles and fishes.

Rolling her eyes heavenward, Meagan summoned more patience to deal with this witless wonder and then stalked off after him, wondering if she would be forced to tow the naked knight from the creek and haul him back to his pallet to suffer a setback. Lord, all she needed was to spend several more days growing accustomed to the man she loved to hate.

As Meagan crouched in the brush, she could not will herself to look the other way as Trevor shed every article of clothing and limped toward the stream. His muscular body tensed as the cold water curled about his ankles and Meagan sighed admiringly at his perfect physique. He was all man, every well-packaged inch of him. She had seen his hard, muscular body when she attempted to cool his raging fever, but now she marveled at his lithe movements, her wonderment tenfold. For what seemed an eternity Meagan studied everything about him, noticing the way his coal black hair sparkled in the waning light, the way his bronzed body glowed with droplets of water, the way his shoulders tapered to his lean abdomen. She was so enthralled by the quiet pleasure of observing him while he was unaware that she failed to notice Lear creeping up beside her to rub his cold nose against her neck.

Meagan's shrill shriek sent the birds to their wings in the trees above her, and she stumbled forward, sprawling over a fallen limb. Embarrassed red made fast work of staining her scratched cheek as Lear trotted up to lick her face. Her head swiveled around when she heard Trevor snickering as he swaggered to the stream bank, the water ebbing to expose the dark matting of hair on his chest, the finely tuned muscles of his belly, and . . .

With a startled gasp, Meagan buried her head in the dirt like a frightened ostrich and clenched two fistfuls of grass rather than partake of the full front view of Trevor's godlike torso. How she wished the earth would open to swallow her up and spare her this humiliation.

"And to think you condemned me for watching you bathe

at a distance while you peeped at me at close range," Trevor chided mockingly. "Tsk, tsk. I would never have expected such antics from a gently bred young lady. I knew you sought to strip me naked with your insults, but I didn't dream that you would delight in seeing me in my state of undress. Tell me, Meagan. Now that there are no secrets between us, do you approve or disapprove of what you see?"

"Go away," Meagan groaned in anguish, knowing Trevor loved every minute of her humiliation. And the worst of it was that she could not move or even look up without embarrassing herself all the more.

"I thought your intention was to study my physical attributes, or lack of them, by peeping at me through the brush," he smirked caustically.

"I was not spying on you. I have seen you before. I . . ." Meagan gnashed her teeth together. When would she learn to keep her mouth shut? It seemed she was forever stuffing her foot in it.

One heavy brow shot up as Trevor stared at the top of Meagan's head. "Woman, you surprise me. Did you take advantage of me in my unconscious condition as well?"

"You required a cool rub down during your fevered ravings and I had very little choice except to let your temperature soar to fry your brain," she sputtered in explanation.

Meagan breathed a sigh of relief when Trevor's husky laugh faded and he ambled back to collect his garments.

"You may get up now, m'lady. I have covered myself . . . not that it matters," he taunted. "You have already seen me in the raw."

Without a word, Meagan picked up her crumbled dignity, brushed herself off, and marched back to the shack. Tears of humiliation boiled down her cheeks. She had followed Trevor to ensure his safety and he had taunted her unmercifully, accusing her of being as hungry for him as a kitten on the trail of a fresh bucket of milk. The man was infuriating, and she found herself wishing she had slipped him a potion to turn him into a toad when he took his meal. Damn his gorgeous hide! Why couldn't he have been some ugly beast as she had imagined? Why did the mere sight of him make her blood run like a roaring river that was about to flood its banks?

Meagan stopped short when her eyes sank to the bare ground beneath her feet. A puzzled frown puckered her brow as she knelt to uncover a tarnished silver brooch. Her mind froze. Carefully, she dug away the caked dirt to see the Saxon crest that was etched on the broken pin. Meagan's eyes flew to the shack that had shown telltale signs of occupancy before she and Trevor had sought its shelter. Nay, it couldn't be, she assured herself shakily. Meagan tucked the brooch away and continued on her way, but bits and pieces of Edric's comments began to rise from shadowed thoughts, leaving her to wonder if her brother's motives for playing the matchmaker for her and Trevor were more devious than she had first suspected. Nay, surely not, she convinced herself. Edric was not a fool, and he would never stoop to something as fiendish as the horrid thought that had hatched in her mind.

Casting aside her troubled deliberations, Meagan stretched out on her pallet to feign sleep, hoping Trevor would take the hint to spare her further humiliation. But the long hours caught up with her and within a few minutes Meagan drifted into dreams.

Darkness hovered over the royal forest and still Trevor had not returned to the thatched hut. For more than two hours he sat on the bank of the stream, grappling with a myriad of thoughts that had selected that particular moment to surface.

The many faces of Meagan kept whipping through his mind, stirring memories that rose like cream on fresh milk. She had approached him, issuing orders and dropping subtle threats. Then she had avoided him, but her sparing glances were veiled with contempt. Trevor had been amused by her feisty spirit, touched by her bravery, and warmed by the woman he found lingering just beneath that stubborn exterior. She had burrowed her way into every emotion,

117

becoming the cause and cure of his frustrations and ventilation for his occasional anger. She was a challenge, an elusive dream that hovered just beyond his grasp. Meagan was an enigma, a muddling paradox that Trevor was having difficulty putting in perspective.

His body ached for intimacy with hers; his mouth watered just remembering the taste of her honeyed lips. The vision of her supple curves and ivory skin was etched in his mind, and try as he might, he could not quench his craving to caress what his eyes had so hungrily devoured.

Trevor heaved a sigh and gathered his feet beneath him. How much longer could he trust himself with Meagan, wanting her as he had wanted no other woman? She was different from the others who flew into his arms, often uninvited, seeking the security a Norman lord could offer. But Meagan resisted him, even when her body responded to his kiss and caress. Her willpower, though to be admired, was the root of Trevor's anguish. Never had he wooed a woman before Meagan, and now he found himself handling her as if she were a fragile flower. And yet, she was like an untamed creature of the wild, her spirit undaunted. She did not look toward the morrow but lived from day to day, content to remain an island amid the forceful currents that sought to change her.

How was he to look upon another woman without seeing Meagan's sapphire eyes and the color of the sun and moon shimmering in her hair? Trevor slammed his clenched fist into his left hand and growled under his breath. If he bedded another woman without satisfying his lust for Meagan, she would continue to haunt him, chaining him to a dream that would never become reality.

Why shouldn't he have her, he asked himself arrogantly. His position as overlord gave him privileges with any woman he chose. A woman was no more than a man's possession, and Edric had offered his sister for that cause. Trevor felt no true obligation to his Saxon vassal. If he bedded Meagan and then returned her to Edric without a marriage proposal, there would be little Edric could do about it besides complain. After all, Trevor's decision was law.

But what of Meagan, Trevor wondered. Could he force her against her will? Rape her to satisfy his craving? Nay, there would be no pleasure in claiming this wild, bewitching vixen if she fought and clawed at him. It would shatter the dream that preyed heavily on Trevor's mind.

As he pulled onto the black stallion's back, he flinched and cursed to himself. Even the steed belonged to that feisty minx. His life belonged to Meagan since she had rescued him from certain death. Blast it! No matter which way he turned he found her name echoing in the corners of his mind. He had to rout her from his thoughts.

But how could he when she waited like an angel in the haze of heaven? Trevor lingered at the door of the shack, his eyes fixed on the trim form that lay sleeping on the pallet beside his. Silky arms protruded from the cape that served as her quilt, and shiny blond hair sprayed across the straw, painting an inviting picture that Trevor could not ignore. Passion was eating him alive, for he knew that her exquisite body waited just beneath garments that could no longer disguise the natural beauty he had spied at a distance.

His footsteps took him to her side, and he knelt beside her, marveling at the flawless features that glowed in the moonlight. Trevor was drawn like a moth to the flame, his body burning from the inside out, craving that which he swore he would never take. Meagan was like the forbidden fruit that made life sweet, and Trevor found himself stung by a temptation the likes of which he had never known.

Soft, cool lips feathered over Meagan's mouth, lightly caressing, patiently drawing her from the depths of her dreams. A quiet moan of pleasure escaped her as her eyes fluttered open, but she winced when she found herself staring into Trevor's glowing amber eyes. Fear ricocheted through her as the moonlight sprayed over his naked body, making her all too aware of his intentions.

When Meagan would have drawn her cloak more tightly about her, Trevor pulled it away, stilling her struggles with quiet words of persuasion.

"Do not fight me, Meagan, and you will have nothing to fear. A lover's touch brings only pleasure," he murmured as

119

his warm breath hovered over her cheek to seek out the sensitive point of her neck. His lips lingered there to kindle a fire that spread through her entire body before his butterfly kisses skimmed the delicate line of her jaw to reclaim her trembling lips.

"Nay, please," she beseeched, dragging her mouth from his before she lost the will to resist. "I know nothing of men. I cannot please you."

A tender smile pursed his lips as he pressed closer to remove the clothes that separated them. His gaze fell to the creamy flesh of her breasts as he drew away her chemise. His breath caught in his throat as he feasted on each enticing curve and swell. When Meagan attempted to squirm away, he braced her hands above her head and crouched above her, her movements like a dance of seduction, making him vividly aware that a glimpse of heaven could never satisfy him. He wanted her.

"The mere sight of you pleases me," he murmured, his voice heavily laden with desire. "Do not be so quick to condemn your inexperience. I will teach you how to please a man."

Meagan squealed as his hand glided over her abdomen, his touch setting her heart to racing in double time. "There are many women willing to share your bed and you promised that . . ."

"A hasty vow," Trevor broke in as his wandering caress scaled the peak of her breast, leaving her quivering as he trespassed on unclaimed territory. "'Tis in the wind, Meagan. You knew this moment was inevitable, just as I did."

"Nay," she protested fiercely, her head rolling from side to side as she squeezed her eyes shut to block out the flames she had seen blazing in his golden eyes. "'Tis not my wont."

"Look beneath your stubborn pride." His hand trailed to the valley between her breasts and then ascended the other taut peak to send another river of fire boiling through her veins. "My touch is not that of a dragon's claws, but of a man who only aches to know you with a tender caress. And you also wish to satisfy your curiosity about this strange attraction between us," he whispered against her skin.

Yea, it was true. She had envisioned sleeping in his arms, even when she knew the thought should never have entered her mind. But when the dream collided with reality, Meagan was afraid to wake, afraid this moment would destroy the romantic notions of making love to this dark knight. There were times when it was best to thrive on imagination, and Meagan was certain that this was one of those times.

"Relax, lovely angel." His hushed voice drifted into her frantic musings to calm her fears. "The night was made for us."

A tiny moan caught in her throat as his mouth slanted across hers. His kiss became more inquiring as his tongue parted her lips to search the inner softness of her mouth, demanding more than she had intended to give, stripping her breath from her lungs and then generously giving it back the moment before Meagan was sure she would drown in the sensations that spread an unfamiliar heat through her body.

His seeking hand traveled over the shapely curve of her hips and then began another arousing ascent along her spine. When his exploring caress trailed around her ribs to capture her breast, Meagan flinched, disturbed and aroused by his touch.

Never had a man attempted to learn her body with his hands and lips, and Trevor's bold advances were her undoing. She tried to gasp for breath, but his mouth returned to hers, warm, devouring, insistent. Her body quaked as his caresses continued to track across her flesh. The gentle massage crumbled her resistance, leaving her aching to discover the meaning of this compelling sensation that blossomed and rose from somewhere deep inside her.

His searing kiss released her lips to spread a path of fire across her cheek before trailing over her shoulder to circle the peak of her breast. Her lashes fluttered down as his greedy mouth suckled her breast and then gave the same languid attention to the other pink bud. Waves of fire rippled across her skin as he tasted her, searing her with unbearable pleasure that drove her to the brink of insanity.

Her body instinctively arched as his gentle hands

wandered over her belly to part her thighs. His fingertips tripped across her legs, tickling and teasing her into submission before his knowing fingers found her womanly softness, arousing her until she cried out to him to appease the craving she never realized existed until she fell prey to his skillful touch.

Each intimate caress, each hushed word that he whispered against her ear heightened her awareness of the muscular body that was so close and yet so far away. Brazenly, Meagan reached out to run her hand over his hips, and then folded trembling fingers around his bold manhood. Trevor groaned in pleasure as her caress trickled up his belly and then descended once again to touch him as he ached for her to do. With hushed words he taught her how to please him, bringing his passions to a fervent pitch.

Again his hungry mouth found hers, and his body fitted itself to hers, seeking to become an intimate part of her to share a moment that had tormented his dreams.

Her sharp intake of breath and muffled cry stunned him, and he drew back to glance down into her frightened face. The wavering light shadowed and highlighted her tensed features, and Trevor longed to kiss away the fear that was mirrored in her wide eyes.

"Give yourself to me," he commanded huskily. "Body and soul. I crave to know you as no man has."

His mouth opened on hers as he carefully entered her, moving in a patient rhythm until the pain ebbed to be replaced by a strange, budding pleasure that compelled Meagan to obey and respond. She dug her nails into the corded muscles of his back as his sleek body joined hers, his hard thrusts driving into her to possess her. She felt the heat of a thousand suns scalding her perspiring flesh as he took her to dizzying heights of ecstasy and then left her suspended in a world that was decorated with stars and rainbows. Sensation upon sensation mounted until Meagan gasped and shuddered in his embrace, clinging to the only stable force in a spinning universe.

"Trevor?" His name bubbled from her lips, but she had no inkling what she had intended to say. Uttering his name was enough.

Trevor buried his head on her shoulder and trembled uncontrollably. His strength escaped him, leaving him oddly content in the circle of her satiny arms. Her innocent response had pleased and satisfied him as no other lover had, and Trevor felt the gnawing hunger to reclaim the moment of rapture.

As he rolled to his side, wondering at his need to take her again, even when he could not muster the energy to do so, Meagan squirmed away to cover herself.

"It must not happen again," she choked out, ashamed of herself for responding to him like a common whore.

A disappointed frown plowed his brow. He was not accustomed to being cast aside, and he had never found himself content to sleep in a woman's arms after their lovemaking until he had shared an intimate embrace with Meagan. What power did this temptress have over him? Why did he long to comfort and keep her with him? What was wrong with him? He had *never* been protective of a woman. Indeed, he had considered most of them a necessary evil. But each time Meagan flew from him he pursued her, as if he sought to catch the wind.

Tears trickled down her face as she drew herself up in a tight ball, praying that she could forget the turmoil of emotions his lovemaking evoked, but Trevor pressed his hard body against hers, refusing to allow her to remain distant and remote.

Helplessly, Trevor listened to Meagan sob, but he could not share her regret. She had touched him as no woman before her had. Trevor knew that the first night he spent in her arms would not be the last, and he smiled to himself as he wrapped a possessive arm around her waist and wandered into pleasant dreams.

But Meagan was hounded by entirely different thoughts, and she held her breath until she heard Trevor's methodic breathing. Carefully she inched away from him and gathered her discarded clothes. She could never face him again after she had surrendered to his kisses and caresses. Like a creature that had been too long in captivity, Meagan fled deeper into the woods, away from the tormenting pleasures that haunted her, away from the man who had taught her the meaning of passion. For them there could be no tomorrow, she reminded herself as she weaved through the trees with her devoted companions at her side. She *had* to forget that this night existed. Trevor was a Norman and she had become a slave to his desires. Never again, she told herself as she wiped away the lingering tears and sought the swaying shadows. There was one man in England who possessed the power to make her forget everything that had any resemblance to sanity. She could not trust herself with Trevor Burke, and there was only one place she could go for sanctuary. There he could not touch her. She was safe to tarry and forget . . .

Chapter 8

Heaving a weary sigh, Meagan sank down to rest, feeling no need to hurry on her way. After all, no one would be following her, not yet anyway. And if anyone did, it would be too late. Meagan would reach the convent in two days, traveling as the crow flies, picking her way cross-country.

Trevor did not have the strength, the stamina, nor the desire to track her down. His longing began and ended in bed, she mused bitterly. More than likely, Trevor was hobbling back to the fortress to whittle another notch in his bedpost. Meagan cursed under her breath. Trevor's bedpost was nothing but carvings of conquered women, and Meagan found herself spitefully wishing that its supporting frame had been weakened by his sculptured list of lovers and that the damned thing would collapse with him in it, preferably while he was having a tête-à-tête with one of his castle wenches.

How could she have been so foolish as to surrender to the Dark Prince, she asked herself. Meagan groaned miserably, her face flushing beet red when she remembered how she had boldly touched him, craving his experienced caresses, clutching at him as if she would never let him go. Her gaze soared heavenward, blocked by the thick canopy of branches that allowed only scant sunlight to filter into the forest. How could she live with herself after what had happened? Why was she experiencing this maddening emotional tug-of-war? Trevor Burke had stirred her passion with his magic touch even when she tried to keep it buried beneath her bitterness. But like a disturbed lion, those fierce needs to know him as a woman knows a man reared to shatter her self-control.

Day by day, the attraction and curiosity about him had grown until each smile and provocative glance fed a fire that had finally burned out of control. And now each time Meagan allowed her mind to drift, she could see those beguiling golden eyes staring through her, feel his hands exploring her flesh.

Meagan vaulted to her feet and then stepped into the stirrup, weaving her way through the brush as if Satan himself were hot on her heels. She *had* to force all thoughts of Trevor Burke from her mind before the memory of that tender moment, which had no place in her life, took hold of her. What she felt for Trevor was mere physical attraction. She was drawn to him because he was the first man to kiss and caress her in the heat of passion. 'Twas only that her conscience insisted that there should be more to a relationship, she told herself firmly. She was ridden with guilt because she knew she *should* have loved the man she allowed to possess her. Oh, why hadn't he raped her? Then she would have had just cause to loathe him. But nay, Trevor left her blaming herself because he had been gentle with her and she had been unable to tear herself away from the addicting sensations that compelled her to see their tryst through to the end. And that end had been bittersweet, she reminded herself. She could find no lasting pleasure in Trevor's brand of passion. It was lust that overwhelmed both of them. They intensely disliked each other. And yet . . . Meagan frowned at her meandering thoughts. Was this making any sense? She laughed humorously. Nay, it was not. She loved to hate Trevor and now she hated loving him. Somehow her spiteful thoughts had become entangled with her desire for a man who was impossible to resist, and she bore a heavy cross. She had become a hypocrite. She had bedded a Norman. God help her!

Meagan pulled her steed to a halt as nightfall descended on the forest, and then she pricked her ears to the sound that had trickled into her troubled contemplations. The muffled laughter in the distance made her tense uneasily, and she did not dare to breathe until she sought its source. Summoning her courage, Meagan crept toward the sound and then frowned bemusedly when she spied the silhouettes that clustered about a covered campfire. Only the dim glow from the flames cast weaving shadows, and the faintest hint of smoke drifted from the small fire that had been built in a pit and was protected by shields of armor. It was obvious to Meagan that this group of men, whoever they were, had no intention of being discovered or reported to the Norman overlord.

Strangling a small gasp, Meagan squinted to make out one of the men who strode across the camp to squat down beside the fire. She was instantly reminded of Edric since the man carried himself with the same springy step. Meagan squinted again. There was also something familiar about the other two men who were huddled by the fire, but for the life of her she could attach no names to the shadowed figures.

It must have been her imagination, she told herself as she backed away to retrieve her mount. She was making irrational grasps in the dark. The band of men were probably outlaws, scavengers who had lost their land to the Normans, and who lived like a pack of dogs to survive. Although many men had fled to Ireland, there were those Saxons who chose to live a hunted life on native soil rather than to migrate to foreign lands. Meagan could not fault them, but she would not risk rape at the hands of men who might have become vicious and bloodthirsty after the hardships they had endured.

Steering clear of the encampment, Meagan turned east and did not stop to rest until she had put a safe distance between herself and the shadowed figures who lived like creatures of the night, clinging to the shelter of the forest for protection.

Meagan lifted weary eyes and groaned at the stiffness that had invaded her body. A misty rain hovered over Ashdown

127

Forest, and the morning chill settled around her. She wrapped her cloak more tightly about her neck and massaged her aching muscles. Her stomach played a hungry tune against her ribs, but Meagan had bypassed nourishment in her haste to flee from the vagabonds in the forest. After glancing about her to locate something edible and finding nothing within arm's reach, Meagan crawled to her feet and fed herself on the hope that she would reach the convent before sundown. There, she could eat her fill and breathe a sigh of relief. No one would be allowed to drag her home against her will. Home? The word left an empty sensation in her soul. She no longer had a home. Edric would not welcome her with open arms when he learned that she had fled from the Dark Prince. She prayed that Sister Elizabeth would grant her refuge without interrogating her. The sympathetic nun had always been kind to Meagan even when the others had frowned on her high-spirited behavior. Sister Elizabeth had made excuses for Meagan and had stood against the condescending tones of the other nuns, who would have seen her punished more than once during her three-year stay at the convent.

As Meagan reined her steed through the mud and was about to breathe a thankful sigh when she spied the towers of the convent in the distance, she strangled on her breath. Lear's low growl sliced through the fog, and Meagan felt her heart pounding so furiously against her ribs that she was certain it would beat her to death. She had the eerie feeling that someone or something was watching her. Even Garda sensed danger and fluttered from her perch on Meagan's forearm.

A shriek burst from Meagan's lips as a dark figure leaped at her from behind a tree. The same haunting specter from whom she had fled pounced at her.

Trevor's pale face grew red with fury, his eyes blazing like the flames of a forest fire. Meagan would not have been the least bit surprised to find the trees ablaze if Trevor had turned that smoldering glare from her to his surroundings. If looks could kill she would have been burned at the stake, her remains no more than a pile of dusty ashes.

"How did you . . ." Meagan swallowed her tongue as he leveled her another murderous glare. "You were weak and . . ." She gulped and began again as she backed her steed away from the bulky warrior whose rigid stance spelled trouble. "I . . ."

Trevor's hand snaked out to grasp the reins, startling the flighty colt. Meagan held on for dear life when her mount reared and Trevor yanked on the halter to bring the colt's head down. But Meagan lost her seat when the steed kicked up his hind legs and bucked, his frightened snort piercing the air to muffle the thud as Meagan landed face down in the mud. Stunned, Meagan shook her head and then attempted to gather her feet beneath her, but Trevor planted himself on top of her, pinning her to the ground.

"Damn you," he hissed furiously. "I should have you whipped for leaving without permission. Silly fool! Would you risk your life just to avoid my bed?"

Meagan stopped struggling, her lips curling to match the sneer that was stamped on Trevor's face. "No risk is too great if I can avoid that," she spat at him. "You have shamed me and I am no longer fit for another man."

"No *Saxon* man, you mean to say," Trevor snapped back at her in an intimidating tone. "Making love to me was the ultimate humiliation, was it not? You detest me so much that you deny the pleasure you found in my arms."

"The ultimate insult would be to bear your bastard child." Meagan strained against him, hating the reminder that they had been much closer than this for altogether different reasons.

A low rumble came from his heaving chest as he stared down at the bedraggled beauty who wore a layer of mud. Why had he pushed himself to pursue her when he could barely find the strength to place one foot in front of the other without dropping in his tracks? He had punished his body, thriving on raw will and determination. When he finally caught up with this fiery minx, he was forced to nurse more bruises, ones that arose when she slapped him with her hateful insults.

"If that is the reason you fled from my embrace, you worry

for naught, my muddy witch. You will never carry my bastard child. I promise you that."

Meagan heard his words, but it took a moment to digest them. Was he sterile, unable to sire heirs? Although she was relieved to learn that one night's mistake would not cost her further humiliation, it changed nothing. She was dismayed by her response to Trevor, and she longed to strike out and hurt him the way she was hurting, hoping to mend her tattered conscience by rejecting him as she should have done in the first place.

"I despise you for what you did to me. I would have spread myself beneath the lowliest scum on earth before I would have sought out your bed," she hissed, reminding Trevor of a coiled snake that had every intention of poisoning him with venom.

If Trevor thought he could release her arms without having her claw his face, he would have clamped his fingers around her lovely throat and choked her with bubbling enthusiasm. But Meagan was a tigress who when given an inch would stretch it for all it was worth, Trevor mused as he glared at her through a veil of angry red.

Meagan feared that look in his eyes, wondering what vengeful thoughts were whipping through his head. She felt threatened. "Lear!" she called to her shepherd, hoping he could distract the fuming lord so she could worm free and run for her life.

"Stay, Lear," Trevor barked as his head swiveled around to meet the wolf-dog's dark eyes.

The shepherd pulled up short and looked from one stern face to the other, confused by the contradicting commands.

"Lear!" Meagan was frantic. Never had her guardian disobeyed her. He had always been blindly loyal.

"Sit, Lear," Trevor ordered, his voice sharp and demanding.

The dog whined and then sank down on his haunches, and Meagan glowered at the dark knight who sat upon her.

A wry smile grazed Trevor's lips as he peered at Meagan's stained cheeks and muddy blond hair. "I took the liberty of feeding and befriending your vicious mongrel . . . just in

130

case such a situation should arise. Thankfully, Lear does not despise and mistrust me as fiercely as his mistress does," he added with a derisive snort.

"Damn you to hell and back!" Meagan railed as she writhed to relieve herself of the heavy brute who sat perched on her back as if she were his throne.

Trevor's amused chuckle stoked the fires of her volatile temper. "You give me so many reasons to have you executed that I am sorely tempted to follow through with the dastardly deed. You have abandoned me without permission. You have attempted to sic your mutt on me and now you dare to curse me. Methinks you are a frightful witch who should be burned at the stake."

Meagan wished she could sprout a third hand and slap that arrogant smirk off his face. She was smoldering in outrage. Nothing could make her more furious than to be held down and insulted. How she itched to vent her frustrations, but Trevor was not foolish enough to unhand her, even for a moment.

As if he had read her vindictive thoughts, Trevor tightened his viselike grip, and Meagan groaned, her arms tingling from lack of circulation. Infuriated, she squirmed and then muttered several unrepeatable epithets to his name, wondering why she had kept them to herself. Trevor certainly did not deserve the courtesy.

"There was a time when I entrusted my life to your gentle hands, but now I would not dare to turn my back on you for fear of finding my own dagger buried between my ribs." Cautiously Trevor crouched beside Meagan and then twisted her arm farther up behind her until she shrieked beneath the unbearable pain of having her limb ripped from its hinge. "I will teach you the proper manners that become a lady. And before I am through with you, my feisty vixen, you will surely wish you were dead."

Meagan didn't doubt it for a minute. She had heard horror stories about tortures worse than death, ones inflicted on belligerent Saxons by their Norman conquerors.

As Trevor uprooted her from the mud and planted her on her steed to tie her in place, Meagan acquainted him with her look of disgust. "Does the fact that I saved your life count for nothing?" she queried in an acrimonious tone.

"Exactly that," Trevor assured her gruffly. "Your disrespectfulness overshadows your noble deed. I will regard you as I would any other disloyal servant."

"Servant!" Meagan gasped indignantly. "If you think . . ."

"Do not presume to tell me what to think," Trevor bit off as he limped over to retrieve his stallion. "From this moment on, you will do as I command *when* I command it."

Meagan clamped into her iron will and held her tongue even though she was stung by the impulse to shout in his arrogant face. She watched unsympathetically as Trevor called upon his failing strength to mount his horse. There had been a time when she would have spared him the agony of pain, but now she wished it on him like a spiteful curse.

As Trevor led her toward his fortress, seeking out the longer-but-safer route, Meagan glared flaming arrows at his back. If Trevor thought he would find her groveling at his feet, begging for mercy, he had made a gross error in judgment. Force would not subdue her. He had given her dozens of reasons to loathe him, and her irritation with him aided in her bout to overcome the passion she had discovered in his arms that reckless night. Servant, indeed! Trevor Burke was hallucinating if he thought she would cater to his whims. Her stubborn pride would not permit it.

The long hours of riding in dampness played havoc with Trevor's black mood. He was tired, hungry, and irritable. The morning he had awakened to find that Meagan had abandoned him had destroyed a contented dream. Trevor had ignored the stabbing pain in his thigh to pursue that appetizing lass who left him craving the feel of her supple body in his arms. During his tedious journey he had asked himself why he was chasing trouble. He had taken what he wanted from her and he should have been satisfied, but dammit, he wasn't. Meagan was like an addiction, and Trevor was annoyed with himself for allowing that blond-haired hellion to preoccupy him. She was worth her weight

132

in trouble, he had reminded himself. And yet, the thought of Meagan being set upon by man or beast disturbed him. He had not intended to become entangled with this firebrand, but he was. Perhaps Meagan would drag her feet, but by damned, he would have his way with her. The wench had met her match, he told himself arrogantly.

Trevor gritted his teeth as a white-hot pain shot up his thigh. The rugged journey and the inclement weather had drained him, and it was all he could do to keep pressing toward his destination. When the spiraling towers of Neville Castle appeared in the distance, Trevor breathed a sigh of relief. A soft feather bed and good companionship awaited him. There, he could put his plan into action and ease his weary bones and aching muscles.

"Yonder awaits Neville Castle." He gestured to the south and then tossed Meagan a warning glance. "Mind your manners while others are about and you will be spared my wrath."

"You need not preach," Meagan muttered, her expression sour enough to curdle fresh milk. "You lectured me on that subject the first day we had the misfortune of meeting."

"But your memory is short," Trevor pointed out. "Just do as I command without argument. Lord Neville would expect me to severely punish you for your impudence."

"Another Norman pig," Meagan speculated, her nose wrinkling distastefully. "I suppose he is so magnificently arrogant that he cannot tolerate a woman who has a mind of her own and occasionally speaks it."

Trevor twisted in his saddle, his golden eyes raking her with scornful mockery. "A man could overlook an occasional outburst, but your runaway tongue is the rule, *not* the exception. You, m'lady, have spoken your mind so often that I am left to wonder if you have depleted your supply." His gaze narrowed meaningfully. "Watch your step with Ragnar," he cautioned. "Neville rules his fief with an iron hand. Perhaps it would be wise to inform you that the first Lady Neville did not meet Ragnar's expectations, and . . ."

He let his remark dangle in the foggy air, knowing the inquisitive imp would prompt him to continue.

133

"What happened to her?" Meagan didn't really want to know, but as Trevor anticipated, her curiosity got the best of her.

"Rumor has it that Ragnar saw to it that the lady drowned." His shoulder lifted and then dropped lackadaisically. "But Ragnar swears that she was lost in a swift current and that no one was able to rescue her." A wry smile tugged at his lips. "He seeks a new wife, and I should think that Edric would be pleased if I could strike up a match, since he is so anxious to wash his hands of his unruly sister. I shall make a mental note to approach the subject with Ragnar."

Meagan strangled on her breath. "You wouldn't dare . . ."

"Wouldn't I?" His dark brow arched tauntingly. "The idea has a certain amount of sadistic appeal. But if I find that Ragnar would not make a suitable mate, I have another knight in mind who might also cause you considerable distress."

Trevor bit back a chuckle as he watched the color seep from Meagan's muddy cheeks. Ragnar was not as bad as Trevor insinuated, but Meagan didn't need to know that. It did his heart good to watch her squirm uncomfortably.

Meagan focused apprehensive blue eyes on the fortress that grew larger on the horizon, and she fell silent, certain that Trevor would leap at the opportunity to see her wed to some brutish oaf who would beat her for voicing an opinion. Trevor would gloat over the misery he caused her, she predicted. Damn that Trevor. He had just added another reason to her extensive list of excuses for why she should hate him.

Chapter 9

Ragnar Neville quickened his step when he recognized Trevor hobbling toward him. "What has happened?" he gasped as he wrapped a supporting arm about Trevor and propelled him toward the forebuilding.

"I was attacked by a boar," Trevor explained briefly. "Lady Lowell and I request rooms for the night."

Ragnar sent his servants scurrying to prepare the chambers for the overlord and the disheveled young woman who fell into step behind them. Within a quarter of an hour he had his guests situated in their rooms, and Meagan found herself settled in a wooden tub, thoroughly enjoying the luxury of a bath. She vigorously scrubbed away the layers of mud that clung to her and then lathered her hair to transform the tangled mass of dingy brown to shiny silver blond. Although she would have preferred to sit and soak until her body had fully recovered from the punishment she had forced upon it, she stepped from her bath to dress in the clothing Ragnar had graciously offered to her.

When she returned to Trevor's room, as he had ordered, his consuming gaze poured over her deep purple attire and then he nodded approvingly, warmed by the transformation and aroused by the enchanting sight of silver-blond hair shimmering in the lamp light and bewitched by blue eyes that were as clear and bright as a bubbling spring.

"Ragnar will be spellbound," Trevor mused aloud. "No doubt, he will question our relationship, wondering if I will

135

object if he bestows his full attention on you." Trevor took a step closer, his senses asssaulted by the tantalizing fragrance that hovered about her. "What would you have me tell him?"

Meagan wrung her hands in front of her, faced with the possibility of being dumped in Ragnar's lap. "M'lord, I know I have caused you trouble, but . . ."

"An armload of it," Trevor interjected, checking his aroused desires and then casting her the evil eye.

"But you will find no complaint with my behavior this night," she promised him faithfully. "I know you would hand me over to Lord Neville, just for spite, but I have decided I would like the opportunity to return to your good graces." The thought had not occurred to her until this very moment, but Meagan suddenly found herself with little choice except to soft-soap the lout.

Trevor chuckled at that. "M'lady, you and I have been on opposite sides of the battlefield from the moment we met. You cannot return to somewhere you have never been."

Meagan itched to shake him until his teeth rattled. He delighted in infuriating her, and he was forcing her to tread carefully when she yearned to tell him what she thought of him, sparing no derogatory adjectives. But she would not fly off the handle, she told herself firmly. 'Twas time to resort to feminine finesse in dealing with this ornery scoundrel.

A wicked sparkle glistened in her eyes as she sashayed up in front of him, determined to appeal to the instincts of the lusting beast within him. She looped her arms over his shoulders and her lips parted invitingly, leaving Trevor drooling to taste the kiss that had every indication of being as intoxicating as wine.

"Is it worth the trip, m'lord?" she purred seductively.

Trevor caught himself the split second before he tumbled headlong into her tempting embrace. Summoning his willpower, he set her hands from him and then aimed her toward the door. "I have no intention of falling prey to your spell when I have viewed the conniving witch who lurks just beneath the surface. Come. We shall see if you can deceive Lord Neville with your blinding beauty."

Meagan gnashed her teeth together and then retracted her

claws. Resolutely, she descended the stairs beside the limping warlord and then swallowed her apprehension when Ragnar climbed to his feet, his green eyes raking her so thoroughly that Meagan felt the need to shield herself as if she were parading through the Great Hall like Lady Godiva, wife of Leofric, earl of Mercia, who had ridden stark naked through Coventry on her white stallion. Meagan could read Ragnar's thoughts and she swore he would not object if she decided to enact the lady's daring ride.

Although Ragnar was mildly attractive, Meagan found herself comparing him to Trevor, finding that the burly knight ran a distant second. His medium brown hair was chopped off in the uncomplimentary Norman style that left her wondering if one of his servants had slapped a bowl on his head and had haphazardly clipped his hair while blindfolded. Ragnar was muscularly built, but again she realized Trevor's striking physique placed him in a class all by himself. Meagan searched Ragnar's face, hoping to perceive a gentleness amidst his rugged features, but each time she sized him up he fell short.

"M'lady," Ragnar breathed as he feasted on her comeliness. "It has been an eternity since I have had the pleasure of such lovely company and I cannot conjure up another face that compares to yours."

"Blundering fool," Trevor muttered disgustedly. "Your tongue is hanging out and I swear you are in danger of tripping over it."

Meagan elbowed Trevor in the belly, making him grunt uncomfortably, and all the while Ragnar could see nothing except the angelic vision who fluttered toward the dais. "You are very kind, m'lord, but I fear you have made much ado over this plain porridge. 'Tis only these exquisite garments you have lent me that greatly compliment my appearance," Meagan assured him sweetly and then curtsied before him.

Trevor rolled his eyes and then planted himself in the chair. If he didn't put some food in his belly, and quickly, he was sure he was going to be sick. This overdose of flattery was nauseating him. Ragnar was behaving like a love-struck swain, and Meagan was batting her big blue eyes at him. The poor man might never recover from his fascination. It annoyed Trevor that Meagan was behaving so graciously to Ragnar when she had been cool and aloof toward him, except for the night . . .

"It distresses me, m'lady, that you were forced to endure the storm. It must have brought you great discomfort to find yourself without proper protection from this dreary weather," Ragnar went on to say, ignoring Trevor as if he were some inanimate object to be walked around or stepped on.

Meagan slid Trevor a discreet glance and then frowned curiously. Ragnar did not seem the fierce, unsympathetic brute Trevor had described. Indeed, he was quite the gentleman, or as close as any Norman could come since the two words were a contradiction in terms.

"It has been an unbearable few days," Meagan agreed and then muffled a snicker behind a cough when Trevor's head swiveled around to glare at her.

Swallowing his irritation with a hunk of bread provided by the pantler, Trevor kept silent, finding himself omitted from the conversation. Ragnar was so busy chattering with Meagan that Trevor had naught else to do but sit and eat.

After they had taken their meal, Ragnar invited Meagan to tour his fortress, leaving Trevor to hobble along behind them or return to his chamber. As Ragnar escorted Meagan down the steps he broke stride and then colored in embarrassment.

"Forgive me, Trevor. I did not mean to exclude you."

Trevor's reply was a disgusted grunt as he nailed Meagan to the wall with a hard glare, quick to blame her for Ragnar's lack of courtesy.

"Do you wish me to send a wench to you?" Ragnar questioned.

Meagan tensed, knowing she had no right to be jealous, but the thought of Trevor taking another woman in his arms upset her, even when she swore she despised him.

The faintest hint of a smile skipped across Trevor's lips when he detected the dark glow in Meagan's eyes. Had their tryst meant more to her than she admitted? Was the jealous green monster lurking in the confused depths of Meagan's mind?

"'Tis the custom," Trevor commented blandly. "Since you seem to have taken such a liking to Lady Meagan, perhaps I *should* search elsewhere for companionship."

Ragnar smiled secretively. If Trevor would consider bedding another woman while the lady was in his care, surely there was nothing between them. At least he hoped not. Meagan aroused him, and he craved a few moments alone with her and any affection she might grant him.

Trevor's subtle strategy proved successful. Meagan was so agitated with him for accepting a wench that she could not fully enjoy Ragnar's company. Several times Ragnar was forced to repeat himself because Meagan was preoccupied in thought. Finally, she focused her full attention on Ragnar, determined not to dwell on the infuriating man who had stolen her innocence and was, at that very moment, kissing some castle wench senseless.

"You are breathtaking," Ragnar murmured as he paused by Meagan's chamber door. "There is something about you that reminds me of my late wife. 'Tis your eyes, I think."

His head bent toward hers to take privileges Meagan was not prepared to offer. Meagan sidestepped before he could pin her back to the wall. She had experience with a Norman's cornering tactics and she wanted no part of them. Once had been enough.

"May I be so bold as to inquire what happened to her?" Meagan smiled up at him, hoping to smooth over the fact that she had dodged his intended kiss.

Ragnar breathed a defeated sigh and then peered off into the darkness. "'Twas a freak accident," he explained. "The duke of Normandy insisted that Idona remain in court when we sailed for England. I had met the lady only once, but she was pleasing to the eye. When William suggested the marriage I had no objection. It was an honor to become a member of the noble family." Ragnar sighed heavily and then continued, "After England was secured and the king granted me a fief, Idona was to come to me. A storm in the channel hampered the voyage and Idona was washed overboard. Although her servant attempted to save her, they both perished in rough waters. So you see, my marriage, although it spanned a year, allowed us not even a full day together."

Meagan cursed under her breath. Damn that Trevor. He had intentionally made Ragnar out to be a beast when in fact it was Trevor who deserved the title. But why did Trevor want her to be wary of Lord Neville? If she was forced to take a husband, she could do worse than Ragnar, Norman or not.

"M'lord!" Meagan gulped when she came to her senses to find Ragnar's mouth playing on hers. She braced her hands on his chest to hold him at bay and peered wide-eyed at him. "We have only met," she admonished and then ducked away when his face moved steadily toward hers.

Ragnar smiled apologetically, but he was not sorry for stealing a kiss. It was worth the reprimand. "Forgive me, m'lady. 'Twas not meant as an insult," he hastily assured her. "'Tis just that I am overwhelmed by your charm. Would you find complaint if I asked Lord Burke's permission to . . ." Ragnar paused to carefully formulate his words. "That is to say . . . I would be most honored to stand among those worthy warriors who seek to make you their lady."

My, but these Normans wasted no time with courting, Meagan mused as she pasted on a pleasant smile and offered it to the overzealous knight. Ragnar would have seen her wedded and bedded before he had known her a full day. Although he was not harsh or unkind, Meagan knew it would be a loveless marriage. Nay, as she had informed Trevor, she would prefer to remain unattached rather than marry a man who could not become both friend and lover. Ragnar's kiss served to prove that he could not set fire to blood even if he had a week or a year to see to the task.

Ragnar mistook her silence for a coy affirmation. After pressing a kiss to her wrist, he pivoted on his heels and made a beeline for Trevor's chamber to discuss the possibility of arranging a marriage.

The impatient rap on Trevor's door brought him from his troubled reverie. *"Entrez-vous,"* he mumbled as he pushed up to an upright position on the bed.

"M'lord, I beg a moment of your time." Ragnar's gaze scanned the room, finding the fair-haired woman he had sent to Trevor was nowhere to be seen. A muddled frown plowed his brow as his eyes circled back to his overlord, who sat abed—alone. "Alodie did not please you?" Ragnar couldn't imagine that. The wench had a penchant for lovemaking and many of his overnight guests had complimented her expertise.

Trevor gnashed his teeth. The woman had not pleased him because he could not bare to touch her. Alodie was as attractive as that feisty she-cat he had tracked through the forest, but the depressing truth of the matter was that she was not *Meagan*. And Trevor would not be satisfied until he tamed that gorgeous minx, who spited him at every turn.

"I had no complaint with the woman," Trevor begrudgingly explained. "'Tis just that the grueling journey and my injury have left me . . ." His voice trailed off, leaving Ragnar to finish the thought.

Ragnar nodded understandingly. "Perhaps another time." Slowly he drew himself up before his superior and then looked Trevor straight in the eye. "I have interrupted your privacy to voice a matter close to my heart. I am enchanted with Lady Meagan and I wish to make my intentions known. Has a mate been selected for her?" he blurted out.

Trevor felt as if Ragnar had doubled his fist and knocked the wind out of him. His previous plan had not accounted for Ragnar's hungry impatience for Meagan, and it took a moment for Trevor to gather his composure.

"Meagan's brother has requested a match, but I have not yet decided if the other knight is suitable for Lady Lowell," he replied in a bland tone.

"I do not mean to sound presumptuous, but I believe the lady has no objection to my offer of marriage. She seemed at ease in my company and I was warmed by hers."

No doubt Ragnar's lust was at a rolling boil, Trevor grumbled to himself. Leave it to Meagan to attract men like flies buzzing about honey. Damn that woman. She could disrupt the best-laid plans.

"I shall keep your offer in mind," Trevor grunted and then gestured his head toward the door, abruptly dismissing the knight.

When the door closed behind Ragnar, Trevor snatched up his makeshift cane and stalked across the room, his face set in a grim frown. Had that temptress allowed her suitor to take outrageous privileges with her? The answer to that question was one that haunted Trevor as he hobbled down the hall to Meagan's chamber. He wanted to know what had transpired between them, and he wanted to know that instant! His curiosity was eating him alive, as was the jealousy. Egod, that woman had an uncanny knack of setting fire to a myriad of emotions within him and Trevor was in no mood to battle the blaze.

Meagan gasped and fumbled to hug her discarded tunic to her breasts as Trevor barged through the door like a charging bull. "Do you heathens know nothing of courtesy?" she snapped curtly. "Man made doors for the purpose of knocking before one intrudes on another's privacy."

"Doors will never serve as barriers between us," Trevor growled as he marched across the room, forcing himself not to dwell overly long on the soft, creamy flesh that lay bare to his gaze. He need not look upon her to remember that she was perfectly shaped and pleasing to touch. The sight and feel of her was implanted in his brain. "I demand to know what went on behind my back! Ragnar had visions of making you the next Lady Neville even before I put the matter to him."

Meagan kept her cool, even though the fuming lord was parked in the middle of her boudoir while she wore not a stitch. "I fail to see why you are upset. Was it not your intention to push me off on Lord Neville? I have not interrogated you about your tête-à-tête with the castle wench and 'tis none of your concern what Lord Neville and I did or didn't do," she retorted flippantly.

Trevor ground his gnarled cane into the floor, his temper gushing like an erupting volcano. "Answer me, woman!" he roared.

Her bare arm shot toward the door, her glower silently

assuring him that she was wishing him one-way passage to hell. "Get out! I do not have to answer to you," she flared, her voice matching his in ferocity.

His footsteps carried him forward until they were only inches apart. "You will always answer to me," he gritted out. "Your fate lies in my hands. How you react toward me will determine your future . . . or lack of it."

One delicately arched brow raised slightly. Although Meagan was standing on shaky ground, her devil-may-care attitude got the best of her. "You cannot possibly know how I itch to slap your arrogant face," she told him, her pretentious tone camouflaging the bite of her words. "If you tarry much longer I fear I cannot be held responsible for my actions. If you persist in blundering into my private quarters to issue threats I will retaliate with violence, the one thing you Normans understand."

Trevor grabbed hold of her tunic and hurled it across the room, forcing Meagan to streak toward the bed and dive into the quilts. When she tucked the covers beneath her chin, she glared at him, her face blazing with fury.

"Damn you! If I were a man I would call you out and plunge a lance through your hard heart!" she hissed venomously.

Trevor stomped toward her, wagging a lean finger in her indignant face. "I warn you, woman. You are treading on thin ice. And you will not avoid the issue by dragging me into an argument. Unfortunately, you have become my responsibility, and I will not have you dallying with Neville or any other man without my permission. My word is law, like it or not!"

"While you have the freedom to bed any woman who meets your whim?" Meagan sniffed disgustedly. "You see a woman as your chattel to be bartered and traded for political purposes. I am my own person and I will not be dictated to!" she informed him, her voice rising until she was shouting in his face.

Trevor clamped his hand over her mouth to shush her and then plopped down beside her. "Mind your tongue. I will not have the guards bounding into the room to see if the Saxons

143

and Normans have declared war a second time." When Meagan gained control of her flaring temper, Trevor broke into a reluctant smile, unable to smother the warm tide that washed over him when he stared too long into her blue eyes. "I am not ashamed to tell you that I sent the wench away. 'Twas you I craved, my fiery minx, just as I do now."

Meagan was shocked by his confession and stunned when his lips captured hers in a kiss that was tender, yet insistent. Her traitorous body responded as if it possessed a will of its own. Knowing that he had denied himself another woman soothed her resentment. Before she realized it, her arms curled about his neck to draw him closer, forgetting that she had spent the better part of three days vowing that he would never get close enough to stir the passions that had consumed her that fateful night.

As his searching hands slid beneath the quilt to cup her breast her heart slammed against her chest and Meagan feared it would permanently lodge between her ribs. Trevor's touch was like a shock wave that affected every part of her being. The more desperately she fought against his seductive magic, the more deeply she became entangled in passion's web. Meagan was painfully aware of how hot the flames of desire could burn. When Trevor caressed her there was no reasoning, no justice in the shameful way her body betrayed her. She was moving with the flow of an undercurrent that left her dizzy and breathless.

Trevor's moist lips abandoned hers to skim across her neck and then descended to the ripe mound of her breast. His tongue circled the taut peak, and then he left a trail of searing kisses as he pursued the shapely curve of her waist.

A tiny gasp escaped her lips as his skillful hands and arousing kisses sought out the sensitive points of her body and triggered reactions that left Meagan questioning her sanity.

"You battle me, *cher amie,*" Trevor murmured, his voice heavy with disturbed passion. "You defy me, curse me, reject me, and then when I dare to touch you as I yearn to do, you melt in my arms. I am at a loss to understand you."

Meagan had no answer to explain her quicksilver moods.

144

She did not want to desire him, but she seemed helpless when he caressed her so tenderly. No words formed on her lips to deny that he had the power to transform her from a defensive child into a passionate woman, and Trevor allowed her no time to speak. His mouth returned to hers, parting her lips to probe the soft depths while his inquiring hands continued to draw responses that left her relaxed and pliant in his arms. Meagan was just beginning to understand the meaning of unconditional surrender. Her body cried out to his, aching to bring an end to the sweet torture that drove her mad with want. She clutched him closer, unable to appease the fierce need that rose from somewhere deep within her soul and spread like wildfire through her trembling body. Trevor pressed closer, cursing the fact that his tangled garments separated him from what he craved most.

"M'lady?" Ragnar's quiet voice drifted beneath the door to shatter the spell in a fraction of a second.

Meagan's wild eyes flew to Trevor, sending him a silent plea to vanish into thin air before she was thoroughly humiliated. A wry grin dangled from the corner of his mouth as he touched his finger to his lips and then rose to bury himself in the heavy folds of drapery that surrounded Meagan's bed.

"Yea, m'lord?" Meagan questioned, her voice quivering from the side effects of Trevor's soul-shattering kiss.

"I wish to bid you goodnight." Ragnar stepped into the room without awaiting an invitation to find Meagan abed, just as he hoped she would be.

Damned Normans, Meagan thought sourly. Not one of those barbarians waited for permission to enter a lady's chamber. They marched in as if they owned the entire world and everyone in it.

Ragnar was all eyes, his gaze working it sway over every inch of exposed flesh. Disappointment settled on his craggy features when Meagan clutched the quilt around her neck. But Ragnar was still spellbound by the picture she presented. Her blond hair sprayed about her like a shimmering cape woven with silver and gold. Her creamy skin glowed in the dim light and Ragnar's mouth was watering like a starved shark that had spied a long-overdue meal.

"I spoke with Lord Burke," he said hoarsely and then choked down his heart after it had catapulted to his throat to hammer against his neck. He moved deliberately toward her, raking Meagan so thoroughly that she glanced down to see if her quilt was transparent or if the hawk-eyed Norman had the incredible knack of seeing through the thickest of fabrics. "Trevor and I are close friends. Now that he knows of my interest in you, I think he will seriously consider my desire to make you my wife."

Meagan flinched as Ragnar occupied the spot Trevor had vacated. "Was there something else you wished to speak to me about, m'lord? I am very tired and I . . ."

"Only this . . ."

Ragnar bent over her, leaving her no choice but to accept his kiss or flee, exposing her nakedness to his ravishing gaze. His lips clung to hers, and Meagan was again stung by the painful knowledge that Ragnar Neville could never set her pulse to racing or wilt her resistance the way Trevor could. The Dark Prince put his knight to shame, Meagan mused disheartenedly.

When Ragnar finally dragged his lips from hers, Meagan conjured up a meager smile and then gestured toward the door. "'Tis not proper for you to tarry in my room, m'lord, and the hour *is* late," she reminded him tactfully.

His coarse features softened as he trailed his index finger over her satiny cheek. "You sorely tempt me, Meagan, but I shall deny myself the pleasure I seek because you are well worth the wait. The day will come when I have no cause to leave your chamber until the sun bids me to rise and attend my duties."

When Ragnar gathered his feet beneath him and strode across the room, Meagan breathed a sigh of relief, but it was short-lived. Trevor stepped from concealment, grinning outrageously.

"My, my, what a touching soliloquy from such a fierce knight. Methinks you have captured that mighty warrior's heart," Trevor mocked, although he sorely felt the pinch of jealousy. If *he* had offered such tender words to Meagan, she would have laughed in his face.

"You lied to me," Meagan snapped as she presented her back to him, unaware that the quilt had slipped down to reveal the shapely curve of her hip to Trevor's hungry gaze. "The rumors that Ragnar disposed of his wife are untrue. There was no foul play."

His shoulder lifted in a noncommittal shrug as he filled the empty space beside her to run his hand along her spine. "I did not say I believed the story. I merely repeated remarks I have heard from Saxon tenants. Whom shall we believe, Meagan, your countrymen or mine?"

Meagan turned back to him and propped her head on her hand, her platinum hair cascading over her bare shoulder in such a provocative manner that Trevor had difficulty keeping up with conversation. She studied the darkly handsome warrior for a long, pensive moment, grappling with his subtle point.

"Have I wrongly misjudged you as well, m'lord?" she mused aloud. Perhaps Trevor was not as evil as she would have preferred to believe. The thought allowed another layer of bitterness to crumble as she gazed at the shiny raven hair that framed his rugged features.

Trevor pushed forward, his warm lips hovering over hers. His golden eyes danced with deviltry as he whispered back to her. "I doubt it, my fiery angel. And do not think to deter me from my intentions for your future with a compliment. Nothing has changed."

In an instant they were back to swords and daggers. Meagan flounced to her back and yanked the cover over her head, refusing to meet his taunting gaze.

"Then leave me be, Norman pig. I can see that you and I will never be compatible. If you are determined to see me wed, as Edric is, then give me to Ragnar. At least I can tolerate him."

"Are you insinuating that you cannot endure *my* presence?" he snorted. Angry flames leaped through him, provoked by Meagan's acceptance of Lord Neville. "It will not be Ragnar who takes you for a bride. I will not give my consent to that. Ragnar has failed the test. The man I have in

147

mind for you is exactly what a termagant like you deserves. He will not buckle beneath your charms as Ragnar has. He will rule you with a firm hand." He pulled the quilt away from her face to meet her snapping blue eyes, his expression stern. "Hear me well, Meagan Lowell. You can drag your feet and complain of an injustice to your heart's content, but the inevitable will come. You will wed the man I select for you."

A bemused frown knitted her brow as she peered at Trevor. "At least tell me his name." when Trevor unfolded himself from her bed and limped across the room, her quizzical gaze followed him, as did her insistent question. "Who is this beast whom I shall be forced to marry? I have a right to know who he is."

"You forfeited all rights and privileges when you stole off into the night and then lashed out at me with that razor-sharp tongue of yours. You will learn the name of your intended when *I* choose to offer it to you. Besides . . ." Trevor turned back for one last punishing glance at her tempting figure and exquisite face. "I must speak with this Norman lord to see if he is agreeable. Edric and I might find it necessary to furnish him with a heavy purse to strike this match."

Meagan wished she had a weapon in her hand. She was itching to carve this infuriating man into tiny pieces. "You are a hateful beast, Trevor Burke," she growled at him.

"A dragon," Trevor corrected, flinging her a satanic grin. "You have called me that often enough and now I have begun to believe it myself. Your insults can no longer penetrate my spiny scales and I would not think to disappoint you since you see me as a fire-breathing monster."

As the door closed quietly behind him, Meagan muttered under her breath and then squirmed to find a more comfortable position that would ease her irritation. But no matter which way she turned a pair of amber eyes materialized from the darkness to mock her. Damn, Trevor was up to no good. He was out to destroy her life, refusing to provide straight answers to her pointed questions. Meagan

148

was uncertain how to react to him. When she had attempted to soothe his temper that afternoon, he had pried her arms from his shoulders. And yet he had come to her, tormenting her with unfulfilled caresses. Then he seemed immune when she drilled him with insults. Meagan threw up her hands in a gesture of futility. Trevor was constantly changing like the restless wind. She never knew from what direction he would come at her. She could never anticipate his force or his gentleness.

Meagan groaned in frustration and then slammed her fist into her pillow. Trevor was unpredictable and it was a waste of time to analyze him. The only way to salvage her sanity was to avoid him completely. Once he returned her to Edric, she would flee to the convent before he could chain her to the frightful brute he had selected for her husband. Trevor had become vindictive. She wondered if the Norman Trevor had in mind for her was as vicious as the savage who had taken Trevor's mother. Although Trevor despised his uncle's treachery, he had fallen into the mold. Did he intend for history to repeat itself? Nay, it would not, Meagan assured herself. She would be safely tucked away at the nunnery before Trevor could fetch his frothing beast and drag him across the Lowell drawbridge.

With that encouraging thought buzzing through her mind, Meagan closed her eyes to allow sleep to overtake her, trying not to think of how her body had turned when Trevor had graced her with a kiss hot enough to melt the moon and leave it dripping on the sky.

Chapter 10

A thoughtful frown creased Edric's brow as he listened to the leaders of the revolution describe their plans and report the distressing results of other uprisings against William the Bastard.

"The loyal knights of Devon and Cornwall fell before the King's forces," Morcar, the brother-in-law of Harold Godwinson, informed his attentive audience. "'Edric the Wild,' lord of Herfordshire, is planning to attack Mercia as soon as he has gathered his army."

"'Tis rumored that the king himself will take the field in the north if the Mercians attack the king's strongholds," Edwin Leofric, Morcar's brother, went on to say. "When we were held captive in William's court we saw the strength of his forces. It will take a well-trained army to cripple the Bastard. News has reached us from our informants that William has sworn revenge on the Mercian rebels and will soon move his infantry toward Stafford."

Edwin Leofric glanced up at Edric. "We are pleased with the subtle plan to take command of Burke Castle," he complimented. "My men have seen to it that William's messenger never reached the fortress to inform the Dark Prince that the king has summoned him. But our time is short. If Burke does not report to the king within two weeks, William will become suspicious."

"I cannot take credit," Edric explained. "'Twas Granthum and his stepbrother who have pieced this plot together. I did

151

but supply the lady who could catch the Dark Prince's wandering eye and distract him."

"You have great confidence in your sister, Edric. I should like to meet this rare beauty whom you claim will bring William's right-hand man to his knees," Morcar chortled.

"But you will only be allowed to see her from a distance," Reid Granthum grunted as he flashed the handsome rebel a condemning frown. "Meagan is mine, betrothed to me by Edric's father. If I did not need her to lure Burke into a trap, I would not allow that murdering heathen near her. I have already lost my sister to that barbarian and I intend to see him pay for his sins. Meagan will receive compensation for the pain she must suffer when I claim my lands and William the Bastard is driven from England."

"I did not question your right to Lady Lowell," Morcar smirked, surprised by the red-haired knight's fierce possessiveness. "I only wish to see this dazzling beauty for myself." His taunting glance focused on Edric. "It baffles me that Lady Meagan could be this ugly brute's sister."

The tension eased with Morcar's teasing gibe. It was obvious to all that the comment was made in jest, since Edric Lowell was the most attractive Saxon in the crowd.

Reid chortled as he glanced at his fellow countryman, his jealousy dwindling. "Forgive my outburst, Morcar. I have waited three long years to claim what is mine. Once you lay eyes on Meagan you will know why I am so anxious to have her for myself."

It had taken every ounce of self-restraint Reid possessed the first time he spied Meagan riding in the distance. But he had not dared to reveal himself to her. She could suspect nothing. Nay, it was far better for her to be ignorant of their plans until the matter was settled and he could come forward to claim what was rightfully his.

Edric had been hesitant to use his sister for bait, but Reid had been adamant, refusing to send someone other than Meagan to Trevor Burke. It had taken threatening persuasion to sway Edric, but finally he had come around to Reid's way of thinking. But then, Reid had given him little choice, he mused as he slid Edric a quick glance and then focused his full attention on the conversation that passed back and forth across the campfire that was concealed beneath Saxon shields.

Although Meagan had intended to snub Trevor during the last leg of their journey she found it unnecessary, since he paid very little attention to her. Trevor had a great deal on his mind and was busy making a mental list of duties that he must attend to after his long absence from the fortress. But his obligations were cast aside when he returned to the castle to learn that Conan had fallen into a trance shortly after Trevor left on his hunting trip.

Trevor hurried up the steps with Meagan in tow and then cringed when he found the hoary sage lying in bed, his glassy gaze fixed on the ceiling.

"Conan, can you hear me?" Trevor gave him a sound shake to rouse him from his stupor. "Conan, wise soothsayer and friend, awake! 'Tis I, Trevor."

After a few apprehensive moments, Conan's deathlike gaze moved to settle on Trevor's concerned face. "The boar was an omen," he rasped. "I felt your agony and I lingered with you while the angel of death came to await your soul."

Meagan's legs buckled beneath her when she heard the seer's husky words. She had doubted the old man's powers until this eerie moment. No one knew of Trevor's injury. Conan's knowledge must have come from a vision, Meagan thought shakily.

The sage's gnarled hand curled around Trevor's forearm. "Heed my warning, Trevor. I speak from a hazy dream. What you see as truths are disguised lies. Those who seek your trust hunger to destroy you. And the day approaches when the world will be set ablaze. Then you will know a pain worse than death, one more maddening than enduring the agony of the swine's tusk penetrating your flesh. Beware of your shadow, my son. Danger lurks so close to home that it will haunt your sleep."

When Conan looked past Trevor to stare at Meagan, she wilted like a fragile rose beneath the blazing summer sun.

She gulped nervously and took a retreating step when Conan's dark eyes drilled into her.

"This woman also visited my dream. Friend or foe I do not know. But she was there, just beyond my understanding."

Two pair of penetrating eyes fastened on Meagan and she felt her heart slamming against her chest. It was on the tip of her tongue to deny the accusations, but Meagan doubted that either man would accept her claim of innocence. Yet the sage's dream was too vague for her to argue. Slowly, she retreated toward the door, her eyes dodging Trevor's and Conan's probing gazes.

"I will be in my chamber, m'lord. Summon me when you are prepared to return me to my brother."

Meagan expelled the breath she had been holding as the door creaked shut behind her. If she had not given Trevor cause to despise her, Conan had. His dream made her out to be some sort of ghastly villain, and only God knew what the old man was raving about. How could *she* possibly be a threat to Trevor?

Grappling with that thought, Meagan strolled back to her room. Would Trevor become more intent on seeing her wed to one of his countrymen? Was this other Norman a ruthless man who coveted Trevor's prestige with the Throne of England? Was that why Conan saw her hovering in the shadows of his eerie dream? Was she to become the wife of Trevor's would-be assassin? Was that the pain Conan foresaw in Trevor's future?

She would *not* have a hand in Trevor's fate, she told herself firmly. She would return to the nunnery and Trevor would never see her again. He could not accuse her of treachery, because she would soon be out of his life forever and there would be no marriage at all!

When Meagan entered her room, Devona came to attention, her concern mirrored on her pale features. "M'lady, I was beginning to wonder what had become of you. I had begun to fear that something dreadful happened when you did not return within the week."

"I have not suffered," Meagan assured her. "'Twas that Lord Burke was injured and unable to travel until he had

154

regained his strength."

Meagan ambled toward the window to stare out over the sprawling meadow, preoccupied with Conan's haunting words. And then a memory stabbed at her soul, remembering the cluster of men she had seen in the forest. Could they have something to do with Conan's vision? Should she inform Trevor that she had seen a band of men lurking in the woods? But what if they were her fellow countrymen? She could not betray them to warn her Norman lord, a man who sought revenge on her and who would mistrust her reasons for offering the information. Meagan found herself balancing on an emotional tightrope, torn between her physical attraction to Trevor and her loyalty to the Saxons, if indeed that was who the mysterious men were. And there was a strong possibility that the men were rebels. Two years earlier trouble had broken out in Exeter. Another raid on Norman strongholds had come from Ireland, but the forces had been crushed by the king's experienced warriors. When Edwin and Morcar Leofric had escaped from the palace the following year, there had been more talk of rebellion.

The appearance of outlaws in Ashdown Forest, Conan's strange dream, and the ill feelings that existed between Normans and Saxons were forewarnings of another tempestuous storm. Meagan shivered uncontrollably. William was a brilliant military strategist, and she feared that another clash would prove disastrous for the die-hard Saxons who refused to submit to the Norman feudal system.

Lord, what could she do to prevent another war? Was Edric involved? Devona had informed her that Edric had become very secretive, refusing to share his innermost thoughts. Meagan slumped against the windowsill, confused and frustrated. Where could she turn? Could she trust her own brother, a man who had shoved her at Trevor for his own selfish purposes?

Swallowing her troubled thoughts, Meagan turned back to see Devona slipping quietly from the room. Later she would contemplate the matter, she assured herself. Now she needed to rest. Her journey had been long and unnerving. Trevor had treated her like a possession to be toted home and kept in cold storage until her brother could take her off his hands. Damn, her life had been uncomplicated until she met Trevor Burke. If only she could turn back the hands of time, Meagan thought disheartenedly. She should have fled into the forest, never to lay eyes on the darkly handsome knight who had come to haunt her dreams.

Meagan's bloodcurdling shriek shattered the silence and she bolted up in bed to stare into the darkness. Her frustrated thoughts had fed her nightmare, leaving her trembling and afraid of her own shadow.

"M'lady? What is wrong?" Devona was at her side to press a cold cloth to her perspiring brow.

Meagan collapsed on her pillow and gulped hard. "Too much, I fear. I do not know how to begin to right the wrong or if the evil I perceive is a camouflaged blessing. I know naught which way to turn," she mused aloud.

Devona stared at her, confused by the riddles. "Perhaps you would like a bath. It will soothe your troubled dreams."

Nodding mutely, Meagan sank back on her pillow to stare up at the gold silk drapes that surrounded her bed. Why gold, Meagan asked herself miserably. She needed no reminder of the color of Trevor's eyes. Must every object remind her of Trevor? She could see his craggy features materializing about her, his face hovering so close, offering a temptation. And then he was cruelly mocking her. Meagan squeezed her eyes shut, forcing back the thought of his handsome, but haunting, face. All Meagan desired was to return to Lowell Castle and then to flee to the convent where she belonged. Perhaps in a hundred years she could learn to forget the man who was tearing her apart. Meagan felt as if wild horses were strapped to each arm, attempting to drag her in two different directions at once. Why did she fear betraying Trevor, and why was she magnetically drawn to him when he was her worst enemy?

Rousing from her deliberations, Meagan moved mechanically toward the tub that sat in the corner. A thoughtful frown plowed Meagan's brow as she lifted the perfumed soap and absently washed her arm.

"Has Edric had any unusual guests of late?" she questioned.

"Unusual?" Devona frowned puzzledly.

"Yes, strangers who have come for private conferences," Meagan prompted, trying desperately to make some sense of a myriad of thoughts that were drifting about her head, just beyond comprehension.

Devona eased back in her chair and mentally sorted through the men who had come and gone from the fortress. "A few," she replied. "But as I told you, Edric has become distant and remote. He no longer allows me into his thoughts. Edric often went riding alone at night and occasionally did not return until dawn. When I questioned him about his disappearances he would shrug and say that he wanted to be alone to contemplate. Whatever he is planning, he has been most secretive. I doubt that he spends his nights staring at the stars . . . alone. At first I wondered if he was visiting some wench in the village."

"Nay, I think not," Meagan mused aloud.

"Have you some clue about his activities?" Devona queried, easing to the edge of her seat. "If you could shed some light on his odd behavior I would be most grateful."

Meagan's shoulder lifted in a casual shrug. "Edric has said nothing, but I am concerned about a band of men I saw in the forest and . . ." Meagan gestured to her soiled tunic and then motioned for Devona to retrieve it. "I found this near a shack. Does it look familiar?"

Devona gasped incredulously when Meagan fished into the hem of her tunic sleeve to extract a tarnished brooch. "Where did you say you found this?"

"Trevor and I sought the shelter of an abandoned lean-to while he was recuperating from his injury," Meagan explained. "At first I wondered if it had remained buried for all these years, but I am beginning to think that perhaps its owner has recently taken refuge in the forest."

Wide eyes circled from the brooch to Meagan. "What does this mean, m'lady? Do you suspect Edric . . ." Devona could not voice the rest of her question, her apprehension

157

strangling her.

"I can only hope that I am wrong. If Edric is involved in some sort of conspiracy the outcome could prove disastrous. The king has too great a force at his command to fall before a mere handful of rebels. Surely Edric knows that all of England must unite to oust William the Bastard, and even then the Saxons would face defeat."

The color seeped from Devona's features, terrified by the thought of Edric taking arms against an unconquerable force. "You must confront him with your suspicions. If you are correct you must convince him to abandon this madness. I cannot bear to think of Edric rotting away in the king's prison."

"Men are such fools," Meagan sniffed distastefully. "They suffer from delusions of grandeur. They pride themselves on warring against unfavorable odds, and they live to die an honorable death. A revolution would prove nothing but Saxon stupidity."

Devona nodded in agreement. "When will they learn that enough blood has been shed?"

"Fools rarely profit from their mistakes and they often repeat themselves, floundering on battlegrounds where angels fear to tread," Meagan muttered cynically. "No one is more anxious to see England restored to the Saxons than I am, but the battle will be futile unless we enlist the aid of allies. I wish just once that a man would ask a woman's opinion of war, I would dearly love to . . ." Meagan swallowed her sentence and shrieked, plunging into the water as the door slammed against the wall and Trevor filled the entrance.

Devona scrambled to her feet to position herself between Meagan and Trevor, shielding her mistress as best she could. "M'lord, the lady is . . ."

"I know very well what the lady is," Trevor snorted as he stalked across the room, sending Meagan sinking deeper into her bubble bath. "You are excused, Devona. I want a private word with Meagan." When Devona wavered indecisively, Trevor grabbed her arm, uprooted her from the spot, and propelled her toward the door before she could protest.

"That is the second time you have dared to intrude on my privacy," Meagan sputtered when she came up for air, furious to see Trevor looming over her.

Golden eyes swam over her glistening flesh like a heated caress that dried her from inside out. Although Meagan attempted to cover herself, she knew she was wasting her time since she was blessed with only one pair of hands and they were too small to serve as suitable covering.

"I have made my decision," Trevor announced, fighting to keep from becoming sidetracked by the delicious witch who was stewing in her kettle. My, but he couldn't have selected a better moment to make his entrance even if he had planned it, he mused as his appreciative gaze dipped to the swells of her breasts that were barely concealed from view. He had always been of the opinion that a woman's body was beautiful, but Meagan's left his description sorely lacking. She was breathtaking, spellbinding. . . .

"Hand me the towel," she snapped tersely. "Say what you have come to say and then get out."

Trevor leaned over to fetch the towel and then planted himself in a chair, refusing to allow Meagan a moment's privacy. "I have sent a message to your brother to join us here, posthaste."

"When he arrives, do you still intend to keep your promise about the proposal to Devona?" Meagan questioned, wondering if his irritaiton with her had thwarted any chance of repaying Edric for his deceitfulness.

Trevor nodded slightly as he unfolded himself from the chair to stare down at the enchanting display that had successfully managed to detour his thoughts. "God, but you are lovely," he breathed hoarsely.

Meagan tucked the towel about her and flashed him a disgruntled frown as she carefully rose from the tub. "Answer me," she demanded impatiently.

A devilish smile caught one corner of his mouth, curving it upward as he reached out to trail his index finger over her bare shoulder. "I am still contemplating the matter. Perhaps if you could convince me . . ." His hand glided across the swell of her breast, branding her with a white-hot fire, and Trevor's voice evaporated.

Meagan caught the spark in his eyes, a forgotten dream, a reminder of the night they had shamelessly kissed and touched. Afraid of close contact, Meagan took a retreating step and then bumped into the tub. She flapped her arms to maintain her balance, but just when she was certain she would fall into an unceremonious heap in the tub, towel and all, Trevor's arm encircled her waist to clutch her to the solid wall of his chest.

A low chuckle bubbled from his lips as he lifted her from the floor and then tucked his arm beneath her knees. "You seem to be willing to go to great lengths to avoid me, Meagan. Are you afraid of me?"

Dodging his probing stare, Meagan glanced down to ensure that her meager covering still served its purpose. "Nay," she insisted, but her voice crackled with the fire that his physical contact kindled.

"You lie," he whispered as his face inched closer. "I can feel your body trembling against mine. You fear that I will touch you as I did that night in the shack, the night you fled."

"I do not fear your touch," Meagan protested. "You and I mean nothing to each other." Trevor's doubtful glance had her squirming in his captive arms. "Put me down!" If she did not gain her freedom, and quickly, Trevor would know for certain what she was trying to hide. The feel of his muscular body pressed to hers fed a growing hunger that had become an addiction. Meagan detested her weakness for him. It frightened her, but she would be damned if she admitted that to Trevor, since he only sought to feed his male pride.

"You protest too much, m'lady," he teased, his amber eyes dancing with amusement. "Show me some proof that you are not apprehensive of my touch."

Damn him! Why must he torture her so? Was this his special kind of punishment for her insolence? Why couldn't he let the days pass quickly until Edric came for her? Was she to be humiliated and intimidated every waking hour? Well, if that was the game he had in mind for her, two could play it, Meagan reminded herself. She was not about to be bested by Trevor Burke. She could control herself and remain unaffected by a mere kiss if she put her mind to it.

A deliciously wicked smile captured her ivory features as she curled her arms around his neck and tossed her blond hair aside to allow him to see the determination in her eyes. "Is this proof enough, m'lord?"

Her lips hovered over his like an arousing caress, using the techniques she had learned from her skilled instructor. Her tongue sought the hidden recesses of his mouth as she pulled him closer, her body pressing wantonly against his. Her fingers tunneled into his raven hair and then she traced the corded muscles of his neck, sending a rush of goose bumps rippling across his skin. Meagan could feel the accelerated beat of his heart drumming against her as she breathed into him a fire that was hot enough to melt a knight's armor and leave the scalding molten metal dripping in his boots.

Trevor groaned in unholy torment, his breath ragged, his pulse racing like a stallion thundering across a battlefield. She left his knees weak and Trevor staggered on his mending leg, certain it would buckle to leave them sprawled on the floor. This was not the reaction he had expected from Meagan, but he was not one to whine about his good fortune. He had this tempting siren right where he wanted her.

When Meagan sought to withdraw to grace him with a smug grin, Trevor refused to break the embrace. His mouth slanted across hers, forcing her lips apart to savor the sweet taste of her. He was like a mad bee buzzing about nectar, craving the flavor of a rare flower and refusing to fly until he had drunk his fill.

Meagan's lungs burned and she gasped for breath, but Trevor had stripped the air from her throat. She was living and dying in the same moment, and she wasn't certain when he set her to her feet to remove her towel, but she found herself standing naked before him while his gaze devoured her. His hands brushed across her hips and then he clutched her to him again, letting her feel his raging desire for her. His caresses wandered higher, leaving her trembling like a leaf in a wind storm.

Their eyes locked and in an instant Meagan knew she was about to break every well-meaning vow she had ever made concerning Trevor. And then, as if a bolt of lightning flashed before her, Meagan saw Trevor as she prayed she would never see him. She was staring love in the face, a hard, chiseled face that was surrounded by thick, black hair, and she was peering into golden eyes that burned with such an intense flame that they could brighten the darkest night.

How could she have fallen in love with this Norman knight? It was beyond conception! He was all wrong for her, she told herself frantically. Their political views were at opposite ends of the spectrum. They were too much alike to complement each other. They clashed like two warring armies, their strong wills battling for supremacy. Meagan raced through several other reasons why they were incompatible, but despite their contrasting differences and inharmonious similarities, she loved the Dark Prince who could make mincemeat of her emotions, leaving her aching to feel his hard body molded intimately to hers.

Trevor drew back, baffled by the stunned expression on her face. Meagan looked as though she had come face-to-face with a ghost. Her jaw sagged from its hinges. Her sapphire eyes were glazed with something close to horror and disbelief. She stood rigidly before him, seemingly unaware of her nakedness, staring at him as if he had sprouted another head on either side of his neck, as if a horrible monster were about to gobble her up.

Grabbing her shoulders, Trevor shook her until her teeth rattled. "Meagan, what has come over you?" he demanded to know.

Meagan was jolted to her senses and then squealed as she darted across the room like a shooting star before disappearing into the quilts on the bed. Trevor's long strides took him to her side and he peered incredulously at her wild-eyed expression.

"Upon my word, woman, I do not know what to make of you," he hooted as he threw up his hands in exasperation. "Oftentimes I question your sanity . . . or lack of it!"

"Go away!" Meagan choked out, refusing to look up at

162

him. "Don't ever come near me again."

Trevor leaned over her, bracing his arms on either side of her shoulders, unsure of why he felt so annoyed with her. Perhaps it was frustrated passion, he told himself after a moment's consideration. The wench was tying him in knots. He wanted her as he had that night in the shack and he could never be satisfied until she was warm and yielding in his arms. Once had not been enough, would never be enough. She had left him to burn alive. She was a sorceress who had cast some wicked spell over him. He had become like a man who had been deprived of food and water for days on end, and he would stop at nothing to devour the meal that hovered just beyond his reach. He would use force if he must, but he would not walk away unappeased, not this time. He had held himself in check at Neville's fortress, but the tension had built like a tempestuous whirlwind that sent tidal waves rushing toward a distant shore. Trevor felt uncontrollable passion flooding over him, and like a drowning swimmer on his way down for the final time, he succumbed to raw instinct.

Crouching above her, his eyes like cold, hard chips of stone, he clamped his hand over her mouth to shush her when she tried to scream. Her attempt to shout him out of her room left him all the more frustrated.

"I warned you that it was unwise to stir my wrath, Meagan," he growled. "Taunt me with that appetizing body of yours, fight me if you will, but nothing will keep you safe from me. Not now or ever . . ."

His lips ravished hers with forceful insistence and Meagan panicked. She had never witnessed the fierce, unyielding side of this Dark Prince. He tore the quilt from her grasp, leaving her body exposed to his hawkish gaze.

"Do you seek to make me less of a man by making me beg for your affection?" Trevor muttered, his voice ragged with mounting desire. "I never beg. I take what I want." His logic was being twisted and stretched out of proportion as Meagan writhed beneath him, terrorized by the cold gleam in his eyes. Trevor was furious with her and with himself for finding no civilized way to break this stubborn minx's spirit.

163

She had been sent up from the fires of hell to torture him with her beauty and harass him with her belligerence. He was being put to the test, forced to prove himself a man or a two-legged mouse. His patience had snapped. His pride was at stake, and Trevor was certain Meagan meant to burn it to a crisp. "You will yield to me, woman. Now . . . Ouch!" Trevor retracted his hand when Meagan clamped her teeth into his finger. Growling, he pinned her beneath him the split second before bared claws scratched across his face. "Damn you!" he roared, his voice echoing about the room like the crack of thunder.

"Don't touch me!" Meagan shrieked hysterically and then grimaced as his fingers bit into her forearms. The tears that she had so carefully held in check burst forth to boil down her cheeks, realizing at last that there was nothing she could do to stop him from forcefully taking her. "Please . . ."

Trevor stared down at her flooded eyes, watching the hot tears roll like a bubbling river. She had provoked him to violence by refusing his embrace. Never had he roughly abused a woman, and he had sworn he never would after the way his mother had been treated. Trevor felt as if a knife had been plunged into his back and then twisted with painful deliberateness.

Had he gone mad? One or the other of them was crazed, he mused as he sank back on his haunches to peer into Meagan's flushed face. Now all he had to do was determine which one. His bruising grip eased from her arms and his body sagged as he listened to Meagan sob. It seemed that he could do nothing but anger and hurt her when his only intention was to bring them both a moment of pleasure. But it was too late for that. He had destroyed the fragile web that their one night of lovemaking had begun to weave. There was nothing left between them but a sea of bitterness, one too deep and wide to cross.

As he rolled to his feet, he cursed his barbaric tactics. Meagan had every right to call him a beast. That was exactly what he was. When she would not allow him to have his way with her, he pouted like a spoiled child, exerting his superior strength to dominate her. But what had he accomplished by manhandling her, he asked himself resentfully. Heaving an exasperated sigh, Trevor strode across the room and then halted in his tracks when he spied the brooch that had tumbled from the edge of the tub. He scooped up the jeweled pin and then twisted around to glare accusingly at Meagan who was oblivious to all except her own torment, loving a man who despised her and who sought to abuse her for his own revenge.

Trevor set the brooch aside and left the room, mistrusting Meagan more than ever. Perhaps he had been too hasty in his decision, he mused as he stalked down the steps to order a bottle of wine to be sent to his chamber. Maybe he was searching for something in that blond-haired witch-angel that wasn't really there. Was he seeing her only as he *wanted* to see her? She had sent him subtle signals and he had doubted that the naïve maiden understood them herself. But perhaps she was fully aware of what she was doing to him.

Meagan eluded him. He had always been adept at reading people's faces, but Meagan was the exception. What was the cause of the torment he had seen in her eyes? Finding that brooch in her possession disturbed him, and he prayed that his conclusion was incorrect. God help her if he was right, Trevor muttered as he stalked down the hall.

Chapter 11

Raising tearstained cheeks to the dim glow cast by the oil lamp, Meagan glanced about the room, finding herself alone, haunted by an emptiness the likes of which she had never known. Was this love, this twisting, burning ache that inflamed her soul and squeezed her heart like a vise? This was not how Meagan had envisioned love. It was to be a warm and fulfilling, an intangible bond that the sharpest sword could not sever. Even in her worst nightmare she had never dreamed that she would fall in love with a man who detested her. And Trevor did, she reminded herself miserably. Why else would he force himself on her? A muddled frown captured her brow. But why had he turned away before he had appeased himself with her? Was there one shred of conscience within him?

Meagan sat up cross-legged on the bed. Could she dare to hope that Trevor cared enough not to rape her when she resisted him? Meagan heaved a sigh and then peered across the room to watch the shadows skip across the wall. She could continue to battle her attraction for Trevor, or she could accept what she could not change. She could deny herself the passion she had discovered when he held her so tenderly, or she could go to him, giving him no cause to abuse her, proving that there was more pleasure in love than in lust. Inexperienced though she was, she could give herself to him, freely, shamelessly. And if Trevor could not see that she was offering her love then he was as blind as a bat and no more intelligent than the winged creature that lived in the dark.

Muffling a sniff, Meagan gathered her feet beneath her, brushed away the lingering tears, and walked over to the trunk to retrieve the pale blue gown that Devona had made for her. The gossamer fabric clung to her like an extra suit of skin and left one shoulder bare. Meagan had found it too revealing and seductive, but now it would serve its purpose. The moment she stepped into his room he would know why she had come to him. If he sent her away, then she would know that Trevor wanted nothing more to do with her. She would surrender to him in tenderness, but never under force. Perhaps he could learn from her that brute strength could not tame even the wildest heart. It *was* true that honey attracted more flies than vinegar, she reminded herself, managing a faint smile. Perhaps she would wrestle the mighty warrior to the floor and coat him with honey to sweeten his disposition, she mused as she clasped the silver brooch on her left shoulder.

Summoning her determination, Meagan moved silently down the hall to pause before the oak door that separated her from the man she loved, despite their differences, despite her better judgment. But love him she did, and before the night was over, she would know if he felt more for her than animal lust. Inhaling a deep breath, Meagan pushed open the door to find Trevor planted in his chair with a bottle of wine tucked under his arm, a mug in his hand, and Daralis draped over his shoulder, her lips hovering along the side of his neck.

Meagan froze, her blood turning to ice. The impulse to turn tail and run was great, but Meagan held her ground, leaving Trevor to decide which one of them would go and which one would stay. It took every ounce of self-control she possessed to raise her chin and await his preference. But she was determined to stay until the bitter end to learn which one of them had the better chance of winning this dark knight's heart. Meagan frowned slightly when she hit upon that thought. Trevor was skeptical of love and she was left to wonder if any woman could crumble his hard heart without resorting to a chisel.

Trevor's blurred gaze swept Meagan from head to toe, dazzled by the streaming platinum blond hair that tumbled over her bare shoulder, aroused by the provocative gown that left enough to his imagination to allow it to run rampant. The shimmering fabric clung to her breasts, revealing the pink peaks that lay so temptingly beneath it. The folds of her gown dipped into her trim waist that was encircled with a silver leafed belt and then flowed over her shapely hips to cascade to her bare feet. She was like an angel hovering close to the ground, bathed in the glow of the lantern that gave her ivory skin an incandescent appearance. Clear blue eyes that were surrounded with long, thick lashes focused on him, holding him spellbound. Her sensuous lips parted slightly, as if in invitation, and Trevor felt his heart slamming against one side of his ribs and then the other, as if a crazed drummer were pounding on two snare drums. His entire body vibrated in rhythm. Although he had been drinking hard and fast since he exited from Meagan's chambers, he was not too numb to feel the effect of this enchanting vision that hovered just beyond his reach.

Daralis had come to serve him drinks, offering to ease his frustrations, but he had no inclination to touch her. Trevor knew he would find no satisfaction in bedding Daralis when the taste of Meagan's kiss still lingered on his lips. And yet, Meagan's sudden appearance and provocative attire triggered his suspicions. What did she want from him? Was there a dagger concealed in her belt? Had he angered her to the point that she had come to carve his heart from his chest? Would she rely upon sedutive sorcery before she buried her knife in his heart? The fact that she kept Reid Granthum's brooch among her possessions was proof that she was tied to the rebel cause. But could he send her away when she tempted him? And yet, could he allow her to stay when Conan warned him that danger lurked in the shadows? Was one night of pleasure worth the risk of dying in her silky arms? Trevor had waded through hell, weak and injured, to retrieve this unpredictable witch. He had flown into a jealous rage when Ragnar announced that he wanted Meagan for

169

his wife. Now Trevor faced another kind of torment, wondering if Meagan was the "disguised lie" to which Conan referred.

The room was so quiet that Meagan feared the dropping of a pin would sound like a ton of lead crashing through the floor. The minutes ticked by and still Trevor stared indecisively at her. Meagan's composure was crumbling, and she feared that if he did not call her to him or chase her away, and quickly, she would shatter in a thousand humiliated pieces.

"Leave us, Daralis," Trevor commanded, his voice raspy with desire. "The lady and I have unfinished business to attend."

Daralis blanched, stung by the insult. Her annoyed glare pinned Meagan to the wall. She envied the lady's beauty and the power she seemed to hold over Trevor. If Daralis thought she could have strangled Meagan and escaped unscathed, she would have clamped her fingers around Meagan's neck and choked the life out of her. The lady would pay dearly for mortifying her in front of Lord Burke, she promised herself. Meagan would lay no claim on the overlord of Wessex. One day Daralis would carry Trevor's child and he would keep her by his side, she vowed to herself. The blond wench would never come between Trevor and his future child. And one day there would be a son, Daralis told herself. She would see to that. She would make Trevor forget that Meagan Lowell ever existed. Once that blue-eyed termagant was out of the way, Daralis would claim the man she desired and care for his child. Her heir would come to rule Wessex, and Daralis would want for nothing. She had paid her dues to the Norman conquerors, and the time would come when she would rule in her own subtle way.

With that determined thought buzzing through her head, Daralis withdrew her arms from Trevor's neck and strode toward the door to disappear down the hall. This would be Meagan's last appearance in Trevor's solar, she swore. There were ways of ensuring that the lady was unable to venture there again. Soon Meagan would be gone and Daralis could set her plan in motion.

When Daralis left them alone, Meagan moved gracefully toward Trevor. Voicing not a word, she knelt before him to remove his boots and then set his mug aside to pull the tunic over his head. A faint smile traced her lips as she combed her fingers through his coal black hair, rearranging the thick mass that lay recklessly across his forehead.

A dubious frown slashed across Trevor's features as Meagan silently prepared him for the bath that had awaited him, one he had procrastinated taking until he was swimming in wine. Now he was swimming in desire, wondering if he had died and gone to heaven. This silky angel's appearance had ignited a fire that must have consumed him, Trevor told himself as her gentle hands glided across his flesh.

"Come, m'lord," Meagan murmured as she clasped her small hand around his and urged him to his feet.

Trevor followed like an obedient pup and then sank down in the cold tub, oblivious of its temperature. Meagan tested the water and then smiled apologetically.

"I fear it needs reheating. Shall I fetch hot water?"

"Nay." There was no need, Trevor mused. He was ablaze. The heat of his desire would bring the water temperature up a quick twenty degrees, and within a moment steam would be rising from the tub to form a haze of clouds.

Meagan took up the soap to lather his chest, seemingly content with her task, loving the feel of his muscled flesh beneath her fingertips. As her hand trailed lower and then ascended his bent leg, Trevor choked on his breath. Her patient ministrations were playing havoc with his sanity. She boldly touched him, washing every inch of his body, and Trevor wondered if his palpitating heart could withstand the physical strain she was forcing upon it. How long would it be before it tore loose and tumbled around his innards? Goose pimples popped out on his flesh, but it was not from the water's chill. Indeed, the steam was rolling. He was experiencing a violent reaction to this seductive sorceress. Another dose of Meagan could prove fatal, but like a lamb led to slaughter, Trevor reveled in the sweet torture that her touch evoked. If he was to eventually die beneath her blade, at least he would expire a contented man, he reminded himself. Again, Conan was mistaken, he sighed recklessly. He was not to endure a pain worse than death, but rather a *pleasure* that overshadowed logic.

Although Trevor had demanded to know Edric Lowell's intentions in sending Meagan to him, he refused to question the reason Meagan was kneeling beside him, giving him a bath that bordered on seduction. He only sought to relax and enjoy her attention.

When Meagan rose to her feet to retrieve the mug of wine, his hungry gaze followed her sylphlike movements until she sank down beside him. Trevor watched as she brought the wine to her lips, and then he melted when her eyes sparkled with radiance. He was lost to that dimpled smile and the perfection of her oval face. And then he moaned softly as she offered him a drink of the wine that moistened her lips.

Trevor was intoxicated all over again. The heady sensations of her unhurried kiss left the room spinning about him. She had affected his equilibrium as well, he realized as the tub sprouted wings to send him sailing around the chamber. Lord, was he dreaming? Trevor pinched himself twice to return the bathtub to the floor, but he could have sworn it had been a gliding like a butterfly the previous moment.

"Do you desire another drink, m'lord?" Meagan whispered as she withdrew far enough to peer into his amber eyes, amused by the stunned expression mirrored there.

"Yea, one sip only served to tease my thirst," Trevor assured her huskily as his index finger trailed over her bare shoulder and then trickled over the soft fabric that concealed her breasts. "Will I be permitted to drink my fill or will you snatch it away from me when the wine bottle is only half dry?"

Meagan chortled at the underlying meaning in his inquiry and blessed him with a smile that threatened to turn him into sentimental mush. "You are the lord and master. 'Tis not my place to deny your whims. I do but hear them and obey. This night I am your devoted servant. Your wish is my command, m'lord."

172

One dark brow shot up as he regarded the submissive maid for a long, pensive moment. "Do you perchance have a twin sister who has hounded me with her obstinance for over a fortnight?" he queried, his tone holding a hint of a taunt.

Meagan's soft chuckle drifted about him, tickling his senses. "Nay, m'lord." She clasped the mug in both hands and rested her elbows on the edge of the tub, her gaze traveling over his handsome face and broad chest like a light caress. "I am not always contrary and stubborn. On rare occasions I have even been called gentle, though I would prefer not to spread the word," she insisted. Her laughing eyes circled the room and then she leaned closer, as if to divulge some deep, dark secret. "There is a dragon hereabout and I must confront him with sword and shield. If he learns of my weak moments he might use the knowledge to his advantage."

Trevor was hopelessly lost to the depths of those pools of sparkling sapphire. If she had requested that he lay the world at her feet, he would have leaped, stark naked, from the tub, vaulted onto his steed, and galloped off to fetch it for her.

When her wine-kissed lips feathered across his, Trevor sank back in the tub like a limp fish that was rolling on a wave. He was content to let her have her way with him until he shriveled up in his cold bath. But it mattered naught, he reminded himself. Meagan was a sorceress and she could transform him into any creature that met her whim—a fish, a frog, or a man. Her touch was magic and he became whatever she desired.

His lashes fluttered up as her lips abandoned his, and his gaze lingered on the wet fabric that clung to her full breasts. Trevor sighed helplessly. This *was* heaven and he was higher than the clouds, drunk on the sight and feel of Meagan, who catered to him like an Egyptian handmaiden.

As she drew him to his feet, her wandering eyes beheld his magnificent physique, unconcerned that she might risk being ridiculed for gawking. With gentle hands she dried his skin and then led him toward the bed. When Trevor balked, refusing to take another step, Meagan glanced back over her shoulder and raised a quizzical brow.

173

"Is something amiss, m'lord?"

"Yea, you hold the advantage." Trevor gestured toward the tantalizing gown that hid what his eyes and body craved to see and touch. "Although I find your garment lovely, I have one complaint with it."

"And that is . . ." Meagan raised her gaze to his roguish smile.

"I should like the gown better if it were draped over yonder chair." His heated gaze sketched her alluring figure with such intensity that Meagan feared the fabric would become engulfed in flames. "This gorgeous package needs no wrapper." His hand moved to unclasp the silver brooch, allowing the gown to drift into a pool around her ankles. "Do you know how beautiful you are, Meagan?" Trevor murmured as his unhindered gaze flooded over her satiny skin. "There are no words to describe what my eyes behold. You are what dreams are made of. Soft, shapely, and compelling are meager words that cannot touch what I see when I gaze upon you."

Meagan was flattered by his compliments, and she was thankful that their last encounter would be a cherished memory, one she could recall when she was a world away from him. It would erase the nightmare of remembering how Trevor had towered over her like a fire-breathing dragon, exerting his strength over her. There was a gentle man beneath those spiny scales, one that only love could perceive. Meagan did not regret coming to him this night, because when she left she would take with her a love to sustain her on all the lonely nights that would follow. She had opened her heart, giving of herself with no other motive than to share Trevor's embrace. She would not ask for his love in return She would not demand marriage. She would take only what he offered for the moment and be content with it. Perhaps one day he would recall their time together and he would realize that she had reached out to him with love.

"I have known no other man as I have known you," she said quietly. "No one else possesses this strange power you hold over me. 'Tis not your superior strength that commands my respect. 'Tis your gentleness. Make love to me, Trevor."

Her hands cupped his face, holding his steady gaze. "Is it vain to want this night to be special? I have had very little practice at being a woman, but I cannot deny that you stirred me when we slept together under the stars." Her trembling hands splayed across his chest, her misty eyes following the path of her wandering caress. "I wish to build a memory, one that fulfills what one night of lovemaking has taught me." The faintest hint of a smile pursed her lips as she met his flaming gaze. "I have always maintained that one should be well-versed in *all* subjects. 'Tis time for me to learn why I enjoy touching you and why I tremble so when you touch me."

Trevor caught her straying hand and held it in his own, his level gaze holding her hostage. "The first time I gave you no choice, Meagan. I wanted you then, just as I do now. But will you still come to me without a struggle when I tell you that I intend to see you wed to a Norman lord I have selected for you? Do you still wish to sleep with me, knowing that soon you will be another man's wife?"

Meagan nodded slightly. She wanted Trevor beyond all else, and he did not have to know that she would be long gone before he could fetch her Norman husband. There would be no other man in her future. "I ask only for this moment with no strings attached. What happens tomorrow is of no consequence. I do not expect favors from you, nor should you anticipate any from me. 'Tis a night for love, nothing else."

Had his ears deceived him? What in heaven's name had come over this lovely nymph? Trevor had expected Meagan to explode once she knew that he had made arrangements for her wedding. Why hadn't she railed at him or attempted to slap his face? Lord have mercy! Trevor swore he could spend the next hundred years analyzing this unpredictable beauty and gain nothing from his comprehensive survey. The only piece of knowledge he would gather for all of his efforts was the fact that she would never react the same in any given situation. How would he ever untangle the workings of her mind when she continued to flabbergast him?

When she took a step closer, her luscious body melting against his, Trevor lost the desire to cross-examine her. He hungered for that which she offered. He craved to hold her in his arms. He would teach this enchanting goddess what none of his other lovers had ever known. This night would find a fresh new star sparkling in the sky, one that outshone all others. And when she gazed into the heavens, that special, twinkling star would capture her attention and she would remember. . . .

Trevor slid his arms about her waist and bent to accept her upturned lips. "Let your heart lead you," he murmured as he broken the kiss to nibble at the corner of her mouth. "Do not be ashamed to tell me what pleases you, for that is my sole intent."

His arousing caresses trailed across her hip and then wove a warm path across her belly. Meagan sighed in exquisite pleasure as his hand moved upward to fondle her breast. Didn't he know that his mere touch pleased her, spreading a fire through her body that she had never been able to ignore? She was keenly aware of the male scent of him and the miraculous way his hands discovered and aroused each sensitive point. How could he not know how he affected her? Her skin quivered beneath his explorations, and her breathing was irregular. He had to know of his powers over her because she responded to every skillful technique and pressed closer to the flame that burned her inside and out.

As his greedy mouth captured the peak of her breast and his hand moved languidly over her hip to bring her thighs in close contact with his, Meagan wilted. For this she had come to him, disregarding her pride in the name of love.

When Trevor set her on the bed she stretched leisurely, like a contented kitten, and then curled up beside him. Trevor was no longer impatient and frustrated. He was satisfied to kiss and caress her until the dark hours before dawn. A quiet smile tugged at his lips as his absent caress trickled across her shoulder and then tracked along her waist. She was like silk and satin. Touching her was sheer pleasure and her kisses were like a breath of spring air.

Meagan came to her knees, her smile a mite mischievous.

"The pleasure you give will be twofold in return," she promised him.

And she was true to her word. When she set her hands upon him, Trevor knew he had not been cheated. Her caresses worked subtle magic on his flesh. She learned each scar that marred his ribs by touch while her butterfly kisses skimmed his neck like a delicate wind stirring across his flesh. Her caresses were constantly moving and then flooding back to restoke the flames that kindled in the wake of her inquiring touch.

Trevor gasped for breath as she boldly fondled him, sending his passions soaring and his heart fluttering, missing several beats before it hammered against the inside of his chest like an imprisoned man beating his fists in a hysterical plea for freedom. He was hot and cold and shaky, and the sweet torment continued, making him wonder who was instructing whom in the ways of love.

In his past experiences with women, he had never allowed any female to take the initiative. His main intent had been to appease his lust and then rout the wench from his bed. He had always been in control, the possessor, never the possession . . . until Meagan came into his life to turn it upside down and sideways.

"Do I please you, Trevor?" Meagan's voice came to him like a soft whisper in a cloudy haze.

The way she made him feel was sinful, he mused with a sigh. He was bobbing on an endless sea, drifting on waves that rocked and lured him farther from reality's shore. He couldn't fight the emotions that simmered beneath the surface; he could only respond to them.

"Too much, I fear," he rasped as he hooked his arm around her, bringing her straying lips to his. "I may never be satisfied to sit in an upright position again, my tempting nymph. To lie abed with you satiates all my needs. I can quench my thirst with your kisses and feast upon the passion you brew. Conquering England does not compare to the victory of surrendering to your touch." His hands cupped her face as he stared into her eyes, seeing both the sun and the moon glowing in their colorful depths. "You have twisted my thoughts until I can make no sense of them. Breathe into this wretched dragon until you have stilled the inner fires of turmoil. Come, sweet angel, make me your obedient slave. Tame this beast within me."

The kiss he craved took his breath away. She made him forget the treacherous world beyond the circle of her arms. His passions raged as her mouth opened on his, her tongue seeking his in a devouring kiss that assured him that she hungered for him as fiercely as he longed for her. His hands moved instinctively to the full mound of her breast before his lips left hers to follow the trail his hands had blazed. His caresses continued to rediscover every inch of her pliant flesh, and her silky thighs opened beneath his guiding pressure as his body captured hers.

Meagan felt the world careening about her. A soft moan bubbled from her lips as desire erupted like a volcano, sending a wave of fire boiling through her veins. Trevor plunged deeply within her, striving for unattainable depths of intimacy, the heat of his passion forging with hers until they were one, possessing, sharing, belonging.

The hazy world became an irradiating universe, and Meagan tumbled in a mindless swirl of sensations that lifted and then plunged her downward like an eagle towering and diving in the wind, gliding with the current that carried her to ecstasy. And then she was being swallowed up, engulfed by the wondrous feelings that riveted through her body. It was a moment of wild splendor that transcended time, holding her suspended until she feared she would die in the sweet pleasures of it all. Meagan buried her head against his shoulder and clung to him for dear life, as if letting go would send her plummeting to certain death. But the incredible sensations continued, and she arched against him, clutching him closer, whispering his name over and over again until there was no breath left with which to speak.

Trevor shuddered above her, overwhelmed by the pleasure that flooded over him. He had survived on raw nerves throughout the day, and now they were frazzled, leaving him utterly helpless. If a shout of alarm rattled through the fortress, alerting him that rebels were storming the castle walls, Trevor doubted that he would be able to withstand another assault. Meagan's attack on his senses had been so thorough and devastating that he could not find the strength to move or the will to do so. As his heart slowed its frantic pace, Trevor braced his arms by her shoulders and peered down into her mellow blue eyes. He could not resist dropping a kiss to her swollen lips any more than she could stay the wandering caress that followed the corded muscles of his back to linger on his hip. She was like a cat purring in satisfaction and Trevor chuckled softly against her mouth as she stretched to relieve the heavy pressure of his body on hers.

"God, woman, you never cease to amaze me. One moment you make me so furious I cannot see clearly, and the next moment you are driving me mad with passion and I cannot think clearly." Trevor brushed his fingers through the blond tendrils that spilled across his pillow. "There is no hope for it. You have bewitched me."

Meagan was warmed by his words, but the moment before she melted like a thawing snowbank she reminded herself that Trevor had slept with more than his fair share of women. No doubt, he had spoken hushed words to all of them in the aftermath of passion. Had he uttered such flattery to Daralis? Meagan did not pursue that question. This was not the time for an argument. She could only hope that this moment was different from all the rest and that she held a special place in his heart, at least temporarily. Although there would be many others to take her place when they went their separate ways, she prayed that the dim flame would kindle a fondness that would continue to burn, and that he would remember this night for years to come, just as she would.

Summoning his depleted strength, Trevor scooted beside her and then propped up on an elbow to study her flawless features. "Will you be so amorous with your future husband, *cher ami?*" he queried softly, an ornery grin draped on the side of his mouth.

Meagan could not resist the temptation to tease him, hoping to stir a twinge of jealousy. Her arms curled about his

179

broad shoulders as she graced him with a saucy smile. "Even more so," she assured him. "He will find no complaints, nor will I give him reason to stray. I will offer passion until he wants no more of it."

Trevor raised a curious brow. "You are not opposed to indulging in lovemaking more than once a night?"

With a provocative chortle, Meagan pressed wantonly against the hair-roughened hardness of his chest and then traced the curve of his lips with a dainty finger. "Nay, not at all. And if my future husband has not the strength to perform, being the aged and cantankerous man I presume you have selected for me, then I shall seek out his loyal knights." One bare shoulder lifted carelessly, and Meagan bit back a grin when she felt Trevor tense at her words. "Once a queen has her king, one or two of his knights might be enough."

"You would sleep with his own men?" Trevor crowed, falling for her taunt, never certain whether or not to believe Meagan.

"But of course," she insisted breezily. "'Tis not uncommon for husbands to keep mistresses or to accept a wench while visiting a neighboring castle. I see no reason why a wife should not enjoy such privileges. As you said, physical needs are strong. I realize now that the pleasures of sleeping with men are some of the most satisfying experiences to be found."

"Shameless nymph!" Trevor grunted disdainfully. "If your husband learns of your infidelity he will be outraged. I do not wish to think of the punishment you would endure."

"But surely you would not expect me to tie myself to an old man, such as yourself, who cannot provide a full dose of passion for a young, active woman, such as myself," Meagan countered, a devilish sparkle dancing in her eyes.

Trevor winced as if he had been stung. And indeed he had been. Her taunt set his teeth on edge. "I do not consider myself old," he snorted indignantly. "But I am prone to agree that a feisty witch like you might wear out her husband before his time with such amorous demands."

"Perhaps," Meagan replied, taunting him and loving

every minute of it. She could boast outrageously since she knew she would never have a husband. "If my intended cannot satisfy me I will not hesitate to find one who can." A wicked smile played at the corner of her mouth as her hand dipped below his waist, making Trevor inhale sharply. "Could you appease your lover if she requested love more than once a night, m'lord?"

Her touch was fire, her provocative smile inflaming the embers of desire. A rakish grin slashed across his craggy features as he hooked his arm about her, his hot breath tickling her neck.

"I may be almost twice your age, my fiery vixen, but you have no cause to question my virility."

"Questioning you is the farthest thing from my mind," she purred as she raised parted lips to him. "Show me proof that age has not dampened your desire."

The feel of her supple body molded to his was like lightning searing through his limbs. Trevor trembled as the storm of passion billowed about him. He lifted Meagan above him, fitting her hips to his, wondering if any woman could match this seductive lass who pleased and bewildered him. Try as he may, he could not conjure up another face or another night that compared to this one. Meagan was the essence of beauty, and she had taught him things about lovemaking that he had somehow overlooked in all his years of experience. She could breathe magic into the moment with her lively spirit, and she challenged him with her teasing antics. If she doubted his prowess, he would prove his worth, he told himself as her butterfly kisses skimmed his cheeks and eyelids.

Trevor's thoughts were swept up in the whirlwind that sent him tumbling among the clouds. The sensations that riveted across his flesh were like the impatient drumming of driving rain, demanding that he ease this maddening craving that Meagan could so easily evoke. He was as helpless as a feather caught in a tempest, tossed and pitched with such fierceness that Trevor swore this passionate storm had blown the stars around in the sky, mixing them up until they were twinkling at opposite ends of the universe. And then, in the wake of the calm that chased the storm, Trevor drifted back to reality to be gently laid in the silky circle of her arms.

After a long, breathless moment, Meagan squirmed above him, and Trevor stilled her movement. "I yield," he admitted raggedly. "No more . . . Lord, woman, do you not believe in sleep?"

Meagan rolled to her feet and padded across the room to fetch her discarded gown. Loving him was an exhilarating feeling, and although Meagan would have cherished spending the entire night in his arms, she didn't dare. A confession of love would betray her, and the temptation was too great when she gazed into his golden eyes and trailed her hand across his handsome face. It did her heart good to hear the mighty warrior admit that his passion was spent. Perhaps he *would* remember this night. If Meagan could not win his love, at least she would be the one to leave him. It was much easier to walk away than to be the one who remained behind.

"Where are you going?" Trevor questioned incredulously.

"I am not the least bit drowsy, m'lord," she taunted unmercifully. "I think perhaps a stroll downstairs is in order. I seek to become better acquainted with your knights. Maybe a few of them also suffer insomnia."

Trevor groaned miserably and then collapsed when he tried to drag himself into a sitting position. "My men will be unable to resist you, and I do not wish to punish them for the temptation. I forbid your promiscuousness," he grumbled.

Meagan clasped the brooch on her shoulder, smoothed the gown over her hips, and then ambled back to torment Trevor once more in parting. "You need not worry, m'lord. I shan't tell my future husband of my wanderings, and you have no reason to take offense. You will not be held responsible for my actions. I am my own woman. I also know that I am not the first woman you have bedded, and you must know that you will not be the last man in my life. What difference could it possibly make if I visit your men?"

"Come back here, Meagan. I will not stand for this!" Trevor snapped irritably.

Meagan chuckled recklessly. "Then by all means stay in bed, m'lord. I can see myself out." She tarried by the door and glanced back at the disgruntled Trevor, her eyes taking on a mellow hue, her smile ruefully tender. She knew this would be the last night she would spend with him. "It was good between us, Trevor. There is no denying that. Goodnight. . . ."

When she disappeared from sight, Trevor stared up at the ceiling and then shook his head in disbelief. A secretive smile crept to his lips and he felt a warm tide surging through his veins. He was lost to the vision that hovered above him. Her glossy hair tumbled about her. Her perfect body curled contentedly against his. Her sensuous lips opened in invitation, and the taste of her kiss was like summer rain, cool, quenching. . . .

Mustering his strength, Trevor crawled from bed and strode over to pry away the wooden panel that revealed an opening that overlooked the Great Hall. Trevor had installed the peephole to keep a watchful eye on the activities in his castle while he was in his chamber. He squinted to make out the forms of his sleeping knights, who were stretched out on the benches that also served for tables during the day. To his relief, he did not spy Meagan wandering among his troops.

With his mind at ease, Trevor returned to bed to wander through his muddled thoughts. Although Meagan was quickly becoming his foremost concern, the appearance of the tarnished brooch disturbed him. He wanted to trust Meagan, but there were lingering doubts, ones that he simply could not overlook. Why had she come to his room? Did she seek more than passion? Was she attempting to gain his confidence? Conan's words kept ringing in his ears and, although he did not want to believe the worst about the bewitching goddess who had visited his solar, he had to consider the possibility. Stranger things had happened, he reminded himself cynically. And he could not deny that Meagan did strange things to him. Indeed, the aftereffects of her embrace had left him shaken, stirring emotions that Trevor thought he had under control.

A contented smile hovered on Meagan's lips as she sank

down on the edge of her bed, careful not to awake Devona, who was nestled on the pallet on the far side of the room. Although she had teased Trevor with the possibility of searching out another man, Meagan had no other desire but to be alone with her dreams. There would be no other man tonight or any other night. What she had shared with Trevor was enough to last her a lifetime, a dream come true.

The light rap on the door stirred her from her silent reverie, and Meagan breathed a hope that Trevor had come to ensure that she had returned to her room, rather than meandering about the Great Hall to seek out his replacement. A curious frown knitted her brow when she opened the door to find Daralis standing before her, offering a cup of wine.

"Compliments of Lord Burke," she murmured. "His wish is that you sleep well."

Meagan took the cup and watched Daralis disappear into the shadows. Had Trevor crawled from bed to see her return to her room and then summoned a servant to fetch her wine? And why Daralis, she asked herself. Was it his way of telling her that he considered Daralis no more than a servant in his home? Meagan sipped the wine, remembering how she and Trevor had shared the brew with their kisses. A quiet smile pursed her lips as she wandered back to bed and closed her eyes to dream, reliving the splendorous moments she had spent in his arms.

Chapter 12

Trevor dragged his weary body from bed to meet the dawn. There were several matters that demanded his attention before the flow of tenants flooded the Great Hall. Although the local squabbles and domestic problems that he was forced to solve were matters that he would have preferred to avoid, he could not overlook them. He had been away from his demesne for more than a week, and he expected the day to become a nagging headache.

After shrugging on his garments, Trevor strode over to shave the stubble from his face. Glancing down, he smiled slightly. It was good to stand on both feet without the throbbing pain that had hindered him. His wound was healing, thanks to his lovely nurse. Trevor chuckled to himself when he landed on that thought. Just thinking her name stirred a myriad of emotions—anger, frustration, confusion, desire. . . . Yea, an armload of that, he mused. Meagan could arouse him as no other woman had. Her future husband would have his hands full with that feisty she-cat prowling around his castle. Meagan left no stone unturned when she was suffering a flare-up of mischief, and she could uncover a man's most sensitive points when it was her intent to seduce him. Trevor was acutely aware that his life had been too methodic and mundane until that sweet but mischievous angel winged her way toward him to set him on fire.

Trevor nearly jumped out of his skin and slashed his chin

with the razor when he noticed that someone was standing behind him. "Dammit, woman! You do not enter a man's chamber without announcing yourself," he growled at Devona and then wiped the blood from his cheek.

Devona shrank away from his booming voice. "Forgive me for startling you, m'lord. I would not think to burst in on you if not for this grave matter." She inhaled a frantic breath and then plunged on before she lost her courage. "'Tis Meagan. She is deathly ill. She thrashes in her bed as if she were haunted by demon spirits. Her face is so white, her lips blue . . ."

Trevor breezed past the servant and dashed to Meagan's room, the ghastly sight making his heart flip-flop in his chest. "Meagan, can you hear me?" Trevor questioned as he knelt beside her, grasping her waving arms to keep them pinned to her sides.

"I have tried to rouse her," Devona informed him, her voice quivering with concern. "But nothing seems to bring her around. She just tosses and turns and then collapses for a time."

Trevor sank back on his haunches, baffled, frightened by a fear that sizzled through his body. The thought of losing Meagan tore at his soul, leaving a void of emptiness he prayed he would never have to endure.

Devona chewed thoughtfully on her bottom lip, confused by the expression on Lord Burke's face. She knew how furious he had been with Meagan the previous night. Devona had lingered outside Meagan's solar while the two of them clashed like two warring armies. Finally, she could stand no more and fled, knowing there was nothing she could do to intervene. When she returned, Meagan was gone, and later Devona had awakened to hear Daralis speaking to Meagan. Her first thought was that Trevor had slipped a potion in the wine as a method of revenge, but now the overlord seemed as distressed as she was. If it was not the wine that had poisoned Meagan, what had come over her?

"Do you truly care if my lady lives or dies?" she questioned as she touched Trevor's sagging shoulder.

What the hell kind of question was that? Trevor stared at

186

Devona as if she were addle-witted. "Of course I care," he snapped in annoyance. "I have no wish to see her suffer. Do you see me as some frightful beast, just as Meagan does?"

Devona dropped her head and dodged his probing glare. "I only know that the two of you have been at each other's throats. I thought perhaps she had angered you once too often and that you had poisoned the wine you sent to help her sleep last night."

"What!" Trevor shrieked. "I sent no wine to her room."

Wide green eyes settled on Trevor's fuming face. "But your servant informed Meagan that the wine was delivered with your compliments. I was awakened when Daralis rapped on the door." Devona gestured to the half-emptied cup that sat beside the bed. "Meagan drank part of the wine before she retired."

Daralis! That deceitful bitch! Trevor stormed toward the door and then felt his stomach twist in an agonizing knot, causing him to break stride. Suddenly he remembered another woman who had suffered as Meagan did. When he had first come to rule the manor, Melissa Granthum, a comely lass whom Trevor had taken a fancy to for a time, fell ill and died suddenly. Had Daralis poisoned her, as well? The thought made Trevor's skin crawl as he bounded down the steps to search out the treacherous servant.

The door of the servants' quarters splintered as Trevor shoved his heel against the wood, refusing to wait for one of the women to unbolt it. His murderous glare flew around the room to inspect the startled faces and then anchored on Daralis.

"You devious bitch!" Trevor raged as he yanked Daralis to her feet and then backhanded her across the face.

Daralis whimpered, covered her stinging cheek, and then ducked away when Trevor raised his arm again. "M'lord, what have I done to upset you?"

"Do not pretend innocence," he growled, barely able to contain the urge to choke the life out of her. "You poisoned Meagan!"

The color flooded from her face, leaving nothing more than the welt of his handprint on her cheek. How had he known? There had been no one up and about when Daralis returned with the poison herbs to stir into the drink. She had been careful, just as she had been three years ago when she feared that Melissa Granthum would win Trevor's heart before Daralis had the opportunity to lure him into her arms.

"Meagan's servant heard you enter her chamber to inform the lady that *I* had sent a drink to her." His lips curled menacingly as he grasped a handful of her dark hair and twisted it around his hand like a rope, threatening to pull it out by the roots if Daralis did not confess to the dastardly deed. "But it was *you* who prepared the drink, wasn't it, Daralis?" he hissed furiously. "And it was *you* who poisoned Melissa's wine not long after I claimed this manor." His accusing glower was like a lance driving into her heart, and Daralis sagged in his hard grasp. "Do you think I am such a blind fool that I cannot see you for what you are? You mean nothing to me." Trevor was being cruel, but he ached to lash out at her, releasing his pent-up frustrations. "I took what you offered and I gave nothing in return. But now you will receive your just reward, bitch. If Meagan dies, you will die with her."

Trevor shoved her away, sending her sprawling on the bench. Touching her repulsed him, and he cursed himself a thousand times for allowing that devious wench near him. "You shall serve as an example to others who think to deceive their Norman lord. Speak your last words, Daralis, for you will soon meet Satan."

He wheeled and stalked across the bailey to order two of his squires to prepare Daralis's torture. His hurried strides carried him back to the Great Hall and into Conan's room. There was only one man who had the power to save Meagan from the deadly poison. Trevor eased down beside the old sage and nudged him awake.

"Lady Meagan is dying," he choked out. "Only you have the knowledge to make her well again."

Conan's dark eyes focused on Trevor's grim features. "I will not interfere," he said simply.

Trevor clutched his shoulders, shaking the seer until his

188

brittle bones rattled. "I cannot stand to see her suffer. I demand that you go to her."

"And if I manage to save her, it will cost you dearly. You know that, don't you?" His husky voice settled over Trevor like a foreboding cloud of doom. "She is closely entangled in the dream. Her death can untwist the fate that awaits you."

"I prefer to endure the prophecy than to watch Meagan thrash in agony and die a painful death," Trevor argued.

"Even when you know that one day she might deceive you and that you may be forced to take her life with your own hands or sacrifice your own?" Conan parried, his brooding gaze drilling into Trevor.

"Fate be damned!" He vaulted to his feet to pace the narrow confines of the doomsayer's room. "I will decide if her future actions deserve my wrath. I will not sit idly by to watch her wither away. If she is to be my destiny then so be it. I cannot live forever, but I want what little happiness I have known with Meagan." Trevor pivoted to face the ailing wizard. "You have the power to spare me this grief. Give her back her life, Conan. She is my sun and I revel in the warmth of her smile."

"You wish temporary happiness at *any* cost?" Conan challenged.

"At *all* cost," Trevor insisted, his solemn gaze fixed on the aging sage.

Conan heaved a heavy sigh and then nodded reluctantly. "Very well, my son. I will do what I can. But heed my words." He waved a gnarled finger in Trevor's grim face. "All things are not possible. Do not blame me if 'tis too late to save her." His dark eyes pinned Trevor to the wall, demanding his undivided attention. "And if Meagan lives, you have sealed your fate. You reach out to her from across a hazy sea, just as I have envisioned in my dream. If you call her back, the looming shadows will engulf you. Dangers lurk in the corridors and the storm rapidly approaches, bringing with it a fire that will char the world beyond recognition."

Trevor felt as if the weight of the universe had been dumped on his shoulders. Conan's dreams were frightening. It was little wonder the sage was haunted by his visions. His

189

gift of foresight was a difficult burden to bear. But more often than naught, Conan's warnings had spared Trevor a great deal of tragedy. This time Trevor wondered if he would be forced to pay his dues, ones he had miraculously escaped paying in the past. For ten years, Trevor had responded to Conan's warnings, but now he defied the seer's claim. If Trevor took Meagan at all costs, his own life hung in the balance. And yet, one day of basking in the radiance of her smile was worth the week of catastrophe he might face. He had made his decision and he would accept whatever fate awaited him.

"Tell me what ingredients you require to brew a curative. They will be in your hands within the hour," Trevor murmured as he met Conan's sober expression.

"Eupatorium and mentha to counteract the poison," he muttered acrimoniously. "Yarrow, oxalis, and jewelweed. The other ingredients I keep in this pouch." Conan retrieved the foul-smelling sack from his belt and then gestured toward the door. "We have no time to tarry. The poison spreads like wildfire and it will take time to prepare the brew."

After Trevor called his servants and sent them scurrying to fetch the herbs Conan needed, he returned to Meagan's room to wait, dying a little inside each time she thrashed and rasped his name before falling silent for what seemed an eternity.

"Leave us alone," Conan said bleakly as he hobbled into Meagan's room and flicked his wrist to dismiss Almund, Devona, and Trevor. "I will summon you if I need your assistance."

Tearing off an arm would have been less painful than leaving Meagan while she writhed and moaned, Trevor mused as he backed away from the bed, his pained gaze never leaving her whitewashed face. It broke his heart to see a woman who had been so full of life lying in bed, her features tormented with anguish, her complexion so pale and waxen that he wondered if an ounce of blood flowed through her veins.

For hours on end, Trevor paced the hall, refusing food and drink, ordering the stream of tenants who gathered in the Great Hall to return another day. Like a man balancing on a tightrope, Trevor strode back and forth down the hall, wondering if the poison had done irreparable damage. If only he had called her back to him the previous night, forcing her to sleep in his arms. . . . But nay, he had allowed her to walk away while he grappled with his suspicions. God, if only he could turn back the hands of time . . .

"Trevor." Conan opened the door, his weathered face somber as he gestured for Trevor to join him in Meagan's chamber.

His concerned gaze flew to the bed, and Trevor halted in his tracks, standing stock-still as he stared bewilderedly at Meagan. Her skin was still whitewashed, her arms were peacefully folded over her breasts, and her hair was adorned with a circlet of blue wildflowers. There was not the slightest sign that she lived and breathed, but as Trevor peered at her it kept running through his mind that at any moment her lashes would flutter up and she would smile at him. But she made no movement. She just lay there as if she were . . . Trevor choked on his breath and his haunted gaze flew to Conan, who stood beside him with his head reverently bowed, as if praying for her soul.

Trevor adamantly shook his head, refusing to accept the tormenting thought that blazed across his mind and shattered his aching soul in a thousand pieces. Meagan dead? His heart refused to accept the bitter truth.

A spine-tingling bellow erupted from his heaving chest as he vented his frustration and grief. His wailing cry was like a parade of banshees marching in the howling wind. The castle rang with the warrior's mournful cry and then fell deathly silent.

Devona clutched Almund's trembling hand. She knew why the overlord was roaring like a wounded lion. Meagan was dead. The darkness spun furiously about her, and she wilted in Almund's arms, feeling as though part of her had perished with her lady. The emptiness that gnawed at the pit of her stomach was like a potent acid. She wanted to cry, to scream, to lash out, but she was dumbstruck with disbelief. And then, after what seemed an eternity of living in an emotional void, the tears welled up in the back of her eyes and she sobbed hysterically, haunted by the memories of seeing Meagan bounding through the Great Hall to torment her brother and riding against the wind on her magnificent black stallion. But the sweet memories could not chase away the tremendous pain of loss, Devona mused broken-heartedly.

As she allowed Almund to lead her down the steps, her legs threatened to crumble beneath her. Devona paused at the foot of the stairs to peer through the sea of tears. Dozens of melancholy faces rose to meet her, and Devona clutched Almund to keep her feet.

Without a word she weaved through the quiet congregation to shed her grief in the stables, where no one would hear her pitiful wails. Meagan was dead. God, what a horrible twist of fate.

Chapter 13

Trevor fell to his knees, his fists clenched at his sides, his body trembling with unshed tears. He fought to keep what was left of his composure, but he feared he was like a crumbling dam that was about to give way to a flood of emotions. Was this the pain worse than death that Conan had foreseen? Trevor swore by all that was holy that he would mutilate Daralis for putting him through this living hell. He would derive demented pleasure from drawing his sword and slashing her to pieces. If anyone deserved to die, she did. And he would see to the matter just as soon as he could collect his wits and still the ache that tore at his soul. He was angry and bitter, stung by a guilt that shot through his very core. A crimson red haze of wrath blinded his vision, and tears threatened to scald his eyes. He felt the fierce urge to hurl furniture against the wall, to demolish the room that had once been Meagan's, one that no one would ever inhabit again.

Conan clasped his gnarled hand on Trevor's trembling shoulder to stir him from his troubled reverie. "Learn well from this experience, my son. Remember the despair that closes in on you. But also remember that the pain you are feeling does not even compare to the agony your future holds."

Trevor truly doubted that. What he felt was an unbearable pain that no medicine could ease. It sliced through him like the sharpest sword, leaving his soul to bleed. "I cannot imagine a pain worse than this," he muttered brokenly.

"But there is one you will face in days to come," Conan told him softly and then tapped his tensed shoulder. "Yet now you grieve for naught, except to prepare yourself for the future. Take heart, m'lord. The remedy has countered the poison. The lady lives. She remains in a trance caused by the strong potion I was forced to give her."

Trevor dared not believe it, could not believe it. His glistening lashes swept up to peer into Meagan's ashen face, afraid to grasp at false hopes only to plunge headlong into the depths of despair. "'Tis not the time to test me, Conan," Trevor muttered resentfully. "Perhaps your eyes can see some sign of life, but mine cannot. The angel of death will not leave her room empty-handed."

A husky chuckle tumbled from Conan's lips as he gestured toward the bed. "Move closer, my doubtful son. I do not lie. Press your lips to hers and then tell me that the woman you have dared to tie to your fate has left her mortal form."

Cautiously, Trevor sank down beside Meagan, grasping at the thread of hope that he feared to be a figment of Conan's imagination. He bent his head to hers, taking her lips as gently as a breath of wind fluttering through the trees. His hand slid over her breast, seeking to find a heartbeat beneath the exquisite flesh he had come to know by touch. His tension ebbed when he felt the faintest flutter of life beneath his shaky hand and the wispy breath that caressed his cheek. Misty amber eyes focused on Conan as Trevor eased away from Meagan.

"*Merci, mon ami.* I am indebted to you," Trevor murmured.

Conan nodded slightly. "Stay with her. Summon her soul to yours. When the potion takes effect she will return to you, but do not become impatient. 'Tis a long way back from where she has gone."

After Conan shuffled out the door, Trevor traced his finger over Meagan's pale cheek. A tender smile skimmed his lips as he took her limp hand in his and pressed a light kiss to her wrist. He lingered beside her as Conan advised, and it was late afternoon before Meagan made the slightest movement to assure him that she would recover.

Meagan raised heavily lidded eyes and moaned softly. Her entire body felt as if it had melted into the feather mattress. Her lazy gaze came to rest on Trevor's dark face and she smiled slightly when she saw him hovering in her hazy dream.

"Trev . . ." she rasped. Speaking seemed to exhaust her, and she was baffled by the strange sensation that plagued her. It was as if heavy weights had been strapped to her arms and legs to resist movement.

"Do not try to speak," he insisted as he clutched both of her hands in his, wishing that his mere touch could give her renewed strength. "You must rest, *cher amie.*"

Despite his order, Meagan struggled to sit up, but Trevor's firm hand forced her back to her pillow, earning him a disgusted frown.

"Daralis poisoned your drink," he informed her. "It will take time to recover. Conan has given you a strong potion."

"Conan?" Meagan repeated incredulously. She doubted that the cantankerous sage would lift a finger to help her. "But why? He despises me."

"Nay, he does not." Trevor smoothed her platinum hair from her face, his expression so gentle that Meagan felt herself melting back into the mattress once again.

"Then perhaps you should tell him that," she suggested sluggishly. "I do not think he knows it."

Trevor chuckled softly and gave his raven head a negative shake. "Conan despises no one. 'Tis just that he fears that one day you will betray me. Will you, Meagan?"

Nay, she would not, but she could not speak for her brother and it was he who worried her. Meagan was stung by the premonition that Edric had something fiendish up his sleeve.

"I should like a breath of fresh air," Meagan remarked, avoiding the pointed question.

Trevor rolled his eyes heavenward. The woman had just escaped death and she demanded a tour of the castle. "Nay, I do not think . . ."

Gritting her teeth, Meagan swung her weighted legs over

195

the edge of the bed and inhaled a deep breath, struggling against the dizziness that swam about her. Trevor grumbled under his breath and scooped the determined minx up in his arms.

"We make a fine pair," he smirked caustically. "I still bear a limp from my bout with a boar, and you are still dazed from your potion of poison. If my leg buckles beneath me and we tumble down the steps, do not complain, m'lady. You have already worn my patience thin."

Meagan draped her arms about his neck and laid her head against his shoulder. If this jaunt sapped her failing strength it would be well worth it. The feel of his sinewy arms about her was by far the best medicine. "I would not think to complain," she sighed contentedly.

Trevor let loose with a snort. "Nay? I swear you stay up nights dreaming up new ways to torment me. 'Tis what you do best, m'lady." A wry smile softened his chiseled features. "Second best," he amended, his voice like a soft caress.

A hint of color worked its way into her cheeks as she dodged his provocative glance, attempting to allow the subject to die a graceful death.

A round of cheers rose from the Great Hall when Trevor carried Meagan down the stairs, but her happiness dwindled when Trevor carried her across the bailey to see Daralis strung between two supporting beams, her arms and legs stretched to the limit. Daralis' mournful whimpering tore at Meagan's heart. She had expected to thirst for revenge, but she found no contempt for Trevor's handmaiden when she spied her dangling in midair.

"Cut her down," Meagan demanded as her firm gaze swung back to Trevor.

"Nay, I will not!" Trevor growled vindictively. "The bitch cannot suffer enough to suit me."

"I will not have her death on my conscience," Meagan insisted, blue eyes clashing with gold ones. "Perhaps you can live with her blood on your soul, but I cannot. There has been enough blood shed on England's soil. Her only crime is that she loved you too much. She would stop at nothing to have you."

"Her kind of loyalty is lethal," Trevor reminded her harshly and then chided himself for allowing Meagan to drag him into another argument. He had no desire to bicker with her. He only wanted to hold her close and wait for her blue eyes to regain their lively sparkle. "'Tis not the first time she has stooped to poisoning someone who stood in the way of what she wanted. Lady Melissa Granthum was another of her victims, but no one knew what illness had befallen her. Had I not seen your symptoms I would have never known the cause of Melissa's death."

Meagan fell silent. There were many speculations concerning Melissa's death, but no one could say for certain what had become of her. It left Meagan to wonder if Reid Granthum harbored a double-edged hatred for Trevor. No doubt Reid thought, as many Saxons did, that Trevor had disposed of Melissa. Reid had lost his land and his sister to the Norman overlord, and Meagan was certain that wherever Reid was, he thirsted for revenge.

When Trevor carried her into the stables, Meagan frowned bemusedly. "I requested fresh air, not the stench of stables that are sorely in need of cleaning." Her senses were sensitive after her near collision with death, and Meagan grimaced at the foul odor that wafted its way toward her.

"You promised not to complain," Trevor reminded her, flinging her a reproachful glare. "I only sought to fetch my horse. I know of a quiet, inconspicuous corner of the world where you can breathe all the fresh air you desire, if you can show a meager amount of patience."

Devona's sobbing drifted toward them and Meagan squirmed from Trevor's arms to seek its source, surprised to see her dear friend lying face down in the hay.

"Are those tears for me?" she questioned curiously, turning back to Trevor.

Trevor grumbled to himself. In his own grief, he had left Devona and Almund in the hall to hear him screeching like a madman. They had assumed, as he had, that Meagan had lost her bout with the poison wine.

"Devona," he called to the distressed servant. "Arise and dry your eyes. Your lady lives."

197

Lifting tearstained cheeks, Devona glanced over her shoulder to see Meagan in the circle of Trevor's protective arms. A gasp of disbelief erupted from her lips as she scrambled to her feet and then dashed toward them.

"M'lady, I thought . . ."

Meagan smiled tenderly, moved by the relieved expression on Devona's grimy face. It was good to know that there was one among them who would have missed her if she had sailed off to castles in the air . . . if that was to be her ultimate destination. Meagan gulped. Perhaps she should change her ways, just in case she was booked for a journey in the opposite direction.

"You are not yet rid of me," she teased lightly.

"You scared ten years off my life," Devona breathed as she wiped away the lingering tears and dirt. "I never thought to see you again. Almund!" Devona darted outside to carry the good news to the stable boy, who had wandered off to grieve alone.

When Trevor lifted her into his arms while their horses were being saddled, Meagan struggled for freedom.

"Put me down," she ordered. "I feel much better. You need not pamper me."

Trevor refused to release the delicious bundle he cuddled against his chest. "I will not risk your fainting in the straw. You might accuse me of rubbing your face in the dirt and the leavings of my prize stock." His eyes locked with hers to observe the tiny sparkle that he had waited to see flickering there. And then he leaned closer, his warm breath caressing her neck. "We were much closer than this last night. And as I recall, you seemed quite content where you were."

Why was he flirting so outrageously with her? Meagan was miffed by his attentiveness. Was this all a dream? she asked herself. Or was it that he felt responsible for her plight and sought to cater to her out of pity? That must be the reason, Meagan decided. Trevor had sworn to treat her as his slave until this incident. Once she had fully recovered, he would return to his old self, tossing her around like a punching bag to polish his talents for hand-to-hand combat.

"Last night was an entirely different matter," she hedged.

His brows formed a hard line across his forehead. Her tart reply caused his buried doubts to resurface. Trevor well remembered that Meagan had refused to answer when he asked if she would stab him in the back if he presented it to her as a target.

Trevor set aside his cynical thoughts when the black stallion was led outside. After swinging into the saddle, Trevor leaned out to pull Meagan from one of his knight's arms and then settled her across his lap.

The feel of his muscular body against hers as they rode across the meadow was both comforting and arousing, stirring sensations that Meagan did not expect to experience so suddenly after her calamity. Apparently, nothing could curb her desire for this handsome warrior. The man could work miracles, and Conan had nothing on Trevor, at least not to Meagan's way of thinking.

They rode in silence for a quarter of an hour while Trevor fought to hold Poseidon to a walk. The steed snorted and threw his head, unaccustomed to plodding along at a nag's pace when his master or mistress climbed on his back. Meagan leaned down to stroke his tense neck and he finally quieted beneath her coaxing touch.

Trevor watched the stallion grow calm when Meagan soothed him. It stung his male ego to realize that this vixen had the same devastating power over him. He had not survived his thirty-three years by buckling beneath a woman's touch, he reminded himself stubbornly. He had to be wary of Meagan, keeping one step ahead of her, in case Conan's premonitions proved correct. He made a mental note to question the older servants of Granthum manor about the connection between the Lowells and the Granthums. His curiosity about the reason Meagan carried the tarnished brooch was eating him alive.

Meagan lifted her arm to offer Garda a perch and then glanced back to see Lear and the greyhound trotting along beside them. The dogs had finally accepted each other, but as Trevor had predicted, they had battled more than once, and both of them had emerged with notched ears and bare patches of hide after the fur had flown. The faint smile on Meagan's lips evaporated when she glanced back to see Trevor staring off into space, deep in thought.

"Is something troubling you?" she inquired and then darted him a mischievous grin. "Are you having serious misgivings about summoning your sage to work his magic on me?"

Trevor's gaze swung back to Meagan, surveying the flowing blond mane that curled over her shoulder and the provocative gown that had captured his undivided attention the previous night. His suspicions faded into the shadows of his mind as he peered at the enchanting beauty who sat in the circle of his arms.

"Nay, Meagan. I do not regret it for a minute. Besides, I have conferred with your future husband and he was most agreeable to the marriage. He would be bitterly disappointed if I could not deliver what I promised," he declared, a devilish smile catching one corner of his mouth.

He could have rattled on all day without saying that, Meagan thought sourly. She had hoped to hear some minute confession that Trevor cared enough not to allow her to perish. "But as for your own personal whim, I suppose you would have been relieved if Conan's potion had failed to rouse me," she sniffed.

"Ah, here we are." Trevor gestured to the west, drawing her attention from the pointed question to the inviting stream bank that was surrounded by sparsely scattered trees. The sound of water trickling over the rocks of the creek bed intermingled with soft songs of birds overhead, and Meagan sighed appreciatively. She dropped the previous subject to inhale the scent of wild flowers and fresh air. It was as Trevor had said. This corner of the world could even make one forget that war had raged across this peaceful land. For that moment they were the only two people on earth, and Meagan did not intend to destroy the serenity of the setting by bickering with Trevor.

"'Tis beautiful," she breathed as Trevor set her on her feet and then kept a protective arm around her waist as he slid from Poseidon's back. "Is this your quiet place where you come to rid yourself of troubled thoughts?"

For the life of him, Trevor couldn't remember thinking a discouraging thought. Meagan had successfully managed to chase away everything that had a resemblance to reality. Finally, he nodded affirmatively after returning from his fantasy of making love to her in broad daylight on plush green grass.

"Yea, but you are the first to enjoy my refuge. In the past I have come alone to sit and think," he murmured, his eyes following the shapely curves of her figure, engrossed in the pleasing picture she presented.

Meagan tested her legs to ensure that they would not give out on her and then wormed from Trevor's arms to skip across the rolling sea of tall grass that rippled in the gentle wind. She inhaled a deep breath, lifted her arms to the heavens and spun in a circle, glorying in being alive and well again. She felt whole and strong, surrounded by the sights and sounds of nature. Meagan was thankful she had not missed this day. It was all too perfect.

A lopsided smile tugged at Trevor's lips as he watched Meagan float about the creek bank like a butterfly, gliding and circling with magnificent grace. Her silver-blond hair lifted and then settled about her as if an unseen hand had smoothed it away from her exquisite face. The color of pink roses blossomed on her creamy cheeks as she hovered by the stream to drink. Her pale blue gown clung to her enticing figure like a flowing caress, one Trevor had made with his eyes, over and over again. He was hard pressed not to pursue her to live the fantasy that had preoccupied him moments earlier. Although it was his wont to take her in his arms and mold her delicious body to his, the voice of reason warned him to tread lightly with Meagan. She was bound to exhaust herself on this outing and he would take no chance of living through the hell of watching her collapse into another deathlike trance.

After drinking her fill, Meagan stretched leisurely on the bank to stare up at the wispy mare's tails that floated high above her, and then she reached over to pluck a stem of yellow heather from a nearby bush. After inhaling its delicate fragrance, she smiled quietly, watching Lear and the

201

greyhound romp through the grass and then lope toward her. A soft chortle tumbled from her lips as the dogs planted themselves on either side of her, nuzzling against her for attention. When Garda fluttered down to perch on her shoulder, Meagan breathed another tranquil sigh. But then she winced when Trevor's long shadow fell over her. For a moment she had almost forgotten that she was not alone, reminded of the peaceful days at the convent when she had strayed to seek the solitude of nature. Meagan lifted her eyes to Trevor, her face alive with happiness.

"I think I shall spend the rest of the day on this very spot," she declared as she set Garda to the ground and then lay back to stretch like a contented kitten that was about to curl up for a nap in the sun.

Trevor was again assaulted by overwhelming desire. Her innocent movements were so seductive that he was forced to still the urge to ravish her. Clamping a tight grip on himself, Trevor sank down beside her and then propped up on an elbow to gaze into her radiant face, bewildered by the miraculous transformation. Only a few tormenting hours earlier she had been pale and motionless, her life slowly ebbing away. Now her blue eyes sparkled like the morning star and her lips were a kissable shade of pink.

Before Trevor realized what he had done, his lips fluttered over hers and he sighed as the sweet taste of her kiss melted on his mouth. Silky arms glided over his shoulders and his body trembled with a need that rose to shatter his composure. His inquiring hands were upon her, moving unhurriedly over the full swells of her breasts and then slipping beneath the bodice of her gown to fondle the taut peak. A groan of torturous pleasure erupted from his chest as his lips trailed along the trim column of her neck to seek out the thrusting pink buds that seemed to beg for his attention. Trevor was at a slow burn. When her body instinctively responded to his caresses he could feel the fire in his loins.

Would he ever be able to resist this delicate maid? Had she made him a slave to passion, *her* passion? Trevor could not seem to think past this blue-eyed enchantress. She had taught him much in her innocence, and he found his need for her transcending physical desire. He felt weak and vulnerable in her presence, like a puppet dancing on a string, swaying beneath her whims. Had he lost every ounce of willpower? How could he keep fighting to hold himself at bay when he was his own worst enemy? Could he no longer look upon this silver-blond nymph without craving to touch her?

When her lips parted to grant him free access to her honeyed mouth, Trevor knew he was on the brink of losing control. Passion had taken a trembly hold on him, shaking his senses loose. Lord help him. He had waded into quicksand and he was sinking fast.

Meagan raked her fingers through this raven hair, drawing him ever closer, ignoring her pride. After her bout with death, she hungered for his embrace, longing for a memory that was more cherished and dear than their previous night together. She wanted him, needed him, and nothing else mattered. If only she could recapture the bliss she had found in his arms once more before they parted, she could survive, existing on the sweet memories that could overshadow the heartache of leaving the man who had become the quintessence of her dreams.

Her body arched to meet his exploring hands, surrendering to the rhapsody of a melody that played somewhere in the distance. His kisses and caresses left her drifting on a puffy cloud of pleasure and she reveled in the blissful sensations that flooded over her.

Suddenly, Trevor jerked away, shattering her dream as he muttered under his breath. His accusing gaze flitted over his shoulder to land on the beady-eyed falcon that had pecked his back, reminding him that he had overstepped his bounds.

"Shoo, buzzard," he growled irritably.

Garda flapped her wings and then settled them back in place, her dark eyes glued to Trevor, who breathed a frustrated sigh, knowing the feisty fowl had more sense than he had. Lord, if he didn't get a grip on himself he would be tumbling in the grass with Meagan, their passion spent and Meagan's newfound strength drained. Had he gone mad?

Where was his sense of decency? Obviously, he was carrying what little he possessed in his belt, and he had rolled over, squashing it flat. Meagan needed time to recuperate, he told himself. Trevor scooped her up so fast that it made her head spin, and he marched back to his steed to promptly deposit her in the saddle.

"I think you have had enough airing for one day," he informed her.

And his senses needed a rest, Trevor decided. This lovely sylph had devastated them, and he had to give himself time for his head to clear. He could take no more of her arousing presence without crumbling like a fallen statue, his confidence shattered, his passion running rampant.

Meagan stared puzzledly at him as he stepped into the stirrup and swung up behind her, taking great care not to make physical contact with her. Had he tired of her so soon, she wondered disheartenedly. Did he no longer find pleasure with her? Was the previous night the victory he sought, and once he conquered her did she no longer hold a challenge or his interest? Meagan answered affirmatively on all counts and then slumped dejectedly, reminding herself that she had expected no more of Trevor. He was a strong, unrelenting warrior who thrived on victory and quickly became bored with his conquests, impatient to seek out other triumphs. And yet, she had hoped . . . Meagan smiled ruefully. She could not live on hope. She had to face the fact that she was not woman enough to win Trevor's love, and she must learn to accept it, just as she had adjusted to the realization that England would never be the same. It had been difficult, but after her encounters with Trevor Burke, baron of Wessex and master of her soul, she knew that she could not walk away unaffected by the changes the Normans had wrought, especially those caused by the man who rode behind her on the magnificent black stallion that had once been hers.

The journey back to the fortress was a depressing one for Meagan. The warmth of the sun and her disappointment in Trevor had sapped her strength. Her eyelids had grown heavy, and she sank back against his hard chest, her silky hair tumbling over his shoulder. She fell asleep in his reluctant arms, wishing she had not ventured out at all. Learning that Trevor was anxious to be rid of her smothered her enthusiasm, and sleeping was far better than wallowing in self-pity.

As Meagan's body molded itself to his, Trevor tensed, aroused by the unappeased desire that still bubbled through his veins. A mellow smile traced his lips as he rested his chin against the top of her head. If she knew to what extent he had gone to tear himself away from her luscious body while they lay together in the grass, she would be grinning smugly. Meagan was a sorceress, using her body to reduce him to burning passion. But she could not control *all* his thoughts, he reminded himself. It was best for a man to keep his wits about him when Conan envisioned that the world was about to go up in smoke. Meagan was a devastating distraction, but he had important matters to attend. He could not while away all of his hours with this seductive minx, he told himself. Rumors of a full-scale war were circling Wessex, and Trevor and Ragnar had discussed the matter at length before parting company. Trevor could not dally with Meagan, shirking his responsibilities to the king. Soon word would come for him to serve the forty days he owed William, and he could not be caught with his armor drooping and his head in the clouds. Once Edric Lowell came to the castle to learn of Trevor's decision, he would turn his mind to political matters. Trevor had not earned his position in William's military counsel by lolling around like a lovesick squire. If he did not focus on the important matters concerning his demesne, he would be of no use to anyone.

With that determined thought milling through his mind, Trevor gently pulled Meagan into his arms, strode through the Great Hall, and ascended the stairs to put her to bed.

Although Meagan had awakened, she feigned sleep, afraid her longing gazes would assure Trevor that he claimed her heart. She had attempted to convince him that she loved him through actions, but she could not voice the confession. Pride turned the key to lock the words in her soul. It would be too humiliating to profess to love a man who had used her for his pleasures and then made arrangements to have her wed to one of his fellow Normans. Though she would not complain about his decision, she would never wed the man he had selected for her. Indeed, she would marry no one, since it was a forbidden institution for nuns. And that was exactly what she would be once she sneaked back to the convent she should never have left in the first place.

A faint smile brushed across William's lips as he read the letter delivered to him by Trevor Burke's messenger. Now he knew why his favorite warrior had delayed his arrival in London. More than a week had passed since William had sent his request to the overlord of Wessex, and he had become concerned that his courier had met with trouble. But after reading Trevor's correspondence, he assumed that the royal messenger had delayed his return trip to journey with the Dark Prince, the man under whom he had served during the invasion.

His fears at ease, William sat back to dictate a letter to his chaplain, and then he summoned one of his servants to deliver a second correspondence to Baron Burke.

Chapter 14

The late summer sun rose and set on another day, and Meagan knew for certain that Trevor wanted nothing more to do with her. He had left her to her own devices while he heard the complaints from the villagers and solved their squabbles as best he could. It hurt her deeply to see him behave as if she had suddenly contracted leprosy. He had ordered her to remain in her room to rest and sent meal trays to her chambers.

By dusk of the second day, Meagan was climbing the walls without a ladder. Finally, she decided to venture to Conan's solar to thank him for giving her back her life. Meagan owed him a great debt, and although the wizard was suspicious of her, she could not allow him to think she was ungrateful as well as disloyal to his lord.

Meagan rapped lightly on the opened door and tensely waited for Conan's dark eyes to settle on her. Conan frowned at the young woman's intrusion, wondering if her intent was to persuade him into thinking that his visions were false.

"What is it you wish of me, Meagan?" he demanded in his gravelly voice.

Drawing herself up proudly before his scrutinizing gaze, Meagan stepped inside without invitation. "I have come to thank you for what you did. I am left with a debt that will be difficult to repay, but I intend to try," she assured him.

His dark eyes made a slow, deliberate sweep of her petite

stature, well aware of why Trevor had been driveling over this sultry dryad who had emerged from the woods to enchant him. Her beauty, although skin deep, was distracting, Conan mused as he turned his back on Meagan and shuffled over to his chair to stare out the window.

"I seriously doubt that you *can* or *will* repay me in the manner I would request, young lady," he sniffed caustically.

"You have no right to judge me by your muddled dreams," Meagan blurted out, forgetting that she had intended to practice the art of diplomacy on this hoary sage who seemed to resent her mere existence. "Because of your closed-minded opinions, you have placed suspicions in Lord Burke's head that have no right to be there. How can you possibly think I pose a threat to him? I am merely a woman. I do not delve into sorcery and 'tis plain to see that I could not stand against this warlord's overpowering strength and expect to enjoy victory." Meagan glared daggers at the high-backed chair that swallowed up the frail form of a man who cloaked himself in long, flowing black robes that contrasted with his silver-white hair and beard.

"A woman may not be strong enough to bear arms but she is clever enough to deceive those who carry them," he mocked without twisting around to acknowledge that his ridiculing remark was aimed at her.

Meagan winced after being slapped by his insult and then stalked around in front of him, refusing to be intimidated by his poetic barbs. "My intentions are, very simply, to leave this fortress when my brother comes for me. I will have no further ties with Trevor, since I plan to return from whence I came." Meagan slammed her mouth shut, wishing she had not allowed her tongue to outdistance her brain. But then, why should she worry? Conan intensely disliked her, and he would never divulge information to Trevor, because he preferred that they remain as far apart as two people could get without dropping off the edge of the earth. And Conan would probably give her a gentle shove if he found her teetering on the edge of the world, she reminded herself bitterly.

"Trevor has set fate in motion by calling you back from

the dead. If you had taken the entire mug of wine, my potion would have been of little use to you," Conan remarked with a sigh. Meagan glowered at him, knowing Conan would have thrust the entire drink down her throat to ensure that she did not wake if he had been on hand that night. "You can flee to the edge of the earth and it will not matter." Meagan choked on her breath, wondering if the wizard was psychic and had just read her thoughts. "Your destiny has been linked with Trevor's. He knew of the dangers when he implored me to save you. Again, I pleaded with him to avoid setting off this chain reaction." His haunted gaze returned to Meagan, making her very uncomfortable. "A lesser man would have chosen the safer route, but not Trevor. The day rapidly approaches when you, too, will be faced with a difficult choice. I perceived this while I tended to you." Conan toyed with his cane and then massaged his temples before anchoring his level gaze on Meagan. "You will soon possess the power to destroy him. I cannot clearly see what force you have at your command, but you will have the opportunity to repay the debt or ignore it."

His words hung heavily in the air and Meagan practically strangled on them. Horrified, she gaped at him. "I do not wish to destroy Trevor. Yea, I will confess to you that I came here with anger and resentment in my heart, but now I have come to know Lord Burke and I accept him as the man he is," she argued.

His shoulder lifted and then dropped as he thoughtfully brushed his index finger over his silver moustache. "Perhaps 'tis true," he conceded. "But 'tis no matter. You will be plagued with inner turmoil. Its source I do not know, but 'tis in your hands that the final decision rests. You will hold the dagger and you alone must decide whether to plunge it into his heart or cast it aside. And even if you choose to repay your debt to me, as I would hope, Trevor will still consider you disloyal. Your course is even more treacherous than Trevor's. No matter which way you turn, you cannot be content with your lot."

Meagan nervously wrung her hands in front of her, confused and frightened by Conan's interpretation of a vision. "And what would you have me do?" she queried in a quivering voice.

The faintest hint of a smile bordered his lips as he lifted his eyes to the lovely maid. "You know of my deep regard for the overlord of Wessex, a man who befriended me, who watched over me when I was too old and weak to defend myself. Trevor has taken me in, assuring that I want for nothing when others would have cast me out as useless baggage." Conan inclined his head, measuring her with his gaze. "I think you know what I would ask of you, Lady Meagan. I am not certain that you possess the fortitude to give it if it means personal sacrifice. And for that reason, I cannot fully trust you. My apologies for voicing my skepticism, but I have always been one to speak my mind and I am too old to change my stubborn ways."

Meagan could think of nothing appropriate to say. To confess that she loved Trevor above all else would not satisfy the sage. To say that she would never betray Trevor when she could not foresee the future would be of little comfort to Conan. Since she was at a loss for words, she dropped her head and moved silently toward the door until Conan's husky voice halted her.

"You cannot follow your heart, Meagan, and you cannot depend on pure logic, for you will be in great conflict. I would spare both of us the agony of awaiting the outcome if it were within my power to do so, but my gift is to see and forewarn. My failing strength makes it impossible for me to intervene."

Meagan slipped outside the door and then leaned back against the wall to heave a perplexed sigh. Conan talked in riddles, but he had instilled a fear in her; she could not name or analyze it, but it was there, just the same. She could make no sense of his vision, and she feared that she would not like what she saw when the future emerged from its cloudy haze and she was forced to face the dilemma to which Conan referred.

A self-satisfied smile hovered on Edric's lips as he focused on the towering fortress that rose before him. He had been elated when Lord Burke's messenger arrived, requesting that he gather his belongings and journey to Burke Castle as quickly as possible. Along with his delight in thinking that Trevor intended to announce his upcoming wedding was his elation in seeing Devona again. The time he had endured without her was agony, pure and simple. Devona was a necessary part of his life, and a fire kindled within him at the thought of the nights they had spent sharing soft words and lingering kisses.

Edric shook his head to shatter his straying thoughts and then glanced over his shoulder, hoping the band of traveling musicians was only a few miles behind him. He had notified the troubadours as Reid had ordered and then set out for Burke Castle without delay. Edric was apprehensive about suggesting an immediate wedding, fearing that Trevor would become suspicious of his intentions for a whirlwind marriage. He could only pray that Meagan had bewitched Lord Burke and that he would not be opposed to settling the matter posthaste. Although Edric pitied Meagan, his hands were tied. The marriage had to be consummated to ensure its legality. There would be no time to bicker over the credibility of Meagan's claim to Wessex lands and its military force. The sooner this grisly business was finished the better, Edric mused. Soon Reid would be too busy to heckle him. The man had made a nuisance of himself, and the less Edric saw of him the happier he would be.

The familiar irritation hatched within him when Edric and his three knights pulled their steeds to a halt and stared down at the Norman overlord who was on hand to greet them. Edric chafed, thinking that not once had he been allowed a regal entrance into the Great Hall. Trevor had an uncanny knack of stripping Edric of even the simplest pleasures. A perplexed frown formed on his blond brow when Ragnar Neville strode up behind Lord Burke. What the sweet loving hell was that Norman doing here, Edric thought disdainfully. He had not anticipated that Neville and his eight knights would be visiting Burke Castle on this particular day. Damnation, Neville's appearance was bound to complicate matters.

Trevor's faint smile of welcome evaporated when he looked past Edric's entourage to see a handful of troubadours appear on the hill.

Swiveling his head to follow Trevor's narrowed gaze, Edric breathed a sigh of relief and then hastened to explain. "I happened upon the vagabond musicians during my journey and suggested that they entertain you, m'lord. I hope you have no objection."

Trevor shrugged slightly. "Nay, it will only add to the festivity," he said absently.

Biting back a secretive smile, Edric stepped from the stirrup and handed his steed's reins to Barden Keyes. Trevor had insinuated that he had an announcement, and Edric felt like beaming in satisfaction. Meagan must have charmed the muscular warrior out of his chain-mail shirt, he thought delightedly. Perhaps it would take very little persuasion to get Trevor to consent to a hasty wedding. Since the musicians were on hand, it would be difficult for Trevor to bypass a celebration. After all, Lord Burke had all the makings for a holiday—jesters, knights, an available bride . . .

"I suppose you are most anxious to see your sister," Trevor remarked, bringing quick death to Edric's silent reverie.

"But, of course," he insisted and then smiled broadly. "I trust Meagan was on her best behavior and that you were not disappointed with her."

"The lady is lovely," Trevor replied, swallowing his own devilish grin. "A bit feisty and contrary, but bewitching."

Edric gloated every step of the way to the Great Hall, but he cast aside his thoughts when he spied Devona descending the stairs beside Meagan. Their eyes met from across the sprawling room, and Edric detected the sparkle in her gaze. He was reassured that although Devona had been furious with him for toting Meagan off to Burke Castle, she still harbored a strong love for him that no misunderstanding could conquer.

While Edric was ogling Devona, Trevor fixed calculating

212

eyes on his vassal. It seemed that Meagan had not lied to him on that count. Edric and Devona did not realize there were other bodies in the Great Hall. It was as if the two of them stood alone, sending messages in their longing gazes.

When the group of musicians filed inside, Trevor glanced over his shoulder, wondering if it was truly coincidence that brought the traveling minstrels to his castle. Trevor possessed a suspicious streak as wide as the English Channel, and Conan's constant warnings made him all the more cautious.

"Set up the trestle tables for our guests," Trevor called to his servants. "I am sure they would enjoy refreshments after their journey."

When Trevor motioned for Meagan to join him at the dais, she did a double take. Trevor had carefully avoided her for more than two days, and she found it strange that he requested her to sit in the seat Conan usually occupied. Her apprehension was twofold when she spied Ragnar Neville ambling along beside her brother. Sweet merciful heavens! Had Trevor decided to wed her to Neville after all? Had he only taunted her with the possibility of tying her to some cruel barbarian? Had Trevor summoned Neville to meet Edric and arrange the match? Meagan feared she would come apart at the seams if Trevor did not enlighten her, and quickly. The day was not progressing as she had anticipated, and she would have given a king's ransom to know what was buzzing through Trevor's complicated mind.

A wry smile trickled across Trevor's lips when he saw the myriad of questions in Meagan's eyes. "Sit down, m'lady. I do not intend to make a feast of you, if that is what you are thinking."

"I am thinking that I would dearly love to know what *you* are thinking, m'lord," she muttered as she discreetly gestured toward Ragnar who planted himself in the chair beside her. "I have the eerie sensation that this pomp and circumstance is the ritual that precedes catastrophe . . . mine in particular."

Trevor chuckled as he sank down in his seat. "Have patience, nymph, and keep in mind that things are not always what they seem. I will foretell your future when the time is right."

The time was *now* as far as Meagan was concerned. Trevor had her squirming in her chair with uncontrollable apprehension. Meagan detested surprises. Her wandering glance circled to Ragnar to see him gawking, and Meagan rolled her eyes toward the lofty ceiling, summoning patience to endure Trevor's tormenting game. This day would be a disaster, she thought disgustedly. She could feel it in her bones.

After Trevor had fed his numerous guests, he announced his plans for the afternoon activities, leaving Meagan dangling on the edge of her chair to know whether or not Ragnar Neville was to become her betrothed. She could have cheerfully choked Trevor for forcing her to endure the agony of waiting to hear his intentions for her.

It was with tempered patience that she adjourned to the meadow to watch the tournament of war games Trevor had arranged for the day. Meagan eased down beneath the canopied gallery, a hint of boredom tugging at her delicate features. She had always preferred to participate rather than watch such events, and when she was a child her father had consented to let her join in the less rugged sports. But she doubted that Trevor would give permission for her to venture from the gallery.

A meager smile touched her lips as Ragnar, in his full suit of armor, approached her and then bowed from atop his steed.

"M'lady, I beg to carry your scarf to bring me good fortune during our games," he explained.

Ragnar waited a patient moment while Meagan tugged at the sash on her belt and then presented it to the knight. Her eyes drifted to Trevor, who sat upon his magnificent stallion, looking as ominous as Satan himself in his dark chain-mail armor and black surcoat, his sword and scabbard hanging by his side. Meagan had to admit that he was an awesome sight, one which kept attracting her attention during the jousting. Trevor had little difficulty ousting his opponents from their saddles as they stampeded toward each other. Even Ragnar, who wore Meagan's scarf, found himself dumped on the hard ground when he faced the Dark Prince whose shield bore the head of a dragon.

Trevor had ensured that neither Edric's, Ragnar's, nor his own knights would be seriously injured during the games, by using blunt lances. For that Meagan was thankful. She was in no mood to watch the bloody matches that closely resembled genuine combat.

Meagan snapped to attention when Trevor announced that the final event would be held after the baron dubbed one of his deserving squires as a full-fledged knight. After scurrying from her seat, Meagan glanced about her to seek her servant and then made a beeline toward him.

Almund Culver eyed Meagan warily as she bounded toward him, her face alive with mischief. "I swear you are up to no good, m'lady," he accused. "That look in your eyes spells trouble."

"Nay, not trouble, pleasure. . . ." Meagan corrected and then dragged Almund along with her to the tent containing the suits of armor for Trevor's knights and squires.

Trevor shouted orders to the knights and squires who had fallen in line for the final competition of the day and then took his place behind Ragnar. His wandering gaze strayed to the gallery to see that Meagan had retired to the castle. No doubt she had tired of men's play and had sought out her own amusement. It came as no surprise, he mused as he rested his spear against his thigh. Meagan was too nervous to know her fate. Sitting and waiting played havoc with her disposition.

After each rider had taken his turn at hurling his spear through the small ring that hung from the timber post, several knights were eliminated, but Trevor was still among the competitors. Trevor heaved a weary sigh as he watched Ragnar thunder toward the target, his spear breezing through the circle. Edric had missed with his third throw and had joined Devona to watch the outcome of the competition. A curious frown plowed his brow when he noticed the small squire who sat upon Meagan's steed. Almund? His gaze drifted to Ragnar, who was also studying the young lad who was galloping toward the target.

A pleased smile traced Trevor's lips as the lad's spear sailed through the air in another accurate toss. He had grown fond of the lame lad who had been Meagan's constant shadow while she was wandering about the bailey.

After half an hour there were only three contestants left in the competition. Ragnar missed his target, but the small lad who rode the black colt met with success, and a round of cheers erupted from the gallery.

Trevor took careful aim as he cantered toward the post. As the spear arced through the air, Trevor tensed, realizing he had been bested by the small lad even before the target bounced sideways, letting the spear fall to the ground.

When Trevor had retrieved his weapon, he trotted his steed back to the victor and smiled down at the young lad. "Remove your helmet, boy. I wish to see the face of the worthy squire who has bested me." The color faded beneath Trevor's ruddy tan when a pair of glistening blue eyes peered back at him.

Meagan's low chortle wafted its way through the mighty warrior who slumped in the saddle. "Do you suppose I have sufficiently impressed my future husband?" she taunted.

Trevor's gaze slid to Ragnar and then he smiled wryly. "I think you might have humiliated him. Perhaps we should not divulge your identity so the noble knight can save face."

Meagan nodded agreeably. Her intent had been sheer enjoyment and distraction. She had no need of embarrassing the proud warriors. Trevor knew who had defeated him, and it did her heart good to see the bewildered expression that was carved in his features when she lifted the helmet just far enough to expose her face to the baron of Wessex.

"Tell me, m'lady," Trevor insisted as he urged Meagan toward the castle. "Will you always make it a habit of surpassing me with your athletic talents?"

Her shoulder lifted leisurely as she grinned behind her

helmet. "Would you have me *let* you win, m'lord?" she countered.

Trevor grunted disgustedly. "Nay, Meagan. Never that."

The excitement of competition dwindled as Trevor nudged Poseidon and left Meagan to trot along behind him. Perhaps Trevor would never love her, but Meagan was certain she had made a lasting impression on him. The proud warrior would not soon forget that he had run a distant second to a woman, not once but twice. Her skills in the hunt were as sharp as his. Meagan sighed heavily, knowing that she would forfeit any challenge if she could earn Trevor's love. But that was asking the impossible.

Chapter 15

A secretive smile pursed Trevor's lips as he glanced at Meagan, who sat beside him on the dais. The previous day had been her undoing. Although she had humiliated him in the final event of the tournament, Trevor had some small satisfaction in watching her steam and stew over her fate. No doubt she had endured a fretful night wondering when he would divulge his plans for her.

Trevor eased back in his chair and peered at Edric, who was still making love to Devona with his gaze and had been since the moment he laid eyes on her. "Vassal Lowell," he said, dragging Edric back to reality. "About the proposal we discussed."

Edric's head swiveled around and he pricked up his ears. "Yea, I was wondering when you would inform me of your decision. I have been very curious."

Trevor doubted it. Edric had been so busy fantasizing that Trevor was certain he had forgotten that he even had a sister. "I have decided . . ." He strategically paused in midsentence, leaving Edric, Meagan, and Ragnar on the edge of their seats while he casually sipped his ale. "I have decided that I would like to take a wife after all. The woman of my choosing is worthy of the position of Lady Burke. She is comely, knowledgeable, gentle, and warm." He gestured toward the woman who sat at the first table below the dais. "'Tis Devona Orvin."

"What?" Edric crowed, unable to draw a breath without

219

choking on it. "But she is only a servant." He was dismayed by this cruel twist of fate, his heart hammering so furiously that he was sure it would beat him to death.

"Perhaps," Trevor acknowledged. "But lovely Devona possesses the gentle qualities of nobility, does she not?" His tone carried a hint of challenge.

Edric felt his mantle strangling him, and he tugged at it to relieve the pressure. "Yes, of course, but . . ."

"Do you consider yourself a child merely because you were born one?" Trevor inquired and then, without awaiting a reply, he hurried on with his rapid-fire questions. "Does a man not have the power to transform a maiden into a woman? Is a duke considered a king before he places the crown upon his head?"

Although Edric would have preferred to argue the point, he couldn't since the Saxons had refused to acknowledge William the Bastard until he forcefully acquired the throne of England.

"It seems to me that we *are* what we *become,* not what we were yesterday or the week before." Trevor slid his pallid-faced vassal a sly glance. "If a man can create a woman from a virgin, and if a king can proclaim his lady queen, why would it seem unnatural to raise a valuable, well-deserving servant to the station of lady?"

"But it was Meagan I sent to you on approval," Edric sputtered. Lord, the plan had seemed simple, but with this new twist Edric could not bear to think of depositing *his* Devona in the Norman's hands, not even for a minute. Devona loved him. Edric knew that just as surely as he knew the sun rose in the east, or at least that it had for the past twenty-eight years.

Trevor's shoulder lifted carelessly. "And I am most thankful that you sent Devona with Lady Meagan."

Edric's wide eyes flew about the crowded hall to peer helplessly at the troubadour who sat inconspicuously beside Marston Pearce. Then his frantic gaze circled back to Trevor. "M'lord, I do not wish to offend you or voice complaint, but . . ."

While Edric struggled to assemble his wild thoughts,

Meagan silently applauded Trevor's finesse. He was eloquent in speech, just as he was experienced in bed. Meagan blushed profusely at the direction her thoughts strayed and then pushed the arousing memories aside to watch Edric squirm like a rat caught in his own trap.

"The fact of the matter is . . ." Edric stared at the strawberry blond whose bewildered gaze was glued to the Dark Prince. He could not sacrifice Devona to *any* cause. If all else failed in Reid's scheme, Edric would still have Devona. "Devona and I are of one heart and soul, m'lord." Edric slumped back in his chair, as if blurting out his confession drained every ounce of his strength.

Although Meagan was delighted with Trevor's expert handling of her brother and still curious to know what Trevor had in mind for her, a strange tremor raced down her spine when her eyes fell to the jester who sat beside Marston Pearce. The man had kept his head down, making it impossible to see his face, but Meagan was certain she had seen him somewhere before. Odd, she mused as a muddled frown furrowed her brow. Why should a stranger garbed in a pointed hat and loose tunic seem familiar? Meagan cast aside her contemplations to focus her attention on Trevor, who was gloating over his success of putting Edric in his place. Not that he didn't deserve it, Meagan reminded herself. Her brother had it coming.

Trevor spared Meagan a quick glance. Now it was *her* turn to balk, he thought to himself. "I was not aware of your affection toward the lovely Devona." Trevor pensively brushed his chin and then nodded as if he had suddenly come to a decision. "Since you have proven yourself invaluable in your services to me and to the throne, I will withdraw my proposal." His eyes drifted to Almund's whitewashed face, and then he glanced at Edric, tossing him a faint smile. "I find that I must accept your original proposal to marry Lady Meagan, since I have decided that 'tis time I take a wife."

The split second before Trevor made his announcement, the jester looked up to the dais, and Meagan gasped in alarm. It only took a moment to recognize the man in the clown's garb. Reid Granthum! *He* was the man she had seen by the campfire in the forest. And it must have been Edric with him, Meagan realized. Despair closed in on her as bits and pieces of information that had been drifting around her head finally fell into place. Conan's premonitions came back to haunt her, and Meagan suddenly knew why Edric intended for her to wed Trevor. God, why had she been so blind? Because she had been so distracted by her love for Trevor, she told herself miserably.

Panic gripped her as her gaze flew through the crowd to study the faces of the troubadours that had been unrecognizable in the forest when she stumbled upon their camp. Meagan felt an uncontrollable shiver fly across her skin as her wild eyes circled back to her brother. Edric had not intended to see her wed to Lord Burke for his personal gain, but for *Reid's!* Granthum's appearance at his former manor cemented the pieces of the puzzle that Meagan had been unable to put into the proper perspective, but now it was painfully clear why she had been used for bait. Meagan had been betrothed to Reid, but if she wed Trevor she would claim the land and military force of Wessex . . . in the event of her new husband's death.

Meagan felt sick inside. The troubadours had conveniently arrived to ensure that after they entertained the baron of Wessex, he would not live to see another dawn. Reid Granthum intended to murder Trevor when the marriage was consummated and Meagan controlled a share of Wessex! Her horror-ridden gaze anchored on Conan, who was staring at her with a strange calmness. The wise sage's visions were materializing right before her eyes. She was peering into a nightmare of the worst sort! God have mercy. If she consented to the wedding, she would hold the death sword as Conan had predicted. But without the marriage, Reid could not take the soon-to-be-widowed Lady Burke as his wife, inconspicuously laying claim to Wessex without a complete overthrow of the Norman throne. And if Meagan revealed her suspicions to Trevor, she would cut her brother's throat. If she held her tongue, Trevor would be murdered. Meagan was torn between her love for Trevor and her devotion to her brother. Although she would have cherished the position of Lady Burke, loving Trevor with all her heart, she could not wed him and jeopardize his life.

Her soul twisted in tormented anguish. She *had* to sacrifice her love for Trevor to spare him. She *had* to remain silent, fearing Edric's involvement in the assassination attempt that would follow the wedding. Devona would never understand if Meagan betrayed Edric, and Meagan could not live with herself if she betrayed Trevor.

A thoughtful frown knitted Conan's brow as he watched the haunted expressions darting through Meagan's eyes. Their gazes locked for a long moment and then he focused on Trevor, sensing a danger for the overlord. When his dark gaze resettled on Meagan's colorless face, she had no difficulty decoding the silent message he sent her. Conan was challenging her to repay her debt, and she could not deny him his wish, even if it meant forsaking her love for Trevor.

"Nay!" Meagan railed, her thoughts haunted, her wide eyes fixed on the aging sage who held her captive with his solemn gaze. "I cannot wed you!"

Trevor's dark brows formed a hard line across his forehead as he glared at Meagan, annoyed by her disrespectful outburst. He had anticipated an objection, but not an adamant one. "Your brother and I have come to an agreement, woman. You are in no position to speak when Edric serves as your guardian."

Meagan's fiery glare scorched her brother, her expression so full of contempt that Edric wilted back into his chair, using Trevor's bulky frame as a shield to protect him from Meagan's smoldering eyes.

"You forget that Lord Neville has asked for my hand," Meagan argued frantically. "Will you disregard the previous proposal from one of your most devoted knights?"

Her remark set Trevor's teeth on edge. It annoyed him that Meagan had managed to put him at odds with his longtime friend. Damn that minx. When he had her alone in his solar, he would shake the stuffing out of her for causing such a disturbance and forcing him to question Ragnar's loyalty.

Trevor leaned forward to peer at the disgruntled knight

who until a few moments earlier had expected to take Meagan as his wife. "Can your loyalty to your superior be dissolved by this woman, Ragnar? Will she pit friend against friend?"

With head bowed, Ragnar murmured, "Nay, m'lord, my first loyalty lies with you. I will voice no protest to your marriage."

"Ragnar, you cannot do this!" Meagan clutched his arm, her gaze beseeching. "Surely the king will understand if you . . ."

"Silence!" Trevor's voice rumbled through the Great Hall like the crack of thunder, ominous and threatening. "Lady Meagan will wed me at dusk, and the troubadours will entertain us on this festive occasion," he declared.

Meagan collapsed in her chair. She was terrified, knowing what darkness would hold for her and Trevor. She sympathized with Conan, who had foreseen impending doom and found himself handcuffed. If she was forced to wed Trevor, she must see to it that the wedding was not consummated. When the would-be assassin came to ensure that the lord and lady shared the same bed, Meagan would not be in it! Somehow she must convince Trevor to sleep alone this night . . . and every other night until the danger was passed. But how? He would be humiliated if she avoided him on their wedding night, and he would be a dead man if she surrendered to his passions.

Her thoughts swirled, searching for a dilemma as she ascended the stairs to prepare herself for a wedding she wanted but could not enjoy at Trevor's expense. How could she save him, her mind screamed. Meagan choked on her breath, remembering Conan's other prophecy. Could she expect the world to go up in flames as well? What else could possibly go wrong? What had she overlooked? Meagan feared conjuring up answers to those questions. It was far too dreadful to face.

Trevor's golden eyes followed Meagan until she disappeared from sight, and then he frowned puzzledly. Why had she thrown such a tantrum? Had he misread the sparkle in her eyes that afternoon by the stream when she raised parted lips in invitation? He could have sworn her heart had softened toward him and that she might come to care for him as a wife cherishes her husband. But Meagan seemed to prefer Ragnar over him. Damn, Trevor could make no sense of her violent reaction to the proposal. He thought time and their physical attraction to each other would dissolve her bitterness, but maybe he was wrong. Perhaps Meagan could never forget the fact that she detested Normans and that Trevor was, and always would be, her enemy.

His pensive gaze settled on Conan, whose weather-beaten face was twisted in torment. What trouble did the sage foresee? Had Trevor fallen into some trap that he had not anticipated? He knew he was asking for trouble by wedding that feisty vixen, but was it more than he had bargained for?

When Marston Pearce approached the dais, Trevor dragged himself from his musings and focused on the minstrel.

"M'lord, my musicians and I are proud to serve you on this grand occasion. Shall we clear the hall to make ready for the entertainment?"

With a slight nod of approval, Trevor dismissed the musician and then sank back in his seat to contemplate the reason why Meagan had protested the marriage. Surely he could discover her motive if he gave the matter serious thought, he told himself confidently. But after a full hour of deliberation, Trevor was no closer to solving the riddle than he had been when Meagan flounced up the steps to seek asylum in her room.

Feeling like a caged cat, Meagan paced her chamber, her head spinning in frustration. There *had* to be a way to prevent tragedy, and she had only to consider the alternatives calmly and deliberately. She had already discarded the thought of fleeing from the castle, since Trevor had stationed a guard outside her door in case she abandoned him as she had that night in the shack.

Since Devona had tarried in the Great Hall with Edric, Meagan was forced to struggle into her clothes without

225

assistance. As she twisted her hair up on top of her head and set the ceremonial veil in place, a thoughtful frown tugged at her features. How could she ensure Trevor's safety without making him suspicious? Meagan placed the circlet of white wildflowers on the crown of her head and peered into the mirror, wondering why her wedding day had to be plagued with such dismal overtones. What was she to do? If Reid and Edric had their way, she would be a wife and widow before sunrise. Somehow she would prevent the assassination, even if it meant allowing Trevor to think she had a hand in the conspiracy. Fate had allowed her no choice if she was to spare Trevor's life. And it was worth any price, she told herself firmly. She would not let him die.

The impatient rap at the door made Meagan jump as if she had been stung. Gathering her composure, she glanced back over her shoulder to find Edric waiting to accompany her to the chapel. When he attempted to take her arm, Meagan jerked away, repulsed by the physical contact with her treacherous brother.

"Meagan . . ." Edric called softly to her as she hurried ahead of him, making her way toward the pentice, the covered passageway that joined the second level of the castle to the chapel tower. "Although you cannot know the reasoning just yet, 'tis best that this marriage take place. It will not be as painful as you might anticipate."

It was not difficult for Meagan to read between the lines. She knew exactly what Edric was trying *not* to say. She suffered another agony, knowing that she would be deposited in Reid Granthum's eager hands the moment Trevor was dead. Conan was right, as always. Trevor should have allowed her to perish from the poison wine. He would have saved them both a great deal of misery.

"Do not think you can cool my blazing temper, brother," Meagan bit off as she marched across the pentice, entertaining the thought of leaping over the railing, shinning down the supporting beam, and spiriting off into the forest, praying that Trevor would give chase and avoid his appointment with death. But there were swarms of knights in the bailey, and she would not have a snowball's chance in

226

hell of reaching the drawbridge before one of them captured her. "What you have done is loathsome, and I will not have you clearing your conscience by airing your eloquent speeches about what is right and necessary."

Edric clamped his mouth shut. It was impossible to talk sense into Meagan when she was in one of her black moods. Later, he would explain and she would forgive him for insisting that she wed Lord Burke.

As Meagan entered the chapel, Trevor fixed his eyes on the shapely beauty who was about to become his wife. Meagan looked as if she were about to explode with frustration. What in heaven's name was wrong with that little termagant? There were at least a dozen women who would have been delighted to exchange places with her. Indeed, Daralis would have killed to acquire the position, he reminded himself. Why was Meagan dragging her feet? Did she consider him such an unworthy prize? By damned, she could have done much worse! What did it take to make that minx happy?

"Women," Trevor muttered under his breath. Who could understand them? Meagan was so unpredictable that he never knew what to expect from her until the moment was upon him.

When Edric deposited Meagan beside him, Trevor discarded his muddled thoughts and focused his full attention on the priest. It was difficult to concentrate on the ritual when Meagan was fidgeting beside him, bracing herself on one leg and then the other, glancing about her as if she expected her knight in shining armor to come charging through the door to whisk her off to safety. Confound it! Would she not allow him to enjoy the only wedding ceremony in which he intended to be a participant rather than a bystander? First she had carved him to pieces with insults, then she had hopelessly seduced him until she had become his addiction, and now she was behaving as if she would have preferred to clean the latrines rather than endure this marriage ritual. Lord, the woman must have stayed up until all hours of the night inventing new methods to torture him, he thought sourly.

Time ticked by at a snail's pace, but the cogs of Meagan's brain were cranking. Finally she brewed a scheme that might save Trevor. When Trevor nudged her to repeat the vows, Meagan rattled them off, her mind too preoccupied to realize that she had tied herself to the Dark Prince until he took her in his arms to drop a hasty kiss to her unresponsive lips.

As Trevor ushered her across the pentice, his curiosity got the best of him. He paused, curling his index finger beneath her chin, and then stared at her through the veil of white. "Why, Meagan?" he questioned softly.

Her frown settled deeply in her exquisite features. "Why?" she repeated, unable to interpret his vague inquiry.

"Why were you so set against the wedding? The king would see me properly wed. Edric was eager for this match. Why was the thought of wedding me so distasteful? Have I been so cruel? You have given me numerous reasons to punish your impudence and yet I abstained. What must I do to win even the smallest amount of your affection?"

Meagan wanted to throw her arms around his neck and assure him that nothing would have made her happier than claiming the position of his wife, except hearing him confess that he loved her. But her hands were tied, leaving her no choice. Trevor had to think that she was annoyed with him. Reid was waiting like a vulture to seize what had formerly been his, and Meagan was caught up in a role that she was forced to portray.

"You could have informed me of your plans instead of filling my head with visions of some ghastly Norman who would reign over me with his lash," she muttered.

"And if I had informed you of my intentions you would have attempted escape," Trevor guessed and then graced her with a wry smile. "Although I find you very distracting, I cannot fully trust you with my thoughts since I have found it necessary to track you down when you have fled. I have not recovered from our last chase through the forest, and Conan advises me to keep a watchful eye on you, m'lady. I would imagine that divulging my plans to the likes of you could be disastrous."

228

He had yet to learn the true meaning of disaster, Meagan mused dismally. If he only knew how much healthier he would have been without making her his wife! Meagan pried his hand from her chin and then stalked off, flinging her parting remark over her shoulder. "You decieved me, m'lord. I cannot forget that. The price of my devotion to you comes high and you would do well to remember that."

As Trevor followed in her wake, another puzzled frown surfaced on his rugged features. What the devil had she meant by that? Finally, he shrugged away the muddled thought. He and Meagan would work out their differences when the music died in the hall and they were alone in their chamber. She would come around to his way of thinking once he had ample time to convince her that sharing his name was not so distasteful. But in the meantime, he would celebrate his wedding and bide his time until Meagan was his pure possession.

A sly grin pursed his lips as he aimed himself toward the Great Hall. This groom was well-warmed and ready to consummate the vows. And with the proper atmosphere and subtle persuasion, Meagan would find no complaint when he snuffed the lamp and drew her down beside him in bed. She would see him in an altogether different light when the dawn sprinkled across the lord and lady's chamber and the priest was assured that husband and wife shared more than a common name.

Chapter 16

"Let the music begin," Trevor ordered as he rose to his feet and raised his mug to the round of cheers that rippled through the Great Hall.

Meagan rolled her eyes as she watched Trevor sway like a willow in a wind storm. He had been sitting at the dais, calling to the butler to refill his mug each time it went dry. Since he had not paced himself he would be cup-shotten long before the minstrels completed their first song. Meagan tugged on his arm and pulled him back into his chair before he teetered on his perch and tumbled from the dais. She had intended that he be well into his cups before they adjourned to their room, but she preferred that he wasn't swimming in his mug of ale, forcing *her* to carry *him* up the steps to the solar.

"Must you expose your foolish side to your court, m'lord?" she chided. "You will drink yourself into a stupor."

"Do not preach, woman," Trevor grunted and then threw down half a mug of ale. "A man's wedding is reason for celebration, or at least I have heard it rumored so."

"Even at *my* expense?" Meagan sniffed as her condescending gaze followed the mug to his lips for his second gulp of brew.

Trevor pushed back in his chair and tossed her a roguish grin that revealed even white teeth. "Later, you will receive compensation if I have embarrassed you with my drunken behavior," he promised, the gleam in his eyes assuring her that his intentions for the night included very little sleep.

Later, he would be fighting for his life, Meagan thought disheartenedly. And this ale-knight would be in no condition to defend himself when the room and everything in it was spinning like a carousel. Dammit, was she to handle this grisly business single-handedly? Could she not count on this drunken knave the one time it was imperative that he have his wits about him? Meagan heaved an exasperated sigh as she watched the butler pour the blurry-eyed lord another drink. It would be up to her to watch over Trevor like a guardian angel, she mused as she broke off a chunk of meat and bread to feed to the falcon and shepherd who would soon be called upon to assist her in her duties as bodyguard for the inebriated lord of Wessex.

As the music of the harp, oliphant, and vielle drifted toward the dais, Meagan eased back to keep a cautious eye on the jester who paraded around the hall in his cloak, cap, and bells, entertaining the court by juggling. Servants mingled with the crowd to refill mugs and offer refreshments, but not one movement escaped Meagan's attention. She observed all activities until Marston Pearce bowed before Lord Burke and then smiled up at her.

"Your lovely lady is blessed with an angel's voice. Would you think it too forward of me to request her song? Her enchanting melody has been music to my ears since the first moment I heard her sing."

Trevor spared Meagan a quick glance, wondering how the troubadour knew his lady. But Trevor did not doubt that Meagan could sing like an angel. The nymph was multi-talented. He already knew that.

"Bless us with a song, Meagan," he requested.

"M'lord, I would prefer . . ." Meagan objected, only to be cut off by Trevor's insistent voice.

"Do not deny us such pleasure. I am anxious to hear you raise your voice in song rather than listen to you lecture me on the evils of drinking," he smirked.

"Please share your talent with us, m'lady," Marston chimed in. "I have waited many weeks to hear you sing again."

As Trevor propped his chin on his hand, Meagan's soft, husky voice filled his head. Her melody was like a skylark greeting a peaceful dawn, bringing a contentment that left Trevor drifting in a mellowed haze. For several minutes he could only stare at the comely blond who held him spellbound with her song. When the music ended, he was stung with disappointment and insisted that she bless him and his guests with another song. The entire crowd of knights and servants had ceased their chatter to listen, and Trevor was eager to allow his head to cloud with the sound of music and the voice of this seraph. Applause rumbled through the Great Hall when Meagan eased back into her chair, blushing modestly at the ovation.

"I am truly blessed," Trevor murmured as he leaned close, his warm breath caressing her neck. "I will fall asleep listening to a lullaby each night." A grin dangled on one corner of his mouth as he trailed his finger over her creamy cheek. "Have you other hidden talents, m'lady? Though I have discovered a few, I am left to wonder what other surprises you have in store for me."

When the music began again, scantily dressed dancers weaved their way toward the dais, and Trevor's glassy gaze shifted to the women's seductive movements, leaving him hypnotized.

"I would consider you the rarest of all gems if you could charm me with a dance to compare with this." His sluggish voice held a hint of challenge and Meagan rose to the dare.

If the drunken lord wanted to see her dance, then by damned she would do it, since it might well be the last time he witnessed any type of entertainment. She would entice him to their room and see that he was fast asleep before he could consummate their marriage. His vice of drinking would serve a useful purpose tonight if she could coax him upstairs before he stumbled in his tracks.

Meagan glanced at Trevor and then her gaze soared toward the ceiling. This was the man she thought she loved? His dark hair was in disarray, his mantle was sagging, and his golden eyes reminded her of a map charted in red. He did not seem the fire-breathing dragon who had caught up to her in the forest or the gentle lover she had known in darkness. He was vulnerable now, and Meagan would take great care to see to his safety.

Her gaze swung to Conan, who sat to the right of Trevor. A quiet smile brushed the old man's lips as she nodded mutely, assuring him that she would see to the unpaid debt as best she could.

Trevor was not too drunk to miss the silent exchange between Conan and Meagan. The fact that the wary sage was no longer glaring at her with mistrust miffed him. Had this wily sorceress charmed the cautious sage? Trevor watched curiously as Meagan summoned Marston Pearce and whispered in his ear.

"If 'tis the dance you wish, m'lord, 'tis the dance you shall have," Meagan assured Trevor before she descended from the dais.

When Meagan and the minstrel disappeared from sight, Trevor's muddled gaze narrowed on Conan. "Have you no complaint about my decision to wed Lady Meagan?" he questioned point-blank. "No words of warning?"

One shoulder lifted and then drooped beneath his black robe. "It would have been a waste of breath to issue a second warning, would it not? I beseeched you to abandon the lady once before, but you defied me. I cannot live your life for you, though I think someone should since you have become so reckless of late," he added, his calculating gaze riveting over Trevor. "But there is naught else to do but sit and watch your fate unfold."

Had the old man mellowed? Trevor studied the oracle's blurred image. "I had expected a protest from you. Has Meagan bewitched you, as well?"

"Nay, my son, but now your lady and I understand each other," he explained vaguely and then directed Trevor's attention toward the far end of the hall where Meagan had appeared. "You challenged her to dance for you and she returns in that purpose. But it leaves me to wonder what other purpose will be served."

Trevor was too preoccupied with Meagan to question Conan's remark. His hungry gaze flooded over the provoc-

234

ative costume Meagan was wearing as she threaded her way through the crowd. The transparent skirt was woven with gold and sparkled as she moved gracefully toward him. Her headdress was inlaid with jewels that glistened in the light like stars twinkling in the sky. The Egyptian-style costume and the appetizing figure within it were hard on Trevor's blood pressure. The thoughts that were buzzing through his head while Meagan swayed to the seductive music furnished by the minstrels were enough to drive a sane man mad. She was luring him into her web, leaving him dizzy with a desire that threatened to consume him.

Meagan was amazed at her abandon. She had often mimicked the movements of dancers when she was alone in her chamber, but never in her wildest dreams did she imagine herself dancing in a crowded hall to entertain her husband. It warmed her to feel Trevor's eyes on her, as if he had been captivated. His gaze was like an arousing caress to which her body responded. He was seducing her with his eyes, and she in turn enticed him with lithe movements, twirling and spinning in perfect rhythm with the music.

And then his eyes locked with hers and, as if drawn beneath a spell and commanded to rise, Trevor gathered his feet beneath him and strode toward her. The devilish grin that parted his lips was fair warning for what Trevor had in mind for his seductive wife. Meagan attempted to dart away, but Trevor's hand snaked out to pull her into the tight circle of his arms. The kiss he planted on her lips carried enough heat to set the night sky ablaze, and Meagan felt it spreading through her body like a wildfire. Although she was stirred by the passion that flickered in those beguiling golden eyes, she was embarrassed by his blatant show of affection, considering he was surrounded by rebels who anxiously awaited him to bed his bride so they could dispose of him.

"M'lord, we are making a spectacle of ourselves," Meagan sputtered and then gasped when Trevor scooped her up in his arms and swaggered toward the stairs. "Put me down!"

"Never!" Trevor growled playfully. "You have bewitched me, woman, and I seek to appease the craving that has been gnawing at me since you enticed me with this delicious body

235

of yours."

As he strode across the Great Hall, Meagan squealed indignantly. "M'lord, you forget yourself. You have guests to entertain." Her frantic gaze landed on the jester, the only member of the crowd who had not succumbed to uproarious laughter. Not a living soul was blind to Trevor's intentions as he whisked his wife up the stairs to his solar, but Reid's expression held no amusement. He was glaring murderously at both of them.

Meagan trembled uncontrollably, haunted by the sneer on Reid's face. "Please, put me down," she requested. "Do not disgrace me in front of our guests."

"Disgrace?" Trevor snorted. "Our guests would be disappointed if I did not exert my prowess after you lured me to your side with that provocative dance of yours. What did you expect me to do? Fall asleep of boredom?" His massive chest rumbled with laughter as he carried Meagan up the staircase. "Our guests will feast in our absence, but my hunger cannot be appeased by what is served as the evening meal. My ravenous appetite must be satiated in an entirely different manner."

A round of cheers echoed through the stone fortress, followed by slightly off-color remarks that Meagan would have preferred not to hear. She choked in humiliation and then cursed Trevor's poor sense of timing. This was not the type of exit she had planned for the evening. Indeed, she had intended to have him staggering beside her as they ascended the steps, leaving Reid and his conspirators to wonder if the drunken lord had fallen asleep before he could seduce his new wife.

When Trevor set her to her feet Meagan fled to the far side of the room to plaster herself against the wall. "Keep your distance from me. You are drunk," she snapped.

Trevor felt the quick rise of indignation. "And you are a termagant," he scowled. "At least *I* will be sober on the morrow. But I cannot imagine a dramatic change in *your* behavior."

"I will not be mauled by a lusting drunk," Meagan assured him flatly.

Trevor pulled up short, watching Meagan, who was poised to break and run if he made an abrupt move toward her. One dark brow quirked as he regarded her puzzledly. "Surely you do not intend to deny me my husbandly rights after that provocative performance?" he squawked.

"I most certainly do!" Meagan insisted. "I did but obey your command to dance in the presence of your guests, but I *refuse* to share your bed this night."

"By God, woman, man was not meant to sleep alone, especially on his wedding night!" Trevor wagged a lean finger in her defiant face, but his gawking gaze sidetracked him momentarily. The sight of her heaving breasts beneath the revealing fabric and the shapely curve of her hips chased away his thoughts, and it took a moment to round them up to pursue their argument. "I will not have my guests snickering when I am forced to rejoin them to drown my mortification in a mug of ale. I left them with the impression that I intend to bed my wife."

Meagan could see the columns of steam rising from his mantle, assuring her that Trevor was dangerously close to losing his temper. "Then perhaps you will challenge me to a game of chess," she purred sweetly. "No one needs to know what goes on behind this closed door. I shall fetch some wine and . . ."

Trevor let loose with a gruff snort and marched toward her like an invading army reacting to the signal to charge. "I will not be playing chess on my wedding night." His arm shot toward the bed. "Lie down or I shall forcefully plant you in the midst of yonder quilts." His golden eyes flashed like streak lightning, momentarily blinding her. "You seem to forget that you have become my chattel. I can use you as I please. If I desire your body, then 'tis mine for the taking, *when* and *where* I so chose," he reminded her truculently. "Get thee to bed, woman . . . now!"

Meagan put out a stubborn chin and refused to budge from her spot. "I will not spread myself beneath you, Trevor Burke, lord and master of Wesset, *especially* not tonight!" Meagan flung at him. "You may demand the loyalty of your knights and squires, but I will never bow as your slave."

Why had he married this high-spirited, temperamental, contrary wench, he asked himself in exasperation. Meagan was the most frustrating female he had ever come across. Yea, he had craved the challenge of taming her, but Meagan was a bundle of trouble and Trevor was beginning to doubt his ability to control her without resorting to brute force. Occasionally, she had melted in his arms, but usually he found himself fighting his way through an obstacle course of stubbornness before she surrendered to the churning passions that she refused to acknowledge. Again, he reminded himself that this angel was armed with fire and that he had constantly been scorched. Blast it! Was he not to be allowed an ounce of pleasure on his wedding night?

While he was preoccupied in thought, Meagan dashed across the room and then squealed when Trevor lunged at her. Choosing a path of least resistance, Meagan wheeled to bound across the bed and then buried herself in the drapes, her heart pounding so furiously that Meagan feared Trevor could locate her merely by listening to her drumming pulse.

"Stop this nonsense!" Trevor growled as he yanked on the drapes, searching for his elusive wife. "Hide and seek is not the game I had in mind for the night."

When Meagan heard him drawing nearer to her hiding place at the foot of the bed, she darted toward the door with Trevor hot on her heels. Trevor's reactions were numbed by the ale, and as he turned the corner he caught his foot on the bedpost. Meagan's mistake was breaking stride when Trevor howled in pain. Before she could unlatch the door, Trevor charged toward her and then blocked her path.

A sardonic gleam flickered in his eyes as he hooked his arm around her waist, chaining her to him. "You will not elude me tonight," he rasped.

Although Meagan squirmed for release, Trevor dragged her to bed and then bent his knee upon the quilts, tumbling with her and then crouching above her to hold her in place. His anger evaporated when he glanced down to see the panic in her wide blue eyes. Why did she seem so distraught? It was not the first time they would make love, and it certainly would not be the last. There was magic in their embrace.

238

Meagan knew that as well as he did. What the devil was wrong with her?

His thumb brushed across her flushed cheek, and he frowned curiously at the alarm in her exquisite features. "Why do you fight me, Meagan? You know there is nothing but pleasure to be found in my arms. I long to kiss and caress you." His breath whispered over her neck, sending a wave of unwanted goose bumps rippling across her skin. "I ache for your touch, the feel of your luscious body pressed to mine. I have no wish to hurt you, especially not tonight. Do you see this marriage as some form of punishment?"

Meagan yearned to tell him that she loved him, but even her deep affection for him had limitations. She could not sacrifice her own flesh and blood. A life as Trevor's wife would be no life at all because he would fall beneath the sword. To speak of love when she rejected his embrace and denied his husbandly rights would make him all the more suspicious of her. Nay, this was not the time for confessions.

Meagan clung to indifference, hoping to convince him that his touch no longer stirred her, but her body betrayed her. Her flesh quivered beneath his exploring caresses, and she choked on a sob when his mouth captured hers in a breathtaking kiss.

The seductive costume was drawn away and his fingertips were on her skin, demanding a response to his tantalizing caresses. His hand folded around her breast before his lips strayed to the taut peak to send torrents of arousing sensations riveting through her body to feed the fire that rose to consume her.

Meagan could no more deny the maddening need for him than she could command the world to stop spinning for one brief instant. He had become her reason for existence. He was the master of her soul, no matter what she had been forced to say to the contrary.

Ragged words of want and need brushed over her skin as his moist lips skimmed her abdomen. A surrendering sigh tumbled free as his practiced caresses wove intricate patterns over her breasts. Meagan wondered wildly if he had sprouted an extra pair of hands. It seemed his exploring touch missed not one inch of her trembling flesh, massaging, taunting, drawing responses that she was powerless to control.

Her nails dug into the hard muscles of his back as she arched to meet his seeking hands, gasping beneath the tidal wave of emotions that swelled and tumbled over her. Meagan was engulfed by raw passion, sensations so forceful and consuming that she swore she had been trapped in a whirlpool that would never grant release. His sleek body glided over hers in senseless possession, and her thighs parted under his impatient insistence. His firm mouth softened as it melted on hers, as if he ached to bury himself in her soft body.

Trevor reveled in the union that left him feeling as if he had captured one moment of perfection. All the doubts and suspicions that had plagued him earlier were drained by the undercurrents that swept him beneath reality's surface. His body surged toward hers, plunging deeply within her and then retreating only to be drawn into the rapture of total possession. His soul seemed to reach out to hers, summoning her to yield to emotions that transcended physical pleasures of the flesh. Their lovemaking had created its own unique design, and Trevor gasped as his body instinctively strained against hers to relinquish the last of his strength. But still he soared, uninhibited, as if he had ascended from the depths of ecstasy to sail toward the stars, feeling their warmth, basking in pleasures that defied description.

Time stood still while they explored a mystical universe without leaving the confining circle of each other's arms. Trevor was baffled, wondering how he could feel so pacified while he still hungered for this willful woman. She struggled against him, ran from him, and then surrendered in wild abandon. She had touched every emotion, and he had been unable to put her out of his mind since the first moment he took her in his arms to taste the sweet nectar of her kiss. Trevor had pursued her, cornered her, protected her, and had refused to let her go. But even though he had chained her to him in wedlock, he had yet to capture her spirit. He knew that this feisty vixen would never be his possession. She was

240

as free as the wind, undaunted by his strength and seemingly immune to every technique he had applied in his quest to tame her.

Heaving a weary sigh, Trevor rolled beside her to drape his arm over her waist. His rambling thoughts faded as the effect of the ale dulled his senses. He had partaken of far too much brew and had become intoxicated on the sensations that washed over him in the aftermath of love. When Meagan inched away from him to don her garments, Trevor was drifting in his dreams, oblivious to the fact that he slept alone.

Although Meagan would have preferred to follow Trevor into his fantasies, there was much to be done. Carefully, she eased open the door to find Lear standing guard over the chamber. When she summoned the shepherd inside, he came upon all fours and lumbered into the room to keep a closer watch on the sleeping lord. Assured that Trevor would be safe until she returned, Meagan scurried through the corridor and hurried across the pentice. After making her way down the supporting beam, she hopped to the ground and then darted across the abandoned bailey to seek out one of the young female servants who had not been allowed to join in the activities and risk being mauled by the overzealous knights who were swimming in ale.

Meagan gave explicit instructions to the young maid and then made her way back to the castle by the same route she had taken to sneak away. It was her intention to stash the maid in Trevor's bed, hoping to convince the rebel assassins that the marriage had not been consummated because the drunken lord had bedded the wrong woman. Meagan was trying to buy precious time so she could persuade Edric to relinquish his cause. Trevor's death would not ensure Saxon control of England.

Breathlessly, Meagan pulled herself up the rough timbers and then edged along the bracing post on the underside of the pentice. Her eyes darted about her as she scampered back inside to wait for the maid to weave her way through the Great Hall and join her in the lord's chamber.

A relieved smile bordered her lips as the petite, red-haired maid turned the corner and walked silently toward her. But her smile vanished when Lear's warning growl curled beneath the door that had been locked from the inside. Meagan's face paled as she pushed her shoulder against the door, attempting to force it open, but it wouldn't budge. Trevor's assassin had slipped inside during her absence, and there was nothing she could do to stop the attack. Fear pelleted through her, wondering how the sleeping lord would fare with the man who was consumed with revenge and who might not care whether or not the marriage had been consummated. Reid faced his enemy, the overlord who ruled Granthum lands, the man Reid thought had murdered his sister.

God help Trevor, Meagan mused apprehensively. He was going to need all the divine assistance he could get.

Chapter 17

Trevor dragged himself through his drunken daze when the shepherd's low growl shattered the silence. A wry smile pursed his lips when he remembered that he had fallen asleep in Meagan's silky embrace. As Trevor pried one eye open to peer over at his wife, his mellowed expression vanished, and he tensed when he glanced up to see the cloaked figure that crept toward him, his dagger glistening in the waning light.

Reid's snarl dripped venom as he lunged toward Trevor, hungering to bury his blade in the baron's bare chest. Their bodies groaned, stalemated by matching strength, and Trevor gritted his teeth as the sharp-edged dagger wavered just above his heart. He had no time to survey his would-be assassin's face. His attention focused on the point of the blade that split the hair on his chest. Summoning every ounce of strength he possessed, Trevor kicked the man away, sending him stumbling backward to regain his balance. But Reid was intent on his purpose. His lips curled in a sneer as he cocked his arm to hurl the knife.

Lear lunged at the darkly clad intruder the moment before he released the blade, causing Reid to miss his target. Trevor ducked away from the oncoming dagger and then sprang at the man, who viciously cursed him. When Trevor's booming voice threatened to bring the walls down around them, Reid spun on his heels and darted to the door, fumbling frantically with the lock, and then disappeared into the darkness.

Muttering under his breath, Trevor wheeled back to gather his garments. He could not give chase to the villain without wearing a stitch. When he charged toward the door, another furious growl erupted from his lips and a condemning glare swam over his features. There, clinging to the shadows, was Meagan, his treacherous wife.

"Et tu, Brute?" Trevor hissed at Meagan. "Why did you bother summoning a man to do your dirty work?" His gruff voice dripped heavily with sarcasm. "Do not tell me that you did not have the stomach for such dastardly deeds."

Without awaiting her reply, Trevor dashed down the corridor and then cursed angrily when he noticed that the troubadours had vanished into thin air. The dawn of understanding hit him like a hard slap in the face, and he muttered several unrepeatable epithets as he stalked through the forebuilding to find that Daralis had been cut free and had escaped with the minstrels who had scattered into the woods like ants returning to their den to hide. The traveling musicians were a great deal more than they appeared, Trevor realized. They were rebels who scouted the countryside, familiarizing themselves with the Norman fortresses, intent on taking their enemy by surprise.

Damnation! How could he have been so blind? Because he had been sufficiently distracted by his seductive wife, he thought bitterly. It had been all too convenient for her to lure him to bed with her exotic dance and cloud his head with songs. Conan was right, Trevor growled as he spun on his heels and stormed back to the castle. Meagan's loyalties were questionable. She had seen to it that he was sound asleep when she allowed his assassin to sneak in on him. Trevor had been only inches away from falling beneath the rebel's blade. And if he had perished, Meagan would have taken control of Burke Castle. She was a rebel from the top of her lovely head to the tip of her toes, and she would never feel anything for him but contempt. Her actions had affirmed that, Trevor grumbled sourly.

Why hadn't he kept his wits about him? Because he had become enamored with a crafty witch who had every intention of carving his heart from his chest and feeding it to the wolves. The scheme had been carefully planned, and Meagan had been the bait to lure him to his death. She appeared to be as soft and lovely as an angel, but she was the devil's advocate, masquerading behind her beauty, waiting to dispose of him once the stage had been properly set.

He should have allowed Meagan to die from the poison wine, he told himself harshly. It would have been better to lose her than to live with this agonizing sense of betrayal. The pain that stabbed at him overshadowed the torment he had endured when he thought she had died. Knowing that she lived and would continue to loathe him was enough to twist his heart in two. Damn her! She forced him to slay her for her treachery.

His keen gaze swept the knights who slept on the benches that had been set against the walls to serve as beds. Trevor snorted derisively and then cursed his foolishness again. He and his men had been caught unaware, behaving like drunken idiots while the rebels rubbed shoulders with them. Hell and damnation! Never had he been so humiliated. And Meagan was to blame. That witch could have been the death of him.

Intent on revenge, Trevor took the steps two at a time to find Meagan. He was so furious that his entire body trembled, and the murderous thoughts that whipped through his mind begged to be appeased.

Damn it, where was she? Trevor's head swiveled around her empty chamber and then he stalked down the hall to her brother's room, wondering if Edric had the good sense to flee with the rest of his rebel army.

Meagan breathed a sigh when she found that her brother had escaped, but then she frowned when she found the note lying on the night stand. It seemed that he and Devona had set out for Lowell Castle shortly after the wedding celebration. Devona had wished her well in her marriage to Trevor, and Meagan smiled ruefully, knowing that she would never find the happiness Edric and Devona shared. Meagan was destined to endure a one-sided love and become

Trevor's scapegoat. He had always been suspicious of her, and now that the evidence weighed heavily against her, he would thirst for her blood. To plead her innocence could well mean Edric's death, and Meagan could not name her brother among the conspirators, especially when she could not say for certain to what extent Edric was involved. She would not jump to conclusions as Trevor would do when he returned. If only she could beg for Trevor's mercy and return to Lowell Castle to speak with her brother, she thought whimsically.

"So you sent your brother and his lover away, thinking to spare their lives," Trevor spat as his muscular form filled the open doorway.

Mustering her courage, Meagan turned to look him square in the eye. "Edric knew nothing of this plot against you," she lied without glancing away from the smoldering rage in Trevor's eyes that threatened to reduce her to a pile of charred ashes.

"You lie," he hissed as he stalked forward to loom over her.

"Nay, m'lord," she insisted, her tone more confident than she felt when Trevor was breathing the fire of dragons down her neck. Meagan lifted the note for his inspection. "Edric took Devona home after the ceremony. He knew nothing of this plot against your life. They even wished us well. Would they have bothered with a congratulations if they had known that you would not live to see the dawn?"

Trevor snatched the letter from her hand, hastily read its contents, and then wadded it up. As he hurled it against the wall a hard frown settled into his coarse features. Now he didn't know what to think. He had no proof of Edric's connection with the rebels, but the fact that he had asked the troubadours to entertain Trevor threw shadows of suspicion on the Saxon vassal.

When Trevor hesitated, indecision etching his brow, Meagan hurried on in explanation, praying that she could convince Trevor of Edric's innocence. "My brother's reason for offering me to you were purely materialistic. He sought only to strengthen the bond between the two of you, hoping to solidify his position with the Norman Crown. Edric did not fight with Harold Godwinson," Meagan reminded him as her eyes met his scalding gaze. "Can you blame him for grasping at security? Is that not what you pursued when you joined William? You had nowhere to call home and you linked yourself with the duke of Normandy for material gain. Edric has attempted the same feat. You cannot call him a traitor and still justify your reasons for declaring your loyalty to the king. If your uncle had not died, you would have returned for revenge, and you would have used your wealth to restore your chateau. Edric has his family lands and all he seeks is to protect them. He is not in favor of rebellion. I can assure you of that." Meagan had voiced another lie, but she *had* to protect Edric. He was all the family she had left.

Trevor stared her down for a long, silent moment. He wanted to believe her, but he had been burned once too often in his dealings with Meagan. If she declared Edric to be innocent, then she convicted herself. Meagan had known of the plot. She had said as much. And yet, she kept silent, proving that she condoned the rebels' intentions. She would have watched Trevor die, and no doubt would have applauded his murderer.

"Perhaps Edric was ignorant of the conspiracy, but you were not," he said in a deadly tone. "I found the Granthum brooch in your possession." When the color seeped from Meagan's cheeks, he knew she was guilty as charged. "I made it a point to check on your association with the Granthums, and I learned that you were once betrothed to Reid Granthum. Was he among the troubadours? My would-be assassin, perhaps?"

Meagan hung her head. Did she dare to voice her innocence? Would it matter? The fragile bond between them had been severed, and Meagan doubted that things could ever be right between them, not now or ever.

"Answer me!" Trevor bellowed as he grabbed her arms to give her a sound shaking, sending her head snapping backwards.

"Yea, it was Reid Granthum who sought to dispose of you

247

and then reclaim his lands and his betrothed. But I did not know of the plot until I saw Reid dressed as a jester." The confession tumbled from her lips. She *had* to try to explain. She *had* to convince him that she loved him far too much to allow him to die. "Only then did I realize what he had in mind for you. I left Lear to watch over you and I went to fetch a serving maid to take my place in bed beside you, hoping the rebels would think our marriage had not been consummated. But Reid was too poisoned with revenge to care what reasons had brought him to your chamber. You stood for all that he had lost and he thirsted for blood. He intended to kill you, whether or not he could gain control of Wessex."

Trevor shoved her away, as if repulsed by their physical contact. He wanted to believe her, but he could not trust her. She would lie to save her own neck. Her explanation could easily be twisted into a confession of guilt. If she wanted to spare his life, she could have informed him of her suspicions, he reminded himself. But nay, she had kept silent, hoping to play to either advantage. If Reid had succeeded, she would have wed him, but since he had failed to slay Trevor, Meagan was all too anxious to insist that her loyalty was with her new husband.

"I cannot believe you," Trevor muttered, his voice acrid with anger. "You will remain here as my prisoner until I have tracked down Reid Granthum and his band of rebels. When I hear the confession from his lips, I will know whether or not you have deceived me." Trevor took a bold step forward, standing rigidly before her, his lips thinning in a hateful sneer. "And if I find your brother among the die-hards who think they can overthrow the king with the same treachery they used when they came to serenade me, I will have your head. If you have lied to me, I will not spare your life, wife or nay!"

His tone was so deadly that Meagan's blood ran cold, and she gulped fearfully. Never had she seen Trevor so furious, and she pitied anyone who pushed him past this stage of agitation. He was like a volcano that was about to erupt, and Meagan did not wish to be within ten miles of him when he finally did. She had often called him a dragon, but at this moment she realized he fit the description when he was sufficiently angered.

Trevor focused his piercing amber eyes on her, opened his mouth, and then slammed it shut, deciding against the remark that waited on the tip of his tongue. As he wheeled around to exit from the room, he stopped short, surprised to see one of William's couriers hovering by the open door.

"M'lord, I have a message from the king. Forgive the intrusion, but he specifically ordered that it be delivered the moment I entered your fortress," the young man explained, his eyes straying to the bewitching woman who was garbed in her seductive costume.

Trevor did not miss the messenger's blatant interest in Meagan, and it annoyed him that he could still be stung with jealousy when Meagan would have seen him murdered on his wedding night. No doubt this sorceress could charm William out of his crown if he had the misfortune of feasting his eyes on this stunning nymph, he thought resentfully.

"Go to your room and change into something respectable, woman," Trevor barked sharply as he wheeled to glare at Meagan in her provocative attire.

As Meagan rushed from the room, fighting back the sea of tears that attempted to flood her eyes, Trevor broke the royal seal and read the letter.

Trevor,
    I received your message and I congratulate you on your marriage. I hope your lady will serve you well.

Trevor grunted disgustedly. His lady had served him up to the rebels, he mused scornfully. He had made a gross error in judgment by wedding that deceitful witch.

Although I would prefer to grant you ample time to know your new wife, I must insist that you report to the palace as I requested in my previous letter.

A muddled frown captured Trevor's brow. He had

received no other correspondence from the king since William had summoned Trevor to London the previous month to brief his barons on the uprisings that he anticipated in the west and north.

> I require your forty days of service and those of your knights. Rebels have set Mercia ablaze and I must battle them at Stafford. I have planned a full scale attack to squelch the Saxon rebellion, once and for all.
> French and English mercenaries have been elicited and I will begin my march against the rebels when I have sufficient strength to crush them.
> I have just returned to London to begin negotiations with the Danish fleet that has joined the Saxon rebels. They have a price and I intend to pay it. Once the revolutionists are left to fight alone I intend to teach them a lesson they will not soon forget.
> You have fought bravely and well in the past and I need you by my side. When the Saxons are brought beneath the sword you and your new bride will be reimbursed for this untimely inconvenience.
> I will expect you within the week. Please extend my apologies to Lady Burke and assure her that I would not intrude if matters of state were not so critical.
>
> William

When Trevor finished reading the letter he glanced over at the courier. "I will be leaving for the palace at dawn. Fetch food and drink and select a fresh steed from my stables," he ordered before he brushed past the messenger and aimed himself toward Meagan's room.

Her eyes were swimming with tears as she watched Trevor approach. She longed to dash into his arms and block out the misery that twisted her heart, but she knew Trevor would be unreceptive to her touch. He would never believe her, and he would treat her as a traitorous captive from this day forward.

"I have orders to join the king in London and I will be leaving immediately. You will be confined to the dungeon until my return," he told her coldly. "I would have treated you with nothing but kindness, Meagan, but you could not bury your bitterness for your Norman ruler. You will pay for your betrayal. Think on that while you are caged in your gloomy cell."

With that he pivoted and strode toward the door. Then he paused to lift the message from William. "Your Saxon lover does not have a prayer against our forces. William has called for mercenaries to assist him. Soon they will flood the palace to join the rightful king of England." His brooding gaze riveted over her as his lips curled in contempt. "You were a fool to think a handful of musicians could defeat us. While you rot in prison, I suggest you pray to God that I will be lenient with you."

When Trevor disappeared from sight, Meagan bowed her head and sobbed until two of Trevor's knights came to lead her away. What was she to do? She had to alert Edric, warning him to avoid the rebels. If he showed his face among them, he would die. But how could she deliver the news to him when she had been stripped of all rights, except to exist in the dark dungeon until Trevor decided what was to be done with her?

Meagan wiped away the tears that streamed down her cheeks and glanced about the cubicle that would be her home for more days than she cared to count. Despair swarmed about her as she sank down on the bench, the only stick of furniture in her cell. Although she had known that Trevor would never accept her explanation, she was still plagued with bitterness. If Trevor felt anything for her at all, he would have given her the benefit of the doubt, she told herself. But nay, she meant nothing to him, not in the ways that truly mattered. He had wed her, but he wanted nothing more than a warm body in his bed when darkness closed in on him. Meagan laughed humorlessly. Did she think she could change Trevor Burke? Had she been so vain to think that he might learn to love her as deeply as she loved him? Meagan scoffed disgustedly. She had been a blind, romantic fool, sacrificing herself for a man who was too cynical to realize that if it had not been for *her* he would be dead.

Grumbling at her stupidity, Meagan bounded to her feet to pace the confines of her cell. All this in the name of love? Meagan sniffed bitterly. Love was hell, and she was living in her privately furnished room in the eternal inferno. Trevor did not trust her. The pain that came with that knowledge was torment in itself. No amount of torture could bring more agony than this, she thought disheartenedly.

Meagan sank back on the bench and heaved a dismal sigh. If she could not save herself, she must at least find a way to help Edric. He *had* to know that Trevor was waiting for him to incriminate himself. And Trevor would be hungry for revenge, anxious to erase the name of Lowell from the face of the earth. Damn that man! Meagan cursed under her breath. She had lost what was left of her common sense when she allowed herself to fall in love with Trevor Burke. Yea, mayhap she *did* deserve this punishment, but *not* for the reasons Trevor had stashed her away while he devised some fiendish method of torture. Her crime was falling in love with the enemy, and she did not doubt for a minute that there was a roaring fire in hell where she would eternally roast for yielding to the temptation of surrendering to a Norman warrior whose heart was carved from granite.

Chapter 18

A week of deafening silence had passed in the musty dungeon, and Meagan had counted every crack in the mortar, hoping to preoccupy herself and salvage her sanity. Each morning when the guard brought her meager meal she had requested an audience with Conan, hoping he would listen to her pleas. But the guard had informed her that the ailing sage had been hibernating in his room since Trevor and his knights left for the palace in London.

Each time despair hovered about her, Meagan had shouted it away, refusing to allow her spirit to be broken. When Conan would not come to her, she pleaded with the guard to take her to the oracle, but he refused, informing her that Trevor had left strict orders not to grant Meagan the simplest of wishes.

Meagan jerked up her head when she heard the creak of the door and then breathed a thankful sigh when the aging sage hobbled into her dingy quarters and sank down on the bench beside her.

Conan wheezed and gasped to catch his breath after struggling down the steps. Finally he eased back against the wall to survey the disheveled beauty whose captivity had left her pale and listless. Gone were the vibrant sparkle in her eyes and the color of roses that once blossomed in her cheeks.

After dismissing the guard, Conan focused his full attention on Meagan. "I have heard Trevor's rendition of the incident that nearly cost him his life, and I assume you have summoned me to hear your version." He sighed heavily and then stared at the far corner of the cubicle. "I have had another dream that leads me to believe that fate commands you to cross paths with your husband once again. It will come before the fires of hell that will leave England a desolate waste."

Meagan was strangely drawn to the stooped sage. There had been a time when she saw him as the evil force who threatened her existence, but she had come to understand Conan and no longer feared him. He was merely a cautious man who was deeply devoted to his lord. The fact that he was willing to listen to her explanation encouraged her.

"I found that your vision materialized before my very eyes when I spied the former ruler of this fief among the troubadours who came to entertain us. Suddenly it all became painfully clear." Meagan inhaled a deep breath and then continued as Conan squirmed to resettle himself on the uncomfortable bench. "I realized that if I married Trevor his life would be in jeopardy. When I sought to deny the match I only angered Trevor. Once the vows were spoken I intended to plant another woman in his bed, hoping the rebels would think the marriage had not been consummated and that they would have nothing to gain by killing him. Granthum knew his claim on me and the land of Wessex would not stand up in William's court." Meagan dropped her head to study the stains on the front of her tunic. "The attempted murder failed, and my payment for intervening is Trevor's hatred. He refuses to believe that I had no part in the conspiracy."

"Why did you not confess your suspicions to him before the ceremony?" Conan questioned as his penetrating gaze anchored on Meagan. "He might have believed you if you had approached him on the matter instead of single-handedly thwarting their plans."

Meagan winced uncomfortably. Could she lie to the wise sage? She doubted it. Conan had the uncanny knack of forcing the truth from her lips with his probing stares, and Meagan was certain he could see through any lie she might voice.

"Because I sought to spare my brother," she confessed in a quiet tone. "I am not certain to what extent Edric is involved. That is why I beg you to grant my freedom. I must go to him. If Edric has the slightest connection with the rebels, Trevor will kill him. I must convince Edric that fighting the king means certain death."

"Did Trevor inform you that William has called in mercenaries to double his forces?" Conan queried.

Meagan nodded affirmatively. "Yea, he assured me that the Saxons would suffer for their lunacy."

Conan curled a gnarled finger beneath her chin, his expression somber. "Why did you save Trevor's life? You knew I could not call in your debt. You held the death sword in your hands. Your rebels would have met with success if you had not intervened, and you would have held great power in Wessex."

The words bubbled from her lips like a gushing volcano. "Because I love him more than I cherish the Saxon reign of England. If he had perished my heart would have withered and died like a fragile blossom scarred by a late spring frost. I did not want to fall in love with him, but I have. There could be no victory in his death."

"And what of your brother?" Conan questioned point-blank.

"He is all the family I have left. If Edric dies it will become an insurmountable obstacle between Trevor and me. Although I love Trevor, I could not live with the man who issued Edric's death warrant. I have sacrificed myself for my brother and for Trevor. 'Tis my wish that my secret be kept. I cannot condemn my brother as Trevor has condemned me until I know for certain that Edric is a willing participant in the rebellion."

Conan sat in silence for what seemed an eternity, and Meagan was left to wonder if he would be content to wait until Trevor returned to learn the baron's decision concerning his wife. She clutched his wrinkled hand and raised rueful eyes to Conan, beseeching him to grant her the opportunity to speak with Edric.

"Conan, you must release me. I will return to the dungeon

before Trevor is dismissed from his duties. I have spared your lord's life and I only ask for two weeks of freedom."

Still Conan did not speak. He grappled with Trevor's vengeful words, Meagan's confession, and his troubled dream. Finally, he nodded his consent.

"I have come to trust you, Meagan. Your deeds have proven your words. I believe you when you vow that you wish no harm to come to Trevor. But if you do not return to your cell in the allotted time, I will inform Trevor of our conversation . . . all of it. He too will know that your brother might have had a willing hand in the conspiracy."

Before Meagan realized what she had done, her arms flew about his bony shoulders and she was showering him with grateful kisses. Conan's hoarse chuckle rattled in his chest. It was the first time in years he had been set upon by a woman, and it had been an eternity since he had been stirred to laughter.

"Contain yourself, Meagan. I am an old man, unaccustomed to overzealous women. If you squeeze me in two I will be of no use to anyone."

Meagan planted a hasty peck right smack on his lips, and her eyes twinkled with happiness as she pried herself away from the man who had graciously granted her freedom.

"It seems to me that you have shed ten years when you smile. Perhaps you should make it a daily ritual."

Conan graced her with another gentle smile. For some reason they came easily when he was in Meagan's company. "You are the only one who can give me something to smile about. Guard your step, woman, and keep a constant vigil on your shadow. Now that I have grown fond of you, I do not wish to see you perish." Conan urged her to her feet and then placed a light kiss to her wrist. "God's speed, m'lady. . . ."

Meagan murmured a quiet "thank you" and then pounded on the door to summon the guard. After bounding up the steps she sought out Almund and then stepped back outside to inhale a breath of fresh air, clearing her senses of the dungeon's stench. When Almund brought out their mounts, Meagan stepped into the stirrup and then galloped away with Almund behind, praying she could reach Edric before he did something that might prove disastrous.

"Trevor?" William's insistent voice tapped at Trevor's troubled musings.

Trevor glanced up at the man who was ten years his senior and then smiled apologetically. "Forgive me. I am afraid you have caught me daydreaming."

"It seems to me that you have been doing a great deal of that of late," William taunted. "I suspect that your lady, so quickly wed and so hastily abandoned, preys heavily on your mind."

"Yea, that she does," Trevor murmured, but he did not divulge the reason for his preoccupation with his treacherous wife. He was too mortified to reveal her part in the conspiracy to his king.

During his journey to London, Trevor had been haunted by Meagan's luring vision. The wind had whispered her name to him as he rode, and he became increasingly aware of the color of her eyes each time he glanced skyward. Try as he might, he could not rout her from his mind. She had burrowed so deeply into his very core that each time he tried to discard a thought that centered around her it was like plucking a splinter from his soul, leaving it to bleed with yet another painful memory. He wanted to believe her story, and it disturbed him to think of her wasting away in solitary confinement, but she had yet to earn his trust.

"Lord Burke!" William impatiently drummed his fingers on the arm of his throne and cast the daydreaming knight a disappointed frown. "If you can spare me a few more minutes of your time you can be alone with your thoughts for the remainder of the day."

Trevor snapped to attention, determined not to provoke his king. William had a great deal on his mind, and Trevor had to concentrate on the outbreaks of rebellion that were threatening every corner of the kingdom. Although Trevor had warned the king of the possibility that southern rebels intended to use the same tactics to gain entrance to the

257

palace as they had used at Burke Castle, he had difficulty keeping up with the conversation.

Despite Trevor's obvious preoccupation, William had put his valuable knight in charge of an infantry that was to lay in waiting for the southern rebels, and Trevor was eager to meet the troubadours who had nearly cost him his life.

"I have just received word that the Danish fleet has abandoned the Saxons and intends to sail home. We finally hit upon a sizable sum to gain Danish loyalty to the Norman throne," he assured Trevor. "The Saxons have been left to their own devices and I intend to assure them that England is mine. My cousin, Edward, promised it to me while some of these lionhearted revolutionaries were still sitting in their mothers' laps." William gestured toward the corridor that led to Trevor's private quarters. "Be on your way, and send a courier to me the moment you have secured the South. I will leave an infantry here in London until I receive word from you, and then I will summon my entire strength to the North." When Trevor stood up to leave, William chuckled and then flashed the knight a wry smile. "With your mission accomplished, I suggest you return to Burke Castle before you pine away for this mysterious goddess whom you cannot seem to tear from your thoughts, even when you hold an audience with the king himself. I should like to meet this dazzling young woman one day, Trevor. I intend to see for myself whether 'tis sorceress or maid who has bewitched you."

The king might one day find that cunning young wench stashed in *his* dungeon, Trevor thought disgustedly as he marched up the stairs. William would be dismayed to learn that the lady in question had a rebellious streak a mile wide, and the king would be distraught to learn that Trevor had great difficulty keeping a firm rein on his high-spirited wife.

Trevor was between a rock and a hard spot. He could not inform William of his foolish marriage, and he was at a loss as to what to do with Meagan. But something had to be done, and he hoped to God he could find an answer before he faced her again.

*   *   *

Riding as if the devil were in hot pursuit, Meagan traveled to Lowell Castle in record time, arriving in the middle of the night. The moment she set foot in the fortress, she aimed herself toward Edric's solar and burst into the room with Lear one step behind her and Garda flapping her wings to keep herself perched on Meagan's shoulder.

"What in heaven's name . . ." Edric crowed as he bolted up in bed to shield Devona from the intruder.

"Get up, Edric. I demand to talk to you . . . now!" Meagan shouted. Her irritation had mounted during her harrowing ride, and she exploded the moment the lamplight dissolved the shadows from her brother's shocked face.

"Devona, perhaps you should leave us alone," Edric suggested.

"Nay, she stays. I want her to know what kind of weasel she has fallen in love with," Meagan spouted as she stalked up in front of her bare-chested brother.

"What happened to you?" Edric's bewildered gaze raced over Meagan's soiled, ragged garments, and then he focused on the angry frown that was stamped on her smudged face.

"'Tis not important. What matters is how deeply you are involved in the rebellion," she blurted out.

Edric sank back on his pillow and glanced hastily at Devona before turning his attention to Meagan. "Am I to assume that your husband is alive and well?"

"And irate," Meagan added bitterly. "He believes that I was in on the plot against his life."

Heaving a heavy sigh, Edric shot Devona a discreet glance and then admitted his part in the scheme. "I am deeply involved because you are my sister. Reid came to me with his plan to have you wed Burke. When I hesitated, Reid threatened me. He swore that he would dispose of me and come to rule our family's fief if I did not join the rebel cause. I had no choice but to comply, and I convinced myself that I had to make a stand with the Saxons." Edric inhaled a quick breath and then plunged on. "Reid is a bitter man. He would not allow me to straddle the fence the way Father did when Harold Godwinson asked for our support. Now you know the truth, Meagan. I would have been content to sit back and await the outcome of this rebellion, but Reid would not permit it. He means to rule land in England, one way or another."

Meagan sank down on the edge of the bed. "Will Reid march on London even though he did not secure Burke Castle?"

"Yea, Morcar and Edwin Leofric have summoned him to attack William's flank when the king marches North. Reid has ordered me to accompany him. I am to meet him at noon tomorrow."

"If Trevor learns that you are among the rebels you will die," Meagan informed him grimly. "I swore to Trevor that you knew nothing of this scheme, and if you are among the rebels he will know that I have lied to him. William has purchased a multitude of mercenaries to squelch the rebel uprisings. The Saxons will be greatly outnumbered, and they will commit suicide if they march against William."

Edric grimaced at the news. "And if I do not meet Reid at the appointed time he will come for me. He means to have you, Meagan, and he has made it clear that I will not stand in his way. If he cannot reclaim his former lands then he will dispose of me, wed you, and control Lowell Castle. Reid has every intention of ruling by your side, one way or another."

Meagan bolted up off the edge of the bed and hurried to the door. "Then I must go to him and dissuade him from this madness."

"Nay!" Edric wrapped the quilt about him and sat up in bed, his chin set in the Lowell family tradition of stubbornness. "I will not hide behind my sister. For God's sake, Meagan, grant me an ounce of pride if I am to meet my death, from one vindictive warrior or another," he snapped brusquely and then groaned as he collapsed in bed like a flower wilting from overexposure to the summer heat.

A sly smile pursed Devona's lips as she returned the wooden figurine to its place on the table beside the bed. "I prefer him not to be a dead hero," she murmured and then raised questioning eyes to Meagan, who was amazed that gentle Devona had clubbed Edric over the head, knocking him senseless. "What will you tell Granthum?"

Meagan hurried to fetch the ties from the drapery and

promptly bound Edric's hands and feet. "I will think of something," she muttered and then strained to ease Edric's limp body back into the middle of the bed. "You must not release my brother until I return. It will be difficult to keep him prisoner in his own room, but it must be done."

Devona's eyes twinkled devilishly as she ripped the hem from the sheet and stuffed it in his sagging mouth. "You need not fret over Edric. I will see to it that he ventures no farther than his chamber door." Her expression sobered as Meagan pivoted on her heels and strode away. "Take care of yourself, Meagan. My prayers will be with you."

Nodding mutely, Meagan rushed to her own room to freshen up and change into decent clothing. In less than an hour she returned to the stable to fetch a fresh horse and further instruct Almund that Edric was not to leave the fortress, in case Devona could not keep him confined to his room. Although Almund protested Meagan's second journey, she refused to allow him to accompany her on the next leg of the trip. It would be best to go alone. If she found it necessary to lie her way across England, she preferred not to have an accomplice.

With her jaw set in grim determination, Meagan reined her steed toward the forest, hoping the rebels had not changed their campsite, the one she had stumbled upon while she was fleeing from Trevor. . . .

The thought of him sent a pain stabbing at her heart. Where was he? Had the king ordered him to the battlefield? Meagan squeezed her eyes shut, praying that Trevor was safe. She would sell her soul to ensure that he came to no harm . . . even if it meant facing that maniac, Reid Granthum. She had detected that demented look in his eyes as he scurried from Trevor's solar. Meagan shuddered, remembering how close he had come to disposing of Trevor. The last thing she wanted was to confront Reid Granthum, but it seemed she had little choice.

Intent on her purpose, Meagan picked her way through the forest and then drew her steed to a halt. Her gaze swept over a hundred shocked faces as she swung from the saddle and weaved her way through the crowd to face the rebel leader. Meagan tensed when Reid Granthum's hazel eyes raked her up and down and then focused on her weary face.

"What are you doing here?" he demanded to know. "And where is Edric? Does he intend to sit this war out as well?" The underbite of sarcasm in his voice made Meagan jump as if she had been snakebit.

"My brother is gravely ill and is confined to his bed. A servant attends him night and day," Meagan explained, prefabricating the truth. Edric would be sick when he awoke to find that Meagan had come in his stead, and it was true that Devona was keeping a constant vigil on him. Edric was indeed confined to his room since he was bound, gagged, and strapped in bed.

Reid let his breath out in a rush. "Then we are left with no choice but to ride without him. I should have known the poltroon would find a way to back out of his duties."

"Reid, this is utter madness," Meagan declared, gathering courage with each word she spoke. "The king has sent for reinforcements, and he is prepared to defend the throne. My husband has gone to London, and I have no doubt that he anticipates a rebel attack from the south. You cannot gain entrance to the palace as troubadours now that Trevor knows of your tactics. If you advance toward the palace you will be walking into a trap. Do you not know a lost cause when you see one?"

His fingers bit into Meagan's arm as he drew her close, his lips curling menacingly. "Did you tell that bastard husband of yours of the plot to take Burke Castle?"

"I did not have to. He knew we were once betrothed, and it did not take him long to realize that the attack on his life was the work of a vengeful man who was part of a conspiracy," Meagan assured him, grimacing as his fingers cut off the circulation in her arm. "You cannot have what you want. William is too strong to fall beneath a handful of rebels, and Trevor still rules Wessex."

His face was only inches from hers, his eyes sparkling with both anger and desire. "You were promised to me, Meagan, and one day you will truly be mine. I hold a personal vendetta against your husband, and the time will come when

262

I will slay him. Do not forget that. You are Saxon and you and I were meant to rule, side by side."

Meagan twisted free, repulsed by his touch. "You live in the past, Reid. England has changed, and it will never be the same as it once was. And I have changed as well. I am not the young child who was forced to do her father's bidding. You and I are much too different to rule together." She looked him square in the eye, her expression grave. "William means to crush all rebel uprisings, sparing no one who stands in his way. You cannot defeat him, and if you march on London it will be suicide for you and your men. I wish to allow Saxon tradition to flourish as best it can beneath Norman rule. 'Tis the only way we can survive."

As Meagan pivoted to leave, his hand snaked out to haul her back to his side. "Nothing has changed," he assured her gruffly. "We will march on London and you will ride by my side as proof of your family's loyalty to the Saxon rebellion." A sardonic smile lifted one corner of his mouth as he drew her against him. "Your Norman husband will know that he cannot have what once was and always will be mine. He has stripped me of all else, but he will not have you."

She stared at him bug-eyed. "You are mad!" she railed. "I am another man's wife. Even if you did slay him, I would not wed you."

Reid chained her in his arms, infuriated by her insult. "One day you will beg to claim the title of Lady Granthum. Your Norman bastard has not taken you to bed. I know. I was in his room and he slept alone. You have no reason to be loyal to him. You were betrothed to me and I am the only man who has the right to bed you."

Flesh cracked against flesh as Meagan left her handprint on his cheek. "You have no rights in England. You were banished years ago. I will not accept you, Reid Granthum. You are wasting your time. Look elsewhere for a wife," Meagan hissed furiously.

"Haughty bitch!" Reid growled as he shoved her ahead of him. "Perhaps now is the time to prove who is your master. You have grown much too independent and outspoken. 'Tis time you were taught your place."

263

"Better men than you have sought to subdue me," Meagan scoffed as she wheeled to face the ruthless expression that was stamped on his weather-beaten features. "And as you can see, 'twas a waste of time."

When Reid raised his hand to strike her, his stepbrother wedged himself between them. "'Tis not the time to prove your power over the lady," Marston Pearce reminded him. "We must ride. Morcar expects us in London."

Reid muttered disgustedly. He had waited an eternity to possess this lovely vixen, but he was forced to bide his time once again. Soon, he assured himself. Soon he would have this blond-haired hellion under thumb, and he would return to claim the Granthum lands of which he had been stripped.

"You will ride beside me," he ordered as he roughly yanked Meagan toward her mount and deposited her in the saddle. His eyes narrowed to thin, hard slits. "Do not think you can escape me. I will hunt you down and drag you back with me."

It was Meagan's turn to glare flaming daggers at his chain-mail shirt. Though she itched to curse him, she clamped her mouth shut and kept the silence. Her gaze shifted to the somber faces of the rebels who gathered their weapons and saddled their steeds. The furious red in her cheeks evaporated when her eyes came to rest on Daralis, who was grinning wickedly at her.

Lord, Meagan had forgotten about the murdering wench, but now she was painfully aware of her existence and the threat she presented. Meagan would have to keep a close watch on her shadow, as Conan suggested. The smug expression on Daralis's face spelled trouble, and Meagan could not help but wonder if the wench was entertaining the thought of trying to dispose of her a second time.

Chapter 19

The sun drooped lower in the sky, and Trevor viewed the twilight with finely tempered patience. He had hoped the rebel band would appear in the distance and that the battle would begin. He hungered for combat, anything to take his mind off Meagan. It had been a week since he left Burke Castle and he could not rout the thoughts of Meagan milling about her dungeon cell. She thrived in the wilds, and the vision of her withering away without fresh air and sunlight singed his conscience. Although she deserved her imprisonment, he still harbored a weakness for her. The blue-eyed firebrand was in his blood. He had even prayed that her brother would not be among the rebels who marched toward London and that she had spoken the truth about her lack of involvement in the conspiracy, but he could not truly believe her until he had seen the proof with his own eyes.

"M'lord, I have seen the cloud of dust to the south," Yale Randolph reported, drawing Trevor from his silent reverie.

Trevor peered up at his newly appointed knight from where he lay stretched out in the grass. "Did you venture close enough to count their strength?"

Yale ducked his head, feeling the utter fool. "Nay, m'lord. I did not think of it."

"You did not think of it?" Trevor mimicked sarcastically and then focused his piercing golden eyes on the embarrassed knight. "Do not return to me until you have made certain that 'tis the rebels who approach and not a herd of stampeding cattle that have been frightened from the field. Perhaps I was a bit hasty in granting you knighthood." His condemning tone slashed across Yale like a double-edged sword that was meant to slice the young man's dignity. Trevor was thorough with his intimidation. "A knight must learn to use his head, as well as his lance and shield. It seems we have overlooked that particular facet of your training."

"Yea, m'lord." Yale blushed up to his eyebrows and then quickly took his leave, wishing he had had the good sense to scout out the cause of the rolling dust instead of dashing back to the baron without a complete report.

When the young knight thundered off down the road, Trevor rolled to his feet and paced back and forth beside his stallion. He was anxious to see this matter settled and to be relieved of his duties. William had informed him that his service would be cut short if he squelched the uprising. With the strength of the mercenaries that marched to Stafford, Trevor and his knights would only be needed to restore order to the lands of Wessex. That he could accomplish from Burke Castle, he mused.

"I wonder if the worried frown you are wearing is the result of the upcoming skirmish or your lingering concern for your lady," Ragnar Neville murmured as he watched Trevor wear out the grass with his constant pacing.

Trevor's raven head jerked up to flash the smirking knight a disgusted glower. "Keep your speculations to yourself," he growled, his expression sour enough to leave a honeybee puckering, even while it feasted on nectar.

"You suspect that lovely goddess of wrongdoing," Ragnar predicted, holding his shield before him to ward off Trevor's scorching glare. "I think you have misjudged the lady. Yea, I will admit that she is a feisty one, but I cannot think that she has betrayed you."

"The evidence is not in her favor," Trevor scowled. "Women cannot be trusted. They are whimsical creatures who are easily swayed when they are grasping for security. If you knew the truth as I have seen it, you would also condemn her."

Ragnar's shoulder lifted noncommittally. "Mayhap, but it

appeared to me that the lady had a great deal of respect for you. Could it be that you *want* to believe the worst about her? Do you somehow feel threatened by her?" he prodded.

"I want no such thing and I am certainly not threatened by a mere woman!" Trevor hooted like a disturbed owl.

Trevor had been forced to guard his tongue when the king taunted him for behaving like a lovesick pup, but he did not have to stand there and listen to Ragnar ridicule him for stashing Meagan in the dungeon for crimes the bulky knight seriously doubted that she had committed.

Ragnar did a double take, bewildered by Trevor's vehement denial. "My, but we have become touchy of late," he smirked.

There had been a time when Trevor could laugh and joke about practically any subject, but since he had wed that stunning siren, he stalked around with a permanent frown plastered on his face, and it took very little to provoke him. Trevor had turned over a new leaf after his marriage, and it had not been an improvement, Ragnar thought to himself. Trevor had been barking at his men, biting off their ears as between-meal appetizers, and sulking about camp as if he carried a painful thorn in his paw.

"I am not sensitive!" Trevor bellowed, his voice booming about camp to ricochet off the trees.

"You need not chew my head off," Ragnar snorted. "I only sought to become your sounding board, to help you ease your obvious frustration by discussing your troubled thoughts. But if you do not wish to talk of Lady Meagan then I will hold my tongue."

"I would appreciate that," Trevor bit off, his tone threaded with sarcasm.

At the moment, Meagan was a sore spot, and Trevor had been sufficiently reminded that she was a tender wound that had not properly healed. He was still nursing his bruises after William had taunted him, and he was in no mood to pursue the subject with Ragnar, not until he had gained control of his chaotic emotions. When he could speak of Meagan in a calm, rational manner, he would be only too happy to air his emotions. But not now, not yet, Trevor told himself.

"The lady is none of your concern, and at the moment she is not mine either. I have pressing matters on my mind."

Trevor pricked up his ears to the sound of hooves pounding the ground and then strode toward the approaching knight. "What news have you brought this time, Yale?" he demanded impatiently.

Yale glanced nervously about him, refusing to meet Trevor's stony gaze. "'Tis the rebels." The young man swallowed the lump that had collected in his throat and forced himself to continue. "They number one hundred . . . and one."

A bemused frown plowed Trevor's brow. "So Edric Lowell rides with them," he guessed and then swore under his breath. Damnation, he had prayed that Meagan had not lied to him.

"Nay, m'lord. I could not make out his shield among the revolutionists." Yale squirmed uneasily in his saddle and then yelped when Trevor grabbed hold of him and yanked him from his perch, twisting his chain-mail shirt around his neck so tightly that Yale had difficulty breathing.

"Do not ply me with riddles, lad. Out with it! Tell me who is the one you have singled out from the rebel troops," Trevor ordered, a distinctly unpleasant edge on his voice.

"Your lady, m'lord," Yale squeaked.

A growl of pure rage rumbled through the trees as Trevor shoved the young knight away, leaving him sprawling beneath his horse. "As I live and breathe!" he roared, sending the birds to their wings from the branches above him. "I left her in prison, but even stone walls cannot hold her. I asked for the truth and she betrays me with lies!" He spun around to snarl at Ragnar, who paled beneath his tan when Trevor's livid glare pelleted over him. "Do you still intend to defend my deceptive wife?" Trevor laughed bitterly. "So, 'twas not Edric whom I had to fear, but the lady herself."

Again Trevor was hounded by excruciating emotions that rose from deep inside him and shot through his soul before channeling through every nerve in his body, leaving him trembling in frustrated fury. His jaw clenched, his features as hard as granite as he stepped into the stirrup and shouted orders to his men.

He could barely contain the tormenting sensations that besieged him. It was as Conan had forewarned. No physical pain could touch this deep sense of hurt that tore at his soul. To care for Meagan and to know that her feelings for him were so fueled with bitterness that she would take arms against him, openly defying him, humiliating him in front of his own army.... Trevor swore under his breath and squeezed back the image that leaped into his mind. Yea, his angel had been a disguised devil, one who sought to destroy him. Meagan had played a treacherous game with him. It had all been a carefully calculated act, he realized. She had set him up for the biggest fall he had ever taken. No battle had taken its toll on Trevor, not like this, he reminded himself. Meagan had been his one weakness, his Achilles' heel. But she would pay for mortifying him, Trevor promised himself. She would pay with her life, that which he had given back to her against Conan's warning. God, how could he have been so blind? Trevor forced back his spiteful thoughts and prepared himself for battle, knowing this was the one war he could win and also lose. He was about to relinquish something that had once been precious and dear to him. Trevor would be forced to kill the only woman who had managed to burrow her way into his heart. Now he despised her with the same amount of passion that he had often experienced when he made love to that captivating vixen. Trevor grunted disgustedly, realizing what a fine line separated love and hate. And hate her he did, he told himself. She was his enemy and always had been. He had just been too infatuated with that lively bundle of spirit to realize she was a dyed-in-the-wool rebel.

After sending one division of armed warriors to the east, Trevor directed a second troop to the west. With Ragnar at his side he gouged his steed, mentally preparing himself for a headlong clash with the rebels. Trevor was overwhelmed by such a fierce sense of betrayal and humiliation that he hungered to lash out at the entire world to appease the hurt that consumed him. Part of him had perished even before he ventured into battle. Knowing that Meagan had taken a stand against him was the epitome of disillusionment, and his emotions were eating him alive. He would have his revenge, he promised himself as he reined Poseidon toward the approaching army.

A lump of fear constricted in Meagan's throat when she spied the wave of soldiers rolling across the countryside to surround them. The rebels were trapped and Reid had refused to heed her warning. Had it not been for Marston Pearce, Meagan doubted that she would still be alive. Reid had severely beaten her when she had brought his idiocy to his attention the previous night. At first she had attempted to reason with him, but he was so enmeshed with hatred and bitterness that he refused to relinquish his cause. If Marston had not dragged Reid off of her, Meagan would have perished beneath his punishing blows. Her body was a mass of bruises, and her face was discolored. Every muscle in her body had complained when she pulled into the saddle to follow the demented leader into slaughter.

Meagan tensed when she peered across the distance that separated the Normans and Saxons. Her apprehensive gaze locked with the swarthy warrior who was perched on his coal black stallion. The hatred Meagan saw burning in those flaming amber eyes was her undoing. If looks could kill she would have already been a casualty of war. She had hoped that Trevor would not be among the Norman resistance, but it seemed she was not to be granted the smallest wish to spare her this agony. She knew what he was thinking, and she ached to explain, but he would never listen. She prayed that death would come quickly, knowing that Trevor's intent was to see her fall beneath his sword.

The muscular black stallion came to a halt as his master drew his helmet over his face, and Meagan felt a surge of relief, thankful she would not be forced to look him in the eye when he thundered toward her. Her thoughts were jolted when Reid reached over to rein his steed close to hers.

"Bid farewell to your husband. When the dust clears, his

life will be spilling on this battlefield," Reid vowed as he adjusted his helmet.

Trevor did not miss a single move Meagan made, and he suffered another heart-wrenching pang of fury when he spied Reid Granthum's shield. Never had he experienced anything as agonizing as the gnawing torment that seemed to eat away at him, bit by excruciating bit. She had made a complete fool of him, and he begrudged his weakness for Meagan. He *had* to give her up. He could never take her back now. He could never forgive her this last humiliating betrayal. Not only had Meagan plotted to have him murdered and escaped from his prison, but she had offered herself to Granthum. Trevor gritted his teeth, loathing the thought of Meagan lying in Granthum's arms, responding to his caresses as easily as she had surrendered to Trevor's touch. But what had he expected, he asked himself acrimoniously. Meagan had assured him that he would not be the last man to share her passions. Now he knew exactly what she had meant by that taunting remark.

The immediate world was ablaze with furious red as Trevor lowered his lance, itching to ram the full eight feet of the weapon through Granthum's heart and then turn on his infidel wife. Trevor nudged his steed and Poseidon lunged forward, his nostrils flaring as he charged toward the gray stallion that carried Reid Granthum into battle.

Metal ground against his lance as he speared Granthum in the ribs, momentarily knocking his foe off balance. But Reid clutched the reins and straightened himself in the saddle as he wheeled around to face his enemy and drag his lance back into position for another run at Trevor.

Meagan watched in horror as the two men charged at each other again. This time it was Trevor who careened in the saddle. The sound of shrill whinnies and groaning men reached her ears, and Meagan glanced about her to see hundreds of warriors battling for survival while yet another infantry of Normans swarmed up behind them, leaving the rebels no hope of retreat.

Her attention swung back to Reid and Trevor when she heard the clank of metal and simultaneous groans from the

271

warring men. Their lances had met their intended marks, knocking both men to the ground. Meagan grimaced as she watched Trevor roll to his feet, favoring his tender leg. Within a split second Reid gathered his legs beneath him, discarded his lance and grasped his battle ax, the sharp-edged blade glistening in the sunlight as he moved deliberately toward Trevor. Meagan could not contain her frightened cry as Reid howled like a banshee and swung his weapon to catch Trevor on the shoulder. Blood seeped from the seam of his armor as he sidestepped and then pounced on Reid before he could brace himself for the oncoming attack of Trevor's battle-ax. Wounded, Reid growled in pain, but in less than a heartbeat he advanced on his enemy, refusing to admit defeat to his sister's murderer and his betrothed's husband, a man who had stripped him of his lands and dignity and had stolen all that he held dear. Like a snarling panther, Reid rushed at Trevor, mad with fury and thirsting for blood.

With the quickness of a coiled snake, Trevor clutched the iron-headed mace that dangled from his belt, circling it through the air, waiting for the opportune moment to level a blow that would relieve Reid of what was left of his demented senses. But Reid was a skilled warrior, one who was as adept at hand-to-hand combat as Trevor was. He quickly braced his shield to ward off the blow Trevor directed at him. A pained grunt tumbled from his curled lips as the spiked mace slammed against his shield and jarred his arm, sending him wobbling backwards.

Meagan had seen enough. The bloody battle and the cries of wounded men sickened her. Reining her steed to the south she weaved her way through the warriors who were too busy with defending themselves to pursue her. As she galloped across the meadow, tears misted her eyes, eyes that had seen enough pain and death in a few short minutes to last her a lifetime.

Although Trevor was aware of her flight, his enemy did not allow him to pursue her. Reid grasped his battle-ax with both hands and charged like a mad bull. Trevor ducked away and then spun around to face the second attack, poised with sword in hand, his gaze glued to the one vulnerable spot beneath Reid's breastplate.

Reid sucked in his breath and then fell to his knees when Trevor withdrew the sword that had made lethal contact. The useless shield tumbled to the ground as he braced himself wtih one hand and clutched his wound with the other.

His pained gaze lifted to see Trevor looming over him, his broad chest heaving, his eyes glazed with a hatred to match Reid's. A bitter smile found the corner of Reid's lips as he focused his blurred gaze on the Norman warrior.

"Not even my death will bring you victory, Norman bastard," he hissed venomously. "You may have killed my sister. You may long rule my demesne, but Meagan will never be yours. She rode by my side because she is *my* woman. Remember that, Burke."

As Reid crumbled into a lifeless heap, Trevor stared down at him and gnashed his teeth together. Reid's dying words confirmed what Trevor had feared. Meagan had become Reid's mistress, solidifying her allegiance to the rebel cause, defying the wedding vows she had taken while she stood at Trevor's side. Mutinous thoughts whipped through his head as he stalked to his steed and vaulted into the saddle to give chase to his disloyal wife.

Poseidon quickly closed the distance between him and the slower steed who galloped ahead of him. When Meagan heard the thunder of hooves she turned wild eyes to the bareheaded warrior who galloped toward her like a vindictive demon who was hell-bent on revenge. Meagan knew that he believed she had betrayed him, and a sense of hopelessness overwhelmed her. What purpose would be served to attempt escape? Trevor would hunt her down and dispose of her in time. Why prolong the inevitable? It was a good day to die, and with her would travel the dark secret of a love that could never be and the knowledge that her brother was forced to aid Reid Granthum in his plot to overthrow Lord Burke.

Meagan pulled back on the reins, bringing her winded steed to a screeching halt. Bravely, she maneuvered the horse around to face Trevor's murderous glare.

Trevor whipped his bloody sword from it scabbard, laid it against Meagan's neck, and then surveyed the bruises on her face. His lips curled sardonically as his angry gaze made fast work of raking her trim body to see the other discolorations on her wrists. "I envy the man who marred those delicate features. I assume your rebel lover has left his mark as proof of ownership."

Tilting a swollen chin, Meagan looked him straight in the eye. "Reid Granthum was not my lover," she insisted. "If you were not so blind with rage you would know better than to make such a preposterous accusation. I sustained these bruises because I dared to speak out against Reid, assuring him that he was leading his men to slaughter. I traveled to the rebel camp, hoping to dissuade him from blundering into battle. He forced me to ride with the rebels, knowing how it would infuriate you to see your wife standing on the opposite side of the battlefield."

"Granthum's dying words conflict with your confession," Trevor sneered as he moved closer, the point of his sword pricking her neck as he stilled her movements. "You have deceived me so often that I can no longer distinguish between truth and lies. Pray, tell me how you escaped the dungeon? Did you seduce the guard or did you murmur your incantations to transform yourself into a snake and then slither to your freedom?" The vicious bite of his tone made Meagan wince, but only slightly. One false move and Trevor would slit her throat.

Meagan refused to answer. She would not drag Conan into this. The poor man suffered enough without having to deal with Trevor's wrath. He would be furious to know that Conan had granted her freedom, even if it had been temporary.

"No clever retort? No adamant denial?" Trevor mocked dryly.

"Nay, m'lord." Meagan sighed defeatedly, her eyes swimming with tears. "Do with me what you will. I care not. You have always taken the word of others over mine. If there is not one shred of trust between us, then we have nothing."

274

Trevor measured her with keen golden eyes. Meagan did not seem the feisty young woman he had continually battled. The previous moment he would have cheerfully choked her, or worse. But now he was at a loss to deal with her. If she had fought him, he would have felt justified when he cut her down with his blade. And that had been his intention when he thundered after her. She deserved to die, didn't she? Well, didn't she, he asked himself harshly. Conan had once warned him that the day would come when he would be forced to take the life he had graciously returned to her when she was poisoned. Could he bury his sword in her heart and watch her crumble to the ground? Could he kill the only woman who had ever touched his heart?

Growling to himself, Trevor clutched Meagan's reins and led her back to find that the Normans had sent what was left of the rebel troops scampering into the woods. As they approached, Ragnar glanced up into Meagan's bruised, tearstained face, still unsure that she could be a willing participant in battle. A wave of pity washed over him and he could not help but offer her a sympathetic smile.

"M'lady, it grieves me that you were forced to watch this massacre. I . . ."

"You will take the prisoners to the palace," Trevor broke in. "I have another obligation that demands immediate attention. Disband the troops when you have completed your task. The king has requested that we secure Wessex and wait further word on the uprisings in the North."

When Trevor yanked on the reins to lead her south, Meagan clutched the horse's mane to keep her seat and then glared holes through Trevor's chain-mail shirt, but she refused to speak. She would rot away in Trevor's dungeon, endure the fiendish torture he devised, or even face death if she must, but at least Edric would be spared and the name of Lowell would not be wiped from the earth.

Suddenly a thought struck her, and she glanced over her shoulder, wondering what had become of Daralis. She had seen nothing of the wench since they had confronted the Norman knights. Her astute gaze scanned the surroundings. Had Daralis spirited off into the woods at the first sign of

275

danger? Meagan laughed bitterly to herself. Daralis would not have the opportunity to dispose of her a second time. Trevor would see to it himself.

Meagan slumped back in the saddle and heaved a weary sigh, allowing Trevor to lead her away. She would not attempt to flee from him again. Besides, where could she go? Trevor despised her, and he would tear the world upside down to find her. Even the convent would not suffice as a refuge, Meagan thought disheartenedly. Trevor would storm the walls in order to drag her back again. Yea, it was useless to run this time, she assured herself dismally. Trevor intended to see her suffer, and nothing could save her from him.

Chapter 20

It was long after dark when Trevor stopped for the night and for that Meagan was grateful. The past two days had cost her most of her strength, and nausea had flooded over her, draining her failing spirits. For the life of her she could not fathom what illness had befallen her. Perhaps it was only despair that caused such side effects, she told herself. But knowing the cause was not a cure. Meagan felt miserable, and she refused food when Trevor gathered berries and edible weeds for nourishment.

"Do you intend to starve to death and rob me of the pleasure of torturing you for betraying me?" Trevor snorted derisively when Meagan set aside the meager meal and stared ruefully up at the stars.

When Trevor threw down the gauntlet, Meagan did not rise to the taunt. Instead, she curled up on the ground and closed her eyes. "Being with you is torture in itself," she murmured defeatedly. "You need not look further for some form of torment."

Did she despise him so much that she could not abide the sight of him? She had insisted that she had no part in the battle, but if that was true, why hadn't she attempted to return to his good graces? Trevor threw up his hands in disgust. This woman was a termagant, spiting him at every turn, showing her face in the most unexpected places.

"Woman, what do you expect of me? I am at my wit's end," Trevor growled. "You seduce me with erotic dances and then you attempt to serve me up to your jealous lover. You take Granthum's side in battle and then you ask me to believe that you have been loyal to me when all the evidence points to condemnation. How many times must a man forgive his deceitful wife? What do you want from me, Meagan?"

"Something you cannot give," she whispered. "But at least grant me a little peace. I will be better equipped to fence words with you on the morrow."

Trevor heaved a frustrated sigh as he watched Lear snuggle up beside her. How that mongrel could remain devoted to such a scheming wench was beyond Trevor. He was hopelessly devoted to Meagan, fetching food that she would not eat, following her into battle, sleeping by her side to give her warmth. Trevor muttered under his breath and then sank down on his haunches to munch on the wild berries he had collected. What was he to do with Meagan? Surely Conan would have an answer, he thought hopefully. He would speak with his sage. Conan would advise him, and this time he would listen to the aging seer, Trevor promised himself. It was obvious that Trevor could not trust his own mind when he dealt with Meagan. She was his only weakness, one that confused his thoughts and would not allow him to see clearly. Yea, he would consult with Conan, Trevor decided as he stretched out on the grass, only to be hounded by dreams of the enchanting nights he had held Meagan in his arms.

The dawn did not give Meagan the renewed strength she hoped she would enjoy when she lifted heavy eyelids and peered up to see Trevor towering over her. Meagan groaned miserably as Trevor pulled her to her feet. She felt like death warmed over on a dim flame. Her body rebelled against movement, and her stomach flip-flopped as if a collection of butterflies were performing aerial maneuvers inside of it.

Trevor was baffled by Meagan's listlessness and by her pale complexion. Dark circles hung beneath her dull eyes, and the only color in her face was that of the fading bruises that marred her cheeks. She voiced no complaint and asked no questions of him. That disturbed Trevor. He had anticipated another round of arguments and claims of innocence from Meagan, but she said very little as Trevor led her across the countryside. Even when he flung an insult, she did not respond with a saucy retort. She just sat there on her steed, staring off into space. Trevor was left to converse with his horse, and Poseidon was no more receptive or gregarious than Meagan in her present mood.

During her silent deliberations, Meagan began to understand the cause of her discomfort. The newfound knowledge sent her spirits plunging to the depths of despair. She carried Trevor's child, but he would never believe that. He had assured her in the beginning that she would never bear his bastard child. And she would not, she reminded herself, laughing silently at the irony. The child would be born in wedlock . . . if she lived that long, but it would not be accepted as Trevor's flesh and blood since he believed himself unable to sire a child. As if Trevor did not mistrust her enough already, she would have another burden to bear. What would become of her and her child? The possibilities were too depressing to even consider. And so she didn't. Meagan merely followed where Trevor led her, wondering how everything could have turned out so wrong when she had only attempted to pursue a righteous course. It was as Conan had predicted, she reminded herself miserably. She was destined to suffer. Fate had glared down upon her, and the most eloquent or convincing speech would not raise Trevor's low opinion of her. Trevor glared at her as if she were something that had slithered out from under a rock, and his tone was always laced with contempt.

When nightfall closed in on them once again, Meagan sent Lear to hunt, deciding that she must force herself to eat for the baby's sake. The thought of food nauseated her, but she was determined to choke down whatever game Lear retrieved for her. A faint smile brimmed her lips when she spied the dog loping through the underbrush with Garda fluttering above him. Meagan had been certain she had seen the last of her falcon during the battle when the fowl had

279

flown from her perch to soar above the clouds.

Meagan lifted her arm to summon the falcon and then reached out to stroke Garda's neck when she settled herself on the leather strap Meagan wore on her wrist.

A disgusted frown plowed Trevor's dark brows as he watched Meagan bestow her affection on her long-lost buzzard that seemed to be silently mocking Trevor. Damned bird, Trevor grumbled under his breath as he kindled the fire to ward off the evening chill. He would have stood a better chance of winning Meagan's undying devotion if he had been born with wings, feathers, and a pair of clawed feet. Meagan had a soft spot in her heart for creatures of the wild, but she had little use for men . . . one in particular, he mused sourly.

The sound of voices in the distance drew Trevor's attention, and his head swiveled around to scout out the noises. Meagan raised her eyes in question as Trevor backed away from the campfire and untied his steed.

"Where are you going?" she demanded to know.

Trevor gestured to the west. "Someone approaches. No doubt they have seen the smoke from our fire."

"Do you intend to leave me here to fend for myself?" Meagan's voice hinted at incredulity.

A devilish grin dangled from one corner of his sensuous mouth. "My dear lady, you can enlist the aid of your falcon and shepherd if our guests are unfriendly. And if they cannot serve your purpose, I will become their reinforcement."

Meagan raked the handsome warrior up and down and then sniffed distastefully. "I would imagine your true purpose is to hide and watch these intruders abuse me."

"Why, m'lady, how could you think such a thing when you have always been so quick to defend me?" he queried, his tone dripping with sarcasm. "Have you ever called me vile names, ordered your mutt on me, arranged my murder, fought on the opposite side of the battle . . ."

"Then hide, cowardly ogre," Meagan spat at him. "I have no wish for you to come to my assistance if you think me such a beast."

"M'lady, 'tis my honest belief that *you* are more the

dragon than I am," Trevor smirked and then gracefully bowed out, leaving Meagan to face four shabbily dressed men who picked their way through the underbrush.

Meagan waited tensely as the four men paused before her, their gazes hungrily working their way over her shapely body and then returning to her face after what seemed a humiliating eternity. Four pair of eyes focused on Meagan, leaving her feeling as though she had been stripped naked.

"Would you care to sit and rest?" Meagan questioned nervously, knowing that was the last thing these surly knaves had on their minds. Their intentions were written on their faces in bold letters and Meagan did not like what she read in their expressions.

"What is a pretty little thing like you doing out here alone?" one of the men questioned as he swaggered closer.

Meagan gulped hard, her mind racing through a myriad of excuses, hoping to land one that might seem believable. "I have run away from my husband," she managed to say. Her heart was pounding so wildly that she could barely draw a breath.

Baxter Landry squinted to make out the telltale signs of bruises on Meagan's face. "A brute, was he?"

"Yea, very much so," Meagan hastily affirmed. "I am traveling to my brother's home to take refuge. I could pay you well to see me home." She hoped that Trevor did not miss the exchange of conversation from his cowardly hiding place among the bushes. The lout! It would serve him right if she could persuade these vagabonds to accompany her.

A wide grin stretched across Baxter's woolly face as he stroked his unruly beard. "I think we can come to some sort of arrangement." He craned his neck to peer at his three companions, who were still ogling Meagan. "Although we are badly in need of coins, we would seek another form of payment as well." Baxter strutted toward her and Meagan retreated a step when he reached for her.

"Keep your filthy hands off me!" she hissed. "I offer only money, nothing more."

"Then we shall take what we want, woman," Baxter chuckled as he lunged at Meagan, chaining her in his arms.

"Lear!" Meagan shrieked the moment before his hard mouth descended on hers, stripping her breath from her lungs.

The shepherd sprang at Meagan's attacker, burying his sharp fangs in Baxter's leg while Garda pelleted him with painful pecks, threatening to rip off his ears. Although Meagan managed to writhe free of Baxter's grisly embrace, she was assaulted by one of the other men, who grabbed a handful of her tunic and ripped it from her breasts. Meagan tried to cover herself, but she was forced to the ground, the man's heavy body crushing into hers, his hot mouth plundering her lips.

Meagan could hear Lear's vicious growl as he sought to tear Baxter limb from limb and Garda's furious squawk as she dived down to heckle the man who sought to rape Meagan. Where was Trevor, Meagan wondered frantically. Was he delighting in watching her suffer at the hands of these grimy thieves?

Suddenly, the man who was trying to maul her scrambled to his feet when he saw the dark knight astride his stallion. Trevor looked like the devil himself, springing from the jaws of hell, as he leaped from his concealment with a full coat of armor. Growling like an enraged panther, he charged into their midst, swinging his deadly mace. Each blow he inflicted on his victims brought howls of pain, and their shrieks frightened the horses, causing them to flee into the woods.

Meagan propped herself up on an elbow to watch her knight in black armor send the outcasts of society scurrying into the woods to lick their wounds. Gathering her wobbly legs beneath her, she shook her head to clear her senses, but before she could get her bearings, Trevor wheeled around and galloped toward her. He leaned out from the saddle, scooped her off the ground, and deposited her in front of him. Meagan would have preferred to present her back to him, but Trevor had left her straddling Poseidon, facing him. His touch branded her with fire as they picked their way through the forest to escape the thieves. Meagan pushed aside the arousing sensations that threatened to distract her. She was furious with Trevor for delaying his entrance, and

282

she itched to knock his helmet off his shoulders, head and all.

When she tilted a proud chin and glanced sideways, Trevor smirked sarcastically. "Is this to be my payment for aiding a damsel in distress? I had expected to be showered with grateful kisses."

"Your grand entrance nearly cost me a tumble in the grass," she snapped tersely and then covered herself as best she could with the remains of her shredded tunic when Trevor's hungry eyes dipped below her neck. "You certainly took your own sweet time in arriving. Why did you tarry? I thought your intent was to see me tortured by *your* hands, not those of some scraggly scavenger from the forest."

"I thought you might enjoy your tête-à-tête," Trevor taunted as he removed his helmet to feast upon the display of creamy skin that rose above the torn fabric of her bodice. "You seem to have become less particular about who samples your charms since our wedding night."

Her reply to his biting insult was a sound slap on the cheek. Meagan glared at him and then wormed for freedom, but Trevor kept her chained in his arms, his hard thighs pressing boldly against hers, igniting fires that the entire body of water in the English Channel could not extinguish.

"Did you fight Granthum as well?" Trevor interrogated as his head moved steadily toward hers. "Is that why you suffered bruises?" That question had been gnawing at him since he had heard Reid's dying words. Had she struggled against him and then surrendered? "Do you fight against all men who hunger to take you in their arms?" His hot breath skimmed her cheek as he inhaled the feminine scent that could easily warp his senses.

Meagan leaned back as far as his encircling arms would allow, making Poseidon fidget uneasily beneath them. "I do not appreciate being mauled. I am not some chattel to be used by you or any other man," she assured him, her voice trembling with outrage.

The faintest hint of a smile cracked Trevor's chiseled features as his index finger trailed over her exposed bosom. "Must you always be wooed, minx?" His tone was softer now, his golden eyes flaming with a desire he had spent more

283

than a week fighting to control. He had kept his distance from Meagan, reminding himself that she was still his enemy, vowing never to surrender to his weakness, one that had almost cost him his life. Even when he knew she wanted nothing to do with him, he ached for her. Even when he knew he should have slain her beside her Saxon lover, he wanted her as he wanted no other woman. Meagan was his obsession, and no amount of logic could smother the passion that surged through his veins when he made close contact with this alluring beauty with eyes as bright as the morning sky and hair the color of both the sun and moon. "Do you wish all your lovers to grovel at your feet, begging for what little affection you might spare them? Will it always be this way with you, Meagan? Only on one rare occasion did you come to me, and that has been my torment. I have long wondered why."

Meagan flinched when his arms recircled her waist, bringing their bodies into intimate contact. She wanted to deny him his lust, but the love she harbored for him rose to consume her rational thoughts. It had been an eternity since Trevor held her tenderly, and she longed to forget everything that had any resemblance to reality.

Her hands slid over his broad shoulders as his head slanted toward hers, his lips only a few breathless inches away. "I will always yearn for the man who can tenderly steal my soul and make it his own, one who does not resort to force to stir my desires. I demand a gentle touch. . . ."

Trevor was hopelessly lost to the fathomless pools of blue and the inviting way her lips parted as his mouth lingered on hers. A moan of tormented pleasure resounded in his chest as he clutched her closer, unable to get close enough to the flame that burned him inside and out. His hands were upon her, gliding over her trim waist and the enticing curve of her hips. His touch was embroidered with intimacy as it scaled her ribs, molding his hand around the swell of her breast. His lips clung to hers, and he became intoxicated with a kiss that was more potent than wine. His senses came alive with the subtle fragrance that hovered about her, and his male body strained against hers, seeking to appease the craving to possess her.

Searing kisses trailed across her cheek to nibble at the rapid pulsations on the base of her throat before his lips moved to cover the rosy peak of her breast.

His need for this woman was an addiction that drove all thoughts from his mind, leaving him aching and vulnerable. Trevor paid no heed to the fact that he had allowed Poseidon to wander at will. The gentle movement of his steed as he picked his way through the forest set his caresses to rhythm, and Trevor was caught up in the cadence of the stallion beneath him and the pulsating need within him.

When Poseidon paused and threw his proud head to inspect the goings-on upon his back, Trevor stepped from the stirrup and then gently lifted Meagan into his arms. As he pulled her down into the grass, Meagan drew away his chain-mail shirt to glide her hands over the dark furring of his chest. She was as hungry for him as he was for her. She didn't care if his only interest was to appease his lust. She desired to lose herself to the one man who could make her respond to his skillful caresses. His touch was magic, creating ineffable sensations.

"You know the power you hold over me, don't you, Meagan?" Trevor murmured hoarsely as his hand trailed over her quivering flesh, his flaming golden eyes flowing in the wake of his exploring caresses. "You are the most gorgeous creature I have ever looked upon or touched." A sad smile bordered his lips as he continued his gentle massage, leaving Meagan relaxed and pliant beside him. "Although I have tried to remain remote and distant I cannot deny this maddening attraction. I, like Garda, take to my wings to flee, but I always return, knowing the pleasure that awaits me. No matter how great the danger of my folly, I cannot seem to leave you alone."

Meagan cupped his face in her hands and then tunneled her fingers through his tousled hair. "Then come, my wayward prince; I, too, hunger for that which I can never truly claim. Ours is but a brief, shining moment, but I cannot begrudge one blaze of passion, for 'tis all we will ever have."

The glow in her eyes lured Trevor ever closer, trapping

him, holding him spellbound. His greedy mouth ravished hers, as if he could not get enough of the drugging taste of her kiss. His lips opened on hers, his ragged breath merging with hers, giving, taking, becoming one until they lost all touch with reality. His hands swam across the sea of naked flesh, his body rousing, aching for the softness of hers. His knee slid between her thighs as he stretched out beside her, molding his solid male form to the slightness of hers. His touch became increasingly familiar as it hovered over her skin, seeking to know this exquisite goddess by touch, sensitizing her nerves, leaving her trembling in anticipation of the moment when he would take her with him on a splendorous journey beyond the stars. His caresses roved across her hip and then receded to retrace the sensuous path to her taut breast. His lips fluttered over each pink bud and then trailed over her abdomen, leaving her drifting in such divine torment that a sigh tumbled from her lips.

Meagan brushed her hand over the rippling muscles of his back as his caresses flowed back to reclaim her breasts and then descended to seek out each sensitive point that responded to his skillful seduction. It was *he* who held mystical powers over *her,* Meagan thought as she surrendered to the exquisite feel of his practiced hands. He knew how to set fire to her emotions, making her his pawn.

A coil of longing unfurled within her as he continued his devastating assault. Senses that had remained dormant for more than three weeks were triggered by his touch, keeping her suspended in breathless anticipation as the sinewed columns of his legs slid between hers, the hard contours of his hips blending into hers. Their bodies entwined to become one as passion flowed forth like a roaring river that overflowed its banks. Unleashed desire cascaded through her like wild torrents of a waterfall, drawing her into currents of indescribable pleasure. He had driven her to the edge, sending her plunging downward, leaving her to drown in the sweet torment of his possession. Meagan was oblivious to what the morrow would hold. Their moment of ecstasy could erase the past and forestall the future, capturing time and holding it for a rapturous eternity.

She heard his ragged breath against her neck, felt the reckless beat of his heart against her naked breasts as he drove into her. She arched to meet his forceful thrusts, moving in perfect rhythm while the dark world spun furiously about them. And then another violent upheaval of emotions gripped her and she gasped, overwhelmed by the maddening sensations that sizzled through her, leaving not one part of her untouched. The memories of his lovemaking seemed only a dim shadow that could not compare to the feelings she was experiencing at this moment. Her body and soul had been consumed. He took her higher than she dreamed possible. Nothing existed except the wild, sensuous pleasure he gave and the ardor of her response when she returned it. Pure emotion bubbled and rose as they clung together, awaiting the fall.

And then they spiraled, suspended in midair before they tumbled back to reality. Trevor expelled the last of his ragged breath as he trembled above her. It was a long moment before his heart slowed its frantic pace and his senses cleared, but still he could not move. She had drawn from his strength as she always had, he mused wearily, and clinging to Meagan, feeling her warm breath against his cheek, was a temptation he had never been able to resist. Again they had come the full circle-mistrusting, hurting, and then surrendering to their wild, reckless passions.

It would always be like this with Meagan, Trevor realized. He could never dispose of this feisty, sapphire-eyed beauty, because part of his soul would perish with her and he would become only half a man. Nor could he stash her in his dungeon, watching her wither away like a delicate flower that was sheltered from sunlight. He would never be able to forget the ever-present temptation who paced the narrow confines of her dingy cell. The lure of this platinum-haired minx would tempt him to break his vow of keeping his distance from her. Nay, he could not kill her, and he could not keep her, he mused with a heavy sigh and then drew Meagan's curvaceous body against his.

There could be only one answer to his dilemma, and there was no need to take the question to Conan. Trevor did not have the heart to execute Meagan for her treasonous acts, and he could not bear to sentence her to imprisonment in his dungeon. There was naught else to do but banish her from England and pray that time would allow him to forget the tantalizing feel of her body ardently responding to his caress, forget the taste of kisses that melted like summer rain upon his waiting lips, forget the captivating vision that haunted both his days and nights.

Trevor allowed his eyelids to droop as he snuggled against her shoulder, his senses warped with her feminine scent. He would find pleasure with her until they reached Normandy, and then he would forsake the fond attachment he felt for this enchanting vixen. He would throw himself into his duties for the Crown and his demesne, driving all thoughts of this enticing witch from his mind ... forever. He had tampered with fate and now he would be forced to pay his dues, he reminded himself drowsily. He and Meagan had to go their separate ways. If not, one or the other of them would inevitably perish because of this ill-fated attraction between them.

A bemused frown knitted Meagan's brow when she realized Trevor had changed direction to follow a path that would never lead them back to Burke Castle.

"Have you business to tend elsewhere before we return to the fortress?" she questioned as she squirmed uncomfortably in front of him.

Trevor inwardly flinched. He knew the question would come, and he also knew he would meet with defiance when he informed her of their destination. "Yea, I do have an important matter to attend before I resume my duties at the castle," he hedged.

The frown settled deeper in Meagan's exquisite features. It was out of character for this straightforward warlord to beat around the bush, and Meagan intended to fire questions at him until she knew what he was about. "Where do we ride, m'lord?" she demanded to know.

"Hastings and beyond," he said evasively.

Meagan was growing more suspicious by the minute. Beyond Hastings was the sea. What duty could he possibly have there? Trevor had already ridden far past the boundaries of his demesne.

"Pray, be more specific," she requested, her tone carrying a caustic clip. "I am in no mood for guessing games."

"And you are in no position to demand to know my intentions," he reminded her gruffly. "But since you persist, I will tell you. I have decided to take you to Rocaille Chateau in Normandy for banishment."

His words cut like a knife that left her soul to bleed. Meagan felt something inside her wither and die. Banished from England? Never to see her beloved homeland or her brother? God, how cruel the fate! She was destined to exist without living.

"You should have killed me," Meagan choked out, her voice acrid with bitterness. "I would have preferred an execution to an insufferable existence on foreign shores."

If he had had the stomach for such a grisly chore, he would have left Meagan by her Saxon lover's side. But he couldn't bring himself to bury his sword in this lovely seraph who was the devil's own temptation. Tearing off his own arm would have been less painful than violently taking her life.

"I spared your life. You should be grateful for that," Trevor muttered as he ducked beneath the low-hanging branch and then keenly inspected their surroundings. "But too often I have allowed you to go unpunished. This time I cannot. Your crimes are unforgivable."

"I should be grateful for this?" Meagan echoed incredulously as she twisted around in the saddle to peer at his grim expression. "What future can I anticipate in Normandy? I cannot speak the language and I know no one there." Meagan was frantic. The thought of crossing the channel was like ferrying her across the River Styx to take up permanent residence in Hell!

"This is not intended to be a sojourn for a traveling queen and her entourage," Trevor scowled as he swung from the saddle and then hauled Meagan down beside him while Poseidon drank from a rivulet. "You have been banished for your part in the rebellion and for comitting adultery against your husband." The unhealed wound of seeing Meagan riding by Granthum's side began to fester within him, and the thought of her sleeping in his arms brought all those painful emotions to surface.

Blazing blue eyes riddled over his unrelenting features. "You are a fool if you believe that of me and I was a fool for attempting to dissuade the rebels from marching against the palace." Meagan drew herself up proudly in front of him, unintimidated by the swarthy knight who towered over her like a rock mountain. "If I am to be banished for my supposed crimes without gathering evidence that my words *are* lies, then why not denounce the wedding vows as well? If you want me out of your life forever, then dissolve the wedding and allow me the chance to make a new life for myself with a man who . . ."

Trevor yanked her to him so quickly that her head snapped backward, ripping the words from her lips before she could voice them.

"There will be no other man," he told her harshly. "You are my wife, though unfaithful you have been, and you shall remain my wife until you have expelled your dying breath."

"For what purpose?" Meagan interrogated. The man made no sense at all. Was it spite that forced him to keep her chained in matrimony, allowing her not even one chance at happiness? Not that it mattered, Meagan reminded herself dismally. She would never get over loving Trevor. Perhaps another man could offer her security, but she could never fall in love again, not after her first love had been the lord of Wessex.

Trevor gnashed his teeth together when she posed the probing question. Damnation, he wasn't certain why he refused to disclaim the vows and set her afloat to run aground on Normandy's shores. But he had made her his wife and she would remain so forever.

"You have incredible difficulty remembering your place, Meagan." He looked like black thunder as he stormed back at her. "I am your lord and you will do as I command without questioning my motives."

Perhaps another woman could have held her tongue and behaved submissively when she confronted this fire-breathing dragon, but Meagan could not! Her eyes burned hotter than blue blazes as she glared back at him. She had been beaten and dragged into a battle against the man she loved. She had been unjustly accused of treason and banished from her home and family, and Trevor was too damned stubborn to listen to her true motives. Her temper snapped like a frayed rope. She preferred to die rather than leave her home, and if she must, she would force him to kill her. Death would be far less painful than the existence he offered her as an alternative.

Meagan lunged at him, catching him unaware, struggling to retrieve his sword from its scabbard. Trevor peered bug-eyed at her as they struggled for possession of the blade.

"Little fool! Do you think to defeat me in hand-to-hand combat?" Trevor snorted as he sought to rip the sword from her grasp. Instinctively, he stepped back and raised his sword as he had done so many times when confronted by an enemy.

"'Tis *my* defeat I hope to accomplish," Meagan insisted, her eyes swimming with tears as she clutched the blade and pulled it toward her heaving chest, prepared to die and end the misery of loving a man who had become hardened by battle and so blinded by suspicion that he could never return her affection. "Be done with it! I wish to die on native soil."

Trevor dragged his sword away before she could plunge it into her heart. She was trying to force him to take her life and he could not live with her blood on his conscience. Her defeat would then become her victory, he mused as he attempted to push the sword back into his scabbard. She would die and his soul would torment him all the days of his miserable life.

Meagan was so furious she was seeing red. He would not even grant her death when she would have begged for it. Suddenly, she sprang at him and, with all the strength she could muster, she pressed her hands to the muscular wall of his chest, shoving him back down the stream bank.

"Shall I give you one more reason to kill me?" she flung at

him as she gave him another insistent push. "Go take your *place,* hollow-headed toad!" When Trevor tripped over the driftwood on the edge of the creek and flapped his arms like a bird attempting to take to his wings, Meagan grinned in smug satisfaction and then watched Trevor fall into an undignified heap amid the mud and moss. "Yonder is your lily pad. Sit thee upon it and contemplate why I would want to have you murdered and why I would lead a rebellion against your king when I could have ruled as your lady. And while the bullfrog croaks beside you, ask yourself why I would spread myself beneath Reid Granthum when I could have slept, and quite contentedly, in your arms!"

While Trevor struggled to gain his footing in the swamp that crowded the edge of the rivulet and became entangled by his own scabbard that sought to trip him up and detain him, Meagan pulled herself into the saddle and gouged Poseidon in the ribs, sending him charging through the thicket. Lear turned his head to study the floundering lord and Trevor swore the wolflike shepherd was smirking at him, making him all the angrier.

Trevor splashed in the mud, cursing himself for allowing Meagan to make a bigger fool of him than he already was, and then he roared like an enraged lion when he glared at Meagan's departing back. Damnation, he should have tied and blindfolded that cunning vixen, refusing to announce their destination until they had reached it. What had he expected that high-spirited firebrand to do, dutifully follow him to Normandy without making an attempt to flee or voicing complaint?

Scowling, Trevor slung the moss and mud from his chain-mail shirt and waded ashore. The heat of his furious glare was so intense it could have scorched a desert, but to his dismay, it did not reduce that troublesome wench who trailed off through the forest with her wild hair billowing about her into a pile of smoldering embers. She rode on, putting more distance between them, and Trevor stood on the stream bank silently seething.

When he caught up with that blue-eyed tigress, he would stake her down to something with sturdy roots and then give her the sound beating she deserved for making a fool of him again. Lord, she had him behaving like an imbecile so often that he should have begged William to allow him to assume the duties of his court jester. How could he efficiently rule his demesne when he could not even control that cunning vixen who had shoved him in the creek and then galloped off on his horse . . . *her* horse! Egod! Even that magnificent black stallion had conspired against him, he thought acrimoniously.

Trevor threw up his hands in disgust and cursed himself with every step he took as he followed the shapely silhouette that had faded into the shadows. That woman had turned his world upside down, and he was forever chasing after her like a man dashing blindly after a rainbow and its legendary pot of gold. He had become an incompetent laggard, Trevor berated himself. If he could pursue one sane thought after that mischievous siren turned him every-which-way-but-loose, he would be surprised! Trevor grumbled sourly as he stalked off through the woods, his lordly clothes dripping with mud and moss. That spell-casting witch with hair the color of the sun and moon and eyes as clear and blue as the sky was driving him stark raving mad!

A weary sigh escaped Meagan's lips as she sank into the lagoon to rest her aching muscles. She had meandered through the forest, backtracking, pursuing circles, anything to lose the fire-breathing dragon who chased after her. Thankfully, she had seen nothing of Trevor, and reasonably certain she had lost him, Meagan had yielded to the temptation of returning to Lowell Castle before seeking asylum at the nunnery. Meagan had left Edric tied to his bed, and Devona was probably wondering what had become of her.

And just what would become of her, Meagan mused as she eased onto her back and sighed as the water swirled about her, easing her nervous tension. Would Sister Elizabeth refuse to allow Trevor near her if he stormed the convent? She could not stay one step ahead of Trevor forever, running like hunted prey, surviving like a beast in the wilds. And she could never surrender herself to her angry overlord to be toted off to Normandy. God, he may as well have sentenced her to hell.

As depression tumbled over her like an avalanche, Meagan dived beneath the water's surface and then glided across the rippling pond, attempting to outrun her worries and the darkly handsome face that constantly materialized before her.

While Meagan was drifting across the pond like an unsuspecting swan, Trevor was crouching in the under-brush. For two days he had pushed himself, itching to catch up to the elusive dryad who had continued to elude him and wring her lovely neck for causing him such frustration. He had seen Garda circling high above the trees and he had quickened his pace, knowing the faithful falcon would lead him to his wife. But the hostility that had plagued him became fiery desire when he spied the graceful vision that glided in and out of the sunlight.

Her blond hair flowed out behind her, sparkling in the beams of light that sprinkled through the trees. Her ivory skin glowed against the sunlight's reflection upon the water. And when she eased onto her back to float across the lagoon, Trevor swallowed a forest full of air. Her full breasts lay temptingly exposed to his devouring gaze. Bare arms and legs appeared and then disappeared from the cloudy depths and Trevor could feel the heat of desire frying him alive. He fought a mental tug-of-war with anger, frustration, and passion as he gazed upon this bewitching angel who tormented his dreams and fed his nightmares.

Quietly, he shed his clothes and sank into the lagoon, but the cool water did nothing to extinguish the fire that burned within him. Nothing could smother the flame of mixed emotions Trevor was feeling as he dived beneath the surface and swam toward the frolicking mermaid who thought herself alone in the pond.

A startled gasp burst from Meagan's lips when she felt something curl around her leg and tow her into the depths before she could inhale a breath of air. Her heart very nearly

294

popped from her chest, and her imagination ran away with itself when she was swallowed up by whatever had swum up from the muddy depths to devour her. And just when Meagan thought her lungs would burst and she would be gobbled up by the hideous monster that inhabited the lagoon, she was yanked back to the surface to face the very man she desperately wanted to avoid.

"How did you find me?" Meagan sputtered as she wiped the water from her disbelieving eyes and gasped for air, just in case Trevor did not allow her another breath before he strangled her for escaping him.

"Your falcon betrayed you." Trevor gestured to the circling hawk and then flung her a wicked grin. Long, lean fingers folded about her throat, dragging her closer, his powerful body brushing against hers. "'Tis disheartening, is it not, to learn that even a devoted friend would forsake you?"

Meagan knew that he implied she was a traitor to her lord. Obviously, he had not contemplated the questions she had posed while he was floating on his lily pad like a waterlogged bullfrog, she mused in annoyance. The man was determined to mistrust her, and nothing short of a miracle would convince him that she had his best interests at heart, even when the evidence was not in her favor. What was the use, Meagan asked herself as his fingers bit into her throat. She was doomed, and there was nothing she could do to prevent her destiny.

Lifting a brave chin, Meagan met his flaming amber eyes. "It makes little difference what I say or do. You will never believe that I speak the truth. I won't fight you."

Her body went limp and Trevor growled under his breath. He swore the wench did not know the meaning of fear. Meagan possessed incredible inner strength, and she could stare death in the face without cowering from it.

The fiery glitter in his eyes transformed from anger to desire as he pulled her against the muscled planes of his belly. He was like a giant jungle cat toying with his prey, and Meagan prayed the end would come quickly. Her thick lashes fluttered against her cheek to await the inevitable, certain this time that the lusty beast within him would bow before the vengeful dragon who sought to choke the life from her.

But then the stranglehold on her throat eased and his lips feathered over the trim column of her neck, as if to offer pleasure where he had inflicted pain. Her eyes swept open to see the inner turmoil churning in his gaze before he buried his head against her bare shoulder.

"You have left me with no choice but to send you away, for I cannot bring myself to end your life, even when you have wrought bitterness and shame. God, Meagan, I wonder if I will ever stop wanting you." His voice was husky with mounting passion as he pressed closer, their bodies intimately touching, reminding him of the moments when they had lain together in the heat of passion.

Meagan not only heard his hushed words but she felt them whisper against her trembling skin. His lips claimed hers, savoring the tempting moistness of her mouth before his tongue thrust into its sweet darkness to steal her breath. She melted against him, stirred by his masculine quest, feeling each barrier of defense crumbling as her body cried out for his touch.

She would offer what no other man had taken, and perhaps, just once, Trevor would realize she no longer considered him her enemy. Oh, why couldn't he look into her eyes and see the affection that was meant only for him? Why couldn't he set aside his suspicions long enough to realize she loved him, heart and soul?

Brazenly, she curled her arms around his shoulders and then tunneled her fingers through the damp raven hair that clung to his head. "Now that you have found me, what is your wish, m'lord?" she questioned as her gaze locked with his. "Will I be dragged behind Poseidon in shackles or will I feel the sting of your whip upon my back? What torture do you propose for your defenseless prisoner?"

Torture? Trevor groaned in unholy torment as her wildly disturbing caresses wandered over him. He was the one enduring pain. Her seductive movements were driving him mad with desire. He could no more drag her from the lagoon and bind her in chains than a spider could fling out her web and ensnare the stars. Meagan had made him a slave to her brand of passion, and the forbidden memories converged on him, tearing his heart asunder. He craved the taste of her lips, ones that could melt beneath his like cherry wine. The longing to feel her curvaceous body molded to the hardness of his rekindled fires that no amount of water could extinguish.

Trevor did not bother to reply to her questions. Indeed, he could barely remember her asking them. His mouth swooped down on hers, devouring her with his impatient kiss. As if his hands possessed a will of their own, they began to move across her silky flesh, mapping each alluring curve and swell. Trickling drops of temptation became a roaring waterfall of desire as they submerged into the depths, drowning in the arousing sensations that flooded over them.

He could feel himself losing control. This mysterious angel was the foretaste of heaven, and Trevor hungered for more than a kiss and caress. He knew this gnawing hunger would never ease, no matter how furious he had been with her earlier. This savage need she stirred within him had turned his mind to mush and left him no more than an uncoiling knot of desire.

Her gentle hands slid across the hard muscles of his shoulders and ventured lower. The pleasure of her touch made him ache, and he felt his heart leap with anticipation when her adventurous hand tracked across his hip to trace his thighs. He scooped her into his arms, letting the water cradle her as his hot lips skimmed over her skin and then glided to the dusky peak of each breast, suckling and teasing until he had dragged a quiet sigh from her lips. His hands were never still for a moment, rediscovering each sensitive point, making her respond to his touch in wild abandon.

Meagan felt herself drifting into a world of indescribable rapture. Trevor was a skillful lover. He knew where to touch, how to touch, and he had the power to make her will his own. She was engulfed by the pleasure of his kisses and caresses, and she would have sacrificed her last breath if she could have remained forever suspended in the arousing dream he was weaving about her.

Hot sparks flew up and down her spine as his practiced hands trailed across her abdomen to guide her thighs apart. Wave upon wave of splendorous sensations curled over her as his caresses receded to retrace the same titillating path. His fingertips teased each pink crest into a throbbing peak and then trailed across her ribs to swirl along her inner thighs. Knowing fingers excited her until the burning ache had blossomed and channeled into every part of her being, consuming her.

Meagan could endure no more of this sweet torment. She longed to touch him, to inflame him with the same uncontrollable blaze that had devoured her. She twisted away from him and led him to the pond bank. Her eyes flooded over this lion of a man, worshipping him with her gaze, adoring him with her kisses. She loved the feel of his hair-roughened flesh beneath her hands, and she sought to prove her need for him with her tender touch.

Streams of sweet agony seared his body as the whisper of moist, warm lips spread butterfly kisses over his skin. She ran her hands over his granite shoulders and trailed her index finger over his strong jaw. Her wandering caress glided over his aquiline nose and prominent cheekbones, mapping each distinct feature that was stamped with wild nobility. Her touch was achingly tender as she weaved silken webs of pleasure about him, spinning dreams that he longed to become reality. She touched him and he lost what little sense he had left. She kissed him and the winds of passion swept him up in a whirlwind of emotions. She had fed his growing hunger and then created monstrous new ones. His mind stopped functioning and he was overwhelmed with the primal needs that were as ancient as time itself. He wanted her, craved her, ached to ease a passion so wild and fierce that Trevor wasn't certain he could endure it.

Glowing golden eyes locked with hers as he crouched above her, his muscles bulging as he held himself away. His body tingled in anticipation as her hands settled on his hips to urge him closer, encouraging him with words of want and need, ones he murmured back to her. When her lips parted in invitation, his mouth slanted across hers, drinking freely of a kiss more potent than wine. As his hard body settled exactly upon hers, the leaping sparks of passion became a blazing bonfire, one so intense that Trevor was being fried alive. His nerves fused together like entangled twine as her feminine body yielded to the heavy burden of his weight. With a surrendering groan he drove into her, forgetting everything that had any resemblance to reality. He savored the feel of her supple body arching to meet his hard thrusts, and he clung to her in breathless abandon, swamped and buffeted by sensations that mounted one upon the other until the dark world and all the distant stars within it were spinning wildly about him.

Wondrous sensations that tampered with his sanity boiled through his veins as she took him from one ecstatic plateau of pleasure onto another. They were scaling passion's towering mountain, discovering ineffable splendors on each elevated crest until they had journeyed to rapture's highest peak.

And then, as if besieged by a violent volcanic eruption, he felt the soul-shattering sensations burst within him, leaving him teetering precariously upon the edge. He was falling, his churning emotions scattering in a thousand different directions, taking with them all rational thought and every ounce of strength. A shudder ran through him as he clutched Meagan in a bone-crushing embrace. He was living and dying, suspended in time, dangling in space, afraid to let go of the only stable force within his grasp.

And for what seemed eternity, their souls soared, circling the perimeters of the universe like the spiraling falcon that glided on the wind currents above them. Ever so slowly the veiled darkness of passion faded from his vision, and Trevor fluttered back to reality like a weightless feather settling upon the grass. His tangled lashes swept up and he peered at the angelic face below him. Her silky hair spilled across the carpet of grass like a river of gold. Her sapphire eyes glistened with an emotion Trevor couldn't decipher, a message that he didn't trust himself to attempt to decode. It would have been so easy to believe this lovely nymph when he was overwhelmed by the aftereffects of passion. It would be so simple to disregard the bits and pieces of evidence of her crimes. All too easy, Trevor reminded himself as his sanity returned and his heart began beating at its normal pace.

He heaved a frustrated sigh and then sank down beside Meagan to stare across the rippling waters of the lagoon. He could not allow their mystical lovemaking to influence his logical thinking. Meagan would do anything to prevent banishment, even using her alluring body to sway him, to persuade him to take her back after she had given herself to another man, one who could never come to her assistance again. Trevor had faithfully promised himself that he would deposit Meagan in Normandy and then put her out of his mind forever. His country was in turmoil, his king faced another rebellion, and Meagan was a distraction, one he had never been able to ignore.

There were times when a man was forced to do what he considered best, no matter how much anguish it inflicted upon him. He was William's knight, sworn to hold his king in high esteem. If this traitor and conspirator were someone other than Meagan, he would have sentenced her to painful death. He had already proven himself vulnerable to this enticing witch by allowing her to live in banishment. To forgive her of her crimes and keep her by his side would be proof of his failing loyalties to William.

Without a word, Trevor snatched up Meagan's ragged tunic and pulled it over her head, covering the beautiful young body that brought him such delirious pleasure. He didn't dare risk looking upon her and falling prey to his lust. His need for her had become an eternal spring and even when his passions had been appeased, he could easily lose himself in that endless stream of desire that he saw when he gazed into her eyes.

When Trevor manacled her wrists and led her over to retrieve his discarded clothes, outrage sizzled through Meagan's veins. She realized that he still intended to hold her captive like a disobedient pup that had strayed from

300

its master.

"I will *not* be uprooted and transplanted on foreign soil!" Meagan assured him hotly. "I have done nothing to deserve this punishment!"

Trevor yanked on her arm when she set her feet and then dragged her along behind him. "There is nothing you can say to change my mind. I have made my decision, and I must stand by it until I find evidence that proves my opinion false," he told her harshly. "Nothing has changed. I will admit that I desire you as a man craves a woman, but I have a stronger obligation to my king."

"Then you should have married him," Meagan spat furiously.

"William already has a wife," Trevor threw over his shoulder, along with an infuriating smile that Meagan would have dearly loved to wipe all over his face.

That mulish man! He was so stubborn and set in his ways that nothing could ever change his mind. He wanted to believe the worst about her because he looked upon their physical attraction for each other as a weakness, a flaw the King's loyal knight could not possess if he meant to serve William the Bastard, body and soul. Confound it! Trevor placed his king above his own wife, and she was not to be allowed the slightest consideration. To Trevor's way of thinking she was guilty until she could prove herself innocent, and how the devil was she to do that when she was in Normandy?

"I detest you, Trevor Burke," she spat with childish vindictiveness, so frustrated and furious that she put the thought to tongue without giving it second consideration. "The overlord of Wessex is not fit to rule if he cannot determine truth from lie. And 'tis a lie that I had a part in the conspiracy!" Her voice became higher and wilder by the second until she was yelling in his face.

Trevor chained her in one hand and struggled into his garments with the other. "Spoken like a true rebel," he grunted caustically. "It seems wise to allow the English Channel to separate us, m'lady. We cannot remain on the same shore without antagonizing each other. Our marriage

301

will stand the test of time, and we can only be compatible when I am in England and you are in Normandy."

Meagan was itching to pound him flat and send him drifting across the channel, and she would have done so if he hadn't bound her hands and feet to Poseidon to prevent another escape.

Once Trevor had secured his captive, he stepped into the stirrup and swung up behind her rigid body. "Take your last look at England, Meagan. You could have had the freedom to wander from shore to shore, but you chose to deny the rightful king of England his throne, and you have continued to defy me."

"I only sought to help you," Meagan choked out as the tears boiled down her flushed cheeks. "But you are too blind to see that."

Trevor laughed bitterly as he reined his steed toward Hastings. "You would have helped me into an early grave. That kind of help I can do without. I will do what must be done, and if you were standing in my stead, you could not deny that I have just cause to doubt you. Saxons, men and women alike, have pretended to befriend their Norman lords since William set the crown of England upon his head. It has become a way of life to doubt, and you have given me a score of reasons to doubt your loyalty."

And that was what hurt the most, Meagan mused disheartenedly as Trevor picked his way through the forest. Trevor was cautious by nature and suspicious by habit. Her conspiring fellow countrymen had made him so. He took nothing as truth, constantly questioning the Saxons' motives. And fate had frowned upon her, making her look the culprit, forcing her to endure the punishment for crimes she could never have committed against the man she loved.

This was to be her hell on earth, she thought dismally as they rode to Hastings. She had loved and lost. She would spend her life pining for a man who still considered her his enemy.

Meagan brushed her hand over her abdomen and then breathed a hope that the love she harbored for Trevor would blossom and grow within this child who would never know

302

his father. She would adore her child, offering him all she was unable to give Trevor. The baby would help her endure her banishment, giving her life new purpose. Clinging to that thought, Meagan focused her attention on the jagged silhouette of the garrison at Hastings and tried to imagine what awaited her on the other side of the channel.

Chapter 21

Meagan peered out the second-story window of Rocaille Chateau, which stood on a three-hundred-foot cliff overlooking the Seine River. Below her were the three baileys that were surrounded by massive guard towers. The mammoth castle had an ominous look about it, making Meagan feel as small and unimportant as one of the stones that were imbedded in the garrison.

With a combination of curiosity and remorse, Meagan surveyed the northwestern sky. A faint smile skimmed her lips as she felt the flutter of life beneath her hand, and she wondered whimsically if her child would ever have the opportunity to meet his father. Meagan truly doubted it. Two months had passed since Trevor had veered southeast, deciding that England was not big enough for both of them. Although Meagan had dragged her feet and protested being uprooted from her native soil, Trevor had hauled her to Hastings, deposited her on a long boat, and then transplanted her in the chateau of his old acquaintance, Desmond Farrel.

Trevor had not tarried a day, as if he could not wait to get his unwanted wife off his hands and out of his life once and for all. After dropping a heavy pouch of coins in Desmond's hands, Trevor had retraced his path to England, leaving Meagan on the border between Normandy and France to live with a stranger. That was the last she had seen or heard from her husband, but she well remembered the parting

305

glance he had flung her, and the words he had spoken still echoed in her mind.

"Perhaps in your declining years you will be allowed to return to your homeland. Consider yourself fortunate that I have permitted you to live at all, my deceitful wife. Had I given in to the impulse the day I saw you cavorting with your rebel lover, I would have seen you dead and buried beside him." Trevor had paused, his expression pained as he met her misty blue eyes. "You have become my weakness, Meagan. I have learned to accept that. But the attraction has proved lethal. Once you are out of sight and out of mind, I can focus my attention on my duties, ones you have an uncanny knack of making me forget." Trevor had swung onto his steed and rode away, and Meagan swore the mighty warrior was deaf since he did not seem to hear her heart breaking in a thousand miserable pieces.

Meagan pushed away from the window and ambled back to stretch out on her bed to stare dismally at the ceiling. It seemed an eternity since she had seen Edric and Devona, and she wondered if Devona still held her brother prisoner in his own room since Meagan had ordered her not to release him until she returned. A smile pursed her lips, imagining Edric crowing like an indignant rooster when he awoke to find himself strapped in bed. The impish grin that had momentarily captured her features faded when she recalled the message Desmond had received, explaining the progress of the Norman campaign against the Saxon rebels. Conan's vision had come to pass. Desmond had informed Meagan that William had invaded Stafford, crushing "Edric the Wild," and then had moved northward to demolish York. The vengeful king had sealed off York by burning miles of land and timber. When the Danish fleet had abandoned the Saxons, victory had come easily for William, but it had only been the beginning of a tragic end. The Norman king had sworn not only to punish the Saxons of the North, but also to devastate the countryside, leaving it a barren land. All of Yorkshire would become a charred, desolate waste, unfit for mankind.

Conan had foreseen the end for the Saxon rebels who

challenged the king. A world that had once been a Garden of Eden was now a smoldering hell. Meagan muffled a sniff, wondering why she had grown sentimental of late. She could burst into tears over little or nothing, and she found herself wallowing in self-pity instead of enjoying what meager happiness she could find at the lavish chateau on the eastern border of Normandy.

Although Desmond had been kind to her, Meagan lived a mundane existence, awaiting the birth of her child. The only reminders of her beloved husband were her devoted companions, Garda and Lear. Trevor had seen to it that Meagan dressed in fashionable clothing, and Desmond had taught her to speak French. Meagan wanted for nothing, except that which she couldn't have—Trevor's love and trust.

When Desmond had insisted that he contact Trevor, certain that he would wish to know how Meagan fared during her pregnancy, she had adamantly objected. Her gracious host was unaware of the friction between husband and wife since Trevor had tactfully explained that his reason for stashing Meagan in Normandy was his concern for her safety during the Saxon uprisings. Trevor did not give a fig what became of her, as long as she was not underfoot, Meagan mused bitterly. No doubt, Trevor had not given her a thought since he turned north to cross the English Channel. If Desmond had known that Trevor intended for his unwanted wife to become a permanent fixture at the chateau, he might not have been so eager to take Meagan under his wing.

"Meagan?" Desmond poked his gray head inside and graced her with a warm smile. "You have an unexpected visitor." When Meagan frowned curiously, he continued. "Our guest is one of Trevor's relatives, who has just learned of your stay in Normandy. Do you feel up to entertaining a guest this afternoon?"

Trevor's relative? Meagan's frown settled deeper in her delicate features. She could have sworn Trevor had informed her that he was the last of his species. Heaven forbid that there was another despot like Trevor roaming the

307

earth! Her curiosity got the best of her, and she sat up on the side of the bed, anxious to see what form Trevor's family had taken.

"Yea, I would like to meet a member of my husband's family," she assured Desmond.

Curling her hand around Desmond's proffered arm, Meagan descended the stairs to the Great Hall to await introductions to the elaborately adorned gentleman who eyed her with the same mounting curiosity that she focused on him. There was nothing memorable or mildly attracting about the older man's face, as if his bland features had been randomly selected from a melting pot of characteristics and then hastily plastered into place. It seemed to Meagan that his maker had rushed through his chore in record time. The man's deeply imbedded eyes did not reflect the smile that was loosely pasted on his lips, and Meagan's first impression left her wary of the man's reasons for seeking her out. But Meagan gave him the benefit of the doubt until Desmond voiced the guest's name.

"Lady Meagan, this is Ulrick Burke, Trevor's uncle. When he learned that you were residing here with me for a time, he decided to pay his respects," Desmond explained.

The color seeped from Meagan's cheeks, and she struggled to hold her composure in check. Ulrick Burke was the conniving uncle who had brought about the ruin of Burke land and had disposed of his sister-in-law by giving her to some ruthless barbarian who did not bat an eye at abusing his women.

"'Tis good to meet you, m'lord," Meagan lied through her forced smile. In truth she would have preferred that this treacherous wretch be struck down in his tracks for lying to Trevor and effecting the murder of his sister-in-law.

Ulrick watched Meagan like a starved hawk, detecting the flash of recognition in her eyes. Apparently, Trevor had divulged his past to his wife, Ulrick mused as he bent to press a kiss to Meagan's wrist. Since the moment he heard that Lady Burke had taken up residence at Rocaille Chateau, he had feared that Desmond might inadvertently mention the long-lost uncle. Ulrick could not risk allowing Trevor to learn that his uncle was still alive. Ulrick had purposely sent the news of his own death with his courier when he learned that Trevor and his brother were preparing to depart for England during William's initial invasion. He had hoped that the lie would leave Trevor with little reason to return to Normandy, and Ulrick had been living comfortably on his properties until Meagan Burke suddenly appeared to threaten his existence.

A wave of revulsion rippled through Meagan as Ulrick's cold lips touched her hand. It was a long, torturous moment before he withdrew and she could breathe a constricted sigh of relief.

While Desmond sought to make idle conversation, Meagan squirmed in her chair, wishing the deceitful ogre would take his leave. She would have preferred to roast over a hot bed of coals rather than to tolerate Ulrick's disturbing presence. But to her dismay, Desmond offered the older man a room for the night, one which Ulrick quickly accepted, expressing his interest in becoming better acquainted with his lovely niece. Meagan was not certain she could stomach the sugarcoated lies without a dose of mentha to ease her nausea. When Ulrick retired to his room, Meagan fled to the bailey to breathe a fresh breath of air and corral her scattered composure. The man unnerved her, and Meagan was more than a mite suspicious of Ulrick's reasons for seeking her out.

Did Ulrick expect that she would carry the news of his existence to Trevor, who would, in turn, search out his not-so-dead uncle? And if he did anticipate her course of action, did he intend to prevent it? Would her association with Desmond jeopardize his life as well? Nay, surely Ulrick would not stoop to something as dastardly as murder, she told herself, only half believing it. Perhaps Ulrick had mellowed through the years and had buried the resentment he had carried for Trevor's family. After all, Ulrick had what he wanted. Maybe he had come to Rocaille Chateau to explain and to apologize, hoping Meagan would relay the message to Trevor.

Clinging to the positive thoughts, Meagan inhaled

another breath of air and aimed herself toward the forebuilding, intending to rest. Desmond had constantly harped at her to confine herself to mild activity and shorter days, but it had been difficult. Meagan had been restless and often yearned to gallop across the countryside that she had only been allowed to view from her window.

A muddled frown knitted Meagan's brow when Desmond's cloaked figure moved silently toward her. "Is something amiss, m'lord?" Her question sprang from a strange premonition that suddenly swam over her. Where could Desmond be going at this late hour? He rarely ventured out after dark.

"I am not certain, my dear." Desmond extracted the summons that had arrived only a few moments earlier. "King Phillip of France has requested my presence in court, and I must leave immediately to reach my destination on the morrow." The concern in her gaze drew his fond smile and he reached out to smooth a renegade strand of blond hair away from her lovely face. "Do not fret, little dove. I am not so old that I cannot endure a long night's ride. I will not abandon you for longer than necessary."

Meagan did not have the heart to tell him that her main concern was for herself, having the sinking feeling that Desmond's absence could be all too convenient for Ulrick Burke. "Could you not send a courier to the king and inform him that you will arrive on the morrow, but at a later hour? 'Tis unwise to travel in the cloak of darkness in England, and I would think that Normandy and France have their . . ."

Desmond's soft chuckle brought quick death to her plea, and his gentle hand returned to her face to smooth away her worried frown. "I will be safe with my escort. It is obvious that you have not heard tales of the illustrious king. He is given to impulsiveness, having dismissed his first wife to wed a woman who also had another spouse. One does not cross Phillip. One simply tolerates him while he struggles to keep his kingdom separate from that of William's. You see, child, William's son, Robert, has been at odds with his powerful father, and King Phillip sides with Robert. The landowners of Normandy and France are always being summoned by

310

one or the other to ensure that our allegiance has not shifted in favor of William."

Be that as it may, Meagan was frantic. She needed Desmond's protection. "But I do not want you to go. If you must I wish to travel with you," Meagan pleaded as she hugged him close, afraid that if she remained behind she would be subjected to some fiendish plan Ulrick had devised to ensure that Trevor would never discover that his uncle was still flitting about in his human form.

Desmond pried her arms from his neck and pressed a fleeting kiss to her forehead. "Nay, you must remain here, *chérie*. Trevor forbids such journeys. Now be a good girl and retire to your room. I will return tomorrow night."

As his bulky figure disappeared into the darkness and the hoofbeats faded into silence, Meagan forced herself to return to her chamber, but giving way to her apprehension, she called Lear and Garda to join her. It was better to be safe than sorry, she assured herself. Perhaps Ulrick Burke meant her no harm, but Meagan was no longer a trusting soul. She had seen too many people betrayed by malicious intentions, herself included. Ulrick Burke's arrival and Desmond's sudden departure seemed much more than a coincidence, and Meagan would take no chances, nor could the hours pass quickly enough while she awaited Desmond's return.

As the door creaked open, Meagan was overwhelmed by yet another eerie sensation. An alarmed gasp escaped her lips when she spied a movement beside her, but before she could dart into the corridor, a man's hand clamped over her mouth and she was shoved farther into the room.

"You know of Trevor's past, don't you?" Ulrick breathed down her neck. "You also know what must be done. The news of my existence must never reach your husband's ears." There was a deadly threat in his voice, and Meagan knew for certain that her first impression of Ulrick Burke had been correct, although she wished to heaven she had been wrong.

Meagan choked on the small breath Ulrick allowed her, and her heart thundered against her chest with such ferocity that she feared it would beat her to death before Ulrick could dispose of her. As Ulrick drew the dagger from its sheath, Meagan heard Lear's low growl. The shepherd curled his way around the partially opened door to show Ulrick his full set of teeth.

"Do you think to frighten me off with your mutt?" Ulrick laughed harshly as his dagger slid across her throat, assuring her that he would inflict a fatal wound before Lear could leap at him. "I have seen to it that Desmond will not be around to question my explanation of your untimely death. I have carefully planned my visit after my audience with King Phillip. His intent to confer with Desmond could not have come at a more opportune moment." Ulrick's heavy breath triggered a rash of goose pimples that cascaded across Meagan's skin, and she trembled fearfully in his captive arms.

"You are a fool, Ulrick. Trevor will question my death," Meagan assured him, knowing full well it would come as a relief to her estranged husband. "Sooner or later he will learn that you have again deceived him."

"Silence, bitch," Ulrick hissed as his blade slashed the side of her neck.

Meagan screamed at the top of her lungs as the searing pain burned its way across the left side of her throat. Lear reacted in a split second, springing at the man who held Meagan at knife point and who had every intention of disposing of his beloved mistress. Lear bit into Ulrick's hand until he yelped in pain, forcing him to release his grasp on Meagan. The dagger fell to the floor as Meagan scrambled away, and the wolflike shepherd yielded to his natural instincts. When Ulrick struck out at him, Lear devoured his prey, lunging at his enemy's throat to inflict the same anguishing pain Ulrick had forced upon Meagan. Lear's vicious growl intermingled with Ulrick's agonized cries as the dog knocked him to the floor. Lear clamped his deadly jaws around Ulrick's neck as he frantically groped for the discarded knife and then raised it, poised to bury the blade between Lear's ribs.

Horrified, Meagan listened to her would-be assassin gasp for breath as she grasped her own throat, feeling the blood trickling from her wound. If Lear had not come to her rescue, she would have been lying on the floor with her life seeping from her body. And yet, she couldn't allow the shepherd to murder Ulrick, even though he most surely deserved it.

"Lear!" Meagan choked out. "Come!"

The giant shepherd bolted away from Ulrick before he could slash him with his knife. But Ulrick had sustained several painful wounds, and it took a moment for him to roll to his hands and knees, sputtering to catch his breath. His malicious growl echoed in silence so thick it could have been sliced with a knife, and Meagan retreated another step, certain Ulrick intended to come at her again.

As he struggled to gather his feet beneath him and hurl the blade in her direction, Meagan dashed from the room, blinded by a sea of tears. She couldn't think. She could barely draw a breath without choking on it. Raw instinct drove her from the chateau and into the darkness, stung by the overwhelming urge to put a safe distance between herself and the horrible scene that kept flashing before her eyes. Meagan did not fear the darkness as much as she feared what lay behind her—a man who had been presumed dead once, a man who harbored enough evil to stalk her and ensure that he finished what he had begun.

Meagan succumbed to hysterical sobs as she weaved her way through the brush, afraid of her own shadow, haunted by Conan's warning that danger lurked so close that she must keep her wits about her to elude it.

Oh, why had she called off Lear? Now she would live with the torment that Ulrick was standing in the darkness, awaiting the opportunity to pounce upon her again. Her blood ran cold, remembering the feel of his arms about her, the harshness of his voice, the pain of having her throat slashed by his deadly blade.

As Meagan scurried through the brush, her eyes darted wildly about her, her ears pricked to the sound of danger, wishing she could take to her wings like Garda and sail away from the terrifying memories that hounded her.

The crackling of twigs behind her sent her heart racing

313

around her ribs and Meagan quickened her step and glanced up at the stars to locate her direction. She would go home, back to England, or at least die trying, she promised herself.

Meagan's scratched face puckered into a frown as she peered helplessly at the northern shore of Normandy. In her haste to flee she had neglected to consider how she was to cross the channel that separated her from her homeland. She slumped back to rest and absently ran her hand over the caked blood on the side of her neck. She had narrowly escaped Ulrick's blade, only to find herself standing on the shore, gazing across the rippling waters that were far too wide to swim across. Meagan wished to sprout a pair of wings to fly home, but the way her luck had been running of late, she imagined that her chances of suddenly growing feathers were as slim as the possibility of a woman attaining knighthood.

Heaving a weary sigh, Meagan drew her cloak more tightly about her, hoping to catch a catnap and dream up some ingenious method of ferrying across the channel.

The sound of laughter wafted its way toward her, and Meagan stirred from sleep to peek through the brush, spying more than a dozen men who approached the shore. In the distance two longboats appeared, and Meagan felt a breath of hope stirring within her. She *had* to convince these men to transport her across the channel, she told herself firmly. This was her one and only hope of returning to England.

Mustering her courage, Meagan rose from her hiding place, wiped the grime from her face, and drew her fur cape more tightly about her neck to camouflage her wound. With Lear trotting along beside her and Garda perched on her arm, Meagan ventured toward the Norman knights who were garbed in chain-mail shirts and surcoats.

Fredrick Gilbert's jaw sagged on its hinges when he spotted the comely lass who walked steadily toward them, her head held high, her silver-blond hair billowing about her delicate features. Leaving his companion in midsentence, he

314

strode toward Meagan, his dark eyes cascading over the trim figure that was hidden beneath her expensive cloak.

"M'lady, may I be of assistance," Fredrick murmured as he gave Meagan the once-over, twice, finding only a few scratches to mar this mysterious goddess's beauty. Lord, this gorgeous creature had set his pulse to racing when he was within ten feet of her.

Meagan summoned her dignity and then graced the gallant warrior with a smile as he took her hand to place a light kiss upon it.

"Sir, I must return to England posthaste. I am the wife of Trevor Burke, Baron of Wessex. My lord had sent me to Normandy during the rebel uprisings, but an attempt has been made on my life and 'tis my wish to return to my husband's protection," she replied in perfect French.

Fredrick felt a wave of disappointment wash over him. This enchanting nymph was Burke's wife? It seemed the mighty Norman warrior had all the luck. "My companions and I will be honored to accompany you to the English shore." A rueful smile pursed his lips as he stared into a dazzling pair of sapphire eyes. "I served with Trevor during the invasion, but I had not heard of his marriage." His gaze swarmed over Meagan, but there was nothing crude or offensive in the way he assessed her. Fredrick envied Trevor, a man he had long admired and respected. "Burke has done well for himself. You, m'lady, are enchanting."

Relieved that she would not be assaulted by a mob of unruly mercenaries, Meagan broke into another easy smile, but she silently reminded herself that if Trevor had been here he would have argued the fact that he had been struck with good fortune when he made Meagan his wife. Indeed, he would have sold her as unnecessary baggage to the highest bidder.

"You are very kind . . ." She paused to allow the chivalrous knight to supply his name.

"Fredrick Gilbert at your service." He bowed before Meagan and then rose to full stature to drink another dose of the intoxicating warmth that settled in his belly when he looked upon her. "My men and I will see to it that you safely reach Hastings. I wish we could accompany you to your husband's castle. It has been two years since I have seen Trevor. But William has summoned us to Mercia."

"I will be able to enlist the aid of my own family once I reach England," Meagan hastily assured him, hoping this kind gentleman would never learn that she had been banished from her home. "I am sure Trevor will see you justly rewarded for coming to my rescue once I inform him of our meeting." Actually, Meagan doubted that, but she wanted Fredrick to believe that she and Trevor were on most friendly terms. If Trevor learned that the knight had helped her to escape from Normandy, he would be furious. But by the time he learned of her disappearance, she would be safely tucked away, and all of his searching would not bring him an inch closer to finding her.

Meagan bit back a wry smile as Fredrick led her to the water's edge to await the approaching boats. Soon she would be back in England, and if the country was not big enough for the both of them, then Trevor could return to Normandy to bury his treacherous uncle. She had had quite enough dealings with the Burke family, she reminded herself as Fredrick assisted her into the boat. She would raise Trevor's child, offering him all the love his father had refused. Meagan would claim Trevor's child, something Trevor could never take from her. Her love for the Dark Prince would nurture and grow in a child who would become everything his father was and was *not,* Meagan told herself. This child would be both Saxon and Norman, a combination of his father's strength and his mother's independence. And this child would fully understand the meaning of love, she promised herself as she peered at the shores of her beloved England. The affection Trevor had denied would be the source of her son's strength. In that respect he would become a far better man than his cynical father—the Dark Prince who had refused to believe that she had his best interest at heart since the moment she realized that he had become the master of her soul.

Chapter 22

A sentimental tear crept into the corner of Meagan's eye as she peered at Lowell Castle. So much had happened since the first time she had laid eyes on the barbaric monstrosity. Now her concern was to ensure Edric's safety. When she learned his fate, she would journey to the convent and wait until her child was born. Meagan had not taken the time to consider what was to be done after the birthing. Well, she would just have to worry with that detail tomorrow, she told herself as she forced one foot in front of the other, refusing to rest until she had reached her destination.

Before Meagan walked across the drawbridge, Almund Culver dashed toward her, his face beaming and yet full of unanswered questions. His smile melted into a concerned frown when he spied the scar on Meagan's neck and the tattered clothes that showed definite signs of enduring a long, tedious journey.

"M'lady? What has happened? Where have you been these past months? Edric has been beside himself with worry."

"Edric is here then?" Meagan queried, her eyes wide with surprise. She had wondered if Trevor would oust him from his post, just to spite her.

"Yea, m'lady." Almund peered at her as if she were addle-witted. "Where else would you expect the vassal to be?"

Dead, imprisoned, maimed . . . Each dreadful thought had crossed her mind as she trudged cross-country, carefully avoiding the swarms of humanity that had infiltrated the forest to escape the wrath of the Normans.

"So much has happened during your absence that I do not know where to begin," Almund rattled on. "Lord Burke has made several changes here. The war has gone miserably for the northern rebels. Lord Burke has been at his king's side, beating down any and all resistance that stands in his way and . . ."

"What changes?" Meagan demanded to know. She already knew that the north had been charred beyond recognition, and she was anxious to know how her brother had fared during the upheaval.

Almund wrapped a supporting arm around Meagan when she stumbled over the ripped hem of her tunic. "Lord Burke ordered Edric to take a wife, one he claimed would benefit the Norman system."

Meagan gulped hard, suddenly feeling sick inside. Had Trevor vengefully forced Edric to marry another woman to maintain his position, knowing that he loved Devona? Was that the cross Trevor forced Edric to bear? Damn him! He derived fiendish pleasure in seeing the last of the Lowells in abject misery.

Before Meagan could interrogate him further, Edric appeared at the entrance, his expression mirroring shock. "Egod, Meagan! You look as if you have traipsed halfway across England without a decent night's sleep," Edric squeaked when he viewed his disheveled sister at close range. "Where have you been? Lord Burke refused to tell me what had become of you."

Meagan flung her arms about his neck and thoroughly squeezed the stuffing out of him. At last she felt safe and secure, and her fears about her brother had been laid to rest. "I have been to hell and back," Meagan assured him, muffling a sniff. "Could you perchance spare some food and drink for a weary traveler?"

Edric held her away from him, his gaze somber. "I do not know what trials you have suffered because of me, since Lord Burke refuses to allow your name to tumble from his lips, but I do know that I owe you my life, Meagan. If you and Devona had not seen to it that I remained at the castle, I would have fallen beside Reid Granthum. I will do all I can to ease your burdens, but there is much I do not understand."

"I will explain the whole of it," Meagan assured him tiredly. "But first you must allow me to rest. My journey has been a difficult one."

Although curiosity was eating him alive, Edric bit back his barrage of questions and propelled Meagan toward the Great Hall for refreshment. When she had eaten her fill and had seen to it that Lear and Garda's appetites had been appeased, she spilled her story to Edric and then demanded to know of the events that had taken place since she had left him tied in his room.

Edric eased back in his chair, pondering how he was to keep his banished sister safe from catastrophe without offending Lord Burke, whose dark moods had become pitch black since the moment he had appeared on the drawbridge of Lowell Castle, issuing orders in his harsh, impatient tone. At least the foul-tempered baron was off serving his king, Edric reminded himself. It would give him time to contemplate what was to be done with Meagan.

"Lord Burke demanded that I take a wife of his choosing," Edric announced and then sipped his ale.

"So Almund has informed me." Meagan frowned curiously. "Where is she? Are you living in separate fortresses?"

"Lady Lowell is resting in our solar. She is with child and has suffered a rough bout with morning sickness."

Meagan's face fell like an avalanche. Edric had kept his wife right under Devona's nose and had spawned a child, one that he had refused to grant his mistress? Meagan was silently fuming. The *least* Edric could have done was to keep his distance from the woman Trevor ordered him to wed and see to it that they roomed in separate chambers. Men. They were all alike—lusting beasts, one and all, even her own flesh and blood whom she had protected and thus forfeited her own happiness.

"How has Devona adjusted to this ironic twist of fate?" Meagan muttered, her expression sour enough to curdle milk.

"She has accepted it as she has all else, quietly, nobly . . ."

"Damnation, Edric!" Meagan's fist hit the table, rattling the dishes and slopping ale on the white tablecloth. "How could you be so cruel to Devona? Hasn't she suffered enough?"

"My, but you are in a fit of temper," Edric smirked, bewildered by Meagan's quicksilver mood. "Devona has all she has ever wanted. Why would you think she would have reason to complain?"

Meagan stared at her brother, certain his logic was hampered by the empty cavity between his ears. "You have wed another woman who is with child and you wonder why *I* am in a fit of temper?" she shrieked. "Edric Lowell, you are as dense as an oak tree!"

Edric raked Meagan's shabby attire, wild blond hair, and irate expression and then frowned bemusedly. Meagan was certainly behaving strangely. He had expected her to be elated with the news. "Lord Burke demanded that I marry Devona and I did. Why are you putting up such a fuss? I thought it would please you that we are man and wife, since you have preached to me on the subject on numerous occasions."

The annoyance that had set fire to Meagan's temper evaporated, but still she was baffled. Why would Trevor insist upon the marriage? Indeed, she had anticipated that he would keep Edric and Devona apart for his demented pleasure.

"Oh, Edric, I am so happy for you," Meagan insisted, tears welling up in the back of her eyes. "I did not know that it was Devona you had wed. Almund did not tell me that. I had assumed that Trevor had arranged a political match."

Gesturing toward the stairs, Edric flashed her a wry smile. "Perhaps you would like to wash away the grime and rest before you meet my lady. She would be distressed to see you looking like an unsightly urchin."

Meagan nodded agreeably. A long, peaceful nap sounded heavenly. "We do not wish to upset Lady Lowell in her fragile condition," she chortled, wondering if Edric would be fussing over her if he knew that both his sister and his wife were expectant mothers.

"Nay, we cannot," Edric accorded, his smile widening into a grin. "My wife has taken great pains to ensure *my* protection, and I am equally concerned for her. I keep her in bed as much as possible . . . to ensure that she rests, of course."

There was a rakish glint in her brother's eyes and Meagan did not doubt that Edric had more on his mind than keeping Devona flat on her back for health reasons.

"Of course," Meagan snickered as she pulled herself to her feet, realizing how exhausted she truly was. "And now if you will excuse me, m'lord, I am in need of a long rest myself."

As Meagan dragged herself up the steps to her solar, a pair of brooding amber eyes watched her from the shadows of the corridor. When Trevor had seen Meagan in the distance, all of his bitterness had risen like cream on fresh milk, along with a myriad of emotions that he had battled for over two months. Although Conan had advised him that Meagan might not have been guilty of whatever crimes Trevor thought she had committed, he had refused to listen to any words voiced in her defense. The witch had obviously cast a spell on the old sage, and Trevor could no longer trust Conan's logic when it came to the touchy subject of Meagan. Trevor had thrown himself into battle, waging a war on the Saxon rebels as well as enduring the inner conflict with his distorted emotions. The battle had left many casualties, not the least of which was Trevor's bleeding heart. Try as he might, he could not force Meagan's memories to retreat. They came at him like an invading army, haunting his dreams and feeding his nightmares. The mere sight of his bedraggled wife brought the tormenting memories from their shallow graves, rising like specters to taunt him all over again.

How had Meagan escaped Desmond? It seemed no one could keep that woman caged when it was not her wont. She must have transformed herself into a bat to wing her way to freedom, returning to pour salt on his healing wounds.

"Vassal Lowell." Trevor's husky voice wafted its way

321

across the quiet hall and Edric pivoted, his eyes bugging from their sockets, his heart catapulting to his throat. Trevor pushed away from the wall and closed the distance between them in deliberate strides, his unrelenting gaze holding Edric in bondage until he was staring down into the vassal's peaked face. "How long have you been keeping Meagan here without my knowledge?" he demanded gruffly.

Edric peered up at the towering overlord, whose condemning glare would have had a mountain lion cowering in his den. "She has only just arrived," he chirped, wondering if Trevor would swallow the truth. He looked so furious that Edric was certain the lord's flaming temper would see him reduced to a heap of smoldering embers. "But I think you should hear her reasons for . . ."

"Do not think to rush to her defense," Trevor snapped brusquely. "If I wish to endure another lie, I would prefer that it comes from *her* lips, not yours. You are already treading on thin ice." His hard glare was potent enough to melt the ground beneath Edric's feet, leaving him treading water when the thin ice gave way. "Stand aside, Edric. I intend to speak with my wife . . . now."

"But, m'lord." Edric boldly grasped Trevor's arm to detain him when he whirled away. "Meagan is . . ."

When Trevor's head swiveled around to level Edric a glower, the words died on his lips. It was obvious that he might as well be carrying on a conversation with a stone wall. It would have been as receptive as Trevor in his present mood.

Without uttering a word, Trevor aimed himself toward the stairs, taking them two at a time in his haste to see the witch who had spirited across Normandy, sailed across the channel, and winged her way across England to resettle herself on her perch. Lord, he was itching to break the broom that sorceress had confiscated to fly home on, he mused sourly.

Meagan stretched leisurely on her feather bed and then sighed wearily. After spending a fortnight on the cold, hard ground she made a mental note never to overlook the luxury of sleeping on a soft mattress. It was heaven to relax on a bed that was not crawling with varmints of the night. Her sooty lashes fluttered down, and a quiet smile traced her lips. If only the rest of her life could be as peaceful as it was at this moment, she thought whimsically.

And then the entire castle rumbled as if besieged by an earthquake. The door bounced against the wall, streams of dust trickling from the woodwork. Meagan bolted straight up in bed, gasping in horror as Trevor stomped toward her like a frothing beast stalking its prey.

"Trev . . ." His name escaped her lips in an alarmed whisper.

Instinctively, she bounded from bed to make her escape, but Trevor moved just as agilely, flinging her back in the direction she had come, sending her sprawling on her bed. His narrowed gaze riveted over her as he held her in place, taking note of her ragged clothes, stained cheeks, hollowed eyes, and tangled platinum hair.

"God, woman, you look like hell," he muttered and then wondered why he still felt this wild, irrational attraction for Meagan when she looked like something the cats dragged in. Damnation, she *was* a witch, Trevor decided. Why else would she appeal to him when she was at her worst? He had to be under her spell; otherwise he would have been repulsed by their physical contact. But repulsion was not the emotion that was boiling through his veins. It was a strange concoction of anger, desire, and simmering frustration.

"Then we make a matched pair," Meagan hissed, her breasts heaving, her blue eyes snapping with indignation. "You look like the very devil."

Where did he find the gall to insult her appearance when his raven hair sprayed about his face in disarray and his hardened features were etched with grime? He was covered with dust and smelled like a lathered horse. Obviously, he was born with unmitigated gall, Meagan thought resentfully. Tactful he was not, nor had he ever been, come to think of it. The Dark Prince was domineering, hateful, and downright exasperating. Why had she fallen in love with this

323

fire-breathing dragon, she asked herself. All she would ever receive in return for her affection was *burns* from his flaming breath.

"At least you have saved me a great deal of trouble," he grumbled scornfully. "William has planned a royal celebration after he crushes the resistance, and he expects to meet my *lovely* wife." His tone was so heavily laden with mockery that Meagan felt as if she had been pricked. "It will be difficult to provide the enchanting, loyal product that he anticipates, but I will set about to salvage what is left of your appearance and educate you with the proper manners befitting a wench who is about to meet her king."

"I prefer to miss the festivities," Meagan gritted out. "I do not think I can tolerate my escort, and I doubt that I can be civil to your king when hounded by a man with your grizzly disposition."

When Meagan thrust out her defiant chin and then glanced away, snubbing him, Trevor spied the jagged scar that marred her swanlike neck. The venom drained from his amber eyes as he carefully traced the wound.

"How did you get that?" he questioned, his tone softly inquiring.

Meagan was not to be subdued by the gentleness in his voice. She had seen this black panther purring one moment and then growling in the next instant. It was best to keep her claws bared for the upcoming encounter, knowing there would inevitably be one.

"From your not-so-dead uncle," she spat at him.

Trevor sank down beside her, his fierce grip easing as shock registered on his chiseled features. "Ulrick?" God, it couldn't be. The man was dead. The courier had sworn it to be true.

Meagan nodded affirmatively. "He intended to dispose of me because he thought I knew too much. I tried to explain that his secret would be safe with me since you intended to leave me in Normandy . . . permanently," she added bitterly. "But the vicious brute did not allow me the opportunity to explain. He went for my throat. If not for Lear, my head would have been separated from my shoulders. Not that you would have cared, dear husband. I would think you would applaud your uncle's handiwork."

Trevor's face paled beneath his dark tan. "That miserable bastard," he spat as if the word left a bitter taste in his mouth.

A curious frown knitted Meagan's brow as Trevor's jaw clenched and his golden eyes took on a faraway look. "Do you call him that in anger or in honesty?" Meagan had noticed no family resemblance when she had had the misfortune of meeting Ulrick, but she had only assumed that Trevor carried his mother's traits more strongly than his father's.

"He is the illegitimate son, born out of wedlock. Ulrick lusted after all my father's possessions and he lived to destroy everyone else's happiness. Ulrick thrived on his festering hatred for my father and his family," he muttered, his voice crackling with emotion. "I can never rest in peace until I have destroyed that bastard."

"Lear would have seen to his murder if I had not called him back to my side," Meagan grumbled, wishing she had not been so tenderhearted to a man who made Lucifer appear a saint. "He deserved to die after what he tried to do."

Trevor spitefully wished Meagan had allowed her wolflike shepherd to make a meal of Ulrick. He had thought the man had been wiped from the face of the earth to serve eternity in the devil's inferno long before now. A long, quiet moment passed while Trevor wrestled with the bitter memories he had attempted to bury three years earlier. But they rose before him, twisting in his belly until he could taste the sweetness of revenge upon his lips.

Once he had encouraged Meagan to forget her resentment for the Normans who now ruled her homeland, but Trevor couldn't accept his own advice. Ulrick had caused his family tremendous heartache, and now he had dared to dispose of Meagan to prevent her from carrying the secret to Trevor. The man was rotten to the core, he thought murderously. He could not allow Ulrick to attempt murder and permit him to live. Trevor could never be content, knowing Ulrick was alive and well. He had enough difficulty sleeping nights without wondering if that ruthless bastard would feel threatened and come sneaking out of the shadows to murder him and his wife.

When Trevor's wandering thoughts circled back to the present, a bemused frown clung to his brow. Meagan was supposed to have been under Desmond's care. How could he have allowed this tragedy to happen? Desmond had been his longtime friend, a man Trevor had trusted. It was obvious that he was ignorant of Trevor's belief that his uncle had died before the invasion of Saxon England. But had he ignored Meagan's suspicions of the man who tried to kill her? Egad, was there no place Trevor could stash this woman without trouble brewing about her, he asked himself as he focused his full attention on Meagan. "How did you escape the chateau? Where was Desmond while my uncle plotted to kill you?"

"Ulrick knew that King Phillip had requested an audience with Desmond, and he arrived the same day as the royal courier," Meagan explained, a trace of bitterness seeping into her voice. "Your uncle wanted Desmond conveniently out of the way when he exterminated me. I hate to venture a guess at the lie Ulrick was preparing to give to Desmond upon his return."

As Trevor's scrutinizing gaze traveled over her, his index finger instinctively trailed across her scratched cheek. Although Meagan had battled against her attempted murderer and had managed a rugged journey, she showed no outward signs of starvation. Meagan retained her shapely figure, her breasts full, her hips padded with just the right amount of flesh to leave inviting contours. Trevor was tempted to reach out to run his hand along the enticing swells and curves, but he stilled the absent caress when Meagan continued.

"I was too frightened to remain at the chateau. The instinct to return to England gnawed away at me. When I reached the northern shore of Normandy I was allowed passage with Norman mercenaries who journeyed to York to join William." Meagan did not bother to mention Fredrick's name. No doubt, Trevor would hunt down his old friend and curse him for offering to assist her. "Once I reached Hastings I traveled alone and only arrived at the castle late this afternoon," she added for Edric's defense, just in case Trevor had accused him of harboring a fugitive.

"How is it you have grown plump when you look as though you have waded through a barren hell?" Trevor questioned, giving way to the impulse of trailing his hand over the full mound of her breast and along the contour of her waist.

Her eyes darted away, avoiding his pointed gaze, wishing he had not been so observant. "I gorged myself like a pig at Desmond's chateau, hoping you would not recognize me, if by chance you ever returned," she replied, her tone coated with sarcasm.

Trevor raised his hand to strike her for her insolent remark, but Meagan raised a proud chin. "Go ahead, beat me," she challenged daringly. "It could be no worse than Reid's brutal abuse or Ulrick's deadly carvings. Men seem to delight in proving their strength over women, as if it were the only weapon with which they have to fight."

His grip eased from her arm, and he clenched his fist as he gathered his feet beneath him to march toward the door. He was sorely tempted to thrash her, but it would serve no purpose, Trevor reminded himself. More than once he had shaken this feisty hellcat until her teeth rattled, but he had accomplished nothing. Nay, it was a waste of time to taunt this wench, he decided.

Meagan's relief was short-lived when Trevor stepped back into her room, sporting a devilish smile that made her all the more suspicious. She could deal with the forceful lord, insulting him until she drove him away, but the handsome swain who was grinning at her like a starved shark studying his next meal worried her.

"Now what fiendish torment do you have in mind for me, Trevor? Can I not enjoy one moment's peace before I am whisked off to your torture chamber?"

Mild amusement glistened in his eyes. He knew how to bring this fiery vixen down a notch. "Your room will become a temporary chamber for punishment until I can transport you to a cell equipped with the latest devices to crumble your sanity with indescribable pain." His grin broadened to show

327

even white teeth, and Meagan had to stifle the overwhelming urge to knock a few of them loose.

When a stream of servants, carrying heated water for a bath, filed into the room, a dubious frown carved new lines on her weary face. "Do you intend to drown me in my own tub?" she quipped caustically. "Why not seek out your poison-bearing handmaiden to stir up her toxic brew?"

Trevor swaggered back to pull the reluctant Meagan to her feet. Nimble fingers impatiently worked to remove the grimy tunic and chemise. Although Meagan squealed indignantly, Trevor was not to be denied the spiteful pleasure of stripping her naked. With a nudge he directed her toward the tub.

"Come, witch, I wish to see you stewing in your own pot. With any luck at all you will shrivel up like a prune," he chuckled sardonically.

Meagan sank down to cover herself with what little protection he offered, but Trevor had not missed the smallest detail of her alluring figure. He could name the location of each bruise that marred her creamy flesh, and he could feel her shapely curves beneath his hands without having to touch her. The sensation had long been branded on his mind, and he had only to gaze upon her to recall the feel of one uninterrupted caress.

Clasping the lavender-scented soap in her hands, Meagan gave Trevor the cold shoulder and set about to cleanse her skin, wishing Trevor would take the hint to leave. But the virile warrior continued to gawk, his all-consuming gaze following the path of the soap as it glided across her velvety flesh.

When Meagan heard him wrestling with his chain-mail shirt, she glanced up at him, her mouth gaping. "What on earth . . ." There was no need to complete her question. His intentions were obvious as his lean, bronzed body curled around hers in a tub that was built for one. The water level rose until waves of bubbles cascaded over the rim of the tub to stream across the floor like a river that had flooded its banks and to cut new channels across the planked floor.

"I seek to save the servants the trouble of hauling more

water up the stairs for my bath," he explained as he wedged his long legs on either side of her hips.

Although Meagan was doing her damnedest to remain cool and aloof, she burst out laughing. The feel of his body pressed to hers left her flaming with a desire his touch always had the power to ignite, causing columns of steam to burst into the air like an erupting geyser. And yet, she was amused by the comical picture Trevor presented. He reminded her of a toad who sat with his long legs tucked around his neck, his head thrust forward to prevent jabbing his knees into his chin. Her wish had finally come true, she mused with a giggle. The Dark Prince had finally been transformed into a frog. In the future, when he stormed toward her like a vengeful dragon, she would conjure up this vision of the bug-eyed frog and then laugh in his fuming face. Yea, it would make him furious, she realized, but she could endure his forms of torture if she could cling to this picture of the mighty Norman warrior doing his excellent impression of a frog.

This was not going as Trevor had anticipated. He had expected Meagan to be thrashing and yelping to avoid intimate contact, but she was cackling, her reckless laughter like joyous music to his ears. The bubbly sound dissolved his bitterness. No matter how hard he had tried to despise this vivacious wench, he simply could not. She had the power to make him smile, even when he had forgotten the meaning of happiness. She was a magician who could camouflage the treachery and deceit, leaving him longing to sail among rapturous clouds.

"Lord, woman, you are mad," he chided, but the laughter in his voice belied his insult. "I am not bathing for your amusement." His curious gaze flickered down his torso, wondering what she found so humorous about being up to one's neck in bubbles.

His eyes flitted back to her angelic face. It was the first time he had basked in the warmth of that radiant smile since . . . Enough of that, Trevor chastised himself. He had spent the better part of two months trying to forget how good it had been between them. But now the time of reckoning had come. He had to know if he had blown the enchanting memories out of proportion. Damn his stubborn pride. Damn the lies and deceit. If he was to spend eternity smoldering in hell for yielding to the temptation of this bewitching nymph, then so be it. He *had* to know if the flames of passion could outburn the fires in Hades.

Meagan's laughter faded into silence when she met those fathomless pools of gold. Trevor was luring her to him without voicing the command. She caught herself the split second before she threw common sense to the wind and surrendered to the urge to touch him, to caress his powerful body, to press her lips to the sensuous curve of his.

Grasping at what was left of her self-control, Meagan inclined her head, a sea of silver gold tumbling over one bare shoulder as she studied him warily. "What is your purpose, m'lord?" she demanded to know as she dodged his oncoming kiss.

"I wish to know if all that stands between us has dimmed the fascination you hold for me," he rasped, his voice thick with passion. Cautiously, his dark head moved toward hers and then his mouth feathered over hers, gently inquiring, testing her reaction. "Open your lips to me, Meagan. I want to drink freely of the nectar that once left me dizzy and intoxicated."

Delicious waves of desire crumbled the barriers that had once seemed insurmountable. His tongue probed the inner softness of her mouth and then mated with hers, feeding a flame that had been left to burn, fueled by bittersweet memories of the past. Meagan knew the moment his arms glided around her that her love for him was a torture far worse than any method Trevor might have devised. His embraced was her own private room in hell.

Her heart thundered around her ribs like a stallion galloping in wild, frantic circles. Her breath was ragged, as if he had deprived her of oxygen, leaving her gasping to inhale that life-giving essence which, like love, seemed intangible in its existence. His hands were like a gentle massage that erased the soreness in her body, leaving her relaxed and responsive in his strong arms. The long, harrowing days she had endured during her journey faded as the clouds of pleasure engulfed her. Perhaps the world had gone up in smoke, but Meagan had captured one timeless moment in heaven. Whatever fate she faced, she would accept it if only she could lose herself to the manly scent of this man, if she could quench her thirst with the divine taste of his kisses, if she could revel for one uninterrupted instant in the rapturous sensations of his skillful lovemaking.

"I fear nothing has changed," Trevor mused aloud as his moist kisses skimmed the pink bud of her breast and then languidly wandered to offer the same arousing attention to the other taut peak. "You set fire to my blood, a flame so fierce that it threatens to consume my entire being, but even when it has engulfed me, the flame never burns itself out. I do not know how it can continue to feed when it has devoured me, but it blazes anew each time I dare to touch you."

Meagan was too overwhelmed by the soul-shattering sensations to force her thoughts to tongue. She desperately wanted him, needed him, and speaking the words could never truly describe this hungry obsession that claimed her.

Trevor dragged himself away from her hypnotic kiss and then lifted her into his arms to seek out the plush fur rug that was spread before the hearth. His gaze weighed heavily upon her, wandered unhindered over her delicate features, and then focused on those sapphire blue eyes that mirrored an emotion that he had no time to decode. His body tensed with its instinctive need for her, one that time and bitterness could never erase. It was a growing hunger that had become an addiction. Since the first moment he had pulled her into his arms he had known of his magnetic attraction to Meagan. No matter how many times this enticing vixen lied to him and threatened his existence, he kept fluttering back to her like a mindless moth impulsively drawn to a flame. He well knew the dangers of his weakness for this woman, but he could never resist her. The force that compelled him to her was too great, and he could but surrender to her subtle magic.

When her exploring hand made contact with the hard wall of his chest, Trevor groaned, knowing he would always be vulnerable to Meagan. She could take command of raw emotion, making him an obedient slave. He danced to the mystical tune of her voice, craved the feel of her supple body against his, inhaled the luring, feminine fragrance that clung to her and then hovered about him long after he had eased his ravenous passion for her.

Meagan peered up into his dark, chiseled features, which were carved with nobility and pride, and then felt her heart melting all over her ribs. If Trevor could not see the love sparkling in her eyes, he was either blind or stupid. Why couldn't he understand that all she had done, the trials she had suffered, had been her sacrifice to him? She had unselfishly dared to right the wrongs, but he was wary of her loyalty. It would have been easier to spare herself the misery but she had been unable to stand aside to watch him perish. Her love had survived the torments of hell and she ached to hear him confess that he shared even the smallest amount of the affection she harbored for him.

And then the words she had so carefully held in check tumbled free. It was her last chance to find happiness with the one man who had tamed her wild heart. "Trevor, I love you more than life itself. Can you not see it in my eyes? You have mistrusted my purpose, but I have been faithful and loyal to you, even when you would have left me to wither away. Can you not see the one truth in life?" she murmured, her voice crackling with emotion. "There is but love to feed my soul, a love so strong that even your denial cannot harm it."

"Do not speak." Trevor grimaced and then pressed his index finger to her lips to shush her. He did not wish to face his doubts, ones that had trailed along on his shadow. He only wanted to forget the past while he drowned in the sensations of having her luscious body pressed intimately to his. He ached to make love to her until he released all the pent-up emotions that churned inside him. "'Tis not the time to talk, but to share. I want you, Meagan, as I always have."

His mouth plundered hers in savage obsession, devouring, ravishing her until he had stripped the breath from her lungs, leaving her clinging to him until he breathed life back into

332

her. His caresses were rough with urgency as they raked across her quivering skin, as if he were to be granted only a few cherished moments before his treat was snatched away from him. Wave upon wave of spine-tingling sensations pelleted over her, ones that had remained dormant for months. Passion burned through them with the heat of a thousand suns merging into one. As his hands lifted to cup her breast, his hot kisses flowed over the slope of her shoulder, his lips claiming the ripe bud, suckling and teasing until Meagan moaned in pure delight.

The urgency of his passion dwindled, leaving him to savor the touch and feel of her luxurious body beneath his exploring hands. He would not rush the pleasures that he had been denied these agonizing months, Trevor told himself, summoning his patience. Twice he had sought to ease his frustrations with other women, but he had sent them both away, cursing himself for his weakness for the one woman who had left his soul to bleed, refusing to release him from her spell. Now it was this blond, blue-eyed enchantress who lay beside him, offering to ease his needs, and he could close his eyes, knowing that the woman of his dreams and the woman in his arms were one and the same.

As his roaming caress seared across her abdomen to trace the curve of her hips, Meagan arched toward him, longing to appease the maddening ache of having him near without truly being a part of her. But Trevor had become incredibly patient, enjoying the power he held over her, delighting in her hungry response, and yet teasing her with his seductive fondling. His lean fingers splayed across her belly and then glided over her inner thigh, massaging, taunting, and then receding to retrack the flaming path that left her to burn. Again his hand blazed its tantalizing path to her womanly softness while his lips brushed the peak of each breast and then slowly descended.

Her breathing was erratic, knowing of the tormenting assault that awaited her, wondering if she could endure the sweet fondling that would take her to the edge of sanity. His knowing fingers and warm lips worked their sweet magic on her body. She was living and dying, wrapped in such exotic pleasures that she no longer cared if she had breathed her last breath.

Her delicate fingers investigated the corded muscles of his back and then slid across his hips, stroking his rough-textured skin, begging him to come to her to ease the torturous ache his kisses and caresses had stirred.

As he twisted above her, bracing his forearms on either side of her, he pressed against her, molding his muscular body to hers, but it was not close enough to please Meagan. She wanted him, all of him. She was inflamed with the maddening need of him that transcended physical possession. She wanted to touch his heart, to claim his soul, forging it to hers for one glorious moment that mere words or thoughts could not touch.

Her nails dug into the rippling muscles of his back, forcing him closer, shattering his self-control as she arched to meet his driving thrusts. Trevor could no longer contain his desires, they rose like a disturbed lion, roaring to unleash the chains, fighting their way to freedom. His arms crushed her to him, her breasts flattened against his chest to feel the furious beat of his heart. He swept her along with him in an accelerating rhythm that played an enchanting melody in the essence of her being. The crescendo of the melody built and then burst to pierce the silence, leaving them soaring higher and higher, passing each pinnacle of pleasure and seeking yet another.

The fire that leaped across the logs in the hearth could not match the blaze that consumed them. Their bodies and souls were one, as was the frantic beat of their hearts. The contours of his muscled flesh became hers. His demanding kiss became her breath of life. Theirs was a moment of complete possession. He was hers, sharing an existence in a universe of vivid colors and wild sensations that left them soaring across the sky like a shooting star.

Meagan clutched at him as they skyrocketed toward a new horizon and then succumbed to the tears of pleasure that flooded over her as he shuddered above her, his body surging toward hers in sweet release that had driven him until he had relinquished the last of his strength.

Although Trevor feared that his awesome weight would

334

crush her into the floor, he could not move. It would have taken a team of horses to drag him away, he mused as he mustered just enough energy to raise his spinning head and glance down into her flushed face. Her tangled hair sprayed across the fur quilt, glowing with the light from the fire, as if both the sun and moon had risen and set within the confines of the room. Her kiss-swollen lips parted in a mellow smile as her dark lashes fluttered up to allow him to glimpse the intense emotion that glistened in her eyes.

"Look at me, my love," Meagan commanded, her voice thick with the aftereffects of passion. "Do you think me so cruel and heartless that I could lie about the naked emotion in my gaze? 'Twas more than desire that touched my soul. What must I do to prove that you have taken possession of my heart? There is no greater torture than living with your disbelief."

Trevor struggled to sit up cross-legged and then stared into the fire, watching the curling fingers of the flames. While he was still digesting her confession, Meagan eased up beside him and inhaled a deep breath. She had to be perfectly honest with him. It was the first time he had listened to her words without throwing arguments back in her face.

"You once told me that I would never carry your child, but 'tis not so, m'lord. If I seem to have fared well during my journey without becoming no more than skin and bone, 'tis because . . ." Meagan knew she had planted too much seed for thought in too little time when his head swiveled around to glare at her. She had made a grave mistake, informing him of his fatherhood while he was still wrestling with the possibility that she loved him.

"What?" Trevor howled. His jaw gaped wide enough for a covey of quails to nest. "You are with child?" She had suffered the shock of practically having her throat slit, she had endured a grueling journey, and then Trevor had made love to her like a wild barbarian, unaware that he might have injured her or the baby.

His frown settled deeply in his tired features, his eyes sparking with condemnation. "How can you be so certain 'tis *my* child and not Reid Granthum's?" he quipped, his tone cracking with bitterness. Trevor rolled to his feet, anxious to put more distance between them. "Is that why you have suddenly professed to love me? Did you expect that I would take you back and provide for you and your child?" His stormy gaze swept over Meagan like an angry tempest. "You are beneath contempt, woman. Soft words of love pursued by such a startling announcement only make me more suspicious. I should have known the moment you said you loved me that you were preparing me for yet another betrayal. So your tryst with Granthum has spawned a child." Trevor's granite features showed signs of crumbling beneath the torment that her words had wrought. "Granthum swore with his dying breath that you were his woman. Now I know what he meant when he said I could never truly have you."

Meagan vaulted to her feet; so furious was she that she latched onto a log that lay by the hearth and hurled it across the room at him. "Damn you, Trevor. 'Tis *our* child! I have slept with no other man," she shouted at him.

He ducked away from the flying log and then dodged the second before unfolding his tall frame to glower at her. Lord, but this minx had a temper. "You can protest the truth of the matter to your heart's content," he scoffed. "But your lover assured me that you had been doing more than rallying around the Saxon flag."

"Reid despised you. He thought you had killed his sister. He had watched you claim land that was once his, and you wed *his* betrothed," Meagan parried, her voice rising until she was dangerously close to yelling in his face. "What did you expect a bitter man to do, wish you health and happiness after you had stripped him of his fief, his fortune, and his life?"

Meagan threw up her hands in exasperation, wondering if there was any conceivable way to pound any sense into his wooden head without resorting to the use of a hammer. "You are quick to take the word of your attempted murderer over mine. Do you honestly think I would allow another man to touch me after I had wed you?"

Although Trevor was fuming he was still oddly amused by her tantrum. He could not suppress the trace of a smile as the wild-haired hellion flounced across the room to don her chemise. "I suppose time will tell whose child you carry."

Trevor breathed a heavy sigh. "If I have misjudged you I will get down on my knees and beg forgiveness."

That she would like to see, Meagan muttered under her breath. His stubborn pride would never allow him to stoop that low. God, but this man was arrogant. Time will tell, indeed! He would believe her now or never! He would not come around to inspect his child with a fine-toothed comb and *then* decide if it was his flesh and blood, not if she had any say in the matter.

"And what if this baby has neither reddish nor raven hair, but the light complexion and the fair hair of his mother? Will you accuse me of having incestuous relations with my own brother?" Meagan sniffed disdainfully.

Trevor shot her a withering glance. "Nay, I would never . . ."

"Nay?" Meagan broke in to spout her bitter remark. "You are determined to believe the worst of me. If I am as wicked as you seem to think perhaps I should begin living up to your expectations of deceit and treachery." Deviltry flared in her eyes as she sauntered toward him to give him a firm shove that sent him retreating a step to catch his balance. Meagan pressed her hands to the solid wall of his chest, leaving him in a heap on the bed, and then followed him down. "If you see me as a malicious witch, then I shall become one. 'Tis your wretched soul I seek," she assured him in a haunting voice as she traced her index finger over the crisp hair on his chest and then plucked a few of them out to emphasize her point. When Trevor yelped in pain, Meagan chortled wickedly. "You will never be rid of me, my handsome knave. I will haunt your days and nights. Take me to your king and I will also lure him into my spell. And if you think to sentence me to your dungeon once again, even William will be wailing in outrage."

Trevor was bewildered by that fiery sparkle in her eyes. Even when she behaved like a vindictive wildcat he was magnetically attracted to her. There was no hope for it. This siren had taken hold of his heart and imprisoned it in chains.

"All that you have said about me 'tis true," Meagan declared. Let him chew on this ridiculous confession. She dearly hoped he would choke on it. "Reid was not the

337

mastermind behind the plot to murder you, nor was he the leader of the rebellion. 'Twas I. All these years I have sat alone in my chamber at the convent, devising ways to torture you. Although the nuns preached mercy and forgiveness to mine enemy, I was thinking vile thoughts. 'Twas I who demanded that Edric approach you on the subject of marriage, and then I set out to seduce you. Once I had control of Wessex I intended to dethrone our Norman king, using any technique I could devise. And men?" Meagan's smile broadened, her blue eyes dancing with mischief. "Yea, there were plenty of them to appease my appetite. I hungered to claim the souls of men as a vain woman collects precious jewels."

Trevor propped up on both elbows and peered at the feisty wench who was perched on his belly. "Do you expect me to swallow that concoction of lies?" he smirked. "I am not so dense that I cannot tell a virgin when I have had one."

Her shoulder lifted in a reckless shrug, playing her role as if she were born to it. "Someone had to be the first, and it was to my advantage to allow that man to be you. But you were not the last, of course. I was surrounded by an entire regiment of rebels and 'tis true that all activities did not entail waving the rebel flag. Each night I selected another willing knight with whom to share my passion." Her lips hovered over his like a taunting caress as she combed her fingers through Trevor's dark hair. "The Saxon rebels sold their souls to me, one and all, and in turn I served them up to the devil." Her moist lips descended on his to plant a kiss that carried enough heat to fuse his chain-mail shirt into solid metal. "And now you will take me to your king and I will make him my slave. William will become the figurehead, but 'tis I who will reign over England when the fires of hell have burned themselves out."

Trevor could stand no more. Her arousing touch and tormenting words were playing havoc with what little sense he had left after this battle of wits with Meagan. She had him so confused that he wasn't certain which direction was up. He squirmed to the far side of the bed and then eyed her warily. "I pray Conan can brew up a curative for lying. One moment you swear you love me and in the next breath you

338

confess that you are the devil's mistress. I think perhaps my oracle's remedy and a prolonged visit to the dungeon are the proper retribution."

Meagan rolled her eyes in disgust. The man was deaf, dumb, and blind. Any fool would know that she had unmercifully taunted him. Her only hope now was that Conan had invented a cure for idiocy. Trevor could do with a prescription.

"What? No complaint?" Trevor arched a haughty brow as he shrugged on the rest of his clothing.

"Conan cannot cure what afflicts me, and prison walls will not hold me. Your guard will have his price and I will be only too happy to pay it if he awards me freedom," Meagan countered in a confident tone that rankled Trevor.

His hard gaze riveted over her smug smile. "I will not have you dallying with *my* men. You will not make me the laughingstock of Burke Castle, woman. You have already humiliated me in front of William's regiment, and I will tolerate no more."

Meagan curled up on the bed and chortled at his monumental arrogance. He actually believed she would seduce one of his own men. The blundering fool! This was William's right-hand man? This dense prince? If it was true that birds of a feather flock together, she could only conclude that the king was also a madman.

"No one needs bother making a fool of you, m'lord," Meagan scoffed caustically. "You are adept at managing that task all by yourself, and quite proficiently, I might add."

"Get dressed," Trevor barked as he clasped his belt around his midsection and then adjusted his scabbard. "We have a long ride ahead of us."

"Are you dragging me back to your dungeon?" Meagan raised a challenging brow as she raked the huffy overlord. "I have already assured you that your musty cellar cannot hold me."

Indecision etched Trevor's chiseled features as he glared at the distracting termagant who constantly played havoc with his sanity. He was headed for Normandy to confront his malicious uncle, detouring to deposit Meagan within the confines of Burke Castle. But the cunning minx had the uncanny knack of vanishing into thin air, and only God knew where she would be when he returned. He could no longer trust anyone to keep a watchful eye on Meagan, and he had no choice but to take her with him. Surely she would be as hungry to avenge Ulrick's attack as he was, and she would not attempt to escape him until the return journey to England. But the trip home would be an entirely different matter, Trevor reminded himself. Even if Meagan was with child, she would not bypass the opportunity of eluding him. He would be forced to sleep with one eye open, and he made a mental note to do just that.

"As you said, the dungeon cannot hold you," Trevor concurred. "I am taking you with me to my uncle's chateau to settle unfinished business." Trevor strode over to fetch her clean clothes and then hurriedly helped her into them. "I can never be sure how I will fare with you, but it will save me the torment of wondering how and when you managed to slip between the bars of your cell and spirit off into the night."

"I think 'tis best to let sleeping dogs lie," Meagan advised, dreading another confrontation with Ulrick. "Your uncle is vicious and I do not relish meeting him again, since I very nearly lost my head on my first encounter with that deadly serpent."

"I will not risk having *him* come to *me*," Trevor said firmly. "When he realizes you have escaped him, he will hunger for both our deaths."

If Meagan never laid eyes on Ulrick Burke again, it would be all too soon, but she cherished the chance to spend time with Trevor. Although he might be planning to stash her in Rocaille Chateau indefinitely, she could be with him for a time. And perhaps she would have the chance to convince Trevor to allow her to return to the convent.

She breathed a weary sigh as Trevor led her from the room. Did she dare hope to persuade him to let her come home again to England? Her gaze darted to his stern, commanding features. My, but he was a stubborn man, one who was not easily swayed from his beliefs. She could only hope he would see his way clear to permit her to escort him home.

Chapter 23

A troubled frown etched Meagan's brow when she peered across the channel to see the looming storm clouds that rolled over the choppy waves. She remembered Ragnar telling her about his wife, who had been washed overboard and into the channel, never to return. But before she could voice her reservations, Trevor grasped her arm and led her to the longboat he had secured for their passage. Her wary gaze swept over the vessel, which was fifty feet long and fifteen feet wide. It had beveled and overlapping planks and ribs of sturdy oak that were caulked with animal hair that had been soaked in tar. The stem and stern were gently curved to meet the oncoming waves, and although the boat appeared seaworthy, Meagan was not at all certain she wanted to set foot upon it during the threat of a storm. She had traveled in similar vessels during her other voyages across the channel, but that had been an entirely different matter, she reminded herself as she fixed her eyes on the foreboding clouds.

When Trevor tugged on her arm and she didn't budge from her spot, he cast her a bemused glance. "Surely you are not leery of facing Ulrick? I thought you were anxious to see him pay for his crimes."

One delicate finger indicated the churning clouds that piled high in the sky. "'Tis not Ulrick who worries me. 'Tis yonder storm."

"I will allow nothing to happen to you," Trevor assured her as he shuffled her toward the vessel.

That was an overly generous offer, spoken from a man who had been so intent on his purpose of revenge that he had behaved as if he were traveling alone since they left Lowell Castle, Meagan thought acrimoniously. Trevor had completely shut her out of his thoughts, sparing little in the way of conversation as they traversed England to reach their destination. But then she reminded herself that Trevor had dragged her along with him, simply because he did not trust her in anyone else's care.

"Should the weather threaten, do you intend to divide the channel as Moses parted the Red Sea for the children of Israel, so I may walk the remainder of the way?" Meagan questioned as Trevor scooped her up and set her upon the deck.

"Would that I could, madam," Trevor replied absently before he turned back to give orders to the oarsmen.

Meagan felt her apprehension knotting in the pit of her belly as the wind began to whistle about them. The boat rocked to and fro, taking her stomach with it. And when the driving rain pelleted about the vessel, Meagan instinctively cuddled against the hard warmth of Trevor's chest, whether he wanted her there or not.

A faint smile brimmed his lips as he peered down at the bundle of beauty who had sought out his protection. Odd, he mused as he brushed an unruly strand of her platinum blond hair back into place. Seldom had Meagan nestled in his arms for comfort. She was a strong, independent woman who had always preferred to stand alone. Her behavior stirred a protective instinct within him, and yet he wondered when the Lord commanded man to love thine enemy if He meant for him to carry it to such extremes.

That thought made Trevor stiffen and pull away, offering Meagan his sturdy shoulder to lean upon, but no more. He still harbored doubts about her sincerity, and he was afraid to trust her as he once had. It had very nearly proven disastrous, and only a complete fool would make the same mistake twice, he told himself.

His withdrawal sent Meagan's spirits plunging like a heavily weighted anchor, and she sat upright once again, stifling the pain of rejection. It seemed she was to weather the storm alone, and if perchance she was washed overboard, she would not look to Trevor for assistance. Indeed, this mistrusting soul would hand her a rock and command that she cling fiercely to it, letting it drag her to the bottom of the channel.

Meagan was jolted from her thoughts when her eyes focused on the huge wall of water that rolled toward them. Her heart missed several vital beats as the deafening roar rang in the whistling wind. Her entire body tensed as the boat was sucked into the undercurrent of the water and then rose with the swell. A frightened shriek burst from her lips as the waterfall toppled over them, tearing her from her seat and sending her slamming against the stern. Before she could gasp for breath, another forceful wave crashed against the boat, and Meagan felt herself being washed away.

"Meagan!" Trevor's voice rolled toward her but his outstretched hand could not. He watched in horror as she was dragged off with the wave that continued on its devastating course.

She heard him call out to her as if he stood on the other side of reality, but Meagan was too disoriented to tell which way to turn. The forceful current defied her attempt to swim, and she was destined to ride in its wake. So this was how it would end, she thought as she struggled to the surface to gasp a small breath of air, only to be strangled by another curling wave.

Trevor fumbled frantically in an attempt to shed his sword and scabbard, his eyes glued to Meagan, who disappeared and reappeared on the crest of the wave. As he dived into the channel, the oarsmen made an attempt to maneuver the vessel in his direction, but the lumbering boat did not respond and threatened to capsize as another wave slammed against the bow.

It was as if he were moving in slow motion, unable to reach Meagan before she disappeared from sight once again. His heart thundered furiously against his ribs as he dived beneath the surface, groping to find something that resembled a young woman's body. Trevor held his breath until he feared his lungs would burst and then shot back to the surface to be assaulted by another rolling wave. Inhaling a quick breath, he plunged downward again, praying his second attempt would be successful. After what seemed forever, his flailing arm made contact with human flesh, and he tugged with every ounce of strength he could muster to drag Meagan with him to the water's surface.

He hugged her limp body to him and yelled to the oarsmen to cast out a rope. With the lifeline secured about them, Trevor held his breath as another frothy wave tumbled over them. When the men finally dragged them back into the boat, Meagan's exquisite features were deathly pale, her lips blue. Frantically, he whacked her between the shoulder blades, hoping to revive her, but she did not immediately respond. He pressed his hands into her midsection, attempting to force out the water, and to his relief Meagan sputtered and coughed. For several minutes he diligently worked to bring her back to life, but Meagan was slow in rousing to consciousness. She felt as though she had swallowed half the water in the channel, and her lungs burned so fiercely that she doubted if she could ever breathe normally again.

Her moist lashes fluttered up to see Trevor's concerned face fading in and out of the darkness, and she heard the raindrops thumping against the planks beside her head.

"You should have let me go," she choked on a ragged breath. "It would have been easier for both of us. . . ."

As her eyes drifted shut and she gave way to the circling darkness, Trevor clutched her to him, his gaze sweeping the rain-slicked deck, searching for something dry to wrap around her chilled body, but there was nothing the driving rain and crushing waves hadn't touched.

When Lear crouched beside him and whined, Trevor glanced down at her dutiful bodyguard and then called for him to follow. Trevor kicked at the upturned barrels, pushing them into position to form a circular barrier, and then laid Meagan's limp body within it before rummaging through the crates to find something suitable to cover them. With his makeshift canopy in place, Trevor crawled in beside

344

Meagan and the black shepherd that had stretched out beside her.

Painstakingly, Trevor massaged her body, attempting to revive her circulation while the rain continued to patter about them. If only he had had the common sense to wait until the storm had passed, he berated himself. But nay, he had been overly anxious to set foot in Normandy and seek out his devious uncle. His impatience might well cost Meagan her life and the life of her child. Trevor gritted his teeth as he vigorously rubbed his hands over her icy flesh. Damnation, would he ever behave rationally again, he wondered. Since the moment Meagan had swept into his life like a misdirected whirlwind, he had been in a tailspin. Now his idiocy had caused her to brave a storm that they could have easily avoided. God, this *was* an ill-fated attraction they shared, Trevor mused as he stretched out beside Meagan and drew her lifeless body against him. If he had only clung to her when she attempted to seek protection from the storm, she would not have washed overboard.

Trevor muttered several epithets to his name as he held Meagan in his arms and then prayed she would be spared another tragedy, one that *he* had forced upon her.

As the sun peeked through the gloomy clouds that hung over the shores of Normandy and then sank into the western horizon, Trevor opened the door to the shabby hut he had rented in the small village of free tenants that was nestled on the coast. Meagan had roused several times during their voyage and cart ride into the city, but she was still groggy. Trevor had decided it best to delay their journey until Meagan had been allowed a few hours to recuperate after swallowing a good portion of the English Channel.

When he had carefully settled Meagan on the bed and stripped off her damp clothes, he shook out the fur quilt and laid it over her shapely body. A quiet smile trickled across his lips as he eased down beside her to rearrange the wild, silver-blond tendrils that cascaded about her. His tanned finger traced the gentle curve of her mouth and then trailed along the swanlike column of her neck, admiring the silky texture of her skin.

"It seems we are forever causing each other distress," he murmured. "Sometimes I think 'tis our purpose for being sent to earth." His raven head bent to hers, his warm lips brushing over her before he rose to full stature and strode over to open the door. Trevor instinctively flinched when Lear bounded into the room to take his place at Meagan's feet, and then he ducked away when Garda swooped down at him as if she meant to peck him to pieces for allowing Meagan to endure such a difficult journey across the channel. But when the falcon circled his head and then took roost on his shoulder he chuckled softly. "I did not think you had much use for me, buzzard," he smirked.

Garda fluffed her feathers and swiveled her head to peer at Trevor, sitting cool and aloof on her perch, as if she were only tolerating the man until her lady roused. "I am really not the beast your lady would have you believe," he assured the falcon and then rolled his eyes when he realized he was trying to explain himself to a pile of feathers. Lord, the rain must have seeped into his brain to rust the cogs of his mind! What did he care what that pesky fowl thought?

Muttering about his questionable intelligence, Trevor eased the door shut and ambled around the corner to the tavern with Garda sitting regally on his shoulder, intending to warm his innards with a few mugs of ale while Meagan slept off her bout with the storm.

A weary sigh tumbled from Meagan's pale lips as she dragged herself from the depths of sleep. Her body trembled, and she could not seem to control the shivers that darted up and down her spine. As she lifted heavily lidded eyes a frown formed on her ashen features. She lay in a small room furnished with only a straw bed, table and chair, and small hearth. After pushing up on one elbow, she saw Lear lying on the floor beside her. Her movement brought the faithful dog to his feet, and he padded toward her, seeking whatever affection she might offer. Meagan brushed her palm over his wide head and breathed a deep breath, one that thankfully wasn't accompanied by a wall of water. Lord, she doubted that she would ever set foot on solid ground again.

Her frown settled deeper in her face when she spied her tunic hanging by the fire to dry. "Has the Lord of Wessex abandoned us in his haste to search out his wicked uncle?" Meagan mused aloud as she hoisted herself into an upright position, only to find the room careening about her.

When Meagan had gathered her wobbly legs beneath her and shrugged on her clothes, Lear trotted to the door, patiently waiting for his mistress to follow him. A fond smile grazed Meagan's lips as she bent to pet her shepherd. At least she had one devoted friend who would never leave her side, she thought to herself.

After she had unlatched the door, Lear lumbered around the thatched hut that was attached to a timber-and-stone tavern. Laughter wafted its way toward Meagan, and she followed the sound to the open door. Meagan froze in her tracks, her eyes burning hot blue blazes when she saw the raven-haired knight who sat with *her* falcon perched on his shoulder and a swarm of tavern wenches hovering so close to Trevor that Meagan swore they would melt all over him. He reminded Meagan of a sheik entertaining his harem, and her temper snapped. She had professed to love him, and there he was, cajoling with whores while his wife was left alone to recover from her near brush with disaster in a rented room conveniently located behind the village tavern.

The charismatic smile slid off the side of Trevor's lips when the hum of conversation evaporated and all eyes swung to the door. There stood Meagan, her blond hair trailing about her and her eyes flaming like torches. The neck of her tunic gaped to reveal the full swells of her breasts, and she looked altogether enchanting in her wild, reckless way. It was obvious that he wasn't the only one who thought so, judging by the sordid remarks that flew from the lips of the other men who had paused from their drinking to devour the curvaceous blond.

Trevor had had sincere intentions of taking his meal and immediately returning with Meagan's tray, but he had been

347

surrounded by a flock of females who vied for his attention. It was obvious that Meagan did not approve of the company he kept. If looks could kill he would have been fried alive. It seemed she thought it permissable for her to cavort with other men, while he was to refuse contact and conversation with *all* females. Was it jealousy that flared in her sapphire eyes? It would have pleased him if it were. God knew he had suffered from that affliction on several occasions, and it seemed fitting that Meagan should endure it at least once, he thought to himself.

Meagan didn't know exactly where Trevor had taken her, and she didn't care, nor did she notice the man who sat inconspicuously in the corner, studying her with considerable interest. Gunthar Seaton rose to his feet and quietly made his way through the back door, reasonably certain that he had found the woman Ulrick had been desperately searching the countryside to locate. The description fit this comely maid, and Gunthar had been ordered to return her to Ulrick for a sizable reward. But Meagan had no interest in the man who smiled smugly to himself as he disappeared from the tavern. She was infuriated that Trevor had dumped her in some out-of-the-way hut while he pranced off to find a woman to accommodate him.

When Trevor attempted to rise and approach his annoyed wife, the red-haired wench pressed her hand against his shoulder, forcing him back into his seat. "Stay, m'lord. We do so enjoy your charming company. It has been too long since we have had the pleasure of such a strong, handsome knight," she murmured as she leaned close to his ear. "And I would not be opposed to spending some private moments with you. Pay no mind to the blond maid. She appears too frail and weak to pleasure a virile man like you."

Trevor's lips twitched in amusement as the woman spread butterfly kisses along his neck and Meagan's eyes narrowed into hard, condemning slits. It served her right, Trevor thought spitefully. The boot was on the other foot, and his wandering wife had finally felt the pinch.

Meagan made no attempt to control her temper. She made a beeline for her gallivanting husband and lifted her arm, urging Garda to abandon the traitor's shoulder and roost where she belonged. The falcon fluttered to her and ruffled her feathers as if she were just as appalled by Trevor's behavior.

"It would have been proper to determine if I was dead before you allowed these . . ." Meagan paused, attempting to select an accurate description of the women who drooled all over the dashing knight with coal black hair and glistening amber eyes. Why was she trying to be polite? These harlots knew what they were, and Trevor seemed all too agreeable about accommodating each and every one of them. ". . . these wenches to console you," she finished on a sour note.

"I only came to fetch you a tray of food," Trevor casually explained, watching in delight as Meagan wrestled with her spewing temper. "By I lost track of time."

Lost track of time, Meagan thought huffily. He was *making* time with this flock of fluff! "But all means, m'lord, do not let me detain you from doing whatever it was you were doing," Meagan hissed as she reached over to snatch what was left of the food on the tray and then wheeled toward the door.

When Meagan paused to fling him a glower that would have set the forest ablaze and then sailed out the door, Trevor chuckled and climbed to his feet, undraping the insistent wench who clung like a choking vine. "It appears that my lady frowns on the possibility of the two of us spending private moments together," he chuckled.

The redhead looked him up and down, her green eyes full of blatant seduction. "I would not frown upon anything you did," she purred provocatively as she traced the strong line of his jaw and brazenly glided her fingertips over the hard wall of his chest. "I am disappointed you have wed such a fragile wench. I still contend that a man like you deserves far more."

The wench had sorely misjudged her competition, Trevor mused as he brought her wandering hands to his lips. "My lady would surprise you, I think. She may look like a dainty wildflower, but her appearance is deceiving. I would not dare pit you against her when she is in one of her fits of temper." Trevor winked as he bowed before the disappointed woman. "We dare not antagonize her."

Meagan had the misfortune of glancing over her shoulder just as the buxom serving maid made another bold advance on Trevor. It nauseated her to watch the lout beam at his uncanny ability to draw women like flies. Gritting her teeth, she stormed back to her room, her temper boiling like an overheated kettle.

When Trevor strolled inside like a strutting peacock, Meagan exploded. Before she realized what she had done, the tray had sprouted wings and flown out of her hands. Food and drink dripped from his shocked face and slid down his tunic.

"I hope you are pleased with yourself," Meagan snapped. "You sat there and allowed those trollops to slobber all over you!"

Trevor calmly scraped Meagan's meal from his cheek and clothing and then ambled toward her. "I did nothing to be ashamed of," he insisted in a self-righteous tone and bit back a grin as he watched Meagan spew and fume. If this tantrum served to prove that she *did* care for him, even a mite, and that her confession of love was not another deceitful ploy, Trevor would let her rave. "I was merely being polite, as any other chivalrous knight would do."

"Polite?" Meagan echoed as she flounced onto her cot, presenting her back to her unfaithful husband. "Did you intend to tote your eager wench back here and expect me to make room on the bed for the two of you while you finished what you began in the tavern?"

Meagan had been thoroughly humiliated. Only the previous week she had professed her love, and this woodenheaded knight who had sap flowing through his veins had refused to believe her. Now he was seeking out an obliging wench and dallying with her right under Meagan's nose. She had asked herself a hundred times how she could have fallen in love with this callous, uncaring man, but she had no rational answer. He was everything she couldn't handle in a man, and yet he was the essence of everything she wanted in a husband—strong and firm in his beliefs, even if they contradicted hers. She knew she and Trevor were all wrong for each other, but when she was in his arms all seemed right. A muddled frown knitted her brow. Was she making any sense? Nay, Meagan scolded herself. All she knew was that she loved this exasperating man and that she was deeply hurt that his eyes had strayed to another woman.

When Trevor plopped down on the edge of the cot as if he belonged there, Meagan scooted against the wall, attempting to put as much distance as possible between them. "Go away," she ordered, fighting back the stinging tears that threatened to cloud her vision.

"Since you interrupted what might have been a very interesting evening, I think you should compensate," he breathed against her neck, sending a fleet of goose pimples cruising across her skin.

That two-legged rat! He had his nerve, Meagan thought furiously. But then another thought entered into her mind. Part of her wanted to lash out at Trevor for what he had done, and another part longed to assure him that she could provide affection and passion until she wanted no more of it. The amorous side of her nature won out, and a deliciously wicked smile pursed her lips. She would not send him into another woman's arms when her heart cried out to him. She would offer him what he wanted, and he would have no strength to pursue the red-haired wench. Meagan squirmed to her back, her gaze locking with pools of glistening amber.

Trevor felt his heart melt all over his ribs when he peered into her bewitching face, watching her eyes flicker with that living fire that displayed her feisty inner spirit. He was pleasantly startled when Meagan sat up on the cot, tucked her legs beneath her, and slowly drew the tunic over her head, leaving her luscious body bare to his all-consuming gaze.

"Is it compensation you seek, m'lord?" Meagan purred, using the seductive techniques of the women she had seen draped around Trevor's neck. She fully intended to prove that she could please him as well as the buxom redhead. "Or is it something more than consolation?"

When Meagan came upon her knees and glided her arms

over his shoulders, Trevor felt himself melting into a pool of liquid desire. Her touch was like a white-hot fire, searing him inside and out. His hungry gaze devoured her satiny skin as it glowed in the dim candlelight. And just when he would have clutched her shapely body to his, Meagan gracefully slipped from the cot to stand behind him. Her arms came around his midsection to unclasp his belt and then lifted the hem of his tunic to draw it away from the broad expanse of his chest.

Trevor felt his heart slam against his back and then lodge between his ribs as the ripe peaks of her breasts brushed against his shoulder blades. Her gentle, inquiring hands glided over the taut muscles of his back like a seductive massage while her warm breath whispered along the nape of his neck, reducing him to mush.

"What is your pleasure, my handsome warrior?" Meagan queried as her fingertips created intricate designs on his back and then ventured along his tapered waist, leaving a path of warm, arousing sensations in their wake.

If Trevor could have located his tongue, he would have replied, but he had swallowed it when Meagan's brazen caresses glided over his hips to follow the dark matting of hair that trailed along his belly.

"Do you wish a light kiss? A tender caress?" Meagan did not await his reply. She urged Trevor to his feet and then stepped in front of him to press wantonly against him, her breasts boring into his laboring chest. Again her silken touch trickled over the slope of his shoulder to investigate the powerful muscles of his arms and then settled his hands on her hips as she arched toward him to make intimate contact. A wry smile spread across her lips when she glanced up to see that his chiseled features trembled as if they were about to tumble down his face like a rockslide. "Are you always so shy with your women, m'lord?" she taunted and then moved his hand to cup her breast. "Touch me. . . ." Her lips parted in bold invitation as her fingertips tunneled through his raven hair, luring him ever closer. "Kiss me, Dark Prince . . . like this . . ."

When her tongue traced the curve of his mouth and then

intruded to explore the dark recesses, Trevor's masculine body went up in flames. Her seductive ploy had thoroughly aroused him. The feel of her feminine softness contrasting with the hard boldness of him left him breathless. He had wed a spell-casting witch, Trevor reminded himself as her mouth rolled over his. And at the moment she could have demanded the world be spread at her feet, and he would have seen to it that she had her whim. They were far from England, away from the responsibilities of his demesne and his king. They were alone in a secluded universe that nothing could invade, and Trevor could not think past this delicious moment, could not see past the alluring horizon that dawned in Meagan's sapphire eyes. He wanted her as he had wanted no other woman in his life. She was his obsession, the impossible dream that haunted his nights and chased all rational thoughts from his head.

When her soft lips abandoned his to flutter across each male nipple and then tracked a fiery path across his ribs, Trevor moaned in sweet torment. Her roaming caresses weaved a web of intense pleasure about him, and her kisses spun threads of aching desire. She mapped the muscled planes of his body and inspected the hard contours of his thighs before her hands and moist lips trailed lower, tasting and touching every inch of him in ways that drove him to the brink of insanity. One wild, maddening sensation rose from inside another as she continued to kiss and caress him. Churning emotions spilled forth like an intoxicating wine overflowing its goblet, taking all logical thought with them. Passion, the likes of which he had never known, bubbled inside him, and Trevor wasn't certain he could endure the teasing rapture she forced upon him. She had awakened a need he had held in check, and then she created monstrous new ones. He hungered for her like a man deprived of food and drink for days on end. He was starved for her kisses and caresses, but more than that he craved the joining of their bodies and souls for that one brief, shining moment that defied description. It was as if he were only half a man, an incomplete being without a purpose, until his soul united with her wild, free spirit and soared along the perimeters of the universe.

"Meagan . . ." Her name tumbled from his lips in a pained plea as her delicate fingers folded about him, caressing him, urging him to surrender to the primitive needs that were playing havoc with his sanity.

He didn't care that they were delaying confrontation with his uncle or that Desmond was overwrought with concern about what had become of his ward. Trevor needed this enchanting angel as much as he needed air to breathe and food to nourish him. She had become a vital essence in his life, and she had burrowed so deeply into his thoughts that he knew he could never rout her. It didn't matter that she had betrayed him for her cause or for another man. He wanted her, body and soul, for as long as they had together in this dark world that was alive with soul-shattering sensations.

Long, lean fingers encircled her waist, drawing Meagan to her feet and then off the floor, lifting her upward until her sensuous lips fitted themselves to his. He was drowning in her eager response, suffocating in the delicious scent of her, trembling with a hunger that he wondered if even passion could appease. He wanted her with every ounce of his being, ached to possess this fiery angel who had offered him a foretaste of heaven with her kisses and caresses.

With a maddening groan, Trevor bound her to him with his sinewy arms, and then bent his knee upon the bed, arching her backwards, tilting her head to accept his ravishing kiss. And then, as if she were no more than a weightless feather, he laid her upon the cot and crouched above her.

Meagan's lashes swept up to see the powerful lion of a man who was poised above her, his body of brawn and muscle so close and yet so very far away. His golden eyes blazed like wildfire, feeding on the raw emotions that lay smoldering just beneath the surface. Meagan knew she had routed the thought of another woman from his mind. She knew what he wanted, and she longed to offer herself to him, mind and body.

"Come, my powerful dragon, breathe your fire and inflame my soul. I need you. . . ." she whispered as she looped her arms around his neck.

Her luring words brought him ever nearer, and Meagan sighed in pleasure as his hard, sleek body lowered to hers, his hips settling intimately against hers. Trevor engulfed her, fiercely crushing her to him as his raging passion unleashed its fury and bound him to primitive male instinct. As he became the budding flame within her, his ragged breath caressed her neck and he whispered words of want and need, assuring her that she was the one he craved. He drove into her womanly body, seeking ultimate depths of intimacy, filling her with a warmth and contentment that nothing else could appease. Maddening impatience claimed him as the sweet scent of her swarmed his senses and her body arched to meet his forceful thrusts.

A waterfall of ecstatic sensations cascaded over him as they soared beyond the stars. Her fingertips dug into the hard tendons of his back and he heard her heart thundering in frantic rhythm with his. They were one, exploring the heights and depths of passion, transcending the physical limitations of the flesh, winging their way toward that lofty pinnacle that only lovers could achieve. They were dangling in time and space, suspended in a world of vivid sensations that swelled and then burst, sending them plummeting from their perch.

Meagan breathlessly clung to him as the wild emotions converged on her and then scattered like a thousand shooting stars racing across the midnight sky. As the flames of desire burned themselves out and she drifted back to reality, a shuddering sigh burst from her lips. No words could describe the feelings she had enjoyed when she was in the unending circle of Trevor's arms, giving, sharing, delighting in the sensations that bordered on fantasy. He knew how to please a woman, she mused as her tangled lashes fluttered against her cheek and Trevor's handsome face materialized in the haze of darkness.

In the aftermath of love, Trevor propped his forearms on either side of Meagan's bare shoulders and stared down at her. He traced her kiss-swollen lips and could not resist dropping one last kiss to her sensuous mouth.

"Do you feel up to traveling?" he whispered against her satiny cheek. "'Tis still a long ride to Ulrick's chateau, and I am most anxious to see him after all these years."

Meagan nodded agreeably, but in truth she would have preferred to spend the duration of the night sleeping in Trevor's arms. When she peered up at him an odd expression melted on his granite features, making her frown curiously. She would have given most anything to know what he was thinking.

The faintest hint of a smile rippled across his lips and then evaporated when he saw the question in her sapphire eyes. "Meagan, had we met in a different time and place . . . if we were not serving a different cause . . ." Trevor heaved a frustrated sigh, unable to put his exact thoughts to tongue. He eased down beside her and then bent to collect his discarded garments. "It might have been easier for us to satisfy this insatiable craving that defies logic. If wishing would make it so, I would have wanted you to rule by my side without these insurmountable obstacles between us."

Her spirits tumbled downhill like an avalanche. He might as well have blurted out that they had no chance for happiness, no future. Meagan didn't want to think about how it might have been. She was still too raw inside, too sensitive after having her love for him denied. Trevor admitted that he was attracted to her, but he would not allow her into his heart. Why did she keep trying to convince him that her love was pure and unselfish? He refused to believe it. Why couldn't she accept a lost cause when it was staring her in the face? Because she loved and there was no logic to that emotion.

Meagan climbed to her feet to dress, her thoughts rambling as she pulled on her tunic. Deep in her heart, she knew it was unfair to blame Trevor for being so cynical. She knew he had seen his share of betrayal and that he had endured several attempts on his life by bitter Saxons who longed for his death. Trevor was a cautious man who did not offer his trust until he was certain beyond all shadows of doubt that those who befriended him would remain loyal. He had made her his wife, even when Conan had cautioned him, and now he was riddled with doubts and suspicions. He was afraid of being burned twice, and Meagan wondered if the wound would ever heal. She could follow him to the edge of the earth, and he still would doubt her love and loyalty, she thought dismally.

"I will see if I can find some horses for our journey," Trevor informed her as he clasped his belt around his waist and focused his attention on the far wall. "I will be back for you in a few minutes."

When Lear whined to follow him back outside, Meagan eased open the door and then ambled back to gather her soggy belongings. She was so weary and tired of trying. It seemed she was fighting a losing battle. . . . Meagan jerked up her head when she heard the door fly open, and a startled gasp burst from her lips when a stranger charged at her and then clamped his hand over her mouth before she could voice a cry of alarm. When she writhed for freedom, he pressed his dagger into her ribs, forcing her to admit defeat or perish beneath his blade.

"My master has turned Normandy upside down in search of you, m'lady," Gunthar Seaton insisted as he tightened his grasp on Meagan. "You are coming with me. Lord Burke is most anxious to see you."

Meagan's blood ran cold when she found herself dragged from the shack with a knife pressed between her ribs. If not for the child she carried, she would have struggled against the sturdy knight who held her chained in his arms. Her eyes darted frantically about her, praying that Trevor would return before she was spirited off into the night. Would he believe that she had intentionally eluded him again? That question continued to plague her as Gunthar nudged his steed and took her with him into the swaying shadows.

"Meagan?" Trevor swung open the door, his keen eyes circling the empty hut. Fury sizzled through him and he betrated himself for trusting Meagan to await his return. *Fool!* he screamed at himself. He should have known she valued her freedom far more than she thirsted for revenge against Ulrick. She had run from him so often that it had become second nature to that wild, free bird. Damnation, he thought he could depend on her, but obviously . . . Trevor's discerning gaze swung back to the satchel that lay at the foot of the bed and then to Garda, who had roosted on the rafter. Surely Meagan would have taken her belongings and her falcon if she had fled of her own accord. His calculating thoughts skidded to a halt. This was Ulrick's doing. He could feel it in his bones.

"Lear!" Trevor called to the shepherd as he strode over to fetch the falcon, who objected to being dragged from her perch. "Find Meagan." As the faithful dog and squawking fowl darted off into the night, Trevor vaulted into the saddle and urged his nag into her swiftest pace, but the steed was not built for speed, and Trevor scowled at the slow pace she set.

When Lear veered to the north, Trevor was certain Meagan had been taken against her will. No doubt Ulrick had every available knight and servant in his command searching the countryside and watching the coast of Normandy for a comely blond who had once eluded him. He would not have expected Meagan to escape, but then he didn't know Meagan as Trevor did. Ulrick was not aware of her remarkable ability to survive. She was cunning and resourceful. If Ulrick speculated that she was still hiding somewhere in Normandy, unable to gain passage across the channel, he would not be expecting Trevor to call upon him. A wry smile surfaced on his lips as he followed Lear through the darkness. He had not decided how he was to storm Ulrick's fortress, since he had no reinforcements, but perhaps he wouldn't have to if he could catch his devious uncle off guard.

Chapter 24

Meagan raised beseeching eyes to the burly knight who had bound her to a tree. It seemed as if she had spent half her life tied to some sturdy object that was impossible to uproot. First it had been Trevor who staked her down to prevent her escape, and now it was Ulrick's henchman.

"Please allow me a more comfortable position," Meagan pleaded. "My arms and legs are growing numb."

Gunthar grunted unsympathetically as he twisted around to peer at his captive. "After what you did to Ulrick Burke you deserve no consideration, woman."

"After what *I* did?" Meagan repeated incredulously. "Ulrick was the one who tried to slit my throat to keep his nephew from learning that he was alive after he had been presumed dead."

A bemused frown creased Gunthar's brow as he unfolded his bulky frame from the campfire and ambled over to Meagan. How did this woman know Ulrick's nephew and that he assumed Ulrick to be dead? Was she concocting lies to confuse him? "'Tis not the story we received from Lord Burke before he sent out his search party. He bears the scar upon his neck where your wolf-dog attacked him." And Gunthar was greatly relieved that he had eluded the great shepherd that he had seen at Meagan's side earlier. The beast looked as if he would not think twice about making a meal of a man.

"My shepherd sought to defend me from Ulrick's attack,"

359

Meagan insisted as she tilted her head to indicate the mending wound on the side of her throat. "I do not know what Ulrick is paying you to take me to him, but I will pay you more if you grant me freedom. He wants me dead to protect his deceitful lie."

Indecision etched Gunthar's brow when he spied the knife wound. When he knelt to inspect the scar he heard a low, threatening growl from the underbrush. Without looking, Gunthar knew what beast was issuing the warning. It was Meagan's huge wolf-dog, the one he had seen at the tavern door. A shiver of dread ricocheted through him as he carefully withdrew his hand from Meagan's throat and watched the wry smile spread across her lips.

"If the dog thinks you intend to harm me, he will go for your throat, just as he did Ulrick's," Meagan assured the leery knight. "But he does not attack unless he senses that I have been threatened. One false move and Lear will see to it that you will never view another sunrise."

Gunthar heard the crackling of twigs behind him, and he slowly backed away, casting an uneasy glance over his shoulder, only to see his worst fears materialize from the shadows. Lear bounded from the brush with his teeth bared, ensuring Gunthar that his bite would be as deadly as his bark. Gunthar cursed himself for leaving his shield and sword on his steed. He could never reach his weapon before the monstrous dog leaped on him.

But the attack he had anticipated when he inched toward his horse did not come from the black shepherd that lumbered over to take his place beside Meagan. It came from behind him, along with a growl as fierce and threatening as Lear's. Like a panther springing on his prey, Trevor leaped from the brush, forcing Gunthar face-down in the grass, knocking the wind out of him. His pained shriek sliced the silence as he twisted to face his attacker, who held his arm poised to bury his dagger in Gunthar's heart.

"Trevor, nay!" Meagan railed, praying he would not murder the unfortunate knight right before her eyes. She had witnessed enough mutilations and killings to haunt her dreams, and this man had already begun to question Ulrick's

360

purpose. He did not deserve to die.

"Trev . . . ?" Gunthar peered up at the vicious snarl that curled his enemy's lips. But it was not his enemy who crouched over him, prepared to cut his heart from his chest. It was his friend!

Trevor's arm froze in midair when he stared down into Gunthar's astonished expression. He bounded to his feet, hauling the fallen knight up beside him.

"Gunthar Seaton? Egod! I almost killed you," Trevor snorted and then hugged his friend as if he had not seen him for a century. Indeed, it had been a lifetime ago that he and Gunthar had trained with William's troops, preparing for the invasion.

Meagan glanced back and forth between the two warriors who equaled each other in muscular build and stature, amazed that they knew each other. But that shouldn't have surprised her, Meagan reminded herself. Each time she dared mention Trevor's name someone knew of him, whether she was in England or Normandy. This handsome knight's reputation was known far and wide, especially since he was one of William the Bastard's favorite warriors.

"Where have you been these past four years?" Trevor questioned as he stepped back to peer into the face that had matured with time. He tucked his dagger into his belt and offered a warm smile to the man who had served with him as squire at William's palace long before the invasion of Saxon England.

"I have not fared as well as you obviously have," Gunthar chuckled as he readjusted his clothing, which had been wrapped around him during their tussle. "I was injured in battle and sent back to Normandy to mend. Your uncle offered me a place among his knights, and I have been maintaining and defending his landholdings for the past three years." A proud smile crept to the left corner of his mouth, the side Trevor had not bruised with his doubled fist. "But I have heard that you are among William's favorites. The Dark Prince, I believe you are called by your Saxon tenants."

"It has been such a long time since we sat beside the

campfire, exchanging dreams. Ah, they were delusions of grandeur, were they not?" Trevor chortled as he reached out to retrieve the twig that had snagged in Gunthar's sandy blond hair. "We were young and full of fantasies."

Gunthar nodded and then clasped Trevor's shoulder. "Yea, we were foolish boys playing at being men. Our heads were filled with visions of riches and beautiful women to keep us warm when . . ."

"If the two of you intend to spend the remainder of the evening reminiscing about the ladies you have courted and the battles you have fought, might I at least be granted a meager amount of comfort?" Meagan interrupted. "My back has become indented by the bark on this tree, and if I stay here much longer I fear that I, too, will take root."

A sheepish smile tripped across Trevor's lips as he bent his gaze to his annoyed wife. "Forgive me, m'lady. I was so preoccupied with seeing an old friend that I almost forgot you."

"It would seem so," Meagan sniffed caustically. It appeared Trevor would have preferred she never existed. Indeed, he would have been a much happier man if she had never set foot on the face of the earth. "You need not bother with an introduction. Gunthar and I have become acquainted these past few hours, although I could complain about his manners," she added on a teasing note.

"*Your* lady?" Gunthar looked a mite peaked as he watched Trevor unstrap the shapely blond and then murmur a quiet apology as his lips brushed across her forehead. "I have kidnapped *your* lady?"

A muddled frown clouded his brow. It must have been Trevor who Meagan was glaring at when she appeared at the tavern door. Gunthar had entered from the rear of the tavern after his tryst with one of the serving maids and had not been in the pub long enough to realize that the man who had his back to him and who was surrounded by a harem was none other than Trevor Burke. But then he had not expected to find the baron of Wessex sitting in a Normandy tavern when there was a rebellion going on in England, and his view of the man had been obstructed by the swarm of women he had

362

attracted, Gunthar rationalized. After all, his attention had been focused solely on the bewitching young blond he had tracked for more than two weeks, and he had sneaked from the pub before Meagan had approached her gallivanting husband.

"I would prefer that Gunthar does not know that there is dissension between us," Trevor whispered confidentially. "Can we at least remain on friendly terms while we are in Normandy?"

"You want me to play the devoted wife?" Meagan presumed as she cast Gunthar a discreet glance and then peered up at Trevor.

A faint smile traced his lips as his index finger grazed her creamy cheek. "Will it be so difficult, m'lady?"

It would be as easy as falling off a log, Meagan mused as she wilted beneath his tender touch. "Gunthar will never know that the battle between Norman and Saxon is just as much a part of our marriage as is the rebellion in England," she murmured as she reached up on tiptoe to press a light kiss to his sensuous lips. "I shall make a true effort to assure Gunthar that all is well between us."

A sea of warm memories flooded through his soul when her sweet mouth feathered over his, and Trevor had to will himself to drag his lips from her intoxicating kiss. His arm curled about her waist as he swung her around to meet Gunthar's approving smile.

"Meagan is my wife," he assured the knight whose jaw gaped in disbelief. "Have you been struck dumb, friend?"

Gunthar was not surprised to see that Trevor had an extraordinarily lovely young woman by his side, but he was shocked that he had wed this stunning nymph. In his youth Trevor had vowed never to take a wife, that he was wary of being tied to one woman. And yet, in the short time he had known this comely blond, Gunthar had been plagued with the feeling that there was more to this shapely lass than met the eye. She had known she faced death, and he had not seen fear in her exquisite features, not even once since he had abducted her.

He slammed his mouth shut, and then he frowned when

another thought darted across his mind. "Is it true what you said, m'lady, about Trevor being unware that his uncle was alive, and that Ulrick attempted to kill you to keep his existence a secret from his nephew?"

Meagan nodded affirmatively. "Ulrick came to see me during my sojourn at Rocaille Chateau," she explained. "Before his attempt at murder, he told me that I could not live because I could carry the truth to Trevor. That is when Lear attacked him . . . to save me."

"Before the invasion Ulrick sent one of his servants to me, informing me that my uncle had died. He had hoped to give me little cause to return to Normandy to avenge the bitterness between us," Trevor added, his voice carrying an undertone of resentment. "The servant also informed me that Ulrick had promised my family's land to whosoever King Phillip chose to rule it and that I would not be granted any of the landholdings that had long been in the Burke family."

Gunthar half collapsed after hearing the explanation. He had very nearly delivered Trevor's wife to an unjust death. An apologetic smile tracked across his swollen lips as he stared down at the attractive young woman he had taken captive. "Forgive me, Lady Meagan. Had I known the truth, I would never have seized you or treated you so abominably. I thought I was serving justice."

Meagan graced him with a smile that melted the knight into sentimental mush. "I do not hold you responsible for what happened," she softly assured him. "And I did not doubt that Ulrick would take the truth and twist it to suit his evil purposes."

Trevor dropped his hand from Meagan's waist and wandered over to stare into the curling fingers of the fire. The conversation had stirred a myriad of bitter memories. "'Tis not greed that brought me back to Normandy during the rebellion, but revenge," Trevor insisted as he slowly turned back to his friend, his golden eyes cold and heavy with resentment. "Ulrick would have murdered Meagan to protect his lie and 'tis for that he will pay. There was a time when I would have taken the wealth I gained from the invasion and returned to battle Ulrick for what was rightfully mine, but now it does not seem so important."

"But no matter what your purpose for confronting Ulrick, you cannot storm the garrison," Gunthar reminded him. "Your uncle has a full regiment of knights, mercenaries like myself who are paid well to do his bidding. If he declares you to be his enemy they will take arms against you before you can explain the truth."

A wry smile pursed Meagan's lips as she strolled toward the campfire to ward off the night's chill. "But these men would not think to attack Gunthar Seaton if he returned with his prisoner. And their numbers must be diminished since Ulrick has sent many of his men to search me out."

Trevor eyed his scheming wife skeptically. "What do you propose, Meagan? I swear by that wicked gleam in your eye that you have something devious on your mind."

"Devious? Nay. I should think clever would be an applicable term," Meagan amended as her measuring gaze sketched Gunthar's muscular form and then sized up Trevor's. "When Gunthar returns to the garrison with his prisoner in tow, garbed in his usual attire and helmet, no one will prevent him from crossing the drawbridge and entering the hall." One delicately arched brow raised slightly as she slid Trevor an impish grin. "Do you recall the tournament at Burke Castle, m'lord? No one but you and I knew that I rode in the competition."

"I fail to see what you can accomplish if I deliver you to Ulrick," Gunthar grunted. "If the man sought to kill you once he will make certain there is no mistake the second time."

"You will not accompany me," Meagan informed the befuddled knight. "It will be Trevor who is outfitted in your clothing. Since the two of you are the same size, no one will suspect the disguise since they will not be allowed to see Trevor's face. And while we confront Ulrick, you can follow at a slower pace, explaining our purpose to your comrades before they answer Ulrick's call to kill the man who sneaked into his castle."

Trevor thoughtfully rubbed his chin as he studied his wife.

She suggested a subtle approach, one that would bring him face-to-face with his treacherous uncle without spilling the blood of innocent men. Although Trevor silently agreed that her idea was practical and clever, it left him to wonder if she were indeed the mastermind behind the rebel attack on Burke Castle. But before he could pursue that suspicious thought Meagan demanded his undivided attention.

"Well, m'lord, would you consent to exchanging places with Gunthar? Why invite bloodshed by riding into the garrison like an infantry of one and risk losing your life before confronting Ulrick? After all, this battle is between you and your uncle."

After a long moment, Trevor nodded in agreement. "Your suggestion has merit, although it gives rise to another question that continues to haunt me," he murmured as he lifted her hand to press a kiss to her wrist.

Meagan met his cynical gaze and she had the sick feeling that she knew exactly what Trevor had implied by his remark. She could very well have cut her own throat by offering a strategy that closely resembled Reid Granthum's scheme to take Burke Castle without warring against Trevor's army of knights. But what difference did it make now, Meagan asked herself. Trevor never had believed her to be innocent and he never would. He had already tried and banished her for her supposed crimes, and he had offered her life without pardon. But it was *his* life that concerned her at the moment, and she did not want to see him cut down before he faced the man who had wreaked tragedy and destruction on his family.

As they sat down around the campfire to discuss the specific details of the plan, Trevor became more distant and remote. Meagan could feel the invisible barrier between them, the mistrust that lingered just beneath the surface. Nothing could dissolve his doubts, Meagan thought disheartenedly. She could deny the accusations until she was blue in the face, but in the back of Trevor's suspicious mind, he would never stop wondering if his wife hadn't played both ends against the middle, waiting to claim victory, no matter what the outcome of the Saxon rebellion. She had placed herself in an impossible situation when she had attempted to save Trevor from murder and protect her brother's part in the conspiracy. And she had made the choice, Meagan reminded herself. Now she was forced to live with the repercussions of her actions, ones that constantly shadowed her with Trevor's doubts.

As they rode toward Ulrick's sturdy garrison the following afternoon, Meagan could feel her apprehension mounting. Although the scheme was simple, there was still Ulrick with whom to contend. The man was unpredictable, she cautiously reminded herself. There was no way of knowing what he would do when he realized he had been tricked. The man was poisoned with hatred, and he was ruthless. His past dealings with his half brother's family reflected evidence of that fact.

"Ulrick is mine." Trevor's muffled voice rattled beneath the metal helmet that disguised his brooding features, but Meagan did not miss the undercurrent of bitterness that traced his tone. "When we encounter my uncle, keep your distance. I will not allow him to use you as a hostage against me."

Meagan remained silent as they approached the guard towers, and she was greatly relieved when one of the men called down to the approaching knight, mistaking him for Gunthar Seaton. As Trevor lifted her from the saddle and set her on her feet, she could feel the tension in his powerful body, the potential strength that lay in waiting, the intense energy that would soon be unleashed on Ulrick Burke, a man who had sold and bought this magnificent chateau with his family's blood.

When they approached the dais, Meagan's eyes anchored on the plain-faced man who sat grinning down at her like a starved shark ogling his next meal. She felt her heart catapult to her throat when the memory she carried of Ulrick Burke raced across her mind. She prayed this day would be nothing like the nightmare she had endured when he had crept in from the shadows in an attempt to separate her head from her shoulders.

"You have done well, Gunthar," Ulrick announced as he rose to his feet and descended to the steps. "You will be well paid for delivering this wicked witch who tried to dispose of me." Ulrick's gaze raked Meagan with scornful mockery. "Where is that wolf you keep as a pet? I would have liked to put an end to him as well."

"Lear." Meagan called to the shepherd that waited in the corridor and his appearance took some of the wind from Ulrick's billowing sails.

When the dog bounded across the stone floor, Ulrick retreated a cautious step and drew his sword, intent on disposing of the vicious mongrel that had very nearly ripped his throat to shreds. But when Ulrick grabbed his weapon, Trevor retrieved his, pointing the blade at Ulrick's heaving chest.

"Do you dare to lift arms against your lord?" Ulrick snorted sarcastically. "I did not know you had sentimental value for this man-eating wolf, Gunthar."

Ulrick's eyes rounded in disbelief when Trevor dragged the helmet from his raven head and glared murderously at his uncle. "Nay, it cannot be!" Ulrick croaked in astonishment. Trevor was the last man on earth he wanted to see. Indeed, he had gone to great lengths to ensure that he never encountered his nephew.

"It has been a long time, Uncle." Trevor spat out the words as if they left a bitter taste in his mouth. "And it would have been a great deal longer if you had not made an attempt on my wife's life." Trevor took a bold step toward him, his eyes blazing with all the pent-up fury he had contained since he had learned of Ulrick's evil doings. "I have made a life for myself in England, and I would have buried the past and all the bitter memories associated with it if not for this." His free hand indicated the mending wound on the side of Meagan's neck. "But now you will do penance for this vicious deed and for those you have committed all your miserable life."

Ulrick's wild eyes darted about him as he pushed away from Trevor and then screamed at the top of his lungs. "Guards!" His cry of alarm was met with silence and he

368

called out again as he backed further away from the vengeful knight whose blazing golden eyes raked over him like sharp talons.

Relief washed over Ulrick's face when his knights strode into the corridor, but it was short-lived when he realized that not one of them intended to come to his defense against his dreaded enemy. A lump of fear constricted his throat when Gunthar Seaton emerged from the crowd, his expression cold and condemning.

"You lied, Ulrick. You sent us out to retrieve an innocent woman, one you intended to murder to protect your pack of lies," he growled contemptuously and then gestured toward Trevor. "I will not serve a man who would pit me against an old friend. I came to you, thinking you were as honest and trustworthy as your nephew, but you have deceived me. You have deceived all of us who thought we were serving the uncle of our friend." Gunthar's narrowed eyes swung back to Ulrick who was becoming paler by the minute. "This is one battle you will fight without hiding like a coward behind your lies and your mercenary army. No amount of money could entice us to take your side against the lord of Wessex, a man beside whom we trained and fought for William's rights to the throne of England."

Meagan gulped hard when she saw the wild, desperate look in Ulrick's eyes. She knew even before Ulrick charged toward her that he intended to use her as his defense. With the quickness of a cat, Trevor sprung in front of Meagan, protecting her from his loathsome uncle, who would have stooped to hiding behind a woman's skirts before he would match his skills against another man.

The clash of their swords sliced through the strained silence, and Meagan watched apprehensively as Ulrick made another wild lunge at Trevor, attacking like a madman who had nothing to lose. And indeed he didn't, Meagan realized as Ulrick howled like a banshee and swung his blade with such velocity that the air whistled around him. Ulrick's life was worth nothing, and he was daring and reckless with his moves, jarring Trevor's body when he parried the intended blows. But Ulrick was no match for the powerful warrior, who had battled against worthier opponents than his ruthless uncle. When Ulrick's arm swooped through the air, he left himself an open target for his agile foe. Trevor's sword caught Ulrick's flailing arm and he screeched in pain as the blade slashed his elbow. But the wound only sent Ulrick into a rage, and he snarled like a bloodthirsty lion as he flew at Trevor to avenge his wound.

Meagan strangled on a gasp and spun away as Trevor countered the attack and Ulrick fell beneath his sword. When Trevor knelt beside his uncle, he felt nothing for the man who had caused his family so much tragedy and grief, not pity and certainly not regret that this vile, merciless man had fought his last battle.

"You lived by the sword, Uncle," Trevor told him, his voice void of emotion, his golden eyes gold and unrelenting. "'Tis fitting that you die by the sword."

Ulrick lifted glazed eyes to peer into his nephew's stony features. If Trevor was expecting Ulrick to repent of his sins, he would be greatly disappointed. Ulrick had lived with a hatred for his half brother's success, and he had vowed to wipe him and his family from the face of the earth. Even now Ulrick refused to admit defeat. If he was to die he had every intention of taking Trevor with him. His fingers folded around the concealed dagger in his belt, carefully sliding it from its resting place, determined to plunge it into Trevor's side with what was left of his draining strength.

Horror sizzled through Meagan, and her heart stopped when she spied the movement of Ulrick's hand and saw the blade reflecting the light. Meagan knew she could never reach Trevor in time to prevent the stabbing, and if she called to Trevor he would turn toward her, only to have the knife buried in his chest.

"Lear!" Meagan screamed, her voice echoing around the Great Hall, bringing her faithful shepherd to attention.

The dog pounced on the man who had attempted to kill his mistress and who now sought to murder his master. Ulrick groaned in pain as Lear's jaws clamped around his wrist, forcing him to drop the knife.

And then the flicker of hatred died in Ulrick's eyes as he

370

expelled his last breath and his life spilled from his body.

Trevor sank back on his haunches and heaved a sigh as he reached over to stroke the wolf-dog's muscled neck. Even Ulrick's last fight had not been a fair one, Trevor mused as he gathered his feet beneath him and rose to full stature. Ulrick had been defeated, but instead of asking forgiveness with his last breath he had employed it in an attempt to stab his nephew in the back. If not for Lear, Trevor would have followed his treacherous uncle to his death, and Ulrick would have at last found his ultimate victory.

As Meagan flew into his arms, clinging to him in relief, he bent to press a kiss to the scar that marred her creamy skin. "I have avenged Ulrick's butchery, and if it were within my power to erase the scar left from his knife, I would see it done, Meagan."

Trevor glanced about the Great Hall where he had spent his childhood, studying the fortress that had been stolen from his family long years ago. There were so many memories clinging to these walls, both bitter and sweet. But now the feud between him and his uncle was over, and he could put his long-harbored hatred to rest.

His clouded gaze swung to Gunthar Seaton. "This garrison will remain intact until I learn what provision Ulrick made in the event of his death. You are in charge of the chateau, Gunthar, and I expect you to compensate those who have suffered because of my uncle's ruthlessness. The wealth of this land will be spread among those of you who have served Ulrick and those tenants who have farmed the land."

The blond-haired knight nodded agreeably and then smiled at the honor the Dark Prince of Wessex had bestowed on him. "Are there other tasks you would have me do? Name them and I shall see them done."

Trevor returned his friend's smile. "I am long overdue in Wessex, and William is expecting me to appear for counsel at the palace in a few short weeks. I fear Desmond will be terribly worried about what has become of Meagan since she fled his chateau to escape Ulrick. If I take time to travel to Rocaille it will further delay my return to my demesne. I would ask you to go to Desmond and explain all that has transpired and relieve his fears. Now that the rebellion in England has been contained, I am taking my wife back with me."

"I will leave for Rocaille Chateau posthaste," Gunthar assured him and then allowed another grin to spread across his lips. "'Tis the very least I can do for the Dark Prince and his lovely lady."

"My thanks, Gunthar. I will rest easier knowing you will be in command of this fortress." His gaze swept the solemn congregation of knights, seeing several familiar faces among the crowd. "Each of you has a position here and I hope you will want to stay. I know I can count upon my friend to rule fairly and justly in my absence."

Not one vagabond knight voiced complaint with Trevor's offer, and Meagan could tell by the looks on their faces that they were pleased to serve in whatever capacity Trevor requested. While Trevor was making arrangements with the servants and knights, Meagan wandered through the monstrous garrison, wondering what type of childhood Trevor had enjoyed before Ulrick had stripped his family of their land and titles. Meagan could not imagine Trevor as a young lad playing in this hall. A secretive smile pursed her lips. But one day she would have a child, the image of his father, and then perhaps she could see the little boy in the man she had come to love. Her smile vanished when a depressing thought skipped across her mind. It could very well be that she would only have the child to remind her of the raven-haired knight. She could not have both, she told herself. Trevor had indicated that he was taking her back to England with him, but she knew it was only because William had demanded to meet his loyal knight's wife. If not for that, Meagan was certain Trevor would have ordered Gunthar to return her to Desmond for banishment.

Her rueful gaze stretched the distance between her and the handsome man who was busy giving orders to the knights and servants. Now that Trevor had accomplished his purpose in Normandy, the truce between husband and wife would dissolve. Trevor would resume his position with his king, and Meagan would be cast aside, ostracized for her unwilling part in the rebellion.

It was at that moment that Trevor turned to glance at Meagan, wondering if she meant to slip quietly away before they made their return journey to England. The look in her eyes troubled him. The lively sparkle had dwindled, and she seemed nothing like the strong, independent young woman he had known in the past. His gaze sketched her shapely figure, noting that she was beginning to show evidence that she carried a child. The thought cut like a knife, and Trevor scowled to himself. If it was Granthum's child she carried, how could he truly blame her for attempting to survive the best way she could, he asked himself. Trevor had locked her in his dungeon and she had managed to escape, knowing there was only one place to go for protection—to the Saxons. And Meagan was a true survivor, Trevor mused as his eyes flooded over her exquisite features and followed the stream of silver-blond hair that cascaded down her back. He had sentenced her to a living hell and she had only tried to escape her punishment. Could he blame her for that? Wouldn't he have done the same if the situation were reversed and the Saxons were in control of England?

Heaving a frustrated sigh, Trevor strode back to his wife. What *was* he going to do with her after he presented her in William's court and returned to resume his life at Burke Castle? Could he bear to keep her with him when he was haunted by doubts? Could he bear to send her away, to deny himself the pleasure he had found in her arms, the passion that burned through him like wildfire? She was with child, and he had already dragged her from England to Normandy, forcing her to endure a storm that had very nearly cost her life. He couldn't keep toting her from one location to another forever, unable to decide what was to be done with her, he told himself harshly.

Meagan watched Trevor approach, troubled by the crosscurrents of emotions that passed across his chiseled features. She could tell by the expression on his face that once he had terminated his preoccupation with Ulrick, the doubts rose to the surface like cream floating on milk.

Meagan sought to reassure him just once more before he turned a deaf ear to her pleas of innocence.

Her hand went to his face, smoothing away his frown. "I love you, Trevor, as I have always loved you, even when I knew this ill-fated attraction had no future. You can believe what you wish about my part in the conspiracy to overthrow Burke Castle and my allegiance to a man who would have temporarily sacrificed me to you for his personal gain, a man who intended to use me rather than protect me from a Norman lord he hated so fiercely that he sought to strike out and hurt you with his last words when he had not the strength to raise his sword." Tears misted her eyes as she brushed her finger over the grim line of his lips. "You can continue to deny that what I did was to save you from disaster and to spare my fellow countrymen from certain death, but even your doubts cannot drive my love for you from my heart. I will bear the hurt of seeing mistrust and contempt in your eyes if I must, but I cannot bear your denial of my love. At least accept that." Meagan muffled a sniff and tried desperately to compose herself before she burst into tears and was unable to put her thoughts to tongue. "I ask you to believe only that I love you. It seems a meager request from a woman who will no longer plead for pardon and expects no future."

Her trembling fingers combed through his thick hair, drawing his head to hers, uncaring that they had a captive audience, uncaring that those around them thought all was well between them when nothing could have been further from the truth. "Kiss me, my love, and then look into my eyes and deny the emotion you see mirrored there. If this is to be our last embrace, let it be a cherished memory that will warm my soul each cold, empty night we spend apart."

Trevor could not have denied her kiss or request any more than he could have flown to the moon. He wanted to believe. He did not want to see this affectionate display as another ploy to gain his trust. He only wanted to feel this glorious angel in his arms, to feel the fire feeding on the kindling flames of desire that ignited each time her soft, feminine body molded itself to his.

374

As his head came toward hers he watched the sparkle return to those mysterious pools of sapphire. And when their lips touched and their breath became one, he continued to stare into her opened eyes. The subtle feminine fragrance that was so much a part of her encircled his senses, and his lashes fluttered down to block out all but the warm tide of emotion that ebbed from her yielding body and flowed into his. God, how he wanted to believe what he was feeling, he thought deliriously as his questing tongue probed deeper to drink freely of her response. God, how he wanted to close and lock the door on the past and begin again with Meagan.

But they were returning home, back to the doubt and turmoil, back to England, which had spawned his suspicions and mistrust, back to those who could swear that Meagan was indeed an initial part of a scheme to overthrow the lord of Wessex and march on William's palace. Trevor didn't want to investigate her claim for fear that he would find she had lied, that she was only making one last play for security in a world that had been turned upside down by war and destruction. He didn't want to go home to the memories that were clouded with doubts, but he had responsibilities to his demesne and his king.

When Trevor slowly withdrew, Meagan felt her heart tumble down around her knees. She could see that he was still battling a tug-of-war of emotions. A defeated sigh escaped her lips as she stepped away, her gaze dropping to study the stone floor beneath her feet.

"I will not attempt to escape you, m'lord. Do with me what you will. There is no hope for it. The obstacles that stand between us are as tall as the highest mountain and as wide as the deepest sea. I ask not for my future, but for that of my unborn child, *your* child. At least allow him a chance to live, to grow into a man and one day share a love that his father and mother were never allowed to enjoy."

As Meagan trudged through the corridor with her faithful shepherd by her side, Trevor cursed himself a thousand times over for doubting her sincerity, and he would have followed in her wake if he had not been swarmed by the knights who longed to reacquaint themselves with the man they had known in years past, a man who was followed by his reputation as one of the king's favorites, a man whose reputation had preceded him back to Normandy. They were intent on voicing their loyalty to the Dark Prince before he left the garrison and returned to assume his powerful position beside William.

When Meagan struggled to climb into the saddle, a young squire hastened to her side to offer his assistance. "You are the Dark Prince's lady?" he questioned as he raised a helping hand.

Meagan settled herself on her mount and then looked down into a pair of dark, dancing eyes that were full of hopes and dreams. She allowed a wan smile to graze her lips as she nodded affirmatively.

"One day I will grow up to be like him," the young lad insisted. "I have heard the stories of how he rose from poverty and despair to earn the respect of William. He has become a legend among the aspiring knights of the realm with his valiant deeds in battle. He has obtained the impossible dream. The Dark Prince is a self-made man who has climbed from the ranks to claim a powerful position with the throne. You must be very proud of your husband, m'lady," the boy murmured as he stepped away to bow before Meagan.

"Yea, I am," Meagan softly assured him and then leaned out to straighten the cap that sat cockeyed on his tawny head. "And in your quest for dignity and honor, never forget that the better part of valor is the ability to determine friend from foe. Even the greatest of men must learn to see with their hearts while they rule with their heads. And the courage to admit one is wrong often requires far more strength than that which is demanded in battle." A fond smile drifted across Meagan's lips as she straightened herself in the saddle and lifted her arm to summon the falcon that circled overhead. "May your dreams soar like the hawk." Meagan bent her gaze to the lad, who was digesting her words. "But may you always remember to keep your feet planted on solid ground. And do not dismiss the love and devotion of a friend. For without him, you are nothing."

Trevor had emerged from the forebuilding in time to hear Meagan deliver her quiet sermon to the lad, and he felt more the heel when he heard her words. He had denied his heart in favor of his head, and the inner struggle it caused was tearing him in two miserable pieces. When the young squire bounded enthusiastically toward him, Trevor placed his hand on his shoulder and looked him straight in the eye.

"My lady is wise beyond her years. I hope you cherish the gift she has given you. 'Twas the gift of insight, something some men have shunned and are destined to spend their lives pursuing." Trevor swung into the saddle and then reached into his belt to retrieve the silver-handled dagger that had once been his father's. "And when you have learned your lessons well, come to me in Wessex." He tossed the blade to the young lad, who looked as if he had just been presented with a priceless gift. "There will be a place for you among my knights."

As Trevor urged his steed up beside Meagan's, she tossed him a fleeting glance and then focused on some distant point. "Your generosity moves me, m'lord. You have dangled a dream within the lad's grasp. Undoubtedly, he will one day become your most devoted knight."

Trevor twisted around in the saddle to bid farewell to the beaming lad, who clutched the dagger to him as if it was his most cherished possession. "What is your name, lad?"

"Corbin Roswell," the young squire informed him, his chest swelling with pride when the mighty warrior called back to him.

"I look forward to meeting the *man*, Corbin Roswell," Trevor chortled softly before he twisted back around, his golden eyes anchoring on the shapely blond who rode silently beside him. "It seems Corbin and I have a great deal in common," he mused aloud. "I, too, am in quest of the greater part of valor and I hope to God I find it before this maddening torment of indecision tears me to pieces."

Meagan heaved a heavyhearted sigh as they followed the path that led back to the shores of Normandy, back to the looming cloud of doubt that refused to grant Trevor peace. It seemed the longer they rode, the more distant they became. Trevor did not abuse Meagan with harsh, biting words, but neither did he pamper her. The mental anguish of his silence was almost more than Meagan could bear. He was considerate of her needs and refused to allow her to travel when she grew weary, but his arms never sheltered her during the long, lonely nights when Meagan would have begged him to chase the bitter world away with his ardent lovemaking.

Trevor was battling an emotional war, and she had offered her last plea of innocence and of love. She could only wait and pray that one day he would look upon her with his heart instead of viewing her through the hazy vision of suspicion and doubt. But Meagan wasn't expecting the Dark Prince to reverse his opinion of her before the end of the century. He was a stubborn, cautious warrior who had been burned too many times in the past to bare his heart and risk having it scarred by wounds that were invisible to the eye, but ones that could cut like the sharpest of knives.

Meagan soon found that Lear and Garda offered more companionship than the brooding lord of Wessex. And it was with a heavy heart that she followed him through the forests until the jagged guard towers of Burke Castle appeared on the horizon.

Chapter 25

A wry smile twitched Conan's lips as he watched Trevor, clad in his gold velvet tunic and ermine cloak, pace back and forth across the Great Hall, wearing out the path he had followed for over two weeks. The irascible warlord had prowled about his domain like a wounded lion, favoring an injured paw. Trevor had remained remote and distant for a fortnight, seeing to his duties, avoiding his wife, but always keeping a watchful eye on her. Each time Meagan strolled through the castle or ambled across the meadow, Trevor was in the distance, measuring her every move, keeping watch on her like a posted lookout.

Conan knew of the affliction that plagued Trevor, and he had taken it upon himself to investigate Meagan's claims, sending Ragnar to London to interrogate the rebel prisoners who were being held at the palace. Soon Neville would arrive to journey back to London for the royal celebration William intended to give before he returned to York to watch the last of the rebel resistance crumble beneath the Throne's military force.

Since Trevor had refused his oracle's advice he had sulked and stalked about the demesne, watching his unhappy wife grow round with child. It was as if Trevor had been toying with a creature of the wild, allowing her just enough freedom to leave her craving more. Trevor did not cater to Meagan, nor could he be considered cruel, but man and wife lived a strained existence, sharing the same space while playing a strategic game of cat and mouse. Their civilized warfare had worn Conan's nerves thin, and he was certain that it had played havoc with Trevor's disposition since he grumbled to himself and paced the hall like a—

"I know not what to do with that woman," Trevor blurted out, interrupting Conan's silent reverie. His arms lifted and then dropped helplessly by his sides as he wheeled to continue his frustrated pacing. "My wife? My dreaded enemy? *My* child or Granthum's? I can no longer trust my own mind where that nemesis is concerned. She speaks of love, words I cannot return for fear of falling into yet another trap. Am I to turn my head and pretend *not* to see the deceptions? Must I listen to her pleas and remain deaf to the voice of reason?" Trevor heaved an exasperated sigh and then crossed his arms over his broad chest as he pivoted to peer down at the wiry-haired sage, who was still sporting a secretive smile. "Do you find something amusing about my misery, old man?" he snapped irritably.

Conan halted the drumming of his fingers on the edge of his chair and then shrugged slightly. "'Tis an age-old problem, m'lord, one that noble warriors have sought to conquer for centuries." His dark eyes sparkled as he tilted his head to survey the sour frown that had been permanently stamped on Trevor's face. "I presume you, too, are disappointed that you have not met with success. *Woman* is the one stumbling block that invariably trips up man. You rule with your head, but you cannot conquer the emotion that has taken hold of your heart when you pause to consider Meagan. More than once you have sought to exorcise the feelings that merely mentioning her name evokes." Conan eased back in his chair and flicked a piece of lint from the sleeve of his black robe before continuing. "I have expressed my feelings, certain that I had misjudged her, but you continue to believe the worst about her. Do you expect me to offer more words of wisdom to a man who is inclined to speak of her betrayal rather than to listen to new evidence?"

"So you have turned on me too," Trevor snorted gruffly. "I would have thought that, in all the world, one friend would remain loyal. But even you. . . ." His words died on his lips when he glanced up to see Meagan moving gracefully toward him.

"I wish to ride, m'lord. I have come to ask your permission," Meagan begrudgingly requested.

It took every ounce of self-control she possessed to behave politely to Trevor. She had spent another restless night punching her pillow, wishing it could have been that stubborn knight she was pounding with her frustrated assault rather than a defenseless pillow. Trevor would barely allow her to breathe without asking for permission, and it was all Meagan could do to keep from shouting her irritation in his rugged face.

"Fine, m'lady," Trevor agreed with a curt nod. "But it will not be on the back of your horse, not in your delicate condition. You have approached me on this subject before and I have no intention of changing my decision."

"My delicate condition stems from your . . ." Meagan bit her lower lip and then choked down the remainder of her sentence when she intercepted Conan's guard-your-tongue-or-Trevor-will-be-tempted-to-bob-it-off glance. Her *condition* was the direct result of Trevor's tyrannical reign over her, and it had nothing to do with the fact that she carried his child. "Delicate, indeed!" she muttered under her breath. *Trevor* was the one who had to be handled with care. "Then what would you suggest, m'lord? An ox? An ass? What other beast of burden shall I call upon to bear my weight whilst I set upon my harmless excursion to allow Garda to stretch her wings and Lear to romp through the meadow as I long to do?" Sticky sweet sarcasm dripped from her lips.

Her caustic words floated toward him, setting his teeth on edge, and it further distressed him to hear Conan snickering to himself. "I had in mind a horse-drawn cart," Trevor informed her, striving to maintain a civil tone and failing miserably.

"A cart?" Meagan hooted, and then clamped a tight rein on her volatile temper, one that Trevor had tampered with so often that it took very little to set her off. "I had visions of riding in the normal manner to which I had grown accustomed: on the back of a horse."

"You will take the cart or you will not go at all," Trevor gritted out through his tight smile.

"But I would *prefer* the horse." Meagan's voice was glazed with sugar, as was her smile, but her temper simmered just beneath the sweet pretense.

"My dear lady." Trevor returned her sugarcoated smile for appearance' sake. "I said the *cart."*

"The horse," Meagan insisted, her tone crackling with anger.

"The cart," Trevor growled back at her, his rigid stance assuring Meagan that his tautly stretched patience was about to snap.

They were circling like a cobra and a mongoose, itching to spring at each other's throats, and Conan could stand no more. "For God's sake, Trevor, let her ride," he grumbled as he ground his cane into the floor. "Meagan will not risk harming her child. She only wants some fresh air."

Trevor leveled his seer a harsh glare for contradicting him, but then he relented when Conan nodded to reaffirm his reasoning. Heaving a defeated sigh, Trevor's gaze swung back to Meagan. "Very well, but I want your word that you will not stray too far from the fortress and that you will not race the wind as you have had a habit of doing in the past."

"My word as a lady?" Meagan raised a perfectly arched brow, allowing Trevor to glimpse the flare-up of mischief in her eyes.

His condescending glare narrowed on her impish grin. "Nay, I suppose that would be a worthless pledge," he grunted.

Meagan contained her elation of having won a round with the foul-tempered despot, but she could not suppress a gloating smile as she strode across the Great Hall. At last Trevor had granted her a breath of freedom without following at her heels . . . thanks to Conan, her godsend. He had become her only source of conversation since Trevor spared her only a few words and what little he had to say was spoken with finely honed patience.

"M'lady?" Ragnar Neville sidestepped and pressed his

back against the wall of the corridor to avoid a headlong collision with Meagan, who was too deep in thought to notice him.

Meagan froze in her tracks and then blushed in embarrassment. "Forgive me, Ragnar. I was paying little attention. I did not mean to trample you."

Ragnar melted in his boots when Meagan's sooty lashes swept up and she graced him with a dimpled smile. Taking her small hand in his, Ragnar placed a light kiss to her fingertips. "I hope 'tis not troubled thoughts that occupy you," he murmured.

Casting a fleeting glance in her pouting husband's direction, Meagan smiled slyly. "I fear 'tis so. The tyrant's mood is black, but he has allowed me to venture from the castle without a chaperone. The one who usually trails on my heels has the uncanny knack of spoiling what might have been a very pleasant outing."

"So the beast still froths at the mouth?"

Ragnar's conspiratorial chuckle drew Trevor's disgruntled frown. "A loyal knight does not talk behind his lord's back," Trevor snorted derisively. "If you have something to say, speak out, Neville."

Ragnar's twinkling eyes drifted over Meagan's head to clash with a pair of flaming golden orbs, the derogatory message evaporating Ragnar's amused grin. "I am beginning to see what you mean, m'lady," he said aside. "How long has the baron been brooding?"

"In truth, I cannot remember when he was not plagued by irascible moods," Meagan admitted. It had been so long since Trevor had broken into a true smile that she doubted that he remembered how to contort his face into such a pleasant expression.

"Ragnar!" Trevor barked, making both of them jump as if they had been struck with a whip.

"Temper. . . ." Conan advised as his hand clasped around Trevor's tensed arm. "Your knight has not offended you. He only pays respect to your lovely wife, something *you* have neglected."

"Silence, old man," Trevor muttered. "Is it not enough

that she lures my men? Must you always defend her?"

"The dragon roars," Meagan whispered as she brushed past Ragnar to make her escape before Trevor retracted his permission to leave and sentenced her to her room. "'Tis good that you have come equipped with your armor, but I suggest that you retrieve your shield. I fear you will need it while dealing with the monster of Wessex."

Ragnar nodded in agreement as he dragged his eyes away from the fleeing lady and forced himself to face the golden-eyed demon who was waging a private war with the jealous green-eyed monster. It was not difficult to tell who had won, Ragnar mused as he strode toward the dais. The stubborn fool. It was beyond him that any man could remain at odds with Meagan and still retain his sanity. And Trevor's was questionable, Ragnar thought to himself as he moved up the steps toward Trevor.

A sigh of pure relief escaped Meagan's lips as she stepped outside to inhale the crisp December air. Freedom, she thought delightedly. She craved the taste of it. A happy smile skipped across her face as she crossed the drawbridge with her falcon soaring above her and her shepherd trotting beside her steed.

The previous two weeks had left Meagan to wonder what Trevor intended to do with her once she had been introduced to the king. She doubted that Trevor planned to keep her at his fortress after they returned from the royal celebration in London. Where would he stash her this time? Meagan filed that question in the back of her mind and focused her attention on her surroundings. Although the air was cool it was a pleasant day for riding. A gentle breath of wind rippled across the sea of tall grass, and Meagan followed the luring waves across the meadow to seek out the quiet corner of the world where she could be alone with her thoughts.

As she slid from the saddle to stroll along the rivulet with Lear trailing at her heels, a fond smile hovered on her lips. She sank down to stroke the shepherd's broad head and she chortled softly when Lear nuzzled against her.

"If only Trevor could trust me as you do, my friend," Meagan breathed whimsically. When Lear pricked up his ears, Meagan followed his keen gaze, catching the fleeting shadow that vanished among the trees. "We have company. No doubt 'tis an unfriendly visitor or he would show his face."

A knot of apprehension coiled in the pit of her stomach, and she cautiously rose to her feet to grasp her steed's trailing reins. During her journey across England, Meagan had stumbled upon and then carefully avoided the outlaws who had become scavengers of the forest. She was leery of tarrying too long in one place or daydreaming when she was hunted by the eerie sensation that she was being watched.

"Meagan." Trevor's abrupt voice echoed behind her and she nearly jumped out of her skin. "I ordered you not to stray too far from the fortress," he reminded her harshly as he trotted Poseidon down the slope.

For once Meagan was relieved to see her sour guardian angel. She did not relish facing whoever had been spying on her without a man of Trevor's capabilities at her side. With his grisly disposition, who would dare cross him, Meagan asked herself and then quickly answered, *Only a fool.*

"I am sorry, m'lord," Meagan murmured as she clasped the steed's mane to pull herself into the saddle, a chore that had become more difficult than she had remembered. "'Tis just that I am drawn to this lovely, serene place. Even in winter, 'tis compelling."

A quiver trailed across her skin as Trevor leaned out to assist her to her perch. It was the first time he had touched her since they had set foot on the shores of England. The feel of his firm hand stirred longings that Meagan thought she had learned to control, but one touch was enough to crumble every barrier she had sought to construct to hide the longing of wanting him.

When Meagan glanced up to see the faintest hint of a smile hovering on Trevor's lips, she frowned bemusedly. How had he managed that pleasant expression when she swore he could do nothing but glare suspiciously at her? Meagan was certain that his stony face would crack under the excessive pressure of a smile.

"Our guest expects your presence at the evening meal. It would be rude to keep Ragnar waiting since his face lights up each time you go near him," Trevor rasped as his index finger traced the delicate bones of her jaw.

They rode side by side in silence, and Meagan was truly miffed by the tender smile that lingered on Trevor's lips each time he glanced in her direction. What had come over this dark, moody prince? Had the clever wizard of Wessex devised a way to transplant another personality in Trevor's body? The handsome warlord had suddenly become so charming and attentive that Meagan wondered if she were living in someone else's dream. Trevor had done nothing but scowl and glare at her for a fortnight, and now he was as gallant and chivalrous as any knight could be.

When Trevor lifted her from the saddle to set her on her feet, his hands absently caressed her hips, making mincemeat of her carefully controlled emotions. Had Trevor reached his breaking point? Were these amorous attentions he was bestowing on her the result of lusts that had remained unappeased for the past few weeks? Meagan knew he had slept alone, because she had spied on him, certain her heart would break if she saw one of the castle wenches slipping into his solar during the late hours of the night. But to her knowledge Trevor had remained celibate since their return from Normandy. Why? She couldn't say, but he had received no visitors after he retired for the night.

Meagan gulped in surprise when Trevor's head moved deliberately toward hers, his warm sienna gaze feasting on the luscious curve of her lips, as if they were the first pair he had ever laid eyes on. Her entire body quivered beneath his light, caressing touch, and Meagan feared she would become mellowed mush if she did not retreat from his arousing assault.

"M'lord, are you ill?" Meagan queried as she dodged his embrace. "You are behaving very strangely." Her puzzled regard ran the full length of him and then circled back to his rugged face.

A low chuckle erupted from his massive chest as his arm

encircled her waist to urge her toward the forebuilding. "Nay, m'lady, I feel better than I have in months. A heavy yoke has been lifted from my shoulders. I am only trying to be pleasant."

Meagan cast him a cautious sidelong glance as he propelled her through the corridor, wishing he would expound upon his remark, but he didn't. Trevor looked as if he were about to burst. His face was so radiant that every feature was alive with mysterious pleasure. There was something suspicious about his expression that worried her more than a mite.

"Perhaps you should restrict yourself to something more familiar than pleasantries, m'lord," she advised, her tone hinting strongly at sarcasm. "Although your gallant manner becomes you, 'tis a bit awkward after the way you have been behaving of late."

"M'lady, you wound me to the quick," Trevor assured her, feigning the pain of a verbal lynching.

"And just where is your quick?" Meagan questioned and then gouged him in the ribs, making Trevor grunt uncomfortably when she knocked the wind out of him. "Here, m'lord?" When Trevor grimaced from the second punch just below his breastplate, Meagan smiled, feeling quite satisfied with herself. "Ah, I seem to have found it. And while you are nursing your bruises, I should like to freshen up before joining Ragnar. Your loyal knight is a man of impeccable taste, one after my own heart, one who relishes light conversation and stimulating company."

Trevor's lean fingers clamped about her forearm as he leaned closer, the amusement dwindling in his eyes. "Your *heart* is something Neville will never claim, Meagan Burke," he declared, his forceful grasp emphasizing his words. "And do not think to pit me against him. It will only sour my newly acquired disposition. I have informed Neville of the boundaries and he will strictly observe them where you are concerned. Do not tempt him or you will be punished as well."

When Trevor spun on his heels and left her standing outside her chamber, Meagan frowned bemusedly. She would dearly love to know what was on Trevor's mind, but he refused to enlighten her, and attempting to draw answers from that tight-lipped warrior was as hopeless as prying information from a clam.

Oh, what was the use, Meagan asked herself as she stripped from her garments and then drew the green satin tunic over her head to smooth it into place. Trevor had probably decided her fate, and with it had come a great sense of relief, she imagined. Having her near him had distressed him. No doubt he was gloating after coming to his verdict. Would he be compassionate or ruthless? Her curiosity was eating her alive. How long would Trevor let her steam and stew, keeping her in suspense? Until he considered the moment ripe to startle her, Meagan thought dismally. That was why he was smiling wryly. He was delighting in watching her squirm, leaving her to wonder about her future, or lack of it.

The incessant rap at the door drew her from her troubled contemplations, and Meagan hurriedly checked her appearance in the looking glass and then opened the door to find Trevor adorned in his finery, standing regally before her like a knight awaiting sainthood. A more dashing man she had yet to lay eyes on, Meagan thought, experiencing a mixture of admiration and resentment. She continued to study Trevor as he drew her to his side and steered her down the steps toward the dais.

"Desmond's messenger arrived while you were out riding," he commented. "My dear friend was beside himself with worry until Gunthar arrived to explain the events of the past month. Desmond also informed me that all my uncle's worldly possessions are now mine, his land and chateau in Normandy and France, besides the chateau on the Lys River that I once called home. All that he coveted and stole from my family has been returned to me. Ironic, is it not?" Trevor laughed bitterly. "Ulrick spent his life acquiring land to prove to himself that he was a better man than my father. In the end, he did not bother to bequeath his vast wealth to anyone, and now his holdings fall to me."

"Yea, it would seem that there is some justice in the

world," Meagan murmured absently, wondering when and if she would be rewarded for her troubles.

"Desmond's correspondence was also thick with the apology that you had vanished from sight and that he had been lured away from the chateau during Ulrick's attack. I wonder if he will ever forgive himself for leaving you with Ulrick when you had voiced apprehension about being alone with my uncle," Trevor mused aloud.

"He is a very concerned and considerate man," Meagan replied, a fond smile skimming her lips. "If I had not feared for my life I would have taken time to leave a note, informing Desmond of what had truly happened. I did not mean to worry him. He was very generous and kind to me and I came to love him as a father."

"And he was quite taken with you," Trevor assured her, pausing to stare down into a pair of sapphire eyes that could take him hostage and hold him spellbound. "You seem to have the same devastating effect on *all* your men, young and old alike."

There it was again, that seductive baritone voice and that sensuous smile that could melt her heart and leave it dripping all over the inside of her chest. What the devil was he up to anyway? He knew it would take very little persuasion to crumble her resistance. Why was he torturing her like this? Why was he behaving as if he actually enjoyed her company when she knew he mistrusted her and loathed the sight of her?

Meagan was about to cross-examine Trevor when Ragnar strode up in front of her, demanding her attention. "Lady Meagan, your beauty leaves me breathless. May I request your presence beside me on the dais? I have longed for your pleasant conversation since we passed in the corridor. I can think of nothing more enjoyable than partaking of a succulent meal and feasting on such comeliness."

What? Trevor was not growling at the knight for bestowing attention on her? Had Trevor decided to divorce her and give her to Ragnar, refusing to allow them to live as man and wife? Is that what Trevor implied earlier?

Meagan felt a lump of apprehension constricting her

throat. Although she was fond of Ragnar, he could never replace Trevor in her heart. Seeing Trevor occasionally would be torture, pure and simple. Trevor wouldn't dare cart her off to Neville Castle, would he?

"May I, m'lady?" Ragnar prompted, dragging Meagan from her disturbing thoughts.

When she nodded her consent, Ragnar led her away, but Trevor strolled behind her, voicing no complaint, but remaining like an ever-present threat if she dared to step out of line. During the meal Trevor's eyes came to rest on her. He blessed her with one of his charismatic smiles, and that rattled her. If he did not explain himself, and quickly, Meagan would explode with curiosity. Even his sour moods had been easier to tolerate than this blasted suspense and those secretive grins.

"I am looking forward to journeying to London with you, Lady Meagan. No doubt, William will be as enamored with you as I have been. Will you cast our friendship aside to bestow your full attention on our king?" Ragnar teased.

"I do not anticipate the introduction," Meagan said boldly, knowing her remark would agitate Trevor, but if it did, he revealed no outward signs of irritation. "William has wrought havoc for my people, and although I can do nothing to change the outcome of the revolt, I cannot condone his methods of regaining order."

"William has been harsh on the Mercians," Ragnar agreed. "But many of his enemies have congregated in the North. Force seems to be the only tool they understand. William allowed them to retain their lands, but they have repaid his generosity by terrorizing his fortresses."

"Only because taxation has been unusually steep," Meagan argued. "William has been so thorough in his census that not one newborn calf has been overlooked or allowed to escape the burden of payment to its owner. I wonder if your king intends to tax his overlords for their possessions . . . such as their jewels or their wives," Meagan smirked.

"If such laws come to pass they will be based on the merit of the possession," Trevor remarked as he swirled his ale around the rim of his mug and then cast Meagan a devilish glance. "In that instance, my payment might be minimal . . . if His Grace does indeed place a price on a man's wife."

Meagan felt the overwhelming urge to yank Trevor's mug from his hand and dump it on his head. Clamping her hands around the arm of her chair, she offered him a thin smile that did not disguise the vengeance in her snapping blue eyes.

"Or perhaps wise William will see fit to tax his overlords on merit. The intelligent barons will pay a sum to equal their efficiency while the less endowed members of the feudal system will settle with scant contributions to the Throne." Meagan raised a mocking brow as she leaned forward to fasten her gaze on Trevor. "In that case, m'lord, you may not find it necessary to offer even one coin to your king."

"This meal is delicious," Ragnar broke in when he saw Trevor flinch as if he had been run through by a lance. "My compliments to the cooks."

But Trevor refused to be sidetracked. When Meagan threw down the gauntlet, Trevor quickly snatched it up. "His Grace has implied my worth by placing me in a responsible position and by summoning me to counsel before he decides on his course of action. You, on the other hand, have yet to prove your value. I anticipate that all worthless clutter will be discarded during the spring cleaning. I wonder if you will be in charge of those duties, or among them."

Meagan could have doubled her fist and planted it in the midst of his ornery smile, but she would have had to climb over Ragnar to get to that exasperating knight. Meagan doubted that Ragnar would have allowed her to lay a hand on him, even though Trevor deserved to be throttled.

"Ragnar, why don't you escort the lady to her room," Conan suggested, sensing that man and wife were about to come to blows. "I require a private word with Trevor before I retire."

"I would be honored," Ragnar murmured as he took Meagan's hand and assisted her to her feet. "It seems the direction of this conversation has run amok."

When Ragnar and Meagan were out of earshot, Conan anchored a pair of reproachful brown eyes on Trevor, who was gulping his ale as if he were a camel preparing for a long journey across the barren desert. "How do you expect to return to amicable terms with Meagan if you purposefully taunt her? She will spar words with you all day if you challenge her."

"She started it by ridiculing William," Trevor grumbled with childish vindictiveness.

"Would you care for a few words of advice?" Conan questioned soberly.

"Not particularly," Trevor grunted and then downed his ale. "I doubt that I will like what I might hear."

"But you *will* hear it, nonetheless," Conan assured him tartly. "If you do not make amends tonight and inform Meagan of your intentions, you will find this civil war continuing when peace would have served your cause just as well. Let her go or make your claim, here and now. You have kept her prisoner within these walls long enough. If she is not to rule by your side, then dismiss her. Ragnar would be all too happy to take your leavings. You have toyed with her long enough. Meagan will never be a man's chattel. She will be *more* or nothing at all. Do you understand me, Trevor?"

"All too well, old man," Trevor grumbled.

Begrudgingly, Trevor gathered his feet beneath him and aimed himself toward the steps. Damnation, he would rather be whipped than face that sharp-tongued vixen when he was very nearly swimming in his cups. But Conan was right and they both knew it. He and Meagan had to come to an understanding before they ventured to the palace. If not, Trevor feared that Meagan would purposely brew trouble for them when they encountered William.

A husky chuckle erupted from Conan's chest as he watched Trevor disappear into the shadows. The mighty warrior would not exit as the same stubborn knight who approached his wife. The temptation simmered, and Trevor, who had never been able to resist that silver-blond minx, would not escape with his heart. Not this time, Conan mused as he rose unsteadily to his feet. Tonight Trevor would meet his destiny.

Chapter 26

When Trevor rapped on her door, Meagan frowned at the interruption. The day had worn her nerves thin, and she longed to stretch out in bed, close her eyes, and drift off in dreams.

"Who is it?" Meagan called disinterestedly.

"'Tis I, Trevor."

He had knocked twice in one day without barging in unannounced? Miracles *did* happen, Meagan decided. Trevor had dispensed with that courtesy since the day she had met him, and suddenly he had done an about-face. No doubt Conan *had* stirred up a concoction to dissolve Trevor's annoying qualities.

"I want to know why you have been behaving like a perfect gentleman after storming about this castle like a frothing beast for a fortnight," Meagan demanded to know as she whipped open the door.

His dark brow arched mockingly as he swaggered into the room and then kicked the door shut with his boot heel. "I was not aware that you were in a position to make demands," he chuckled.

"It has never stopped me before," she pointed out, tilting a defiant chin.

"C'est vrai," he agreed as he raked her curvaceous figure, noting the fullness of her heaving bosom and the rounding of her abdomen. "Indeed, it has not. Even when you stood on shaky ground you continued to charge like a fearless knight."

"You have sealed my grim future," Meagan predicted, refusing to rise to the taunt. "That is why your disposition has mellowed."

"You are very perceptive, Meagan," Trevor complimented and then proceeded to shed his ermine cloak and divest himself of his mantle, drawing Meagan's cautious glance.

"Have you decided to give me to Ragnar under some fiendish proclamation that we are not to consummate the marriage?" Meagan blurted out, anxious to know her fate.

Trevor froze. "Do you still profess to love me?"

"Do not change the subject," Meagan spouted. "I demand to know what is to be done with me when we return from London."

"I have no intention of passing my delectable wife among my friends. My generosity does have its limits," he answered and then held her hostage with his probing gaze. "I answered your question, and now I insist that you respond to mine."

"Then what do you intend to do with me?" Meagan impatiently demanded, refusing to be put off. "Your games are worse than being stretched on a torture rack."

A roguish smile caught the corner of his mouth, curving it upward as he ambled toward her, his hungry gaze folding about her shapely contours. "I think mayhap it would be easier to *demonstrate* than to tell you of my intentions, Meagan."

The sensuous way her name tumbled from his lips sent a delicious tingle diving down her spine, but Meagan stilled the arousing sensation, refusing to be seduced by a man who had treated her like a prisoner for over four months. When his hands slid around her waist, Meagan ground her foot on his and then elbowed him in the belly before darting away from his oncoming embrace.

"I prefer a verbal explanation," she said tersely, putting out her chin and then raising her hand to halt his second advance. "Why the dramatic change?"

Trevor heaved a frustrated sigh. Meagan was not making this easy, and he was very unsure of his footing, as he had always been when dealing with this feisty minx. He would be

sking a great deal of Meagan when he begged forgiveness
or the way he had treated her, the heartache he had put her
hrough.

"Sit, please," he requested as he gestured toward the chair.
Meagan promptly positioned herself on the edge of the seat,
er wide blue eyes intent on him as he strode forward to
ower over her. And Trevor, an unsure, crumbling mountain
f strength, shifted uneasily from one foot to the other,
ormulating his thoughts and searching for the perfect words
o begin his explanation. "Thanks to my devoted oracle and
my loyal knight I have learned that you were correct. No one
as made a bigger fool of me than I have made of myself."
Trevor plowed on before he lost his nerve. "I ask that you
orgive this blundering oaf."

Get to the point, Meagan thought impatiently. How could
he forgive him when he had not said what he was
pologizing for?

Trevor retreated when Meagan only stared bewilderedly
t him, refusing to speak. He strode to the window to peer
ut into the darkness. "Conan sent Ragnar to London to
nterrogate Marston Pearce and several other prisoners. At
ast I have learned the truth."

Meagan held her breath, her heart drumming in her ears,
istorting his trembly voice. Did Trevor know of Edric's
nvolvement? God, she had tried so hard to keep Edric safe
rom Trevor's wrath. Had her suffering been for naught?
What had Marston told Ragnar? Had he lied as Reid had?

A tender smile grazed Trevor's lips as he glanced back to
ee Meagan bow her head and clasp her hands in her lap,
eminding him of an angel in meditation. "Marston Pearce
laims that your brother was blackmailed into the rebellion
nd that Reid insisted that you be used as bait to get to me.
He also informed Ragnar that he saw to it that Reid
bstained from intimacy while you rode with the rebels and
hat you made it clear that you would not allow another man
o touch you while you were my wife."

Relief washed over her face, but then Meagan stiffened
when the full implication soaked in. She had voiced her
laim of innocence, and Trevor had called *her* a liar. Her

gaze swung to the handsome knight, sizing him up and the[n] looking down her nose at him. "And you believe Pearce?" Meagan questioned, her tone laced with sarcasm. "A rebe[l] Reid's stepbrother? A man who might have thought to ga[in] favor by relating a story that he thought Ragnar *wanted* t[o] hear?"

She *did* intend to make this next to impossible, Trevo[r] realized. That little termagant! She could not graciousl[y] accept his apology without rubbing his nose in his stupidity[.] This confession did not come easily, and Meagan planned t[o] hound him every step of the way. Gritting his teeth, Trevo[r] plunged on before Meagan could tie his tongue in knots.

"Dammit, woman, I am trying to apologize for behavin[g] like an ass!" Trevor bit off, careful to avoid his tangle[d] tongue. "I realize now that your intent was to protect me an[d] your brother, knowing that you would be suspected o[f] treason. I did not want to believe the worst about you, but i[t] has become second nature to me to mistrust Saxon motive[s.] I have been back-stabbed more times than I care to count. [I] was never certain where I stood with you until . . ." His voic[e] trailed off as he flashed Meagan a hopeful smile. "Until yo[u] professed to love me, or have I destroyed that too?"

Long, thick lashes fluttered up to watch his granit[e] features soften in a boyish grin. "You have made a gallan[t] effort to do just that," Meagan hedged, avoiding a direc[t] answer.

"Have I?" Trevor's golden eyes pinned her to the chai[r,] making her fidget beneath his scrutinizing gaze.

She was not about to bare her heart again and have i[t] trampled. It had taken the better part of two weeks to stitc[h] her dignity back together after Trevor had refused t[o] acknowledge her confession.

"Is there a point to all this?" Meagan goaded him. "If not, [I] should like to retire for the night. Tomorrow's journey wil[l] be grueling and I must rest."

Resigning himself to the fact that he would have to craw[l,] and that he probably deserved to, Trevor strode back t[o] Meagan and then, on bended knee, looked up to view he[r] astounded expression.

"Meagan Burke, you have taunted and tormented me from the first moment I took you in my arms. You have broken every rule I have made. You have wreaked havoc with my thoughts. I have tried very hard to rule over you with my head rather than my heart, and therein has been my torment." Trevor smiled ruefully as he pried her clenched fist open and then brought her fingertips to his lips. "After the night we shared in the lean-to, I knew that I would never be able to let you go, that you would one day claim my name since you had already won my heart. When I assured you that you would never carry my bastard child, I only implied that any child we created would be born in wedlock. I had no intention of giving you to Ragnar or any other man, but I—"

Meagan gasped indignantly and then cast him the evil eye. "Lout! All this time you allowed me to believe . . ."

Trevor pressed his fingertips to her lips to stifle her interruption. "I thought you despised me. You could not tolerate my presence or my touch and you ran from me. I was much too proud to confess my affection to such a feisty rebel, a woman who behaved as if my being a Norman was worse than being afflicted with leprosy." A melancholy smile traced his lips, and his eyes took on a faraway look as he continued in a soft tone. "Since the day I set foot in England I have wished for an extra set of eyes in the back of my head. Reid Granthum was not the first Saxon to attempt to murder me in my sleep. Three other attempts had been made on my life since I came to rule Wessex. Each time I stayed the night at a new fortress, Saxons scurried in the shadows, whispering behind my back, plotting to dispose of me, intending to avenge their fate with my death.

"Even Saxon women have looked upon me as a means to gain security. I never knew for certain if their interest was in me because of the man I was or because they sought to obtain privileges from my position. Confessions of love came all too quickly and easily from their lips, words that had no true meaning. And then along came a distracting woman whose brother seemed all too anxious to have me enamored with her beauty." Trevor reached up to trail his index finger over her flawless features, loving the feel of

Meagan's satiny skin beneath his caress. "I was wary of Edric's motives, but I was also drawn to you, even when I was uncertain of your true opinion of me. I had to consider my position with the Throne, my obligations to my demesne and the possibility of another plot against me. Conan had foreseen trouble and I could not overlook his warnings. Although I longed to throw caution to the wind, I could not. I have fought for all I have gained in life and I was sure I was destined to battle for your love, something I have long wondered if I could ever truly obtain. When you fought me, I knew you despised me, and when you were kind to me I was left to wonder why. You have always miffed me, Meagan."

As if he could not decipher the tenderness in her eyes, Meagan sought to chase away all shadows of doubt and misconception that plagued him. "Do you remember the night you came to force yourself on me when we returned from Neville Castle?"

He gave his raven head an affirmative nod. "Yea, I remember it well, m'lady. I thought you loathed me so much that you had taken a headlong dive off the deep end when I dared to touch you as I ached to do. But then you came to my room and again I was baffled by the abrupt change in your behavior."

"'Twas then that I realized that I had fallen in love with you, despite my strong convictions, despite our differences." Meagan tunneled her fingers through his thick hair and smiled adoringly. "But what I felt for you defied reason, crumbled all the obstacles that stood between us. I came to you that night, offering a love that demanded no commitment. I would have left you, cherishing the memories of that night without daring to hope for more. But then I found myself trapped in the midst of a conspiracy. I could not speak out, afraid I might endanger Edric and unsure of his involvement." A hint of tears sparkled in her eyes as she sighed tremulously. "Conan warned me that I would lose no matter which path I chose, and he was, as he always is, correct. If I married you, Reid would attempt to kill you. If I protested the wedding, you would believe that I could not tolerate you. I protested to protect you and Edric from

398

harm, even when I longed to become your wife, to share your life and any affection you offered me." Meagan glanced away, bracing her courage before meeting his amber gaze. "Am I dreaming an impossible dream, Trevor? Can you offer me more than gratitude, more than compassion, more than lustful desire? If not, pray, let me go. I cannot bear to be near you, wondering if another woman will steal into your chamber to lie in your arms. Let me return to the convent to live out my life."

A quiet chuckle bubbled from his lips as he nuzzled his forehead against hers and then withdrew to brush away the renegade tear that slid down her cheek. "Can you not see beneath this dragon's spiny scales?" He took her hand and tenderly pressed it to his chest. "Here lurks the heart of an overly cautious man who viewed his love for you as his weakness. Ah, Meagan, I have known from the beginning that I was fighting a hopeless battle. Each time you fled from me I pursued you. Each time another man gazed hungrily upon you, I felt a jealousy that threatened to destroy me. If I had not cared so deeply, I could not have been hurt. You can never know the agony I endured, loving you so fiercely, afraid that you wanted to destroy me, dying bit by bit with the fear that Granthum had touched the woman that I loved more than life." Trevor inhaled a deep breath, his senses reeling as Meagan melted in his arms. "I despised myself for loving you and I hated you for betraying me. I was twisted with bitterness and haunted by excruciating torment, envisioning you in Granthum's arms, seeing you standing over me while I slept, waiting for Granthum to dispose of me. But through all the agony, I could not stop loving you. You cannot know the great sense of relief that I experienced when Ragnar told me what he had learned from Marston Pearce."

Trevor eased onto the edge of the bed, pressing her head against his shoulder, cuddling her close. "You are my sun and moon, my essence. You are the sweet angel who makes my heart swell with so much happiness that I fear it will burst. You are the fire that burns with such intensity that I know I can never extinguish this ardent flame of love. Living without you has been hell, but 'tis worth the suffering if you will forgive me for doubting you and reaffirm the vow of love, even if I do not deserve it."

Meagan could not control the tears that tumbled down her cheeks like a flooding river. "I do love you," she sobbed. "There could have been no other man. Each time I close my eyes, 'tis your face that hovers above me. No man stirs me in the ways that you do."

His gentle caress wandered across her trembling flesh as his mouth claimed hers, his urgency stealing her breath from her lungs. Trevor clutched her to him and then pried himself away when his hand roamed over her abdomen to feel the stirring of life beneath it.

"My son seems as possessive of you as I am," he murmured as he pressed a light kiss to the tip of her upturned nose. "I wonder if he knows how difficult it will be for his father to keep his hands off you when his desires burn like wildfire."

"And if you keep your hands to yourself I will surely go mad," Meagan assured him as she took her hand and folded it over her breast. "I long for you to touch me. I crave your kiss and caress. Do not fear for our child's safety. He will be unharmed."

Her gentle coaxing was enough to set his barely controlled passions ablaze, burning him alive. Two weeks of hunger gnawed at him, a fortnight of hell, wanting Meagan and tying himself to the bedpost to prevent bursting into her room and making wild, passionate love to her until the dark hour before dawn.

His skillful hands began their arousing manipulations while he whispered his need for her against her silky skin, drawing away the garments that wrapped his treasured package. The dim lantern light enhanced her exquisite beauty, leaving her flesh glowing like ivory, accenting her flawless features with mystique. Trevor ached to know every inch of her curvaceous body by touch. Watching Meagan curl up beside him like a contented feline was not enough. He wanted to hear her purr. He hungered to feed her passions and his until they united, body and soul, exploring the perimeter of a universe that he could only view when he was held in the loving circle of her satiny arms.

His warm, sensuous kisses flitted across her cheek, descended to her collarbone, and then scaled the crest of her breast, bringing with them such tantalizing pleasure that Meagan wondered if she could endure it. Her body was his, as was her heart. She could do nothing more than respond to his touch. His tongue languidly trailed around one pink bud while his arm glided over her shoulder to tease the other peak to tautness. His idle hand roused to explore the velvety softness of her inner thighs, his fingertips hovering upon her skin like a butterfly skimming her flesh, tickling, teasing, arousing her until she moaned in splendorous torment. Trevor could set each nerve ending to tingling in anticipation. He could stir her heart and set it to racing in triple time.

His wandering caresses weaved intricate patterns on her abdomen before ascending to flick the point of her breast, luring his moist lips to follow in the wake of his exciting touch. Enticing kisses splayed across her hips, sending a tide of pleasure flooding over her and then ebbing momentarily before the rapture of his fondling heightened and washed over her again. The subtle movements of his practiced hands flowed over her body to trace the sensitive flesh of her thighs, leaving her drifting with a current of breathless desire. She instinctively moved toward his seeking fingers, aching to satisfy the maddening craving that his familiar caresses evoked.

"No other man will ever enjoy the pleasure that consumes me when I touch you," Trevor breathed against her skin. "You are mine, Meagan, and I glory in freeing your soul and claiming it as my own. You are my love, a goddess, the essence of my dreams."

Meagan squirmed away, yearning to still the fire that burned its way to her very core. She longed to touch him as intimately as he had touched her, to return the sweet, hypnotic caresses, leaving Trevor craving her with the same breathless urgency that gnawed at her when his hands worked their magic on her flesh.

"And you, my fiery dragon, will whisper words of love to

no other woman. I, alone, will control this lustful beast, keeping you at my beck and call. All others will fear your strength and kneel to call you master, but I will lure you with love until you wish no more of it."

Her gentle hands strayed across the rock hard wall of his chest, circling each male nipple and then tracking down the crisp matting of hair that extended to his belly. His body quaked as she touched him, and then he groaned in unholy torment as her caresses roamed along his scarred ribs to retrace the same sweet, tormenting path. Soft lips feathered across his flesh, and Trevor wondered wildly if this sorceress had melted his bones and muscles, leaving him a quivering mass of jelly that was about to be reduced to its original liquid state.

"God, woman," Trevor rasped. "You *have* tamed this dreadful beast. Do you seek to destroy him as well?"

Her seductive smile wrapped itself around his warped senses until he was consumed by the sight, feel, and fragrant flavor of the one woman he had never been able to resist.

"Nay, my love," she whispered. "I seek to create. . . ."

And create she did. Trevor was assaulted by indescribable sensations as the peaks of her breasts pressed wantonly against him and her bold caresses roved over his hips. Trevor ached to bury himself in the softness of her womanly body, but Meagan refused to release him from her spell until his raging passions threatened to engulf him. The way she made him feel was almost wicked. The way she touched him was enough to strip him of what little sanity he had left. She had always possessed the power to make him forget another world existed beyond the reach of her stimulating caresses and intoxicating kisses.

Finally Trevor could endure no more of the sweet torture. He wanted her, craved her. He crouched above her, his senses alive with the taste and feel of this provocative tigress who had turned him every which way but loose. The muscles of his arms bulged as he held himself above her, marveling at the liquid blue flame that burned in her eyes, entranced by the sea of silver-gold hair that shimmered as it rippled across the pillow. He was spellbound by the sight of her naked flesh.

His male body ached to forge with hers, to satiate this primal craving that demanded fulfillment. And yet, he knew that in possessing her he would become her possession. But Trevor felt no humiliation in surrendering his love and passion to the one woman who was strong enough to gentle the proud, noble beast within him. From this mass of potential strength she had created a tender lover who longed to please her. Her coaxing voice could soothe his savage anger. Her delicate touch could heal all wounds. She was his lifelong dream, the quintessence of love, the one weakness from which he could draw inexhaustible strength. She was his breath of life, his reason for living and breathing. To belong to Meagan was pure, sweet satisfaction.

"Where you lead I will follow," Trevor assured her raggedly. "When you take to your wings, I, too, shall fly. Sweet angel. . . ." Trevor groaned as he carefully lowered himself to her, melting them into one being. "'Tis heaven. . . . I love you. . . ."

His mouth slanted across hers, his lips becoming preoccupied with something more arousing and fulfilling than mere conversation. His muscular body intermingled with the feminine softness of hers, and Trevor was hopelessly lost to the satisfying warmth that consumed him. He moved within her, slowly at first, and then rousing to the demands of a raging passion that had taken complete control.

The proof of their love was in the wild, rapturous union that merged all thoughts and actions into one purpose—to belong to each other for all eternity. Their love transcended time, gliding on pinioned wings to soar beyond the rainbows. Each tantalizing sensation swelled and blossomed into yet another, like the churning clouds of a thunderstorm, mounting and feeding on the winds that lifted and swirled in the sky. Currents of unrestrained passion swept them up, sending them towering higher and higher. The frantic beat of their hearts rumbled in thunderous rhythm as they were towed into the eye of the tempest, where the whirlwind of desire became a peaceful calm. Amidst the devastating gale of passion, the breath of love stirred and their souls merged, enfolded in such serenity that Meagan sighed in blissful pleasure.

It was as if the essence of her being had flowed from her body, as if she were standing apart from the euphoric enchantment that consumed her flesh. And yet she was acutely aware of its existence. It was like living and viewing an ecstatic dream, all in the same moment.

Meagan reveled in the overwhelming feelings that gripped her as they fluttered back to reality. Never had she known such contentment. Yea, Trevor's skillful lovemaking had left her exhausted because he had drained all emotion, but never had she experienced such divine pleasure and sublime satisfaction in his powerful arms.

Her hand absently trailed down his spine and then slid upward as she combed her fingers through his raven hair. Her light touch brought a soft moan from his lips, and Trevor stirred to press a kiss to the trim column of her neck before reluctantly easing down beside her.

"Will you always be this thorough with your love-making?" Trevor propped his head on his hand and flashed her a roguish grin. "Am I to expect only an occasional night's sleep?"

Meagan's counter-smile matched his. "Do you offer some complaint, m'lord?" she questioned, her voice husky with the aftereffects of passion.

"Mmmm . . . nay. I would not think of it, but . . ." His index finger traced the curve of her kiss-swollen lips. "If all our nights are to be this physically exhausting, I must remember to pace myself during the day if I am to endure the night."

"Endure?" Meagan raised an eyebrow at his choice of words.

"Pleasurably survive," Trevor corrected with a chuckle.

Her leg slid between his as she draped her arm over his shoulder, squirming to fit her supple body to the solidness of his. "You may find that the demands of knighthood are not as rigorous as those required of manhood," she assured him in a provocative tone.

Trevor responded to the feel of her luscious curves as they melted against his rough skin. "Are you suggesting that I

404

dispense with tournaments and limit myself to indoor activities, sharpening my skills in bed?" The idea had an arousing appeal, he mused as he dropped a kiss to her full lips.

"Precisely, m'lord," Meagan affirmed as her knuckles glided over the angular features of his face. "There will be no time for war games during your days or nights. I have imagined making love to you during all hours between dusk and dawn." An impish grin captured her delicate face, making her eyes sparkle with deviltry. "What time will we be departing for London on the morrow?"

Trevor was quick to catch the insinuation, and he drew back to cast his shameless wife a dubious glance. "Pray, how am I to sit astride a horse without a night's sleep?" he chirped.

"And pray, how am I to endure the day without a knight's love?" Meagan parried, smoothing away his frown. Her wandering hands ascended his shoulder to toy with the raven hair that curled at the nape of his neck. "Come, Dark Prince, we shall give new meaning to your awesome nickname."

Trevor could not refuse the titillating invitation. His eager body pressed against hers, and again they tasted passion's sweet nectar, whispering words of love, holding back nothing.

For a time they slept in each other's arms, their passion spent, but Meagan awoke each time Trevor moved beside her. Luring caresses brought him from the depths of drowsiness to the heights of ecstasy time and time again, and it was only the quiet rap on the door, long after the sun had blushed down at them, that broke them apart.

"What is it?" Trevor questioned as he abandoned Meagan's inviting lips.

"Have you decided to postpone our journey, m'lord? Must the king himself be forced to tarry until you have flown from your nest?" Ragnar's voice held a hint of laughter. "Midday approaches . . . if 'tis of any concern to you."

Trevor rolled his eyes. He could well imagine the wide grin that stretched across his bulky knight's face, his shoulders shaking in barely contained amusement. "Have you naught else to do but chime the hour? Make yourself useful. Organize the retinue and oversee the loading of the carts," he commanded. "My lady and I will be down shortly to join you."

"Shall I fetch a stretcher, or can you manage under your own power?" Ragnar taunted unmercifully, envious and yet delighted that Trevor had declared the emotion that had wreaked havoc on his heart.

"Off with you, Neville!" Trevor growled. "You sorely test my patience!"

"And I would guess that *patience* is all you have left to work with," Ragnar snickered as he pivoted on his heels and strode down the corridor.

Grumbling at the taunt, Trevor dragged himself from the warm bed and the all-too-willing woman who had kept her promise to occupy the night with something far more interesting than sleep. Trevor rose to full stature and then heaved a weary sigh before glancing over to see Meagan studying him with another seductive smile.

"Do not look at me like that, woman," Trevor chided playfully as he stooped to retrieve his discarded clothes.

"I will always stare at you with desire in my eyes and love in my heart," Meagan assured him. "If you do not like what you see, then turn away, but do not ask me to deny the emotions I have long been forced to disguise."

Trevor sank down beside her, a tender smile bordering his lips as he accepted the invitation of one last kiss. "I love what I see, and I wish to wake to that radiant smile for the rest of my life. I long for you to love me forever and with the same enthusiasm you displayed last night . . . all night." A gold flame kindled in his eyes as his hand strayed beneath the quilts to gently cup her breast, teasing the roseate bud to tautness. "But as Ragnar said, my king awaits, and William has already mocked me for being so preoccupied with my enticing wife that I cannot keep my mind on matters of state." His expression sobered, loving Meagan's feisty temperament and yet wary of it. "Indulge me this request, my love. Do not harass my king with your sharp wit. 'Tis best that he does not know of your fierce loyalty to the rebels.

406

And do not ask to take Garda and Lear with you on this journey. I do not wish to watch that wolf bite holes in William's ankles."

Meagan smiled up at him. "I will leave my guardians behind, since I have nothing to fear when my gallant knight is by my side. And I will behave most admirably because *you* request it," she promised faithfully and then flashed him a mischievous glance. "But I must warn you that I expect payment for my angelic conduct in court."

Trevor breathed a silent sigh of relief. At least he did not have to fear that his rebel wife would take arms against the king in his own palace. "You will receive the proper compensation," he insisted with a roguish grin as he scooped her from bed and urged her to dress. *"All* night, if 'tis your wont."

"I shall hold you to that promise," Meagan taunted as she eased open the trunk to fetch fresh clothes, leaving a shapely backside to Trevor's all-consuming gaze.

"And I am honor-bound to deliver," Trevor murmured as he feasted on Meagan's beauty. "After all, 'tis a knight's duty to serve." When Meagan sashayed toward him, her blue eyes sparkling with deviltry, Trevor backed away, struggling to keep from tripping over his garments, and then raised his hand to halt her advance. "Do not tempt me, brazen wench. Although I would prefer to spend the day alone with you rather than face Ragnar and his teasing, I cannot. The men will harass me unmercifully for dallying as long as I already have."

And Ragnar did, much to Trevor's chagrin. He was further humiliated when Ragnar was forced to grab him by the surcoat and haul him back into the saddle when he dozed from his lack of sleep. Trevor cast Meagan an accusing glance when he was caught catnapping, but his expression mellowed and Ragnar's uproarious laughter faded when Trevor saw the love glowing in Meagan's eyes. He could endure Ragnar's taunts as long as he had Meagan, he reminded himself. She could make him forget that Ragnar Neville even existed. And suddenly he didn't, Trevor realized as he lost himself to the luring blue horizon in Meagan's eyes.

Chapter 27

Meagan checked her appearance for the fifth time since the mesne had shown her and Trevor to their private quarters on the second level of the palace. She had primped for over two hours while Trevor caught up on his lost sleep. Apprehension rose in her throat, wondering how she would react when she faced William the Bastard, king of England. For well over three years she had sworn vengeance, thirsting to confront the brilliant military strategist who had destroyed the peaceful way of life she had known and loved. Now she had promised Trevor that she would not spoil his day in court, portraying the gentle, gracious lady that William expected to meet. How was she to remain civil when she could cheerfully choke the man who was responsible for her brother's demoted position and indirectly accountable for transforming Reid Granthum into a hateful, bitter man?

"You are contemplating how you will hold the rein on your temper when you lay eyes on my king, are you not?"

Meagan blanched when she heard Trevor put her thoughts to tongue. She turned a guilty smile to the handsome warrior who rolled from bed to amble up behind her. "Pray, how does one pay homage to a man she has loathed, sight unseen?"

"It will not be so difficult. Disarm him with your smile and you will have the Throne in the palm of your hand, just as you have manipulated me when beauty appeared before the beast," he teased as his arousing kisses cascaded down her neck.

Meagan surrendered to the feel of his warm lips on her skin and closed her eyes, drinking in the manly fragrance that intoxicated her senses. "But if your king does not approve of me, even when I have put my best foot forward, will you cast me aside to seek out one who meets William's expectations?"

Trevor turned her in his arms, his amber eyes offering reassurance. "I have no desire to endure the agony I experienced when I left you with Desmond. When William watches me watch you, he will know that I have found my prize, one I cherish far more than my demesne and my seat in the king's counsel." A sly smile tugged at one corner of his mouth. "Besides, 'tis not William who warms my bed and feeds my insatiable hunger, 'tis you. My loyalty to my king is shed like a cloak when I cross the threshold of my solar."

"I should hope 'tis not William with whom I must compete in my boudoir," Meagan giggled. "For that is one service I offer my lord that I do not care to relinquish."

"No one will ever take your place," Trevor assured her, his voice crackling with emotion. "Believe that."

Trevor released her to don his clothes and then wrapped a supportive arm around her waist to usher her to the Great Hall, where the Norman nobility awaited the appearance of the mysterious young woman who had seized the dashing baron of Wessex and had enslaved his heart.

"Burke has done well for himself," William observed, sparing Matilda a glance before feasting on the comely blond who approached the dais.

The queen nodded in agreement and then tossed her husband a wry smile. "Methinks your gallant knight's loyalties have shifted, Sire. It seems you have become his second consideration, no longer the first."

"Shall I gracefully bow out?" William questioned aside.

"I doubt that Burke would notice whether you did or not," Matilda chortled.

William's discerning gaze flooded over the circlet of

daisies that adorned Meagan's platinum hair and then descended over her flawless complexion. His scrutinizing eyes sketched her shapely figure that was temptingly wrapped in blue velvet to match the stunning color of her eyes. As his inspection moved downward, William noted that the dazzling nymph was with child. No doubt there would be many Burke knights and ladies in the next generation, he mused, biting back a grin.

Although Meagan's heart hammered nervously against her ribs, she clamped a tight grip on her composure and peered at the king, who sat quietly conversing with his queen. Her wide eyes flooded over the jeweled crown that sat upon his head, surveying his lavish, crimson red robes, admiring the huge emeralds and rubies that were embedded in the brooch on his left shoulder. Her gaze then strayed to Matilda, relieved that the older woman broke into a smile when her attention shifted from Trevor to Meagan.

"So, at last I have the privilege of meeting my competition," William declared as he rose to meet his invaluable knight and his distracting lady.

Meagan swore Trevor actually blushed beneath his tan and her tension eased when William smiled cordially at her.

"May I present Lady Meagan," Trevor murmured and then bowed to his king.

For a split second Meagan tensed again, her knees refusing to bend, but a strong hand curled about her rigid fingers and Meagan's fears dissolved when William stooped to press a kiss to her wrist. He was not at all the harsh tyrant she had imagined, and Meagan could almost like him.

"I was very pleased to hear that one of my favorite knights had wed. And now I can see for myself why Trevor was so preoccupied when I sought to confer with him." When Meagan graced him with a blinding smile, William understood why Trevor had hopelessly fallen beneath this lady's spell. And even in all of her sylphlike grace and beauty there was a mystical sparkle in those liquid pools of sapphire, a glimmer of inner strength that would hold a challenge for her mighty warrior.

"You flatter me, Your Grace," Meagan said smoothly. "I

411

had always considered my husband dedicated to his cause . . . and yours. If he has occasionally spared me a thought, I must also take that as a compliment." Meagan inclined her head to peer up at her ruggedly handsome knight. "For more often than naught, he has distracted me as well."

William smiled in good humor, impressed with Meagan's charm and her obvious affection for Trevor. "Join us on the dais," he insisted. "I am anxious for you to meet Matilda. I should think the two of you will have a great deal in common since she has had the same influence on me that you hold over Trevor."

Meagan breathed a constricted sigh of relief as Trevor seated her and then sank down beside her. She could endure the evening without creating a scene. William was polite and congenial, and it was not difficult to admire him, even if they had been on opposite sides of the war. But the war was over, Meagan reminded herself. England was united under William's rule, and she must begin to consider him and his claim on the throne.

After the guests had partaken of their meal and were entertained by mummers who presented a play for the king and his guests, William invited his knights and their ladies to stroll about the palace before he called conference in his counsel chamber.

As Meagan ambled along the retaining wall of the palace, Trevor drew her around to face his curious smile. "Well, m'lady, now that you have been formally introduced to William, what do you think of him? Is he the ruthless, arrogant tyrant you imagined him to be?"

Meagan gave her blond head a negative shake. "Nay, he seems well deserving of the honor Normandy has bestowed on him."

"But not England," Trevor presumed as he curled a tanned finger beneath her chin, forcing her to meet his penetrating gaze. "My lovely Meagan, will you continue to fight his claim to the throne as I battled against my love for you? Have you learned nothing from your foolish, obstinate husband? When one drags one's feet to deny the inevitable, one only wears out the soles of one's boots."

Meagan's soft laughter tickled Trevor's senses. "Who could argue with such an astute philosophical assessment?" she teased.

The smile that brimmed Trevor's lips mellowed into a somber countenance as he brushed his lips over her knuckles. "You could, m'lady. You have always been a mite defiant. William is king and nothing is going to change that."

Meagan released a quiet sigh as her gaze circled the magnificent palace. "I promised not to embarrass you in front of your king, but I cannot erase all the painful memories, nor can I forget that the palace dungeon bulges with Saxon prisoners. It does not seem fair that they are left to mold and rot in their musty cells when they did what they felt they must do to preserve their homeland."

"All is not fair in love and war," Trevor reminded her. "What would you have William do? Release the radical rebels to regroup and plan another attack? He tried to be generous with them once and he was repaid with this bloody rebellion."

"Nay, but he could pardon those who repent and allow them to take a respectable position within the system," Meagan suggested.

Trevor rolled his eyes. This orderly discussion could become an argument if he wasn't careful. "Do you not think it wise to allow our illustrious king and his counsel to decide the future of the unruly rebels?"

"Are there, perchance, Saxons sitting among the counselors who might be sympathetic to those who fought for what *they* believed to be right and honorable? Has God himself indicated that the Norman feudal system is the *only* workable solution for England?" Meagan questioned all too sweetly.

Trevor gritted his teeth and fiercely clung to the reins of his temper. "I can see that politics will always be a testy subject between us." A heavy sigh tumbled from Trevor's lips. "I will ask William to be lenient with those who are willing to call him king and make a new life for themselves under Norman rule." He couldn't believe what he was

413

saying! Meagan's powerful influence on him had finally channeled into every facet of his life.

A delighted smile blossomed on Meagan's lips as she reached up on tiptoe to shower him with grateful kisses. "Thank you, m'lord. I can only hope your—our king," she hastily corrected, "will be considerate of his fellow man, whether he be Norman *or* Saxon. This rebellion has caused enough bitterness without adding more fuel to the fire. There are already so many Saxons who have been forced to take to the woods to survive as scavengers and outlaws that the forest is crawling with them. I shudder to think it will be that way with every man and woman of Saxon blood."

"I will voice a concern for those who are willing to make amends and come to terms with their reigning king, but I will not defend bloodthirsty murderers who chopped off the heads of some of my own friends," Trevor told her firmly. "And you must remember that the final decision will rest with the Throne. I have often been William's eyes and ears and his advisor in matters of state, but I do not presume to tell him how to think."

"I only expect you to make an attempt," Meagan assured him as her delicate fingers splayed across the ermine collar that lay against the hard tendons of his neck. "And when you return from counsel I will be most anxious to show my appreciation for considering the Saxons who were sucked into the tide of rebellion, simply because they were given no other choice." Her alluring smile held a silent message that Trevor could easily decipher.

"You sorely tempt me, m'lady," he growled seductively as his arm slid about her waist, molding her soft, responsive body to his. "And you know 'tis impossible for me to refuse what you imply."

"I can afford to be most generous when the offer brings such pleasure in giving and sharing," Meagan whispered back to him. "I only wish my fellow countrymen could enjoy the happiness I have found in joining forces with my Norman lord. Peace cannot come without understanding . . . from *both* sides. I, for one, have discovered that there is immense enjoyment in giving and taking."

When the chapel bell chimed throughout the palace, calling the knights to counsel, Trevor stepped away to bow before his lady. "I trust you will find something to occupy your time until I join you in our chamber."

"You can count upon that." There was a merry twinkle in her blue eyes as she boldly assessed his virile body. "I shall while away the hours, contemplating all the ways I can display my gratitude."

"Mere gratitude?" Trevor raised a dark brow as her wandering hands mapped the broad expanse of his chest, sending his heart galloping around his rib cage like a runaway stallion.

"What do you think, Dark Prince?" Meagan also raised an eyebrow, but hers had a very suggestive tilt to it.

A low rumble erupted in his chest as he grasped Meagan's arm and led her back to the hall. "Methinks this had better be the shortest conference William has conducted. I do not know if I can endure the suspense of wondering what methods you will employ to express your appreciation."

Meagan tossed him an impish grin as she sauntered past the knights who had congregated about their king. "I shall strive for inventive, exciting techniques that express what words cannot convey. I pray that they might even surprise and delight a man as worldly and experienced as you, m'lord," Meagan whispered in his ear before she uncurled her hand from his elbow and aimed herself toward their chamber on the upper level of the palace.

As she strode away, Trevor's eyes followed her. The lambent hunger William saw in Trevor's gaze drew his chuckle. He had found an amusing pastime in watching Trevor admire his wife.

"Come, Burke. Your lady can find some simple diversion to occupy her for a few hours while we discuss important matters of state. Surely you can tear yourself away from that enchanting minx and endure my monotonous voice," William taunted unmercifully.

Trevor dragged his eyes off Meagan and settled them on his king. "In truth, can you blame me for gawking at her? She preys heavily on my mind, not to mention the effect she has on the rest of a man's body." A longing sigh tumbled from his lips. "These sensations are new and I am still bewildered by my good fortune. I never thought to find a woman like Meagan."

"In truth? Nay, I cannot," William confessed as he fondly patted Trevor's shoulder and then gestured toward the counsel chamber. "Matilda seems to think that your distraction has dimmed your consideration for the Throne."

A secretive smile pursed Trevor's lips as he walked along beside William, recalling the words he had spoken to Meagan before they left their chamber. Although his loyalty to William was fierce, there were times when he didn't give a fig who ruled the roost. 'Twas *his* roost and the cozy nest he shared with Meagan that usually concerned Trevor.

Would he always lust after that irresistable wench, he asked himself and then promptly answered affirmatively. He had waited thirty-three years to find a woman with Meagan's courage, charm, intelligence, and undaunted spirit. Time would not fade the overwhelming affection he felt for her; nothing could.

"I remain your devoted servant, Sire," Trevor assured William as they ambled down the corridor. "But I cannot deny that the lady also demands my loyalty and occupies my thoughts," Trevor chuckled, flashing William a rakish smile. "Perhaps you should thank her for making me more efficient than I was before. I see to my duties in my demesne posthaste and then turn my attention Meagan. 'Tis a practical combination of work and pleasure."

It was William's turn to grin to himself, imagining Trevor snapping orders and seeing to his tasks without wasting a moment before he galloped back to his alluring wife, no doubt doting on her from dusk until dawn.

"I have waited an eternity to even the score with you, bitch."

Meagan gasped as she wheeled to see Daralis emerge from the shadows of her chamber, holding her knife so that the lamplight glistened on the hair-splitting blade. The de-

416

mented look in Daralis's eye warned Meagan to tread carefully. Daralis would prefer to kill her than to look at her, she mused shakily.

"I have watched you lure Lord Burke into your arms until the thought of you lying with him sickens me," she hissed as her brooding gaze dipped to Meagan's abdomen. "And you thought to trap him by getting yourself with child. But you will not live to glory in your reign." A sardonic smile brimmed her lips as she pounced at Meagan, grasping a handful of hair and gouging her in the ribs to emphasize her point. "You are going to instigate the escape of the rebel prisoners this very night. Once they are free we will seek refuge in the forest and await the birth of your child. But Lord Burke will think 'tis mine when I return to his fortress with babe in arms. I will become his lady, mother of his child, and you . . ." Daralis laughed maliciously as she tightened her grasp on Meagan and urged her down the dark corridor that led to the dungeon. "Lord Burke will be glad to be rid of you once he learns that you escaped with the rebels. This last humiliation will sever any affection he might have felt for you."

"You are a fool, Daralis," Meagan hissed. "You will never accomplish your fiendish threat. The guards will—" She sucked in her breath when Daralis repaid her outburst with another careless jab with her dagger.

"The guards sleep like babies," Daralis cackled. "I slipped a potion in their mugs of ale. I will be a simple matter to fetch the keys and release our countrymen."

Meagan felt a sickening dread flood over her, Daralis had plotted against her, waiting for the opportune moment to strike like a snake lying in wait. Her heart pounded as if it would beat her to death as Daralis shoved her down the musty steps that wound toward the dungeon.

Would Trevor believe the evidence that weighed heavily against her? Would he think her affection was only a charade and that she had planned to effect the escape of the rebels once she arrived at the palace? Meagan's heart sank. She knew how mistrusting Trevor could be. If he believed her responsible for this plot, there could be nothing between them. Daralis would have her vicious wish, and Meagan would die without being given the opportunity to explain.

Her alarmed gaze fastened on Marston Pearce's hollowed face as Daralis shoved the keys into her hand and forced her to unlock the cells of the twenty prisoners who had spent the past months staring at the gloomy walls of their cubicles.

"With you walking beside us, we will be granted safe passage from the palace," Daralis chortled wickedly. "So you thought to impress the king, did you? Now he will loathe you. 'Tis what you deserve."

Meagan gulped with fear as the scraggly prisoners swarmed about her, urging her back up the steps. How could she fight her countrymen? How could she endanger her unborn child? She couldn't, Meagan realized. Again she was swept up in a plot, and there was nothing she could do to prevent it.

"We have all but destroyed the rebel forces in the North," William informed his knights. "The land has been charred and laid to ruin. Never again will it be profitable to gather an army in Mercia and Northumbria. 'Tis what they deserve." His voice carried a thread of bitterness. "When I sent Robert de Comines to Northumbria to assume command of the earldom, the revolutionists burned him alive and then cut his men into pieces in the streets of Durham. The swarm of Saxons sought to demolish my fortress at York and it will take the better part of the winter to rebuild the garrison." William's eyes burned with vengeance, his disposition soured by the destruction and death he had witnessed when he had taken to the field to confront the rebels. "Not only will I see that the Saxons are brought low, but I will leave them starving like scavengers in search of food. Yorkshire will offer them nothing but the blackened remains of what might have been a fertile, prosperous region."

The chamber was hauntingly silent as William slumped back in his chair and then called to his servant to refill his knights' mugs. His narrowed gaze circled the room to survey each solemn face. "You may think me ruthless in this matter.

418

but I intend to seize control of the English realm once and for all. The Saxons grumbled even when I tried to be lenient with them. They may never respect my power and recognize me as their king, but they *will* obey my laws. My enemies have proved vicious and bloodthirsty and I will reciprocate in a like fashion," he said grimly.

"But there are those among the rebels who are willing to make amends and attempt to conform to your laws," Trevor pointed out, bravely voicing an opinion that drew William's sour frown. "If you crucify those who would have conformed you will never have harmony in England and you will invite further conflict. You must be aware, as I am, that some Saxons took arms against you because they feared being ostracized by their countrymen."

"Are you suggesting that I release my mortal enemies and offer pardon to their flock?" William snorted huffily. "I have done that once and I was repaid with a bloody rebellion."

"I certainly do not suggest that you free the radical leaders," Trevor said calmly, his soothing voice resettling William's ruffled feathers. "I only suggest that those who wish peace in your domain are allowed the opportunity that was theirs before the throne changed hands. If you offer them a choice no one can claim you have been unreasonable or unjust. The art of diplomacy does have certain advantages and radical rebels will have difficulty stirring trouble when part of their flock has grown content with the green grass in their pastures."

"But I have found very few Englishmen trustworthy, and I am skeptical of sparing them more kindness until they have proven their loyalty to the Crown."

A wry smile pursed Trevor's lips as he leaned his forearms on the table and peered at his pouting king. "How can a man prove himself when he is herded into a dingy cell and given nothing but time to stew and grow bitter?" he argued.

"What would you have me do, invite them to dine at the dais?" William scoffed sarcastically. "I am beginning to think you have grown soft, Trevor. Have you forgotten that a Saxon is prone to bite the hand that feeds him?"

"Soft? Nay," Trevor assured him, careful not to rise to the

taunt. He only intended to serve William food for thought, not provoke him into an argument. "It was you who insisted that peace and harmony would come only if we mingled with the Saxons and learned their minds. I have found those whom I have treated with respect and have sparingly offered my trust have been swayed toward the Crown rather than alienated from it. I only advise discretion, Sire."

The room hung heavy with silence as William pondered his bold knight's words. "I will think upon it." There was no sound commitment, but then Trevor had not expected one. William had lost many good men to violent deaths, and compassion had escaped him. The idea was fresh and a mite drastic to a man who had been hell-bent on revenge. "But I will not free my enemies without a pledge. There will be no gracious pardons as there have been in the past. 'Tis impossible to know whom to trust." William glanced about him and then frowned in annoyance when he realized the butler had yet to return with the ale. "And 'tis impossible to keep good help! Only three days ago my wife's chambermaid was stricken with a strange illness and died during the night. Even *she* was forced to depend on a Saxon, one who is only half as efficient and responsible as the devoted servant we brought from Normandy. And now 'tis the butler who is lax in his duties," he grumbled, a distinctly unpleasant edge on his voice.

An eerie sensation trickled down Trevor's spine, his eyes narrowing suspiciously. "What was the nature of the illness?" he questioned abruptly.

William's shoulder lifted in a shrug. "Matilda heard the old woman moaning in her sleep and she found her thrashing in her bed before she collapsed into a deathlike trance. The servant died before dawn, and yet she had appeared in good health the previous evening when she attended the queen. At first I feared a plague, but no others have contracted the deadly disease."

Poisoned! Trevor's heart stopped, leaving him gasping for breath and struggling to spit out his next question. "Who is this new serf who has become a member of your royal staff?" he demanded to know.

420

William frowned bemusedly at Trevor's rapid-fire questions and the haunted look on his chiseled features. "Some young wench who begged to serve my lady, pleading that she was willing to take any duties requested of her for room and board. Matilda was too tenderhearted, and the wench has not held her end of the bargain. I believe she is called Daralis. Though I have yet to meet the wench, I have often muttered about her leaving a handful of duties undone."

"Daralis?" Ragnar squeaked as his eyes flew to Trevor, whose face was as white as a sheet.

"Where is she?" Trevor bolted from his chair, his stunned eyes instantly becoming inflamed with fury, his body trembling with barely contained rage.

The frown William wore carved even deeper lines in his features as he peered up into Trevor's face, one that now mirrored a mixture of wrath and even a hint of fear, something William had yet to see reflected in his faithful knight's eyes.

"On the second level, I suppose. Why? What is wrong with you, Burke? Why are you cross-examining me like this?" William questioned warily.

"Your servant was poisoned. Daralis was once a member of my staff. She has already attempted to murder Meagan by the same dastardly means. If she has . . ."

Trevor could not finish his sentence. The thoughts that whipped through his head sickened him, and he could not stand to put them to tongue. Daralis would stop at nothing to get what she wanted. She had thrice proven that. Trevor spun around and dashed toward the door with Ragnar and William scurrying after him, haunted by their own tormented thoughts.

As Trevor pushed open the door to his chamber, another wave of fear washed over him. Meagan had vanished. If Daralis had harmed her, he would . . .

"Call the guards," Trevor ordered his king, giving no thought to taking command. "The bitch has my wife. I would bet my life on it." But *his* life was not what truly concerned him at the moment. It was Meagan's, and he would have given the world to be wrong in this instance.

William's face whitewashed as he wheeled to send Ragnar with the order and then hastened his step to keep up with Trevor's frantic strides as he burst into every nook and cranny on the second floor.

"Damnation!" Trevor snarled as he came to the end of his futile search of the upper chambers. "Where could they have gone?"

A shout of alarm rang through the corridor as Ragnar bounded up the steps to summon his king. "The prisoners have been freed. They have fled through the back entrance."

No sooner had the words burst from his lips than he found himself trampled as Trevor charged past him, leaping down the stairs two at a time in his haste to pursue the prisoners.

Meagan? Trevor's fury flowed like white-hot lava. She wouldn't have, he told himself over and over again. She had given her word that she would be on her best behavior. Was this another ploy? Had Marston Pearce lied to Ragnar, knowing that Meagan's position as a baron's wife would grant her access to the palace to assist in an escape?

His keen gaze swept the silhouettes that darted across the bailey like elusive, dancing shadows. It seemed there was no one to detain the fleeing prisoners. The castle guards were sound asleep at their posts, and the rebels were waltzing about the king's palace as if they owned it! Trevor growled under his breath when he caught sight of Meagan hurrying along the path that led to freedom.

"Meagan!" he roared like the furious, fire-breathing monster she had often accused him of being.

Trevor wished to high heaven that he had been struck blind, unable to see his wife rushing toward the horses that were tethered in front of the overflowing stable. An excruciating feeling of betrayal burned through him, even more severe and painful than those of the past. Had this conniving witch veiled his eyes and fogged his thoughts until he could never look upon her without seeing her as she truly was?

His heart skipped a beat and his doubts parted like the dawn of realization evaporating the low-hanging clouds when Meagan cried out to him in a soul-shattering plea fo elp. Her words were muffled as one of the men beside her lamped his hand over her mouth and Daralis's shadowed mage materialized beside Meagan.

Daralis cursed her rotten luck. If she had been allowed only a few more minutes, the baron would never have known of the escape until it was too late. It had been her intention to et Trevor assume that Meagan had initiated the escape and hat she had willingly fled with the rebels. Now he would now the truth, and her well-laid plans were for naught.

Whipping out her dagger, Daralis grabbed a handful of Meagan's hair, yanking her head back to lay the blade to her hroat. "Hold your ground, m'lord, or the lady dies right efore your eyes," she ground out. Her frantic gaze darted bout her to see the flow of manpower appear from the orebuilding. "If you do not allow us safe passage I will slit er throat."

Trevor froze in his tracks, his narrowed eyes riveting over Daralis's deadly sneer, and then his gaze swung to Meagan, who was still held captive by one of the prisoners. His eyes net hers and in a split second the last of his doubts dissolved nto a fear the likes of which he had never known. Meagan ad not betrayed him. She had been taken as hostage for Daralis's devious scheme. He could guess what the cunning itch had in mind for Meagan once she had served her urpose.

William grasped Trevor's arm, demanding his attention. I will hunt that wench down myself and serve her up to you n bite-size pieces," he vowed, his tone dripping with venom.

"Do we travel unharmed or does the lady perish while you vatch?" Daralis challenged, twisting Meagan's hair around er hand like a rope until she sucked in her breath to keep rom screeching in pain.

Damnation! Why had he refused to allow Meagan the ompanionship of her shepherd? If Lear had been at her eels, Daralis would have found that vicious wolf's jaws lamped around her neck, just as Ulrick had. *Arrogant fool!* Trevor berated himself for allowing this to happen to Meagan. Lear was a far better protector than he could ever ope to be. When Lear was at Meagan's side, she escaped

423

unscathed from impending doom, but when her blundering husband was called to her defense, Meagan faced certain death. One false move would send Daralis into a demented frenzy.

"What purpose will it serve to hand me that bitch's head when I have lost Meagan?" Trevor asked bitterly, refusing to take his eyes off Meagan, as if watching her could somehow save her from catastrophe.

William's hand dropped helplessly at his side, and he silently answered Trevor's question. His angry gaze followed the rebels, who reined their horses toward freedom.

"Your lady will be unharmed," Marston Pearce promised as he led his men away. "Meagan will await your arrival at Hertford."

"Do not speak for me," Daralis hissed. "I have a score to settle with the baron of Wessex. *I* will decide when and where she is to be released."

William jumped as if he had been stung when he heard the hiss of a crossbow so close behind him. His head swiveled around to follow the path of the arrow that sailed through the air to meet its intended mark.

Concealed from view, using Trevor and the king himself as a shield, Ragnar had taken careful aim and waited until Meagan's captor turned to grasp the horse's reins. The soaring arrow had been a signal to charge, and Trevor flew toward Daralis like a bat out of hell before she could plunge her dagger into Meagan's heart. His earsplitting bellow sliced the silence like the hideous howl of a banshee.

Meagan pushed the man's limp body aside and ducked beneath the frightened steed as Trevor pounced on Daralis the split second before the blade could snag Meagan in the back. Trevor spared the wench no mercy, oblivious to her terrified screams as she suffered blow after punishing blow that stripped her of what was left of her crazed senses. And when her whimpering ceased, another deafening silence echoed about the bailey.

Trevor stepped back, his chest heaving, his eyes burning a furious gold flame as he withdrew his sword and returned it to its scabbard crimson red with Daralis's blood.

424

His snarl was like that of a panther frothing at the mouth as he wheeled toward Ragnar. "You could have killed her!" he bellowed in the knight's shocked face. "Have you taken leave of your senses?"

"I am not a novice with a crossbow," Ragnar defended, his voice matching Trevor's in volume. "You were in no position to take aim, but *I* was. All eyes were upon you and your lady. If I did not trust my accuracy I would not have dared to seek out my target!"

"And had you missed, you would have found your blood mingling with the dust," Trevor growled maliciously. Ragnar had scared ten years off his life with his risky shot, and Trevor was not about to let the matter drop without pointing out the foolishness of aiming at moving shadows. "Had I known of your lapses of intelligence, I would not have allowed you to ride by my side these past years. The next thing I know you will have me and my wife lined up against the wall, attempting to shoot apples off the top of our heads!"

Ragnar was dumbstruck. He had given Trevor back his wife, and the knight was raving like a madman. "Perhaps 'tis just that you are envious that 'twas *I* who aimed the arrow to unchain the lady from her captor's arms instead of *you*. Must you be the only knight in shining armor in her eyes?" he questioned, his voice carrying an undertaste of sarcasm.

Trevor went rigid as Ragnar's mocking gaze cut him to the quick. "Jealous of a nearsighted knave who took a reckless shot in the dark?" he hooted. "That will be the day, Neville. If I had not pounced on Daralis to cover your idiocy, the wench would have carved Meagan to pieces."

A gentle hand pressed against each man's heaving chest as they stood face-to-face, staring each other down. Meagan positioned herself between the indignant knights.

"M'lord, without Ragnar's assistance *and* yours I would have missed this ridiculous argument," Meagan reminded Trevor. "What purpose would Ragnar's arrow have served if Daralis was allowed to turn her dagger on me? And what comfort would you have been to me if you had sprung on Daralis while I was still held hostage in my captor's arms?

425

Does it not seem reasonable that both brave deeds complemented each other and that separately both attempts would have failed? My rescue required the quick wit and skill of both knights."

A faint smile grazed her lips as she reached up to smooth away Trevor's harsh frown and then turned to offer the same tender affection to Ragnar, who melted in his boots when she touched him. "As for myself, I am most thankful to be alive, though I regret hearing this bitter discourse between two close friends . . . or men who *were* friends fighting for the same cause until they were seized by an arrogant need to determine which one of them was the bravest and most deserving of praise," she chided gently.

Meagan had both roaring lions cowering like naughty kittens that had been tactfully scolded for their poor behavior. William laughed out loud when both men sheepishly dropped their heads. The lady impressed him and it was not difficult to see that both of his knights were in love with Meagan, though only one could claim the coveted title of her husband.

"Your point is well taken, m'lady." William strode over to draw Meagan to his side, and then he cast Ragnar and Trevor a condescending frown. Curling his arm around her waist, he propelled her toward the Great Hall. "Mayhap we should seek cover before the fur flies," he suggested, flashing Meagan a wry smile. "When our warring knights have laid down their arms and backed from the battlefield, perhaps it will occur to them that they should have given chase to our escaped prisoners. They have already tarried so long that I doubt they could even sniff out a skunk, especially with their noses out of joint."

Meagan chortled as she fell into step beside the strutting king. "Vanity does have its price," she acknowledged. "When a knight stops in midbattle to count his medals, he often overlooks his duties and his initial cause. Recessing to boast in midwar indicates half a man, does it not, Your Grace?"

"Well put, my dear," William complimented his lovely companion. "Perhaps if Burke and Neville combine their

426

kills and intellect I can count upon having *one* warrior who will defend the Throne with the utmost competency." He paused to fling the two slumped shadows a parting remark before propelling Meagan through the forebuilding. "I fear tis too late to pursue the prisoners. A handful of men cannot lay siege to the palace. I suggest you retrieve the pieces of our crumbled pride and retire for the evening. No need to concern yourself with the lady. 'Tis best that I see to her myself since 'twas I who found it necessary to ensure that she was not trampled by the flighty steed while the two of you were buzzing about each other like mad hornets."

As Meagan and William disappeared from sight, Trevor extended his hand and offered Ragnar a shamefaced grin. "More the fool am I for insulting a friend. Yea, I suppose I was jealous that you were able to come to Meagan's defense when I was helpless to move a muscle without bringing Daralis's wrath down upon her," he admitted.

Ragnar accepted the proffered hand of friendship and parried with his own guilty grin. "No more the fool than I for taking such a risk. If you had not sprung on the wench when you did, I would have long lived to regret my folly." His expression sobered as his gaze strayed to the lingering image of the enchanting young woman he could only admire from afar. "Her heart belongs to you and I envy you that possession," Ragnar confessed quietly. "Can you still call me friend when you know of my affection for Meagan? Do you know that not even a day goes by that I do not dream of sharing her love? I cannot lie to you, Trevor. When you announced that you would wed the lady I had chosen to share my name, I was hard pressed to challenge your right to her and give the decision to Edric and the lady herself. Even in my disappointment I knew that you were the one who pleased her most. I care deeply for the lady, deeply enough to consider *her* happiness before my own."

"Had it been anyone but Meagan I would have granted your request, my friend," Trevor assured him softly, moved by Ragnar's honesty and his noble commitment.

A rueful smile spread across Ragnar's lips as he ambled beside Trevor to rouse the drugged guards and secure the

427

palace. "Had it been anyone but this particular lady, I woul[d] not have made the request," he murmured.

"You are a better man than I," Trevor conceded. "I coul[d] not even release Meagan when I thought she had betraye[d] me, nor could I release her to your care when I knew yo[u] would shower her with nothing but devotion and worth[y] love. You believed in her when the evidence weighed heavil[y] against her. If not for you, I would still be battling the tug-o[f] war between my mistrust and a love nothing could rout fro[m] my heart."

Ragnar fell silent. As much as he desired Meagan, h[e] could not have conquered her wild heart as Trevor had. H[e] knew Meagan was fond of him, but her affection could neve[r] run as deep as her devotion to the baron of Wessex. [If] Ragnar had to lose the captivating maid to another man, hi[s] choice was the Dark Prince who had earned the respect of hi[s] king for his valiant deeds in war and his capabilities in peace[.]

Yea, he would continue to dream of the stunning blue[-] eyed blond, but he knew that she belonged with Trevo[r.] They made a dashing couple, and yet . . . Ragnar chide[d] himself for backsliding. Meagan was Trevor's wife, an[d] that was the beginning and end of it. How long would h[e] have to remind himself of that fact, Ragnar asked himsel[f] miserably and then answered—the next hundred year[s] should be ample time to forget the pleasure that could hav[e] been his.

Chapter 28

An annoyed frown etched Meagan's features as she paced back and forth across her chamber, awaiting Trevor's arrival. She had been silently smoldering since she had left Trevor and Ragnar in the bailey. Her irritation with Trevor had mounted until Meagan was certain she would explode like a volcano at the mere sight of her husband.

When he had spied her scurrying along with the rebels, she had known by the tone of his voice that he thought she had fled of her own accord. Damn that man! What more must she do to convince him that her loyalty had been and always would be with him? His voice had trembled with rage and frustration when he bellowed at her. Meagan had heard him ranting on too many other occasions not to know that his mistrust had fogged his reasoning. And then Trevor had turned on Ragnar, leaving Meagan to wonder if the dark knight was only venting his anger on his friend until he could get his wife alone to give her a good piece of his mind. But he had spouted at her so often that Meagan wondered if Trevor could spare too many more pieces without leaving himself a bit short.

Did he intend to rake her over the coals, accuse her of initiating the escape? He dared not condemn her for that! Meagan thought furiously. This was one time she would not plead her innocence while he raved like a madman. In the past she had been forced to consider her brother's involvement, but now she alone faced Trevor on this issue, and she intended to deal accordingly with the suspicious oaf. The most effective defense was a forceful offense when confronting Trevor, Meagan reminded herself. For once she would assault him, accuse him of mistrusting *her*, before he could voice *his* indignation. This time she would convince him of her innocence, and there would never be any doubt left in his mind, because she fully intended to pound some sense into that hardheaded knight who seemed to have metal helmet built into his scalp. When Trevor barged into the room, prepared to lash out at her for disobedience, he would find himself on a battlefield, involved in a full scale war.

Meagan had collected her weapons and they lay within arm's reach. Trevor was about to be ambushed, and she would show him no mercy. He had questioned her devotion and fidelity for the last time. By damned, after this night he would never doubt her again, she convinced herself. If the mighty warrior thrived on battle, she would give him a fight the likes of which he had never experienced, especially in his own boudoir. Disloyal, indeed! Meagan sniffed indignantly, stewing herself into an enraged frenzy. Trevor Burke deserved exactly what he was going to get, and Meagan was going to delight in giving him a full dose of his own medicine. Let him cower and beg, she told herself determinedly. She was outraged with his behavior, and before long he would realize that hell had no fury like an indignant woman wrongly accused of disloyalty.

Trevor heaved a weary sigh as he paused before his chamber door. What could he say to Meagan? He had tossed several soliloquies around his head while he and Ragnar secured the palace, but he had discarded every apology that had fluttered through his mind.

Meagan knew of the doubts that buzzed about him while he frantically sought her out. He had seen that terrified look in her eyes when he had bellowed her name. God help him! He had sounded like Satan calling his evil spirits to counsel. Would Meagan ever forgive him for suspecting her of eleasing her fellow countrymen from the king's palace? Damnation, if he had opened his mouth an inch wider he ould have crammed both feet in it, Trevor chastised himself arshly. He would give most anything to turn back the hands of time and relive that dreadful moment when he had screeched her name. Trevor would have been a happier man f Meagan had not had a clue as to the condemning thoughts that had plagued him. And then, to make matters worse, he aad practically bit off Ragnar's head in William and Meagan's presence. Had he lost what little sense he had left? Obviously, Trevor scowled at himself as he eased open the door to squint into the darkness.

Meagan tensed as Trevor's foreboding shadow spilled across the planked floor. Her hand folded around one of the many weapons that were at her disposal. Meagan cocked her arm to launch the first assault, drawing a pained grunt from Trevor when the flying log slammed against his right shoulder.

"Fie on thee, Trevor Burke!" Meagan cursed, her tone as abusive as her physical attack. "I bared my heart to you and still you doubted me!"

Trevor peered into the shadows, but the only source of ight was the dim candle in the corridor, and he could not make out his lovely, but obviously angry, wife.

This had not been the reception he had anticipated, he mused and then grunted when a well-aimed figurine, which had previously sat on the nightstand beside the bed, sailed through the air to catch him on the left shoulder.

"Meagan, listen to me. I . . ." Trevor pleaded as he took a blind step forward and then froze in his tracks when a dagger flew across the room and vibrated as it lodged in the partially opened door, only a few breathless inches from his left ear. Trevor gulped for air and then cast a quick glance at the blade, which could well have notched his earlobe if it had been Meagan's intent to draw blood rather than his undivided attention.

"Stand your ground, oafish knave," Meagan barked sharply. "You will not come strutting into this room like an arrogant peacock to question my loyalty."

"But I do not—" Trevor interrupted and then squawked when another log sped toward him to ricochet off the side of his head, leaving his flustered thoughts spinning like a runaway carousel.

"Accuse me of conspiracy a second time, will you?" Meagan sniffed disgustedly and then cocked her arm to hurl the chamber pot across the room. "You thick-headed lout! . . . Gardey loo!"

A pained grunt erupted from his lips when the pot smashed against his abdomen, but he was most thankful the vessel had been cleaned; otherwise, he would have had more on his hands than an empty crock and an irate wife. Damnation, when he got his hands on that witch he would shake the stuffing out of her for bruising him, verbally *and* physically . . . if only he could find her among the shadows. Lord, she must have been buzzing around the room like a rabid bat, he decided when an iron candlestick whistled through the air to graze his cheek and then skid across the floor.

"The only crime I have committed is loving you *too* much," Meagan spouted angrily. "I am not such a fool to think I could effect the release of the rebels right out from under the king's nose, and I most certainly did not expect to find Daralis waiting in my chamber with a knife!" Meagan inhaled a deep breath, crept to another strategic corner of the room, and then plowed on, "The wench planned to hold me hostage until our child was born. Then she intended to cart him back to you, claiming that *she* had given birth to your bastard child. None of this was my doing. I came to the palace to meet your king as *you* requested, not to begin another rebellion. Now I know why William rules the roost instead of you. You have been running about this palace like a decapitated chicken, squawking in mindless chaos. At least William has a smidgeon of common sense to his credit while you have proven time and time again that yours has leaked out through the cracks in your wooden head!" Meagan' final weapon left her hand, skimming across the floor to knock Trevor's feet out from under him. The small bench that once stood at the foot of the bed tripped him up, and the mighty warrior landed in an unceremonious heap, his chin slamming against the stool, causing him to bite his tongue. And that was what he should have done in the first place, Trevor painfully reminded himself.

The faint light sketched Meagan's irate features as she stalked past the door to hover above the wounded dragon, who had not one breath of fire left in him since Meagan had besieged him with every available weapon she could lay her hands on. She was magnificent, even when she smoldered with fury, he thought as he scraped himself off the floor and pushed up into a half-sitting position.

A lopsided grin was draped on one side of his mouth as his thick lashes swept up to survey his angry wife once again before he spoke. "Well, m'lady, will you surrender after this devastating assault?"

Meagan let her breath out in a rush and rolled her eyes in disbelief. The Dark Prince was the only man she knew who would demand *her* surrender when *he* had been soundly defeated. He was exasperating! Meagan had no inclination to be sidetracked by his meager attempt at humor while her temper was at a rolling boil.

"Make up your mind, here and now," Meagan demanded sharply. "If you cannot trust me, if you cannot believe in me, then we shall part company and I will seek out the rebels who escaped from the palace. Marston Pearce has shown me nothing but kindness and he will grant me refuge. And Ragnar has shown himself to be a devoted friend. Perhaps I should consider one of them as a lover and husband. They do not always look upon me with suspicion."

Trevor's golden eyes flooded over the intriguing female figure that was wrapped in a gossamer gown of white. The scant light filtered through the thin fabric to outline her enticing contours, molding its amber glow to her perfect body. Trevor felt desire bubbling through his bruised and battered body as his eyes continued to swim over the raging goddess who hovered just beyond his reach.

"You need not search elsewhere," Trevor assured her huskily and then struggled to gather his wobbly legs beneath him. "Yea, I will admit that for a moment my doubts plagued

433

me, but when you cried out to me for help, I knew I had made a disastrous mistake. You know I have grown accustomed to mistrusting Saxons and 'tis second nature for me to be suspicious." His sinewy arms cautiously curled around her waist as he pushed the door shut, blocking out the last rays of light. "Tell me again that you love me. Keep telling me until you have smothered the last of my doubts. I am vulnerable and overprotective of my emotions because my love for you can wound me when nothing else can. I am a jealous, possessive man, Meagan. I want you all to myself and I cannot bear to relive the days when I thought you had betrayed me. I was even envious of William as he escorted you back to the palace. I wondered if he would take privileges with you, even when he knows how deeply I love you. A fool could see that the king was taken with you and I doubted *his* honor. Can you not see how much I love you, that I fear losing you? I have come so close to losing you so often that the mere thought of it drives me mad."

Meagan was touched by his whispered confession. Her anger vanished and she slid her arms over his shoulders, drawing him closer. But Trevor groaned uncomfortably and she withdrew to peer curiously at the dark knight.

"Do you not wish me to touch you?" Her voice held a hint of incredulity. Trevor had told her how much he loved her and yet he flinched when she snuggled into his embrace.

"I crave your caresses," he murmured as he turned her in his arms and aimed her toward the bed, careful not to stumble over the various weapons that were strewn about the dark room. "But my bout with that vengeful witch has left me a mite tender."

Meagan reached up to sketch the teasing smile that hovered on his lips and then chortled as she molded her body to his. "I will kiss away your wounds, my love. Show me where it hurts."

"Here," Trevor rasped, his voice heavily drugged with passion. He took her hand and guided it to his forehead. "And here. . . ." He cautiously inspected the scrape on his cheek. "And my shoulders. . . ."

A shiver of delight cruised across his flesh as Meagan divested him of his clothes to seek out each tender point. He

434

lips feathered across his skin as she drew him down beside her in bed. This fiery angel possessed healing powers, Trevor realized with a sigh of pure pleasure. What Trevor's wily sage had not mastered, Meagan had. Conan was blessed with the gift of prophecy and Meagan held the gift of love. He was a fortunate man, he decided just before reality faded from his grasp. Never had he found such pleasure in pain, and he considered having himself pounded daily if Meagan promised to comfort him.

"Has the pain ebbed, m'lord?" Meagan purred as her gentle hands and moist lips sought out each bruise and scrape, numbing his injured flesh to all except the arousing sensations that danced across his skin and sensitized his nerve endings.

"The pain bows out to the passion you have stirred," he said huskily and then sucked in his breath as her tantalizing caresses strayed across his chest and trickled through the dark furring that descended down his belly. Meagan's magic touch had explored every inch of his body, kindling his desires until his heart thundered with such ferocity that he was certain he would be bruised inside and out. "Lord, woman, you are setting me on fire." His accompanying groan of pleasure assured Meagan that her methods had been effective.

Trevor twisted above her, seduced by her arousing touch. He ached to surrender to the rapture that waited in her arms. Her quiet chortle tickled his senses as her index finger traced an enticing path across his ribs and then sketched the curve of his lips. His nostrils flared to the potent feminine fragrance that clouded his brain and left him yearning to lose himself in the compelling aroma that clung to her.

"What else would one expect from a dragon, my love?" she taunted playfully. "Come, my swarthy beast. Share your flame. Warm me." Her hushed words resounded in his ear. "There will be no fire in the hearth this night since the logs are scattered about the room. My quest for fire lures me closer. . . ."

Trevor needed no invitation. Desire was burning him alive, and Meagan was both the cause and cure of his cremation. His male body moved instinctively toward hers, seeking sweet release while he soared toward the castles in the air, living and dying in that ecstatic moment that pursued and captured time.

Meagan felt his bold manliness against her, and then the blaze of passion was within her, scalding, consuming devouring her until her body was engulfed in molten flames.

Her love for him had endured pain and tormented suffering. His love for her had smothered the last of his doubts. Meagan was his for all eternity. Trevor had chased his last rainbow, had gone in search of a cherished treasure and had discovered a love so strong and compelling that no sword or lance could sever the bond of affection he felt for Meagan.

As they descended from their mindless flight beyond the stars, Meagan smiled contentedly as Trevor cuddled her close. "Is this proof enough of my devotion, m'lord?" she murmured against the hard wall of his chest, feeling his heart slow its frantic pace to beat in rhythm with hers.

A rakish grin dangled on one corner of his mouth as he raised his raven head to peer down into her shadowed face seeing the blinding beauty that even darkness could not disguise. Her exquisite features were etched in his mind, and he had no need to look upon her to see the bewitching young woman whose supple body was molded to his.

"Nay, sweet nymph. A man hounded by doubts is not easily swayed by one display of affection." He grinned "Convince me, love. This doubtful knave has the duration of the night. I bid you to plead your case until dawn."

Meagan flashed him a mischievous smile as her dainty fingers tunneled through his hair to draw his head to hers. "Only the night, m'lord?" she questioned provocatively. "I had in mind to count all the reasons why I love you, and I intend to be very thorough. I hope you did not schedule a morning counsel with your king. I fear this silent conversation might spill into midday."

Trevor considered a retort, but he swallowed it when Meagan's lips melted on his, intoxicating him like a finely aged wine fit for a king. The flame of love blazed anew when their breath mingled as one, feeding a fire that burned righter than a thousand suns.

"I love you, Trevor," she whispered, her voice crackling with emotion, her eyes mirroring her deep affection.

"I know," he murmured back to her. "And I will never doubt you again."

Meagan smiled secretively. Trevor would never question her devotion because she would love away all his doubts. And she was true to her word. When breakfast was served at the king's palace the following morning, there were two empty chairs on the dais, ones that remained unoccupied until late that afternoon when the royal feast was set before the king and his court.

"Do you suppose your king has noticed our absence?" Meagan queried as her wayward hand tracked across Trevor's broad chest.

"Who?" Trevor chortled wickedly, his golden eyes dancing with mischief and desire.

"William," Meagan reminded him, delighting in his amorous embrace.

"I have never heard of him," Trevor insisted just before he lost touch with reality and then scaled rapture's mountain with an angel in his arms.

William impatiently drummed his fingers on the table and then cast Matilda a disgruntled glance. "Should I summon the guards to rouse my zealous knight from his nest?" he questioned and then mellowed when he met Matilda's subtle smile. "Nay, I suppose it would serve no purpose. I doubt that Burke remembers who I am."

And at the moment Trevor didn't. He was enjoying the most pleasant kind of amnesia, one imposed by love's devastating embrace. Meagan had promised to erase all doubts, but she had been so convincing that Trevor was in a mindless whirl, somewhere far beyond the stars that had vanished in the sunrise. Their love had created its own intricate design, one to endure an eternity. And two lovers walked hand in hand, discovering the horizon that waited in world beyond the sun.

Epilogue

"Young Garrick will be in very capable hands," Trevor assured Meagan as he grasped her hand and led his reluctant wife from the room where Conan and Ragnar were peering down at the dark-haired child, waiting for him to make the slightest peep so they could scoop him up from his bassinet and shower him with attention.

Meagan's eyes strayed over her shoulder, fixed on her infant son, unsure she trusted two men to care for such a defenseless child. She had rarely left Garrick to anyone since his birth six weeks earlier, and she was apprehensive about abandoning him even now.

"But Ragnar and Conan know nothing about caring for a child," Meagan protested as Trevor dragged her along with his impatient strides.

"Garrick will be fine," Trevor grumbled and then snatched up the picnic basket and aimed Meagan toward the door. "'Tis *I* who need your loving attention. Methinks you have forgotten that I am the father of our child."

Meagan's mouth dropped open at his acrimonious remark and the sour tone he used to mutter it. Was that why Trevor had seemed out of sorts the past two weeks? He had become irritable and moody, but Meagan had attributed his behavior to the fact that he had been swamped with the duties of inspecting his demesne and seeing to the tithing

439

payments owed by his tenants.

A wry smile pursed her lips as she allowed Trevor to sweep her up in his arms and then deposit her on her steed's back. Trevor was pouting like a child deprived of affection, she realized. So that was what this picnic was all about. He was demanding her undivided attention.

Meagan studied her husband's rigid appearance as he silently rode beside her, his solemn expression chiseled in his rugged features. "I should like to take Garrick and travel to Lowell Castle to see my new nephew," Meagan requested, breaking the stilted silence.

"Fine, m'lady," Trevor answered abruptly. "I will make arrangements to depart at the end of the week."

"Will you be accompanying us?" she questioned, raising a delicate brow.

"Would you prefer that I did not?" Trevor snapped defensively.

Meagan bit back a smile, but she could not resist the gibe. "Since you have been so testy of late perhaps it would be wise if you remained behind and allowed Conan to concoct a potion to sweeten your sour moods."

Trevor's head swiveled around to glare at the taunting grin that Meagan could not contain. "There is nothing wrong with my disposition," he insisted, an unpleasant edge on his voice.

Her shoulder lifted noncommittally, and then she inhaled a breath of fresh air, marveling at the beauty that surrounded her. "As you say, m'lord," she replied glibly.

When Garda fluttered down to perch on her forearm, Meagan reached over to brush her hand over the falcon's neck, drawing a derisive snort from Trevor.

"I had intended that we be completely alone," he grumbled, flinging Garda and Lear a disgusted glower. "Can we make not one journey without that buzzard and wolf eavesdropping?"

Meagan drew her steed to a halt and then swung from the saddle to stroll through the plush grass that formed a lush carpet along the stream bank. "Garda and Lear are not in the habit of spreading gossip." She paused to glance back at

440

Trevor, whose vivid amber eyes were burning with such intense desire that Meagan felt as if he had put a torch to her.

She had been the recipient of his measuring stares of late, but Trevor had not touched her for two months and had moved out of his own chamber to allow her privacy. At first Meagan thought that her blossoming figure had repulsed him, but once their child was born Trevor still kept his distance. Each night he walked her to the solar, pressed a hasty goodnight kiss to her lips, and then took his leave. To say that Meagan had been disappointed by his seeming acceptance of their separation was an understatement. She had yearned for his gentle touch, but she had bided her time, waiting until she could fully prove that her love for him had not diminished with time.

Although Meagan had planned to seduce him this very evening, she decided not to procrastinate until dark what could be pleasantly served with daylight. She yearned to be enfolded in his sinewy arms and to feel his solid body molded to hers. If Trevor was waiting for some sign that she was more than willing to accept him, Meagan intended to drop such an obvious hint that even a fool could not overlook it.

Slowly, she turned back to him, a deliciously mischievous smile hovering on her lips. She would not beg for his caress, she told herself. She would drive him to distraction, using every feminine technique within her power to properly seduce him. Humming a soft tune, she peeled off her emerald-studded tunic and then let it flutter from her fingertips.

Trevor's eyes bulged from their sockets as his gaze flooded over her shapely figure. Surely she did not intend to taunt him when the lusting beast within him roared for release, he thought disconcertedly. His bout with desire had very nearly gotten the best of him as it was. He had removed himself from his own solar to prevent ravishing his enchanting wife and to avoid causing her injury in her delicate condition. He knew better than to take her so soon after the birth of their son, but he was a man on the rack, his patience stretched to tautness. He was torn between the ravenous desire to make love to her and his concern for her health. Yea, maybe his

441

celibacy had soured his disposition, but there were certain things a man could not overcome and still retain his good humor. Abstaining from making love to this intriguing, blue-eyed minx was at the top of his list, Trevor reminded himself shakily as Meagan stripped from her chemise to stand stark naked in broad daylight.

Lord! What was she trying to do to him? Push him past the limits of his resistance? Meagan was driving him mad with her taunting seduction. He had longed to be alone with her, to enjoy what little affection she could offer, but Trevor had not expected to view such a provocative performance.

"'Tis such a warm day that I cannot resist a swim," Meagan purred as she sauntered toward the water and then paused to fling Trevor a silent invitation to join her.

Trevor was on fire! His body quaking, stung by the impulsive urge to rip off his clothes and dive headlong into the rivulet in fast pursuit of this enchanting siren. Before he realized it, his footsteps took him to the water's edge to watch Meagan floating on her back, the glistening water molding itself to her tantalizing figure. Trevor would have waded through crocodile infested waters to ease his frustrated passion, but this enticing scene was too much! His temper got the best of him as he watched Meagan dive beneath the surface and then reappear, her smile beckoning, her curvaceous body calling out to him to touch what his eyes devoured. Didn't she know how difficult it had been to settle for a simple goodnight kiss these past two months when he was starved for more than a gentle embrace? Of course she did, he told himself. This vixen was delighting in watching him suffer.

"Damnation, woman. Do not flaunt yourself in front of me!" he scowled.

"Flaunt, m'lord?" Her silky voice rippled in the breeze and then whispered about him like a tempting caress.

"Do not mock my perseverance, Meagan," Trevor warned, his narrowed gaze reflecting his frustration.

Meagan glided toward the shore, smiling provocatively. "I do not seek to mock your perseverance, only to dissolve it." She gathered her feet beneath her, and as the water ebbed to reveal the creamy swells of her breasts, Trevor gulped air. "Do you no longer find me appealing? It has been two months since—"

"Do not remind me!" Trevor howled. "I have painfully counted the days I have been forced to endure. How much longer must I look without daring to touch what I crave? How many more weeks must pass before you invite me back to my solar? Egod, Meagan, if I must endure many more cold baths I will be as shriveled as yonder toad who sits perched upon his lily pad."

"The time you spend ranting on shore prolongs my agony and yours," Meagan murmured, her sapphire eyes full of promise.

Trevor's grin was wider than the stream in which Meagan stood waist-deep in water. In record time he shed his clothes to join his bewitching wife. Meagan watched him undress, her gaze flowing over his hard, muscular contours. She trembled in anticipation of the moment when she could reach out to touch him, to rediscover every curve of his swarthy physique.

A wave of water rolled toward her as Trevor dived into the rivulet. An aroused shiver flew down her spine when his strong arms encircled her waist. Trevor groaned in torment as his body melted against hers, his longing so fierce that containing his boiling passion was next to impossible. It was like willing a volcano not to erupt and knowing it was only a matter of time before it exploded, inflaming the world with a molten fire that would demolish all in its path.

"I have missed you," Trevor breathed raggedly. His mouth slanted across hers in hungry impatience, stripping the breath from her lungs, leaving her senses reeling in pure delight.

"And I you," Meagan murmured when Trevor dragged his lips away to grant her the smallest breath.

"Had I been forced to endure another day without touching you I would have begged Conan to brew a sleeping potion that would have spared me the maddening agony of loving you from a distance," he breathed as his moist lips skimmed her neck, sending a fleet of goose pimples cas-

443

cading over her skin.

The golden glow in his eyes mingled with the sapphire blue pools that lifted adoringly toward him. Meagan combed her fingers through his disheveled raven hair, neatly rearranging it.

"I have a potion that will cure what ails you, m'lord," she assured him as she pressed closer.

Trevor crushed her to him, overwhelmed by the sensations that sizzled through his body like a bolt of lightning. "Then be quick about administering your remedy. Relieve my anguish."

Meagan leaned back as far as his encircling arms would allow and then traced intricate patterns on his chest. "If your affliction has plagued you for two months, I do not think the curative can be expected to heal you in a short span of time." A wry smile pursed her lips as her wandering caress submerged beneath the water's surface to trace the curve of his hip. "As a matter of fact, I would guess that you will require daily treatment."

Trevor chuckled huskily as he hooked an arm under Meagan's knees and then carried her to shore. "I was hoping you would say that."

"I love you" was written on his craggy features as he stretched out beside Meagan on the blanket of grass. At last he had solved the mystery of life. What he had fought so hard to avoid almost a year earlier had become his most valued prize. Meagan had become all things to him. At last he realized that nothing worth having came without a struggle. But the reward of surrendering to love was victory in itself. The pleasures he had received from taming this enchanting minx were worth the trouble he had endured. This angel had ignited a flame of love that nothing could extinguish. She had given him a glimpse of heaven, and he would never tire of viewing the horizon that dawned in her sparkling blue eyes.

"Love me for all the lonely nights I have suffered without you," Meagan whispered as her arms slid over his shoulder to lure him closer. "I need you, Trevor, always. . . ."

As he came to her they were consumed by love's blazing

e, one that inflamed eternity and fed on emotions that had ng been held in check. And for an endless moment they ere of one heart and soul. The rapturous circle of love had beginning or end, and they soared along the perimeter of universe that only lovers could enjoy.

A contented smile brimmed Trevor's lips as he bent to op a lingering kiss to Meagan's upturned lips. With her by s side he had found his place in the sun, basking in the armth of her unselfish love.

"You will always be my love," Trevor assured her, giving r a fond squeeze.

"And you are my life," she whispered back to him.

In the distance a skylark's song drifted on the wind, rrying their hushed vows with its peaceful melody.

"Conan, are you ill?" Ragnar questioned in concern when glanced over to see the seer's trancelike expression.

The words filtered into the oracle's pensive contempla-ns, and he turned to smile reassuringly at Ragnar. Then he ered down at the small child who was the image of his ther. "I could not be better. All is right with the world," he urmured. "And soon, young Garrick, you will have a sister trail in your footsteps, one whose beauty and spirit will atch your mother's."

"What did you say, old man?" Ragnar frowned, attempt-g to decipher the wizard's inaudible utterances.

"Nothing." Conan smiled secretively. He was the keeper dreams, and this was one that he would not foretell. But ile the rest of the world waited and wondered, Conan uld delight in knowing that one day he would hold a child either arm while Meagan and Trevor ventured to their aceful corner of the world to repeat the vows that wafted eir way across the meadow in the songbird's enchanting elody.